STONE

The Adventures of

RHONE & STONE

book 1

by:

STRIDER

S.R. KLUSMAN

Stone

The Adventures of Rhone and Stone

book 1

2nd ed. IV 2022

Published by: Duramen Publishing

Contact at: DuramenPublishing.com

ISBN: 9798985119640 (paperback)

ISBN: 9798985119633 (e-book)

ISBN: 9798985119626 (audio book)

ISBN: 9798860457805 (hardback)

YA Action Adventure, Sci-Fi Western, Alien Contact

Cover art by: James T Egan, BookFly Design

Dedication

To my wife Pammi. The lady that had to sit through years of writes,
rewrites, corrections, edits, and proofreads, ad infinitum.
So this is for my lovely bride. I don't know why she puts up with me,
but she does.

This book, and my life, are dedicated to her.
Thank you, Pammi. With all my love.

CHAPTER 1

Stoned

I am here.

The unexpected words startled Rhone, and he spun, senses coming to full alert.

But there was no one.

I am here.

Turning cautiously, Rhone scanned the area, thinking he must be hearing things. On second thought, he was hearing things, but his ears hadn't heard it. His head had. Some kind of thought voice in his head. Not a ghost-like whispering sound. It was a real voice, except it wasn't. And with no sound, he couldn't explain it.

Once again, the words came. *I am here.*

"All right, I hear you," he voiced uneasily. "What do you want?" He wasn't sure who he was speaking to, and he asked the question as though he was talking to himself, which he probably was.

I am here. The words came with a feeling of strained patience.

Frustrated himself, Rhone swung around looking for someone, but again, there was nothing unusual, just the countryside he knew so well. Brush, hills, dirt, and rocks. The almost barren land didn't give many places to hide.

Annoyed now, and not wanting to play games, Rhone let his anger grow. "What do you want?" he shouted into the warm air.

Once again, his mind filled with the words, *I...am...here!*

"OKAY, I get that part," he snapped. "Now where are you? And,... who are you?"

He stood wary and unsure as he waited. He didn't like it when things didn't go along with his plans, and this was definitely not on his plans. Focusing his senses, he cautiously searched for the intruder.

He couldn't have said why, but he set a hand on his belt pouch as he warily searched for whoever was trying to trick him.

A strange feeling of satisfaction flowed through Rhone, as the no-sound voice came again. *Yes, I am here.*

It was particularly strange because, while Rhone felt the satisfaction, he wasn't satisfied at all. In fact, he was downright irritated with the entire thing. Frowning at his lack of an explanation, Rhone lightly slapped the pouch against his leg.

Yes! I am here! came the words, filled with both congratulations and mild frustration.

Confused, Rhone slipped the latch free and lifted the flap, suddenly feeling very stupid. Someone had just played a joke on him. There was no other explanation. With cheeks burning, he jerked his head up, fists clenched and ready for a fight. But no one was laughing. In fact, there was no one at all.

Again, he looked in the pouch. And again, nothing. At least nothing unexpected. Even a mouse in his pouch would have been something to consider, if you could imagine a talking mouse. Actually it would have been pretty cool. But no mouse. Nothing at all, except the stuff he normally carried. He mentally went through the list of things that should be there. There were the things he needed for starting a fire. A shiny rock he had been carrying for a couple of years, and a few pieces of dried meat he brought for lunch. Then there was the fishing line with his favorite hook, and a small knife he used around camp. That was all.

He was still considering the situation, when his mind was suddenly filled with exasperation, and the words, *I... Am... Here!*

Rhone spun in confusion, again searching, then back down to the pouch. "What in the dismal world?" he mumbled.

But it was definitely the pouch, maybe.

Slowly, Rhone again opened the flap. Then reaching in, moved the items around, touching everything with exploring fingers. As he reached for the knife, he stopped and pushed a finger at the rock, feeling its warmth. Squinting in the bright afternoon sun, he gave it a good look, then feeling dumb, realized, of course it would be warm. It was a hot day. But intrigued by the shiny rock, he pulled it from the pouch just to look at it again.

The stone's translucent beauty was doubly enhanced by the sun's brilliance, causing it to sparkle until it almost glowed. And as he had done so many times before, Rhone held it up to his eye and slowly rotated the rock, watching the cloudy interior shatter the sunlight into a dazzling display. If he concentrated hard, he could almost see through the stone, but the image broke up in the cloudy facets, dispersing as though absorbed by the thousand crystalline lines that stretched throughout the interior.

The rock was probably a piece of river-polished rose quartz, but it really didn't matter. Its rounded pillow shape was smooth as glass, like it had been tumbled and polished by the river's water for years. It was beautiful, and that was a good enough reason to carry it.

Tossing the rock into the air, he watched as it flashed in the sunlight, then caught it, smiling. He had carried the rock ever since he found it, while walking in the knee-deep water of the river near his home. The shallow water made it easier, and far more fun, than hiking along the shore, where the river's edges were often thickly brushed and soggy. The alder and river willow kept the banks nicely shaded, but often made walking difficult.

Now the rock was one of his treasures. His good luck piece.

But as Rhone held the stone on the flat of his palm, he felt as much as heard the words, *Yes, I am here,* sounding gently in his mind.

Rhone dropped the stone like it was a hot coal from the fire. "Is this for real?" he shouted, the action far more a panic than he wanted to admit.

I am if you are, came the curt reply echoing in his mind.

"But it's a rock," he blurted. "I don't get it?"

Curiosity overcoming his fear, he bent to look at it closely.

Even so, he simply wasn't ready, when it responded, *And you are, what? A biological mass of gooey stuff? Now pick me up.*

It was such a weird thing to hear, or maybe feel was a better way to explain it, that it caught him off-guard. Dropping to a knee, Rhone carefully picked up the little rock, studying it as it lay on his palm. It was warm, but all rocks were warm in this weather.

He simply didn't know what to do, then suddenly realized, he hadn't spoken all the comments. Some he had only thought to himself. Yet he had been answered.

It only left one conclusion. *I must be going crazy.* Reluctantly, and fearing the results, he asked, "Are you for real?"

I am, came the soft reply.

He had asked, but the returning answer still shook him to the core, and it took a moment before he had enough nerve to continue.

With a shaky voice, he asked, "Are you a creature?"

Do I look like a creature?

Covering for his obvious error, he replied, "Well, no. You look like a rock."

Thank you. I am something like a rock. Is that a problem?

Rhone's mom had worked diligently, trying to teach him manners, and now he was embarrassed. "No, I guess not. It's just...I didn't expect...I never even considered..." He paused, not sure how to answer this 'thing'. "What I mean is, I suppose you are, since you are talking to me. But, how?

The answer didn't come immediately, as though the rock was considering its reply before answering.

I think, therefore I am.

Rhone's eyes widened at the answer, and again, he wasn't sure what to say. Until the rock filled in for him.

I have been around for... let us just say, a long time. But then you picked me up and carried me with you. I have been absorbing your energies and your vibrations ever since. The stuff you are made of. Everything is energy, you know, your mental vibrations just as much as your gooey stuff is.

"I think you mean flesh," Rhone answered with a squinted frown. He had never thought of himself as 'gooey stuff' and wasn't sure he was overjoyed at the concept, but next to a rock, he supposed it was true.

His 'rock' wasn't done with its explanation, and Rhone could feel the push of thoughts in his mind, waiting to continue.

As he refocused, the words began to flow again. *As I was saying, I began to gather your feelings, and it began to make sense. When I took your feelings and connected them with your motions, then added your sound waves, connected to certain vibrations of thought, it began to make patterns. Those patterns then connected with a particular... 'picture'? I believe that is the correct word. I am still quite new at this.*

The explanation was so far beyond his understanding that Rhone's mind had simply gone blank.

You must realize, pictures are energy patterns too, but they were quite difficult to understand. I now realize you have eyes, and I do not, but after a period of time, your 'You-ness' made me understand my 'Me-ness'. They are similar, but very different. I think, and you think, but not the same. In the end, I learned to tune in the energy of the different vibrations, much like you learned to speak using your vocal cords, which, if you think about it, is very strange in itself. Still, It is all energy. Different wavelengths and different frequencies doing different things. But it is all energy. You give them and I feel them, and vice versa.

Rhone was amazed. "You just...became? Like magic?"

A feeling, somewhat similar to humor, came through their connection. *No, silly. Not magic. Although, I suppose that would be an understandable explanation too, since magic is like the 'Art' of the science of energy.*

Rhone shook his head, considering the entire situation. "So you are real. A talking, thinking, rock. Nobody is going to believe me."

Probably true, the rock whispered in Rhone's head. *Especially since they can't hear me. I am tuned to your energy.*

That caught Rhone's attention. "No one else can hear you?"

No. Well, it might be possible, if I was around them long enough, but each person's energy patterns is their own. It would be something like trying to read a book in Greek if you did not understand Greek. It would all be Greek to you. Get it?

A feeling of warm humor coursed through Rhone again, but Rhone wasn't impressed. His mind was taking him in other directions. "So a rock can learn?"

No, no, no! How can you be such a blockhead? You take the most obvious things and make them obscure. There was a moment's pause, almost like the intake of a breath, before Rhone heard, or felt, the next words. *Now, Let us try again. I am. Rocks are not. And I am NOT A ROCK!*

The abrupt tone surprised Rhone, making him even more confused. "But you just said you were a rock," he blurted.

If a rock could smile, this would have been the time. A sublime feeling of satisfaction filled Rhone, as the rock said, *No, I most certainly did not. I said, I was something 'like' a rock. Such as, you are something 'like' an orangutan.* Rhone could definitely feel the quotes implied with the word 'like', before it continued. *Like, as in, something similar, as to equate with, but not the same at all.*

Rhone could understand at least that much, and nodded. "I think I get it. So, you are something 'like' a rock, but you're not a rock." But even saying it didn't make it much clearer to his mind.

Correct! Good job. And, 'I am'. Would a rock ever say that? I think not.

This might take a while.

With the rock still in his palm, and suddenly feeling tired, Rhone settled himself heavily onto the gravel. *Too much brain work,* he thought, attempting to get a handle on the concept. "Okay, but I guess I'm back to the question, what are you?"

And I am back to the answer, I am Me.

"Whatever!" Rhone sputtered in exasperation. "I guess we have as good an answer as I'm going to get for now, but I'll let you know, I'm not satisfied." He felt exhausted but had to keep digging. "So, you and I are connected, and no one else who might pick you up would be able to talk to you--"

He was stopped mid-sentence by words coursing through his head.

Of course, they could talk to me! You can talk to a cow can you not? But do you hold conversations with the cow? Do they understand and talk back? You have got to get a hold of your misconceptions and bigotry. You are not the only thinking entities in the universe. Or did you think you were?

This was another surprise, and Rhone didn't have much of an answer. "Honestly, I never thought about it. I'm not sure what to think."

Rhone could feel a subtle vibration from the rock before it spoke to him again. *My review of your patterns shows you had training, schooling. Is that not correct?*

"If you mean, did my mom give me lessons? Then yes. But schooling doesn't mean much out here, and it's just me now."

Rhone could have sworn the rock smiled, as it said, *Well, I believe it is quite time you started thinking.*

Rhone sat huddled, hugging his knees, as the shadows advanced and small animals scuttled under the coarse brush, readying for the coming evening. He still held the rock gripped in his hand when he abruptly raised his head and sat up. "Do you have a name?"

A name? The words came clearly to Rhone's mind. *No, nothing like a name. I am Me, and with others, we are We. We know each other by our vibration, which is not the same as a name. Names, I would think, would be limiting. Although I must be honest, having no experience with such, it is just conjecture. But to be contained by what someone labels you, and not what you are, sounds... problematic.*

There was a pause, and Rhone could almost feel the rock thinking, like wheels spinning in his own mind.

Perhaps that is why dragons did not give out their names. They would be contained by them, and to contain is to control.

The mention of dragons was as startling as talking rocks, but Rhone felt he should correct the rock's misconception. "Dragons are only make-believe, but don't worry about it. I was just wondering."

Why did you ask about names?

Sullenly, Rhone kicked at a rock and answered, "Really, It's no problem. I just figured that everybody had a name. You hadn't mentioned one, so I've just been thinking of you as Stone." He finished with a shallow shrug.

Thoughts that weren't his own weighed heavily on Rhone before words like distant thunder rolled across his mind.

Stone. I like it. Really, I like it. Not just a pile of rocks, but a singular entity. A stone. And even better, just, Stone.

Words filled Rhone's mind, as a shivering vibration warmed the rock in his hand.

Stone... I never had a name before. In all the time I have been, I have never had a name. The rock tried the name again, saying, *Stone. Really, this is wonderful! You have given me a name.* The vibration and warmth grew as it matched Stone's excitement. *I am Stone!*

Rhone couldn't help but smile. He rose to his feet and, like the ringmaster at a circus, held up his hand in a flourish, bellowing to the imagined crowds. "Ladies and gentlemen!... With great pleasure, I bring your attention to the center ring... For the very first time in history... I introduce, he of crystalline perfection... and my most solid friend," and thrusting his hand to the sky in a final flourish, he bellowed the name, "Stone!"

As he shouted Stone's name at the top of his lungs, a blindingly brilliant, golden-pink light flashed into the growing evening, finally fading to the darkness of the oncoming night.

Rhone couldn't see a thing until his vision began to clear, and blinked, still seeing a red spot before his eyes. "What was that?" he asked in awe, finally lowering his arm.

Ahh. Sorry, Stone mumbled. *That was....unexpected. I can assure you, it has never happened before. It was just so... you know... and then...POW. Again, I am very sorry. It is simply inexcusable to allow an unplanned release of energy in such a way.*

"No," Rhone interjected quickly. "It was totally awesome! But you've never done that before? Well, it was way cool."

Yes. Luckily, it was indeed cool, Stone acknowledged, *but differently than you mean. You should be glad it had no heat with it. I could have cooked you without meaning to. Totally unacceptable. Again, I apologize. I am very sorry.*

Rhone could feel Stone's mumble apology echo through his mind.

A moment later, Rhone asked, "You could do that on purpose? Like an explosion or something?"

I suppose it is possible, Stone answered, not sounding certain at all. *Although I have never tried.*

"Well I don't know what you are, but I would be proud to call you a friend."

Thank you. You are indeed kind. But it is also quite possible, I could be a very dangerous companion.

"I'm not worried," Rhone stated easily. "You said it never happened before. We'll just have to think on it, and figure out what happened." He paused, considering. "I can't imagine being able to do something like that, but a couple of hours ago, I hadn't considered something like you."

A gurgling growl erupted from his stomach, reminding him rather abruptly he hadn't eaten all day. But what to do with his new friend?

"Ahhh, Stone. What should I do with you? Do you want to go back in the pouch, set you on a rock, or... what?" He didn't want to be rude to his new friend, companion... rock thing.

Do not worry yourself. The pouch will be just fine. It is not as though I get uncomfortable, and it allows me to be close to you. We connect better that way.

"Okay, sure, as long as it isn't a problem."

Handling Stone carefully, Rhone placed the rock-like entity back in his pouch and started prepping a camp for the quickly arriving night. It was far past time for dinner.

Sitting on a boulder, Rhone stared thoughtfully into the crackling fire, when he quietly asked, "Stone? Can you hear me?"

Yes. Of course, Stone responded, the sound quite clear in Rhone's head.

"Okay. Just checking." After a moment's pause, he asked, "I was just wondering, do you sleep?"

Ah, an excellent question, Stone answered. *It is indeed a difference of ours.* His mental voice dropped into a lecturer's monolog as he continued. *I do not sleep. Not in the way you do. We do rest our minds, but in our normal state, we process everything at such a slow rate that we rest as we work. You see, we have very little outside activity to take up our mental time frame.*

Rhone was intrigued, continuing to stare into the fire as he considered just how little he knew of things.

Stone picked up the thread of thought, starting where he had left off. *When there is no motion to tire from, there is no need for rest from it. As I am sure you can imagine, it is not like we run around much. It took a long time for my mind to acclimate to your speed of action. Your mind jumps from one thing to the next so quickly that its patterns, from brain to action, are almost undecipherable. However, once I had a small pattern interpreted, my knowledge quickly expanded.*

Rhone almost laughed as his mind pictured a pile of hot rocks jumping around.

Stone, on the other hand, patently ignored the thought picture, continuing with his lecture single-mindedly. *All energy is interlinked. Every action has a reaction, and energy is never lost, it is merely changed in form to something else. Energy is forever, and there are patterns in everything. You simply have to find them. It is the quest of life!*

That, and survival, Rhone thought absently.

I heard that you know? came Stone's curt reply.

"Sorry."

This was getting confusing.

CHAPTER 2

Here Today and Gone Tomorrow

Rhone's home wasn't much, and he didn't spend much time there, often preferring to sleep out under the stars. There were just too many memories, few of which were good. Mom said he had been born here and had lived his entire life in the ancient and severely worn homestead, but Mom had never mentioned his father. That was simply how it was. He never worried about it, and now with Mom gone, it wasn't important. Home was just a place to shack-up.

During the winter, when the weather got really cold, the frosty wind would blow down the valley, piling shallow drifts of fine, dry snow against the tufts of stiff grasses managing a hold in the hard ground. Those days, it was nice to have a relatively warm place out of the wind. Other than that, he preferred the freedom of the outdoors, even in the summer heat of the sun-baked rocky valley of his home.

Mom had never asked anything of anyone. She hadn't even asked for medicine. Not even in the final days of her sickness. Rhone was sure it was because they weren't able to pay, and had tried to argue it with her, but she simply smiled and said, "Rhone, they probably don't work anyway. I know the old crook that plays doctor, and I'm sure he's a fake. Don't worry. I lived a good life, and I have you to prove it."

He felt for the truth in her statement, and came away puzzled. She wasn't afraid. Hardly even sad. Instead, she felt complete. But how could that be, when she was dying right before his eyes? How could she possibly be so undisturbed by her own death?

His mom saw the question etched on his worried face, and tried to give an answer he could understand. "Rhone, There is nothing more for me. I have had my time. I could have done better, I'm sure, but I am not ashamed of where I am. We did good, you and I, and now it is your time. Mine is past, and soon, gone entirely. Come over here. Look out the window. See those stars? Go, follow them. This place is not for you. I'm not sure why, but I know it's true. It's in me to know. But you...you have a different path, and I cannot see what that will be. I have tried, but it's beyond my sight. It is for you, and it has something to do with the stars. I feel it, and it's up to you to find it. When you do, follow that star to wherever it leads and find your place. It will be far from here."

The talk tired her, and she fell silent, clutching his hand. Smiling, even through her pain, she drifted off to a calm sleep.

That was their last talk, and it was totally Mom, full of odd sayings and interesting comments. She had always been that way, and thinking about her brought the smallest of smiles to his lips, but his eyes were too full of tears and worry to acknowledge the good of it.

Rhone sat by her bedside throughout the long night. There was nothing he could do. No way to help, other than to assist her sips from the glass of water. She slept fitfully, often jerking as though attempting to free herself from restraints, but there were none. None he could see. Once, she turned her face, creased with wrinkles she was too young to have, up toward the ceiling and smiled. Her hand reached out with a gentle motion, as though plucking the moonbeams from the darkened room. Not long after, she settled her head wearily down into the old feather pillow, and simply...stopped, her face still holding the smile.

The next morning, with tears still washing his face, Rhone went to the rickety work shed and took out the pick and shovel. Their gnarled old apple tree stood its ground not far from the garden plot, and he thought she would like its shade when the scalding hot summer afternoons came. He began to dig the hard rocky soil. It was back breaking work, clawing his way down into the unforgiving ground. His sobs of anger and frustration kept interrupting his efforts, but he kept at it. He would dig it deep and secure, for her.

W ith Mom gone, everything he might have weighed on the good side of the scale was gone, and not much remained to balance it. He was only thirteen when she passed, but that was old enough to care for himself, and over the next few years, not much changed. No one came by, and he never left. There was no need. With the chickens and the little garden, he had all he required. What more could he want? It was a rough life, in a rough land.

Rhone continued his care of the chickens and garden plot, along with fishing and the minor chores needed to keep the place from actually falling down. It remained a place to get out of the weather, and not much more. Having never known anything different, he wasn't even lonely.

Rhone could read and write, and even some mathematics. Mom had been strong on those things, and he had sat for long hours at the kitchen table as she attempted to work their basic concepts into his brain. While he never understood why it was needed, it mattered to her, and he tried to make her happy.

The old worn-out home sat on land that might have had some value, to someone, but it was another of those points he didn't worry about. No one had ever come asking for rent, so perhaps he owned it. Again, Mom had never mentioned it, and now it was too late to ask.

The little plot of garden was the one thing well-tended, and Rhone had been instructed on its care from his toddler years on. The garden, the eggs from the few chickens running around the yard, and the fish he routinely caught in the river running just past the mouth of their valley made up most of what they ate. On a good year, when there was sufficient rain, there would be flour, but it was precious. Grain was cut by hand, harvested from the tall grasses growing wild in the dusty soil of their upper valley and ground in the little hand grinder Mom had been so proud of. Bread was Rhone's one soft spot, and the loaves of fresh, sweet smelling bread would be enough to have his mouth watering as he waited until Mom gave the okay. The crusty, fluffy, beautiful slices were almost enough to make him cry. Even now, the thought of biting into the wonderful treat made his mouth salivate.

But life was not good at granting those wonders. The other side of the coin was that every day required things to fill it. If the chores weren't done, he wouldn't eat. So he worked; tending, watering, gathering, hauling, chopping, splitting, stacking, mending, plucking, fishing and cooking. Occasionally, when he could no longer stand the smell of himself and realized that things were getting a little ripe from the sweat and grime of the garden dirt, mixed with the blood and entrails of gutted fish or rabbit, he would do the washing. Off would come the bed clothes and towels, along with his own ragged things, and out would come the big galvanized tub. But if the weather was good, a swim in the river was called for, and far more fun than the old tub. Wrinkling his nose, Rhone would gather his things and head off, down the dirt road leading from the little valley to the shallow river.

There were also days when it was simply too hot to work. With the blazing sun searing his back, he would wade for hours in the fast flowing river, just for the joy of it, eyes constantly searching for treasures among the sun-gilded rocks polished smooth by the continuous tumbling of the rushing river.

Slogging upstream against the current, Rhone stooped to pluck a bright flash of a treasure from the myriads of rocks he slowly trod past. He gazed at the beautiful piece, awed by its golden-pink depths. Happy with his find, he stuck it in his belt pouch alongside the hunk of dried rabbit meat he had planned on for lunch. For the first time in ages, life felt good.

CHAPTER 3

Skragmoore

The town of Skragmoore wasn't much of a town anymore, and probably never had been. The ruins of old buildings and bare foundations backing up to the hills were evidence that it had been larger, but that only meant it had been larger than it was now. Not that it had any significance to being a place of power, or even a center of trade. It was just a country town, barely large enough to serve the small community of homes that surrounded it, straggling away into the rugged hills.

The land itself was rough, its sharp valleys capped with stony escarpments running between them. The rocky ridges cut the land into a continuous corrugation of heights and lowlands running off into the far distance. The valleys between, ran the gamut of prosperity, from lush grasslands filled with cattle and sheep, to coarsely rugged and brush filled gullies of rock and rattlesnakes. The soil tended to be shallow, and the rain rapidly sank into the porous and rocky ground, or ran off quickly into the shallow, fast flowing rivers. There wasn't much in between.

The sparse and rough population was held together by the commerce of Skragmoore, little as it was, and Skragmoore was run by The Commissioner.

Commissioner Dodge, with his 6'6" height, must have weighed close to 300 pounds. His odd, squat hat almost clipped the door frames when he entered the stores of the town, which he did with regularity as he stomped about, ever vigilant for something to stick his nose into. This was especially true if he smelled a profit in it. He had a dream of riches, and the disappointment of being stuck with a run-down town like Skragmoore left him with a perpetual snarl.

His wife was no better. Mrs. Dodge, no one ever called her Mavis to her face, was the epitome of graciousness at the town functions she held court over. She was curvaceous, in the overly tight, and almost immodest clothing she wore, parading around town as though she was the local debutante, cooing sweetly to the wanna-be gentlemen of the rugged little town. Such was life.

There had been travelers once, coming through the town, spending money at the town's few attractions and dining facilities, but after the weather changed, and whatever else had happened beyond their boundaries, few visitors made it to the little town. Fewer still stayed any longer than needed, finding good excuses to find their way back out. The loss of the exterior coin left the town destitute, or whatever the new politically correct term was for 'being without'. No one had enough money for anything but the barest of necessities.

No one that is, except The Commissioner and his wife. Somehow, even in this poor base, he managed to have his fingers into every pot. Taking the little profits as his due. He was, after all, The Commissioner, granted so by The Council, commissioned to run Skragmoore to its greatest potential. So his charter said, as it hung on his office wall, set in a gilded frame from some past time and scrolled in a flourishing hand of dark ink. It set like a trophy, surrounded by shelves displaying other wonders he had come by in the course of his office.

The skull of a mountain lion hung across the room, and the stories said he had killed it as it attacked his dogs during a hunt. The spear he used sat in a corner, next to a large stone with the bones of some long forgotten species embedded in its surface. Just another treasure he managed to accrue. Still, no one believed his ever-extravagant stories when he sat in the tavern on Friday nights, drinking from his large, beer-filled mug. The town's few courtiers would surround him as he held his un-official court, with each man vying to create a space for themselves in his esteemed eyes. It was a sad sight as his greed visibly deepened with each cup he drank.

The beer however, never made entry into the Dodge residence. Wine was the drink of choice to the up-scale Mrs. The staff drank cider, which she allowed as mid-step between the two. Mrs. Dodge would sit up, waiting for The Commissioner to find his way home after his night out, and glare at him in the most vile of ways, daring him to make a fuss in front of the hired help.

She always spoke of him as The Commissioner. It was so much more grandiose sounding and gave her a little thrill just to say it. She may not have approved of his drinking with the low life, but he was the ranking member of the town, granted so by The Council of State, and accepted by the people. Her life was set, and she was proud of her position next to him.

Whenever she was bored, she would drift into her wardrobe and pull out the drawer of elegant finery she would wear to the next of the town's horrible gatherings. The functions were so terribly drab, she actually felt sorry for the other women who had to appear at the same festivities as she, in all her regalia. They must surely feel as poorly about themselves, as she felt about them. It was very difficult to function effectively, dealing with the masses, but it was her job and she would struggle through the difficulties with hardly a grimace.

Fluffing her hair, she shifted her bosom into place and strained to see her poor reflection in the age-tarnished mirror. Hopefully, things would get better, but she was past tired of waiting. Maybe The Commissioner's next post would be better. It certainly couldn't get much worse.

Commissioner Dodge almost tripped as he left the tavern. His head ached terribly and it had to be the beer. It hadn't tasted right. The stuff must have been old, or off, or whatever beer does to go bad.

Since his head was bad, the beer took the blame, and instead of going home to get scowled at by the Mrs, he had a better idea. He would go see his stash. It always made him happy, and at the moment happy was a long way off. Just a short detour, and he would check on the few treasures he had managed to accumulate, even from a place as lowly as Skragmoore. It was sure to help.

Making his way carefully, so as not to adversely affect his head, Commissioner Dodge checked both directions before slipping into the old building. Like the rest of town, everything about the building was old, except for the door. He removed the lock, turned the intricate knob, and pushed on the thick wooden slabs. The door opened with a dull screech of steel on steel as the hinges complained. The dim room, with its cracked walls seemingly held in place by the thick cobwebs over-lacing them, was as ordinary as could be, saying nothing of what it hid. Crossing the worn wood floor, not even glancing at the dirt-encrusted window that barely allowed the dim light to shine through, he opened a small closet, removing the almost bristle-less brooms then the wooden rod with its hangers. With the little cubby cleared, he grabbed the top of a loose-looking board in the back wall and pulled.

A quiet click rewarded his ear, and the back of the cabinet swung wide, revealing a stone stairway dropping into the earth below. He smiled, one of those smiles a thief might upon effectively opening a safe that wasn't theirs, then cautiously, ducked low and entered the stairwell.

Stopping just inside the opening, he reached to the side, finding the lamp waiting handily on the ledge set into the stonework. A moment later, a match scraped, then burst into flame. When the wick took, settling to a warm glow, he was ready. With one hand on the rough wall, and lantern's golden flame lighting the way, he began his descent of the stone stairwell. The dank room below was obviously old, cut from the very bedrock the building sat on. The room was from the earliest days of the town and had various odd items still tucked into the corners, lying partially buried in dust and cobwebs. Perhaps it had once been a hide-away for goods that weren't necessarily 'above board', at least as far as the law was concerned, but it could simply have been a safe-house feature, in case things went bad upstairs. It didn't matter. It was his now, and he had a use for it.

Directly across from the stairs a heavy-looking door of dark metal set flush in the wall. From its center protruded a large dial with etched numerals along the edge. The dial was connected to an intricate gear arrangement, making a vivid statement of its security. The metal may have been old and lightly rusted now, but it was still more solid than anything else in the ruin of a town. Being called a 'safe' was an understatement.

Even with his head hurting, The Commissioner managed a grin before spinning the dial, first one way, then the other, then back again. Satisfied, he worked the huge crank, unlocking the intricate mechanism. With a few screeching groans, the massive door swung open, revealing shelves full of treasures.

The headache was instantly forgotten as a look of pleasure drifted over The Commissioner's face. Picking up one piece after another, he lazily palmed the items. They were his, and he had worked hard to gain every single item. A few might have made their way to him by some slightly devious method or other, but he deserved every trinket. He had wasted years working to see that the town survived, despite itself, and there would be more. There had to be more. Lots more. He would just have to work a little harder, for a little longer. But he had learned, it was indeed possible to make a cactus bleed. You just had to be very careful how you handled it. It was also why he had men to do the heavy-handed work for him. His hands were clean. His first miserly, thieving, boss had shown him that trick.

As though the memory triggered an unconscious connection, his hands rubbed together, wiping away any possible contamination. But that was the past, and a smile played across his face as his fingers again caressed the goods.

His wandering eyes stopped at a unique polished gem of golden-pink translucence, and he picked it up, gazing deeply into the stone's cloudy interior. His gaze followed the crystalline haze with its shadows and unique facets, until it seemed he could almost fall into its depths. His mind dove deeper, looking for the bottom, until he could almost...

Pulling away quickly, he snickered to himself, embarrassed at his reaction to the trick of flickering light. Yes, this was definitely a unique piece, and worthy of his collection. Carefully replacing the little stone, he smiled, glad he had stopped by, then worked to push the heavy steel door closed. As the resounding metallic clang echoed through the room, the headache slammed back to his attention, banging in his skull as solidly as the door had in its housing.

Making sure to re-lock the mechanism, The Commissioner turned and retraced his steps to the upper level. Mrs. Dodge would be waiting. With a grimace and a sour face, he rubbed the back of his neck. It was time to go home.

Throwing open the front door, The Commissioner called crossly to the help, "Let the Mrs. know I'm home," and headed to the kitchen, hoping there was ice in the bin. There wasn't. A wave of anger flushed its way up his thick neck, and once again he bellowed into the seemingly empty house. "Why isn't there ice?"

A slim figure stumbled into the room dipping his head apologetically. In a timid response, barely heard over The Commissioner's deep breathing, his voice quavered, "I am sorry, sir. There is none to be had. I checked on it personally, but the ice house is empty. It is all gone." He shrugged apologetically. "Remember, we didn't harvest as much last year. The rig broke, and they weren't able to get it repaired before spring." Again he shrugged slightly, hopeful, but his apology landed on deaf ears.

With a caustic growl, The Commissioner denied the explanation. "I don't care about your excuses. My head is killing me, and I need ice. Find some, and I don't care if you have to break down the doors of the pub to do it. You've got fifteen minutes."

With wide eyes, the startled figure looked at the giant commissioner and started to make a reply.

"Go!"

It was enough.

The balding and pathetically skinny figure vanished out the door, leaving The Commissioner standing by the heavy table, supporting himself with one fist. The other meaty hand gripped the back of his neck. It didn't help, but it was better than banging his head on the table.

"Mavis!" His bellow rang through the darkened house, echoing up the stairway to the upper rooms. He seldom used her first name, especially where anyone else would overhear. She hated the name, but at the moment, he really couldn't have cared less what she wanted. He was in need.

When a slight noise at the doorway brought him out of his personal revery, he recognized the form of his wife, casually draped in a filmy, clingy nighty, a shawl loosely flung over her shoulder.

"Poor baby." Her words dripped with sarcasm as she lounged carelessly against the doorway. "Not feeling well again? Couldn't be the drink, could it? I warned you. That town swill you keep drinking will kill you someday. Why can't you stick with the good wine I have brought in for us? It's palatable at least, if not what we would normally have in the civilized world."

The Commissioner's nostrils flared. "I am not interested in your wine. But... maybe they were trying to kill me tonight," he said with a thoughtful pause. "The stuff was terrible. Even worse than normal."

"Then why do you keep drinking the horrid swill? You know I hate having you go there every week."

Growling through gritted teeth, he spoke as though explaining to a child. "I've told you. I need to go, so I can keep an ear on things. When the guys get a few drinks in them, they let go with all kinds of information. Things I need to know if we're ever going to get a better assignment. Do you understand how much we gain by knowing this stuff?"

He gave her what he considered a knowing smile, but she was unimpressed.

"Is it worth dying for?" she asked, without a hint of sympathy. "If you think they tried to poison you, do something about it." And with a swish of filmy material showing off a nice length of leg, she turned abruptly and swept out of the kitchen, back up the stairs.

"There's more if you're interested." Her words came floating back alluringly through the doorway.

Teeth locked in frustration at her uncaring dismissal of his pain, he rethought the moment. At least it would be a distraction. The pain wouldn't be gone no matter what he did, and maybe the ice would be here by then.

Stretching his neck until it crackled, The Commissioner rose from his braced position and stolidly made his way up the stairs.

When the door finally creaked open, The Commissioner was already back in the dark kitchen.

"Well, Did you get it?" he growled at the old man.

He spoke without any form of common social grace. He had no intention of being friends, or friendly, with any of the hired help. They were here to do his bidding, and that was enough. They should be thankful for that. There weren't many opportunities for employment in Skragmoore, and as far as he was concerned, working for the leading citizen of the town was a position of undoubted status.

The skinny little man dipped his head in embarrassment and fear, before bringing the bad news. "No, sir. I'm sorry, sir. I tried, but they said they were out too. I don't believe there is any left in town." With a hopeful burst of energy, he added, "Could I get you some cold water? It might help." The poor man was almost shivering in desperation.

The Commissioner sagged visibly before answering with a, "Damn." Then, rubbing his neck, left the kitchen, too worn to do more than climb the steep steps and drag himself back through the large bedroom doorway.

The little man drooped with relief and quickly made his way out of the house, closing the back door quietly.

Half an hour later, Harold, the skinny little man who worked for The Commissioner, sat sipping his warm beer. His breathing had finally settled down and he was well into his second mug.

"Next time, you better use a ton more of that stuff. You know how big he is," Harold growled uneasily. "For god's sake, Mack. You've gotta use it like you would for a steer. He's big enough to handle it. It didn't do any more than give him a headache." After another sip, Harold, Har to his friends, set the mug down carefully, finally feeling the effect of the brew. "Dad-gummit, Mack. You could've gotten me killed!"

"Sorry, Har. I thought it was plenty. I didn't want him keeling over right there on the stool. He had to go down natural like." Mack, the bartender, had been scrubbing down the counter in the never-ending attempt to keep it clean. Finally putting the rag down, he leaned on his elbow. "So, what now?"

"That's a very good question," Har responded in his gentleman's gentleman tone. He wasn't always a butler, but for this job, it had worked well. "The Commissioner might even suspect something, so we'd better hang low for a while."

"Won't be a problem. But how are you doin'? You looked pretty bad when you came in."

"Tell you the truth. I thought I was done for. Shoot, almost peed my pants when he started hollering like that." He gave a chuckle, now that it was over.

"Dang it, Har, you'd best be careful around there. We'd hate to lose you."

"Yeah, well I'd hate to lose me!" Har said with a snort. Straightening his back, he considered his future. "Gotta be back at it early tomorrow. I want to see what comes out of tonight's situation. Figure it'll just blow over, but then again, the Mrs. might get her nose into it, and all hell could happen. I'll try to keep you informed, but if it goes bad, watch for my hide on the flagpole."

He was joking, but just barely. He had seen some of the things that happened to the people Commissioner Dodge had issues with and did not want to be in that position.

"You be careful, Har," Mack said seriously. "We have time."

Harold gave a nod and climbed a little unsteadily from his chair. "I'll keep you informed."

With a dip of his balding head, Har silently left the tavern.

CHAPTER 4

Learning and Growing

Over the next week, Rhone and Stone worked their way through the process of discovering each other and how they each worked.

Rhone found that Stone knew a tremendous amount about the workings of the mind and how things connected, while Stone discovered the way humans saw the world they lived in. These were not necessarily the same views at all, but not bad, considering that Stone had no movement of his own, just an understanding of things, and Rhone not only saw, but physically 'did' things. Very different things entirely. Action versus inaction, and knowledge by being, versus knowledge by doing. They had many talks, discovering their differences as well as their similarities. Life was good.

Wandering your way through life really wasn't bad, as long as things were going well. It was only when problems arose that troubles obviously began.

Rhone talked as he worked his way up the valley's drive that was becoming more overgrown and trail-like in its unused state. It was just common chatter, about all the things he saw and felt. Actually, he was talking so he didn't have to 'think to himself' to Stone. He could, but it was almost tiring, having to think about thinking out loud. It was an odd kind of mental confusion, thinking about who he was thinking of, or to, so he talked instead. It helped to keep things clearer in his own mind. But talking about what he was seeing was for Stone's benefit, since knowing a thing is not quite like seeing a thing. Both may get the point across, but Rhone had the distinct feeling, seeing was better.

So, you think you are better than me, Stone commented archly, *because you can* see *and I cannot?*

Again, the problem of someone listening in to your mind. Not that it was bad, just that it was always there.

"No, I don't think I'm better. I'm just glad I can see."

Rhone tried to dismiss the argument before it got too challenging. In a contest of 'mind over method', Rhone couldn't win. Stone had too many years head start in mental games.

"But I do enjoy seeing things," he acknowledged. "Everything has structure, color, and texture. I don't really know how to relate those concepts to you. It's like trying to explain a color to a blind pers... ahh, rock."

Ahh, but I do 'see' color, in my own way. Colors have a specific vibration, which I note, your mind 'sees' and translates into an electrical pattern of its own sort. Your visual receptors perceive this light vibration, giving it substance in your mind. It is all very intriguing is it not? We both see, but in two very different ways.

"Uhhh, could be," Rhone replied, not really understanding at all. Sometimes it was just easier to go with the flow. But even the way Stone phrased things was interesting. Like the fact he never seemed to use contractions. It is. Not it's. Correct in all things. But his, 'is it not?' Did that mean, *isn't it?* or, *it absolutely isn't!* Rhone still had so much to learn about his new friend.

They had spent the day keeping cool by wading in the river, and now, as they headed home up the rutted valley road, a boulder came crashing down the hillside, passing closely in front of them. Startled by the close call, Rhone stopped short, looking uphill for any additional falling debris. Normally, he would have paid more attention to where he was and what was around, but he had been 'in his mind' today, and totally oblivious to anything else. Obviously not a good way to be traveling. Bringing his senses back to awareness, Rhone knew there was trouble, which was immediately confirmed by Stone.

There may be a problem here.

Stone's words held the first sign of unsureness Rhone had ever heard from him.

Exactly what I was thinking. Rhone thought back.

His family homestead wasn't in one of the lush farmland valleys. Their valley didn't have much more than low scraggly brush climbing the steep, rocky slopes. They had attempted to make a living in one of the rough and arid draws, and since people seldom came up their valley road, they lived mostly in isolation. Still, he was pretty sure the boulder didn't just dislodge itself. It could have, but didn't feel right. Uneasily, he fumbled for his pouch and the little knife, but quickly found it was thoroughly tangled in the fishing line.

Rhone hated to fight. Even the thought of it made him feel sick. There were winners, and there were other winners, but to date, he had not won many. Actually none, if you needed a full count. He made it a habit to evade any potential confrontation. Besides, being alone had its upsides. You couldn't get in a fight if there was no one to fight.

But sure enough, from behind an old, desiccated stump, that hadn't managed to completely fall apart yet, a tall, rough-looking kid in worn coveralls stood up. The snarl etched on his face made a pointed statement that things weren't going to be good. Then the older teen came clumping down the slope in a sloppy swagger and stopped, crossing his arms belligerently. The move only made him look that much bigger to Rhone.

"Whatcha got?" came the droll voice. The kid was too tall and skinny to have a very deep voice, but it didn't lessen its effect on Rhone.

"Ahh, nothing," Rhone answered, trying to maintain a strong voice, and lifting his arms away from his body, showing no weapons.

His mind raced through the words of wisdom Mom had given him. *Never show fear,* she had said. *People are predators and will walk all over fear.*

But knowing his fear would only empower his attacker didn't make it any easier to control his body's reaction. His legs already felt wobbly.

"You do have something," the kid demanded emphatically. "You've got a pouch. So what's in it?"

Rhone's mind was still reciting more of his mom's words. *Only give ground when you have no other options, or when it's part of your strategy,* and Rhone began backing up slowly.

Is that your strategy? came the accusing voice in his head.

But Rhone slapped the mental connection closed. This was no time to get distracted.

Unfortunately, seeing Rhone backing away made their tall assailant feel more secure. He took another step forward and spat. "Show me what you got, dufe!"

"Ahh, That's not my name," Rhone said with a disarming smile. Or he hoped it would be disarming.

But it didn't work. With another snarl, the kid said, "I called you a dufe. Like a dud, or dummy, you dork. Don't you know anything?"

Rhone didn't like the way this was going. His eyes quickly skittered around the area searching for help. But of course there wasn't any. On the other hand, he didn't see more attackers either, as though that made much difference. One was more than enough.

Rhone tried to be more confident. "I don't have anything you would want, and there's nothing in the bag but fire starter, a fishing line, and a rock," which was true. He had eaten the dried meat earlier and was already wondering what he would do for dinner.

"I said, empty the pouch!" The tall kid was shouting now and thinking pretty highly of himself. "Come on already. Right there on the ground. We'll just see what you're hiding."

A flare of anger shot through Rhone, and finally standing his ground, he shouted back. "I will not!" Surprised at how good it felt, he added, "Why don't you go jump yourself! I have places to go, and they'll be expecting me."

Unexpectedly, things seemed to be going pretty well.

Until words formed in his mind. *Rhone, that was excellent. I did not think you would manage to pull it off. Personally, I have never worried about physical harm, but it is interesting to observe how a threat affects you. Did you realize your heart rate has just risen by forty-five percent?*

The smug satisfaction emanating from Stone, and the fact that he was already angry, caused Rhone to toss back a rude thought. *Well, how would you feel if he smashed you with a boulder?* But he instantly felt horrible about what he had just said to Stone.

His face must have shown something of his disappointment because the skinny kid looked at him oddly. His day was on a fast downhill slide, and now had a good probability of getting beaten up too.

Sorry Stone, he thought quietly. *I really didn't mean it.*

In the short moment of Rhone's communication with Stone, the tall kid stepped forward, now sure of himself and his method. Only a couple of feet away and within punch range, he glared at Rhone, clenching his fist threateningly. "Listen close, dufe. Empty the pouch, now." With a finger pointing for emphasis, he hissed, "Do it!"

Rhone didn't have any options he could see. Involuntarily nodding a couple of times, he slowly unhitched his belt and took off the pouch. Then with shaky hands, he slipped back the flap and dumped the contents onto the dirty gravel of the dusty road.

As the few items fell to the ground, Stone's mental voice shouted, *Close your eyes!*

The words reverberated in Rhone's mind and without thinking, he did as he was told.

Instantly, a brilliant flash erupted, creating spots even through his closed eyelids.

Now pick me up, and run! came Stone's command.

Rhone blinked, trying to see through the dark red spot covering most of his vision. He barely saw the big kid wallowing on the ground, shrieking and covering his face with his hands, but he did hear the obscenities when they began.

He didn't stop to listen. Still seeing spots, he fumbled around, searching the rocky ground for the pouch, then for Stone and his other stuff. Finally, with all found, he crammed them all back in, getting his finger stuck to boot. Without further thought, Rhone headed down the rough roadway at a dead run. He did have somewhere to be. Anywhere but here.

"Thank you," Rhone wheezed between breaths. "I would have gotten thumped for sure." Saving his breath for running, he didn't waste it on saying anything more. A few minutes later, with lungs burning but some distance away, he was feeling pretty good. He had gotten away cleanly, which was something special all by itself. And, he had an ally. Life suddenly felt better.

"I thought you couldn't do that flash thing," Rhone said between ragged breaths.

I said I had not. Not that I could not. And it was a silly statement, considering I had already done so.

Rhone took no offense. "Well, you did, and it was great. Both times. Does it hurt when you do that? I should probably know, just in case."

Rhone's concern was honest. Being saved was great, but not at his friend's expense.

No, not in the least, Stone purred happily. *Actually, It is almost exciting. The release of so much energy in such a way... tickles. I think that is the correct use of your verbiage. The movement of energy across my senses feels quite interesting, and I should have thought to do so before now. It is almost fun. Not painful at all, and I am glad it was effective. To be honest, it was our discussion of sight that gave me the flash idea, but I could not do so successfully until you released me from the pouch and I was in the clear.*

Still breathing hard from his run, and hands braced on his knees, Rhone had in fact almost stopped listening, more concerned with sucking in lungfuls of warm air. But Stone's last words held him. In amazement, he asked, "You didn't know what you were doing? At least it worked. I wouldn't have liked getting punched."

I am glad I could help, Stone answered smugly. *You did not seem to be doing so well on your own.*

Rhone didn't respond, other than to roll his eyes. Sometimes there was no win. But he had gotten away without getting beaten up, so that was something. And he hadn't lost Stone. If the kid had seen Stone, he would have taken him for sure. There was no doubt about that. In fact, the only thing that had gone right was when he was forced to dump Stone out of the pouch. It made him think.

"Stone? What if I carried you out in the open all the time? You could "flash" whenever you needed and wouldn't have to worry about the pouch."

That is true, but you cannot carry me all the time. You need your hands free to do things. Really, I am quite fine in the pouch. But after a slight pause, Stone asked, *What were you thinking?"*

Rhone shrugged. "I thought, maybe I could wear you."

Wear? What do you mean exactly?

"You know, maybe on a belt buckle, or maybe a pendant. Even a long necklace, or a brooch might work. I can think of all kinds of things. Mom had lots of stuff like that, but she never wore them. Anyway, what do you think?" Personally, he thought it was a great idea, but wasn't so sure what Stone would think about being made into jewelry.

Stone took some time considering it. *I do not believe I have a preference one way or the other. Perhaps, if you could explain the differences and how they would wear, it might help.*

"Sure. Let's see..." Rhone answered helpfully. "A belt buckle would be easy, and most people wear belts of some sort. They help to keep your pants from falling down. You would look good set in a buckle, and it shouldn't be too difficult to make." He thought about the other options. "Then there's a pendant. It's a long necklace with a medallion or something large hanging down in the front. They're pretty cool too, but it might get in the way. That could be a problem."

And probably not a good idea then, Stone said graciously. *I do not want to be in the way when you need to be moving,* and good information, since he had never had, nor been, a pendant before. *Please go on.*

"Okay, I thought, maybe a ring, but honestly, you're pretty big for that. So, what about a brooch? It's a really big pin thing."

A pin? But that would hurt, would it not? I did not believe you soft creatures liked things sticking into you. I only say that, because you certainly reacted strongly when you were challenged by the young man. Yes, you most definitely had a reaction to that.

Rhone could feel Stone's chuckling vibration even through the pouch, but he wasn't going down that road. "No, not that kind of pin," he answered curtly. "A pin is also a thing that can fasten. I guess it does go into something, but it doesn't have to go straight in. I don't know how to explain it, but it can go in and back out again, and it fastens things." He was finding it wasn't always easy trying to describe the obvious. "Anyway, if I mount you onto a pin, I could attach you to my clothes, or somewhere." Clumsily, he stopped talking.

Hmmm, Stone vibrated gently, beginning to pick up some human traits. *If you cannot figure out how to say it, then it most probably would not work very well. I could see myself becoming un-pinned at some point, and falling off. Then where would I be? No, I do not believe it would be a good idea at all.* He sounded quite certain of his conjecture.

Rhone accepted the decision and gave a last try. "Well, the last thought I had..."

Excuse me, Stone broke in. *Was it your last thought, or the last item?* He seemed to enjoy his instructive mode of late.

"The last ITEM," Rhone said, speaking overly loud. "The last item, is a choker kind of necklace thing."

A what? Why would you wish to be choked? It does not sound very enjoyable, or healthy.

A deep growl escaped Rhone, and in frustration, said, "This is getting... well... harder than I was expecting. And it shouldn't be. I was just trying to explain what I was thinking."

No, no. It is my fault, Stone said without condescension, but without remorse either. *I simply do not know enough of your ways, and misunderstandings are bound to happen. We will make it work. Now, tell me more of this choker... thing.*

Rhone sighed and tried to blank his mind, hoping his scratchy attitude would settle. "Alright, a choker is a kind of necklace, but instead of being loose and hanging down, it's held close against the neck."

Ah, Stone said, *I believe I understand. I told you we could work through it.*

"So, what do you think?"

A little more cautiously, Stone asked, *Are you requesting my consideration of each option?*

Rhone let out a breath, knowing this might take a while. "Yes, Stone. That's what I said."

Good, I am glad you asked. I have been considering the options as stated, and their various elements, eliminating them one by one. Shall I begin?

"Any time," Rhone said, almost rolling his eyes.

All right then. I believe your first item was the belt buckle. I am certain it would work, but... when you wear your over-clothing, which I believe you do when it is cold, I would be covered. It would then be no better than in the pouch. Perhaps we should discard that option.

Relieved, Rhone gave a nod of acceptance. One down.

As to the ring. I do not know about the size element, but I accept your greater knowledge on the subject. So that is out. Now, on to the brooch, and we have already been through that particular discussion.

"Yeah, and the pendant would swing around when I ran," Rhone said, thinking through today's situation and the trouble a pendant might have caused in the quick getaway.

Stone had quickly made his way down the list. *Which leaves the choker...necklace...thing.*

"Okay, good," Rhone replied. "We have a winner, and I think I can make it work."

Will it be a great deal of effort? We did not discuss that particular aspect.

Feeling the concern, Rhone smiled gently, knowing Stone cared. Now they were down to things Rhone did know. "I can handle it. I'm pretty good with leather."

Very good, Stone rumbled appreciatively. *I believe it is a good plan, and my placement at your neck will allow an excellent view. But, leather? Isn't that skin? Whose will you use, and what is your plan for my attachment?*

"Your view?" Rhone asked, vaguely distracted by the feel of Stone's mental gears whirling. "I hadn't thought of that."

Certainly, when I am against you, there is a better connectivity between us, and I can sense much more. It is when we are around others, and I receive their feelings also, that it is more difficult to separate the senses.

"That's good to know, but would I get burned if you flashed?" Maybe it wasn't such a good idea.

Oh no. That is not a problem, Stone answered with sincerity. *I have determined the frequency needed for light. I could, of course, tune it to heat also, but I am fairly certain you would not want me against you when I did.*

"You're right about that," Rhone answered honestly. He had been burned once when he tripped and came down with his hand in the fire. It had not been his best day, but today was good, and they had a plan.

The creation took time, and Rhone decided he liked the term 'collar' better than choker. The obvious connotation had bothered him ever since Stone had questioned it. Working diligently, he carefully designed the correct proportions for the pattern, then chose a soft, sturdy leather from the stash in storage, shaping it to fit comfortably around his neck.

Cutting a hole just smaller than Stone, Rhone placed his friend carefully into the opening, then lay a second band, similarly cut, but carved with complex curving swirls, on top, leaving Stone sandwiched snugly in place. Once set, Rhone laced the two pieces together, hoping the placement would allow Stone to see the world from the front, and rest against his neck from the back.

He didn't discuss the project as he worked, and Stone didn't question him about it. In some way, it had become like a surprise, which was silly, because Stone could 'see' the work he was doing. Even from the pouch, he could simply scan Rhone's mind.

It may have been silly, but they both held to the undeclared agreement, learning to work as a team.

Finally finished, Rhone whispered tiredly, "It's done," announcing his achievement. "What do you think?" he asked, stepping back proudly.

Stone's warm golden glow sat in the center of the leather collar, surrounded by intricate scrollwork carved artfully cut into the leather.

Stone didn't answer for a moment as he analyzed the picture from Rhone's eyes.

I do not know what to say, Stone mumbled in confused thoughts. *It looks, very functional, which is an achievement all by itself, but it is... so much more.*

Rhone's mind was flooded with the feeling of Stone's amazement, as the little crystalline entity attempted to find a way to express itself.

Functionality is a measure of fulfilling a purpose with practicality, but this is... marvelous, and beautiful. Beauty is a function I have never considered before, other than the heavens. They too are beautiful, and these patterns remind me of the swirling stars.

Rhone beamed, accepting the words as praise. It only took a moment to fasten the new leather, with Stone protruding just slightly through the back, fitting comfortably into the hollow at the base of his throat.

This is *marvelous, Rhone. I can feel your thoughts so much better from here. Marvelous. Simply marvelous.*

CHAPTER 5

Not Exactly What I was Thinking

The new collar felt funny at first, but the more he wore it, the more comfortable it became. Rhone liked the way he could feel Stone's reactions and temperature changes, warm or cool, along with his vibrations. His neck was sensitive to these feelings, and he learned to read them in ways he hadn't considered before, connecting them with Stone's thoughts and words.

There was also pride in wearing Stone. While there was no one in their little valley to impress, he began to think about what it would be like going to town and meeting people. His self-worth grew by leaps and bounds, partially from the simple fact that he had someone to discuss with, and partially from all he was learning. Meeting Stone was an education in itself. Almost everything had changed, and they were relearning the world, together.

"This is incredible," Rhone commented to Stone. "I never knew there was so much 'feel' in things. It's like a whole new world."

It is true, replied Stone. *I too am amazed by our interaction. I thought I had a good understanding of the what and why, but it has required a restructuring of my entire way of thinking. Something as simple as 'seeing' in picture form has added a new dimension to my being.*

Rhone knew very little of the physical universe he lived in. Mom had managed to teach him some, but he had no context to understanding Stone. Now Stone 'rode' on Rhone's collar and 'saw' everything around them, taking in the vibrations and passing on the 'feel' to Rhone.

In return, Stone received the mental pictures of the things Rhone saw, giving him a new view of the world they were in. The partnership was a great exchange for both.

As I lay in the river, way back when, I thought I had a good understanding of the world, Stone explained as they walked along. *I sensed the flow of the water and could tell if the river was full or low by its mass. I felt the fish and other creatures that swam or crawled, and I felt you coming up the river. Truly, I thought I had a good grasp of everything. When you picked me up, I felt the wave of energy from your being, and its warmth. Nothing I had experienced previously had that warmth. Even the sun is different. When you put me into your pouch, I could sense our movement, which is very different from simply lying with other inanimates. I began to wonder if others had these experiences, and what it meant. I quickly learned that thinking, and doing, are very different things.*

Thinking similar thoughts, Rhone listened intently while Stone tried to explain.

As I contemplated these things, I began to notice the connection between our motion and the vibrations of your energy. I started connecting your brain wave's patterns to the motion and the picture patterns you were giving off, and on it went. Luckily, my crystalline structure was able to capture and hold these thoughts and vibrations, and after time, they developed into a recognizable form. I have been amazed since the very first moment of your touch, and my view of the universe has evolved. I cannot even begin to explain how much this has meant to my eternal being.

Stone may not have been able to explain it in a thought, but the ramble of his words certainly filled Rhone's time as he did his chores, splitting firewood and working the garden. The warmth of friendship emanating from Stone matched the glow Rhone was feeling.

"I feel the same way," Rhone replied as he took a break from pulling weeds. "I can't believe what a small sliver of life I was living, or understood. I don't know what I would do if we were ever parted. My life would be left totally empty."

As he said it, he wondered if that was how married couples felt about each other. How could they go on when one was left alone? He didn't know, and didn't want to find out. Almost embarrassed by the thoughts, he changed subjects.

"Hey, Stone. About the guy that jumped us. I know not everyone is bad, but I want to be prepared next time we meet people. So, are there other things you can do? Just so I know."

I believe that is wise, Stone agreed. *As we have just discovered, not all humans are to be considered friendly. We must protect ourselves, yet not be aggressive.*

"Right," Rhone said thoughtfully. "I don't want to get beat up, but what I'm really worried about is someone trying to take you."

Yes, I see, Stone said, considering Rhone's worries. *This is a very nice collar piece, is it not?*

"I think so," Rhone admitted with pride.

Therefore, someone may decide they would prefer ownership, which would not be good. I would be in their custody at that point. A slave in some sense, and they would not even know it as I could not talk to them. Definitely a thing to consider.

Rhone could almost feel Stone sadly shaking his head, even though he didn't have one. It was weird, and he smiled, until he thought of Stone being gone and in someone else's possession. It really was a disturbing thought. What would Stone do if he had to sit for years in some dark box? Besides, he liked having Stone around. It was almost like having a pet.

Stone's snort of disgust made it quite apparent the idea wasn't worth commenting on, but it made Rhone smile even more. The thought of having a pet rock was hilarious.

I Do Not Think So, came Stone's unappreciative reply.

"All right. It was just a funny thought," Rhone acknowledged, trying hard to keep a straight face. "Not that I'm calling you a rock, or a pet, but back to the problem. What can we do? You can't go 'flashing' everybody we meet. Besides, it would probably make them want you even more."

I agree. It would not be right. Therefore, we will have to outthink them. Two minds are better than one, so we have the advantage there.

"It doesn't sound like much of a defense," Rhone muttered. "I know you can feel their intentions, but if they really are bad, we may need to do more."

More than just running away?

Here was one of those places where Stone could outthink him before he even knew there was a problem.

"Yeah, like that," he said, slightly embarrassed, but also a little self-righteous. He had, after all, successfully evaded a conflict, but he put the thought away for now. "So, if things really went wrong, we might be able to...do something." He left it there, waiting.

Stone processed the problem through his crystalline mind like a human might take a deep breath. It was another mannerism Stone had added to his 'vocabulary', although Rhone was pretty sure rocks didn't really breathe.

Of course, we do not, came the retort from Stone, who always seemed to be listening in. *But you are correct. I am attempting to learn your body language. You probably do not realize how much you say in that manner. It seems, your emotions are directly connected to your motions, although you are able to override them if you think about it.*

Rhone hadn't thought about it, but certainly would now. Then in an awkward, comic posture, elbows flapping like wings, Rhone began strutting like a bantam rooster. "What am I saying now?" he asked.

Without a pause, Stone replied, *That you are an idiot, of course.* Which ended the discussion.

Discouraged, Rhone dropped to a sitting position, "All right, I get the point, but what do you think?"

I assume you are considering the issue of our meeting someone?

"Yes. We need some options, before we actually need them," he said seriously.

Very good. Let us play out this scenario and see what happens, Stone agreed.

"I guess that might work," although he wasn't exactly sure what that meant. He had hoped Stone would simply come up with a great answer. He was 'the smart one' after all.

Here, allow me to set the scene, Stone began helpfully. *You and I are again hiking the valley trail. I am on your collar, as normal. A bad person wishes to do us harm and jumps out. Okay, now it is your turn.*

"What? Why me?" Rhone cried out defensively. "If I knew what to do, I wouldn't need to ask you."

That is not a very interesting storyline, Stone stated as if instructing a child. *And you seem to be grumpy a lot lately.*

Rhone growled and rolled his eyes.

All right, I will admit that did not go so well, Stone said, as though sympathizing with Rhone's frustration. *I suppose I could assist a bit more.*

Rhone's growl must have been an agreement since there was no additional comment.

Since you asked, I will tell you, Stone said, switching back to his instructional tone. *I do not know what I can do. I was not aware that I could 'flash' before it occurred, but it is now apparent that I can. Therefore, I feel justified in saying we may not know a thing until it occurs.*

Rhone shook his head slowly. "I might mention, that is not the best time to find out. I would much rather know what to expect, ahead of time, so I don't go blind, or get cooked unexpectedly.

Stone's voice had softened with his apology. *Yes, I do see your point. Yet it is also true, I do not know what things I can do. I have never been in a situation like this before. Rocks, as you say, do not normally have these problems. Therefore, I have no preformed procedures in which to direct you. One thing I have noted of your kind is that you humans are totally out of control much of the time. It has been an extreme challenge just to keep up with your thoughts and actions. So again, I must say, I have no previous experience with these types of things,* and it would all be conjecture.

Squinting through one eye, Rhone considered Stone's comment, then spoke thoughtfully. "I guess we'll just have to experiment then. We can learn more as we go."

And what do you have in mind? Stone asked, suspiciously suspicious.

"Let's make a list of all the ways your energy 'might' be used. Then we can try them out."

Logical and very straightforward. I agree.

The simple agreement surprised Rhone. He hadn't expected it to be so easy, but he couldn't find fault either. Immediately they started building a list of possibilities, with Stone reciting his version of the ways energy might be used.

Electrical, mechanical, chemical, thermal, and molecular, and each can be transformed from one form to another. You must recognize, of course, that Kinetic energy is due to the motion of a body or its system. Whereas, Potential energy is possessed by a body, as a result of position or condition, rather than its motion.

"What the what?" Rhone blurted, shaking his head violently.

Exactly, came Stone's voice, echoing in his head. *You asked for information. Now we need to consider the ramifications. It was an excellent question by the way, and questions need answers. Therefore, I have been as explicit as possible.*

Rhone took a resolute breath and sighed uneasily. "Are you sure you need my help? You seem to have this pretty well in control."

Of course, I need you. I do not know how humans react. A little, since I have studied you, but not in-depth for an entire species. Perhaps that should be my quest. He sounded wistful. *There are so many things I have yet to learn, but for now, I need your input. You know how people will react. I do not. I can surmise, but that is not the same thing, and it could create a dangerous situation. I believe it would be better to be correct.*

Rhone felt small next to Stone's massive knowledge. Honestly, only a tiny piece of the puzzle. In fact, he was nothing without Stone. Just a dumb, uneducated teenager, stuck in the country. It wasn't a pretty picture, but it helped him make up his mind.

"Let's do it."

I do not believe it will be difficult, Stone said cheerfully. *We already know I can produce visible light, and undoubtedly heat, although it is not yet tested. Sound should work too, but I do not believe it would have much volume. I have very little mass needed for resonance.*

"Wait, hold on," Rhone broke in, confused. "You said only I could hear you."

A different thing entirely, Stone replied easily. *Sound is simply a transfer of energy in a wave, moving away from a vibrating source, like me. The more energy put in, the louder the sound. I must admit, this is all new to me too. In space, there is no air to carry the vibrations. Here, there is air, water and earth, and all will carry sound waves.*

Stone was on his soapbox now, spewing knowledge he expected Rhone to remember.

Sound occurs when those vibrations are received by a receptor, like your eardrum. The receptor then decodes those vibrations into data, and the information is then sent by an electrical pulse to the brain, which translates it into a pattern for recognition.

Suddenly interested, Rhone's eyes brightened and he sat up. "So I can hear you when no one else can, because it isn't really sound. It's just in my mind."

That was excellent, Stone said graciously. *You are becoming a very good student.*

Rhone was on a roll and worked his way through the next concept. Thinking aloud he said, "That means you could make noise, if you wanted to."

Yes, I believe I could. Although as we said, it is not noise until something receives it.

"Okay, whatever. But you can make noise vibrations." In frustration, he ground his teeth, thinking, *Aaagggghhh!*

You do realize I can hear that, don't you?

Rhone dropped his head in embarrassment.

Gotcha, Stone chuckled.

Rhone had to admit it was more than fair. "Sorry. I'm still working on being around people." Then in thought, he said. *Let alone you.* He grinned, knowing there was no way he could lose that discussion.

<hr>

The experiment was simple. Stone would attempt to vibrate enough to be heard.

They quickly found that as long as he was close, Rhone could hear it clearly, but as he backed farther away, the sound dropped off quickly, until finally, there was no sound at all.

They tried again with Stone vibrating so heavily, Rhone could actually see the movement, but Stone quickly tired, producing little more than a slight, almost unheard ringing.

I believe this is exhaustion, Stone mumbled, having never felt the sensation before. *I am 'worn out', as you humans say. You must excuse me, but I believe I need rest.*

Rhone did believe him. Stone definitely sounded rough around the edges, not his normal smooth self, but he was satisfied. The experiment had worked, a little. They would keep working on it, until they had their answers.

CHAPTER 6

Regression

The collar experience was a little claustrophobic with the leather strapped around his neck the majority of the day. Rhone took it off to sleep and to bathe, but the remainder of the time, he wore Stone sitting against the hollow of his neck.

For Stone, the constant motion and change of view were exciting. His entire state of awareness had changed. He could visualize through both Rhone's view, and his own perception. It was very different from being in a static, unchanging location for so long, but it brought its own considerations and maybe... memory?

Rhone was working in the garden, attempting to keep it from going totally rogue, when Stone broke the silence.

I have been contemplating my existence, he said quietly, barely over a whispered thought.

"Your existence?" Rhone asked, surprised by the comment. He sat back on his haunches, taking it as a good excuse to rest. "What do you mean?"

As you probably guessed, I have been around a very long time. And yes, I am like a rock, so that is to be expected, but I seem to have a memory error. There should be more.

Ah-ha. Got him there, Rhone thought, smiling slyly as he shielded his thoughts. He was getting better at it. Stone was always going on about his not being specific, or not quite correct in his statements. Now he could get him back. "Would you be more specific please? There should be more of what? More memory, or more time?"

Oh, well done! Stone's unexpected words rang clearly in Rhone's head. *Good job. Your mind is getting quicker.*

The words were high praise, but not what Rhone was going for. He had been trying to get back at Stone. Now what was he supposed to do? He could admit the prank, but that would only make it worse. The best he could come up with was, "Ah...so what's the problem?"

It wasn't great, but it seemed to work.

Stone was thoughtful as he replied. *When I think back, there is a place where it all comes apart. I mean that figuratively of course, and yet. I do not know. There is something. I realize this must sound very odd.*

Odd maybe, but Rhone was definitely intrigued. First off, the fact there was something Stone didn't know, raised Rhone's interest. But as he put his mind to the problem, worry came to the front.

"Wait, what comes apart?"

Something coming apart didn't sound good.

Stone's answer was simple. *Me, and We.*

"Me and we? Like...you and me? We come apart?"

That wasn't good, especially since Stone seemed worried too.

No, No, Not you and me. Me and We.

But Rhone wasn't getting it. "So. You and Me, we come apart, like... not together. In the past?"

He was trying, but couldn't make sense of it.

Of course, we weren't together in the past. We only met a short time ago.

Rhone was beginning to wonder if maybe Stone's mind had developed a crack, or fried or something.

Rhone, Snap out of it. The abrupt reply brought Rhone back to Stone's equally sharp explanation. *You are not listening to me. You are thinking inside you.*

Piqued by the comment, Rhone answered rudely, "Where else am I supposed to think?"

Please. I am trying to tell you, but you keep running off on tangents and stop listening.

Maybe true. Okay, he was, but he was only trying to help. Rhone shook his head as he tried to clear his thoughts. "If you would try again, I'll stay quiet."

But it wouldn't be easy.

Thank you. Now let me explain. Starting over, Stone tried again. *When I think back to my beginnings, what you would call youth, I was different than I am now.*

Rhone quietly wondered if he should think about that, or just stay still and listen.

This is hopeless, Stone moaned in his head. *I did not say, not to think. Just think on the comments I bring forth, not on your own creations. How did you humans ever make it this far in your evolution from the God construct?*

"I don't have any idea what you're talking about," Rhone mumbled, "and what does that have to do with us coming apart?"

They weren't getting very far, and frustration was building on both their parts.

First, Stone said in frustration, *It is not, you and me. It was Me and We, and We came apart. Or, I believe that is what happened. At least, my logic takes me to that conclusion.* Even Stone was sounding confused now. *I have blank places that should connect but don't. Does that make sense to you?* Stone had spoken cautiously, attempting to communicate feelings on something he didn't fully understand himself.

Recognizing the need for understanding in the question, Rhone tried to listen carefully. "Go ahead. It does sound confusing," he encouraged. "Can you remember the last time you felt...whole? Is that a good way to say it?"

Yes, that fits well. And no, I cannot remember when. Only that it does not feel...complete, somehow.

It was a carefully phrased answer that felt good to them both. Maybe they could work through this weird situation. After all, it wasn't any more strange than anything else that had happened.

"So, you do not feel complete. Like you are incomplete?"

A very close description, yes. And no. I feel completely fine, but when I search back, it feels...empty, like there was more that should be there.

"Maybe there was more. You are a rock... thing. Maybe you simply wore away, being polished by the river for all those years."

Oh my, Stone said, totally at a loss. *I did not consider that. I need to review the data. And Rhone, that was well thought.*

Once again, Rhone felt embarrassed by the compliment. He wasn't used to feeling valuable. With sudden effort, Rhone strained his brain, trying to think up other possible answers. Unfortunately, his effort went the wrong way.

"Wait a minute," Rhone said, suddenly recognizing a problem. "Who are, We? Or maybe, was We? I don't get that part. Just getting yourself polished in the river wouldn't answer that. Would it?"

Rhone felt the sudden drop in Stone's energy. *I was so happy at finding an answer, I did not look further. But you are correct. It does not answer the question of We. Therefore the 'We' becomes the correct question, does it not?*

"I guess so," Rhone answered, still working through the 'does it not' thing. "If it wasn't for the 'We' part, we could come up with a pretty acceptable reason, but as I understand, We, isn't you or me. Or is it?"

Of course not. We, are definitely not you. That much I am sure.

"So who are the We?" Rhone queried, just as confused as before.

An excellent point, Stone considered. *Who are We?*

"We, as in plural?" Rhone asked, something tickling his thoughts. "Are there more of you?" His brain said, where there was one, there were probably more, but you never know with these kinds of things. Stone was totally unique to his experience, so who knew?

With a sudden flare of energy, Stone exclaimed, *Yes, of course. There must be more, or it would not have been We. A superb question. How many times have I said, We must always be specific.*

"So, there were more of you, or...them. You, as in plural. You know, others like you." Being specific was very taxing at times.

Perfectly asked, and exactly the question. Now we have the concept.

Getting the hang of it now, Rhone plowed on with his thoughts. "So if you were 'We' back then, and only Me now, meaning you, were you all together as one, or separate?"

This wasn't getting much easier, and trying to think it through had his brain spinning, but he tried one more time.

"Were 'We' like one big rock with multiple thoughts, or a pile of rocks all thinking around each other?"

Amazingly, his words came out exactly as he was thinking, and with no preconceived notion to overcome, he could see both possibilities.

Stone began to vibrate with his growing excitement. *Exactly the question!*

"Well, which is it?" Rhone blurted, not knowing which would be better, or worse, for his friend.

But suddenly, Stone's vibration stopped.

Rhone waited until he began to worry for his friend. "Stone?" he questioned.

Not to worry, came the quiet reply. *I am taking time to consider all ramifications of the situation, but I believe............* again, the voice drifted off into stillness. *We were a single entity! With many sub-components!*

The sudden answer both startled and relieved Rhone. "Great, but what exactly does that mean?" he asked cautiously.

The We and I, were singular parts of a larger unit. Think of it like a seamless community. It is difficult to explain, and I am trying to remember exactly what it was like, but it does confirm the feeling that I am not all here. There is a portion of me I cannot find in my memories.

Stone fell silent again, and again Rhone waited.

I believe I was a segment of a large community of thinking units, connected in thought to each other. So much so, that we worked together as one. Each mind interlocked to the others, yet singular.

Rhone's forehead wrinkled as he tried to picture the We being, and finally gave up, but had to ask, "So what happened?"

I am searching my memory. Now that I know what I am looking for, I believe I will find pieces to some of the puzzle. Already I am finding bits I was not aware of. Disconnected things that now make sense. But as to what happened, all I remember is coming aware as I lay in the river, but there was a time before, when We were together. I must therefore conclude, something separated us.

Rhone's memory flashed back to an odd statement Stone had made days earlier. "Stone, do you remember when you were talking to me about sound? You mentioned something about space." He stood and began pacing.

As Rhone reached for the memory, Stone listened in, both grasping the thought at the same moment.

Yes, Stone answered. *I said, This is all very new to me. In space there is no air, so there is nothing to send sound waves through. But here on earth there is air, water and land. All of which can carry sound waves.*

"So how would you know?" Rhone asked excitedly, beginning to put two and two together.

That there was no air in space? Stone commented with growing excitement.

"Yes, and the comment, 'it's fairly new to me'? What about that?" He really had hit on something.

After a brief pause, a tiny thread of thought seeped from Stone. *I believe you are correct my friend.* But a flood of emptiness followed.

Rhone felt at least some of Stone's loss, and asked, "Are you okay?"

Yes, certainly. I am fine. And thank you for your concern, but I will need some time now. I must delve into my memory and try to find more of the lost pieces. Or, Perhaps I was the one that broke away. My memories may be with the other We.

The hollowness was hard for Rhone to hear. It would be like losing your entire family, or maybe your whole town. He had lost his mom, but even that wasn't a whole town. What would that be like?

Quietly, he said, "You aren't alone. I am here."

Stone chuckled softly in understanding, sending a flash-back memory of their first meeting. Then, *I am here!* rang through Rhone's mind, and they both began to laugh.

Stone had gone silent shortly thereafter, but Rhone continued to think on the problem. He had more questions but wondered if he should ask them. And if he did, would it cause greater feelings of loss, or would it help? Still, he had to try.

"Stone? You said you can feel people at a distance, right?"

That is correct.

"Would you be able to feel another of your own kind? I mean, if you weren't connected to them, like when you were one big rock, thing."

He didn't know how to address the issue of Stone's past, and Mom had always stressed how manners were important. Simply not knowing better, wouldn't take the sting out of words that might come out wrong.

"What I'm trying to ask is, if we found another of the We? Your kind. How would we know? Could you tell, without being connected to them... him... it. Sorry, I feel dumb even asking."

The return answer was definitely from 'Professor Stone', with his good-natured air of authority and knowledge. *In my estimation, it would most definitely be dumber not to ask. And yes. I believe I could feel them, even without being physically connected. There would be an energy signature I would recognize. And Rhone, do not be afraid to ask questions. It is much easier to learn when we know the questions, than if it is merely answers we need to find.*

"Okay. I just wasn't sure. I didn't want to bring up anything that would make you feel worse." Rhone was feeling better about asking, but still shy about when it was right.

Thank you, Rhone. That is truly considerate of you.

"So, I have another question. How far away, or maybe how close, would you need to be before you could feel them?"

Yes. Another good question, and I really do not know, Stone said, in a straightforward, and a very Stone-like answer. *I have never been in this situation before, so I have no information to work from. A guess would simply be meaningless conjecture. But why? What are you considering?*

Rhone was forming an idea, wondering if they could find the others. Stone was thinking it too, or perhaps the thought had been his. He could see both and they were one. He would have to think on that too. Which brought more questions.

"If there were others, then where are they? And what happened to separate them."

Stone picked up where Rhone had left off. *And if the We are here like I am, then we might be able to find them. It is a worthwhile endeavor. A quest. But to do so, we must find the best method in which to go about it. It is a wonderful idea, Rhone. You humans do such exciting things. I have never felt so alive.*

Rhone was still at the question level of the concept, but it seemed Stone had swept right past him, to the do-or-die level. They hadn't even finished with one project, and now they were into another, but he had to admit, it felt right. The rest would have to come when it did.

Closing the door, Rhone took a quick look around and walked away. It hadn't taken much to close up the old house. There wasn't even a lock on the doorknob. He might be back, but maybe not. He had traded the chickens and some of the food stores for things he could take with him, putting it all in his pack along with the few clothes he thought might last a while. Stone was fastened snugly against his neck, and a rough but functional coat was tied across the top of the pack. His bedroll was tied at the bottom. He had slept out often enough, this would be no problem. They were on a quest.

"So what do we do when we find other We? Will they know how to talk, or even understand, or is their system still tuned to being a 'rock'?

Rhone had learned a bit about the We community from their discussions, and hated to use the term rock, but he couldn't think of a better description. There were still a lot of questions to answer.

I have been considering that very situation, Stone said thoughtfully. *I do not believe many We would have developed as I have. Perhaps some, but that is a bit ahead of ourselves. We have not yet come up with a good hypothesis for why I am in a singular form. Therefore, our chance of finding even one is astronomical. When you add the possibility of another having been in a similar situation to learn as I have, it is...unfathomable. So to my quick analysis, they would most probably remain as they were.*

"Then why are we doing this?" Rhone asked.

Because it is possible, Stone answered, giving off a totally unexpected surge of electric static.

Rhone jumped at the shock, feeling Stone's smirk.

A one in fifty million chance could still happen, and it only takes one.

Rhone didn't find it very humorous, but put off his discomfort for the bigger question. Nor was he satisfied with the answer. "If we find one, could they learn to communicate like you did?"

I believe so. I am quite certain I could communicate with them. Whether they would wish to communicate with you or not, I do not know. It would be like me saying you could learn a foreign language, and you could, but that does not mean you would go to the effort to do so. If we find one, we will try. It is the best answer I have.

So many questions and so few real answers, just like the rest of life.

"Well, I think it would be cool to find a whole bunch like you," Rhone exclaimed with passion. "It would be pretty neat."

Neat? Stone questioned. *As in neat and tidy, or neat, the non-exercise transmission of the body's heat energy. Or perhaps you meant neat as an undiluted liquid, but I do not see how these expressions match the subject matter.*

Rhone was getting used to the constant over-classification Stone did, and answered without emotion. "No, you goof. Neat, as in, way cool! You still have a lot to learn, but I can understand. It must be hard, being a rock." He was fully aware of the pun in his words, but doubted Stone would catch it.

Ahhh, As I have said, your human vocabulary is very difficult to master with so many words having multiple meanings. Why would that be when it is all so very confusing?

But with no answer available, Stone broke into a new topic. *Now, to your comment on finding additional We. It is an interesting thought, and while I am in great anticipation, I am also unsure of the outcome. Our first concern would be to find one.*

"You're just a party pooper!"

Stone's mental response to the unique term sent Rhone into a fit of laughter.

The We, do not have such strange sayings, Stone replied archly, giving a mental huff and attempting to gain back his dignity. *We, speak what We mean, and our meanings have sense.*

Still amused, Rhone ignored the comment from his friend and pushed for more answers. "So, how should we go about the search? Should we look somewhere in particular? I found you in a river."

Yes, I remember it very well, Stone rumbled with satisfaction. *I felt you coming through the water and turned my awareness in your direction. Perhaps that vibration is what caught your attention.*

Rhone thought about it. "Maybe, I just remember a shiny rock."

I suppose that too is possible. I could not understand your thoughts back then. Just your unique energy. Once we were together, it took considerable time before it developed into understanding. I worry that I cannot pass on that experience to another.

Rhone felt the disquiet, but Stone understood and covered for him.

Do not worry. We still have many things to learn. Insight may come in time.

"I think that means, maybe," Rhone replied. "But regardless, we still need to work on stuff you 'can' do. We're headed off to, who knows where with no idea how to go about it. Maybe if I help you work through your memories, we could find something that would help."

There, see? Those ideas help us look at things from a different direction. Far different than I would on my own. Our thoughts often lead us along pathways that we already know, yet we do not recognize the divergent path leading to another conclusion. Your eyes see our path with Human insight, but I am not human. Try as I might, I cannot see the path as you see it. Together, we will work to overcome these obstacles. It may very well be your vision that finds our way, for I am separated from my kind, and must now think in shortened pathways that are very disturbing to me.

Rhone wondered how old he would have to be to know that much about everything. In a way, it was comforting.

Stone could sense the question even before Rhone asked.

"Hey Stone, will we need to search while we travel? Like doing a search pattern or something? If we don't have a method, we might miss something."

Much like hunting, when Rhone was on a track, he didn't want to let it go, and as far as he was concerned, going off willy-nilly into the wilderness would gain them little more than sore feet. Rhone's at least. And if Rhone went lame, Stone would be stuck too. It was definitely a team effort.

It was Stone that brought about a new direction in their thinking.

You were asking about my ability to contact the We. It is a good question and one I have been considering in depth. Since apparently, by my own words, We were not on earth, we did not have air, water, or land for our transmission to propagate through. To overcome that particular problem, our energies must have been conducted directly through our crystalline construction, much like your blood system.

"Are you going somewhere with this, or is it supposed to be a classroom lecture?"

Rhone was trying to think, but Stone's constant mumble running through his head made the process of thinking, somewhat less than efficient.

Of course, I am going somewhere. I am attached to you, and you are walking are you not?

"You know what I mean! Do you not?" He could do this too, and throwing the mental punch felt good. But it wasn't right. As soon as he said it, he let out a sigh, sinking down cross-legged in the dirt. "I'm sorry. And I know, I said that about eleven hundred times already."

Nowhere near that many, Stone countered with humor. *Only twenty-seven, by my count.*

Rhone chuckled and scuffed at the dirt with his heel. "Well, thanks. That makes me feel a lot better."

But do you feel better? Stone asked, concerned over Rhone's outbreak.

"Yes. I'm fine. I was just trying to get a handle on this stuff, and can't seem to think straight when my mind is going in two directions at once. But that's my problem. What were you trying to say?"

Yes, well, I was attempting to tell you that I may have a method of finding the We.

Rhone sat up straighter. "What is it? I'm all ears."

All ears? I do not understand how that can be?

Rhone snorted, feeling the shake of Stone's non-existent head. "Never mind. I'll tell you later," he said with a grin.

If you say so, Stone said, still uncertain. *Regardless, let me begin by discussing sound. I have determined that sound propagates over four times as fast in water as it does in air. It is a convoluted equation, dealing with density and the bulk modulus, and is somewhat confusing I will admit, but I believe, even the human mind can derive the basics of the concept. Now, pay attention.* Stone was well into his instruction mode at this point, delivering his lecture with pointed determination. *It is destiny that quantifies the speed it travels. To say 'its speed' is somewhat misleading, because it changes as it is affected by atmospheric pressure, temperature, and the density of the subject matter.*

Already lost, Rhone tried to sharpen his focus and stay up with the information, while Stone, oblivious to the problem, rambled on.

An example would be, that sound travels over four times as far in water as it does in air, because water is more dense. Temperature is another consideration, since sound travels faster in warm air than it will through cold. Are you with me?

Rhone simply shook his head. "I got some of it. Maybe." He had been learning huge amounts with Stone constantly interjecting data into his head all day, and surprisingly, some of it seemed to be sticking. Maybe his memory was getting better too. Squinting in thought, he re-ran Stone's words. "Let's see. So, whatever sound is traveling through…"

"*The 'medium', yes.*" Stone slid the word in casually for verification.

Rhone felt like his brain was frying, as he worked to gather all the parts into one conclusion. "The medium affects the speed and so…" he thought hard, trying to pull it together. "Medium, speed, temperature, and pressure, all affect the distance sound will travel."

Very good. This is but a part of the study of physics. Now, are you ready for more?

Rhone wasn't sure his brain could handle much more, but it was also exciting. "Okay, Let's go for it."

Pleased with the response, Stone dove right in. *We are getting close, so again, pay attention. A direct correlation then is, sound will travel even faster through solid minerals, than either air or water. Why would that be?*

It only took a moment, and Rhone had it. "It's more dense! More density means more speed and greater distance!"

He was proud of himself. This was great stuff to know. But he wasn't going to be a scientist, so what good was it? His world was just too backward, and hard work was the only thing survival had taught him.

As Rhone's thoughts began to drift, Stone quickly brought them back around. *It does have value. Your question brought out information to answer it. That answer brought me a new concept, and now, we have a method, which by the way, answered your original question.*

"We do? What method? We just talked about sound and speed."

We did, but your question, or statement actually, was that we needed a method. See how these things work?

Rhone's excited high dropped like a rock. He was confused again. But it was like that working with Stone. He simply couldn't keep up.

Furrowing his brow, he asked, "How did we get a method out of that?"

Think, Rhone. If we simply travel the world, calling out and trying to be heard. How effective would that be? Ask yourself, how far can you hear? In order to cover everywhere, our attempts could only be twice that distance apart, or we would miss an area. In a term from your mind, it would be a hit-or-miss game.

"Okay, I get that. But what does the speed of sound have to do with any of it?"

Think! If our call goes through a solid, it will go farther and faster. Therefore...

"I get it!" he shouted excitedly. "Well, some of it anyway. We won't have to call as often."

It had come together in a blink, and Rhone was amazed at how thick his skull must be not to have seen it sooner. Deep into his self-congratulations, Rhone started dancing a fancy little jig, when another electric jolt zapped him.

"Yow!" he yelped at the unexpected shock. "What was that for?"

Just testing, Stone commented, turning on his warm glow. *Now, you can dance.*

Which at least got a cracked smile out of Rhone. He had been practicing the little dance maneuver, and Stone had just acknowledged that he did a pretty good job.

I did not say that, Stone commented abruptly. *I would not know the difference between a heel tap and a stubbed toe.*

"Come on, admit it. You like my dancing."

Dancing? Is that what you call that jumping around? I can hardly think with all the gyrations.

"Sure," Rhone grinned. "You talk a good story, but I think you're just jealous." As far as he was concerned, his jibe had struck pay dirt. "By the way, when did you learn to give a jolt like that?"

It did catch your attention, did it not? I am glad to see it worked.

"Worked? It almost knocked my shoes off. But you could have warned me."

He was actually a little irked at having been electrocuted without warning. Okay, it wasn't electrocution, but it was close enough.

Stone's reply was no less than he could have expected. *Had I warned you, it would not have gotten the same response. You needed a reset, and I needed to try out a new theory.*

Dumbstruck, Rhone asked, "Shocking me was a theory? You thought you could, so you did? Great theory."

You were the one going on about, needing measures for *protection,* Stone said, excusing his actions. *As requested, I have been considering the issue, and came up with a concept I thought might be effective. To test it, I needed an unsuspecting individual. Therefore, I believe it was a valid test.*

Grudgingly, Rhone accepted the outcome. He had requested it, so could hardly complain. "Next time, just let me know. Maybe I can do a better evaluation if I know what to look for."

I will try to remember that, Stone said mockingly.

Rhone's forehead wrinkled in the futility of trying to explain some things to a rock. But it had worked. "And what made you think of shocking me anyway?"

As I said, just a theory. Remember, everything is energy. When we were discussing the concept of sending sound waves, I came up with the possibility of changing the vibrations to a current of charged particles. Having already discovered that a static charge can cause a shock, I simply increased the amperage a wee bit.

"Well, it worked. I wasn't actually hurt, but it certainly gave me a jolt."

I will admit, I was not certain how much voltage to give. The first shock was a very small static charge. I increased it for the second, and am glad you were not injured.

"You're glad I wasn't injured?" Again, Rhone was stunned. "You mean, you didn't know whether I would be or not?"

Technically, that is true, but I was fairly certain. It was a test after all, and now we have a method with which to fight back. Is not that a good thing?

Rhone couldn't speak for a moment, afraid he would say something he would really regret later. Gritting his teeth, he counted to five and tried to come up with appropriate words. "Stone... thank you for the great protection method, but next time, would you talk it over with me first? Please?"

Yes, Rhone. I see your point. It was not good teamwork, was it?

"Let's just say, we need to talk over our good ideas, before we try them."

CHAPTER 7

Back in Skragmoore

Harold had finished his daily sweeping of the walks and porches, and casually glanced in the window. A rough field hand stood awkwardly before the big desk of The Commissioner's home office, while The Commissioner himself sat behind it, listening intently. Intrigued, Har shuffled his way past the window, broom in hand, listening carefully but not stopping. The Commissioner did not normally talk with hired help, and it piqued his interest. Maybe this was what they were waiting for.

He only caught a few words before he was past, but even then he didn't have any idea what it meant. With a hand to his back, in the often posed action of an old worn-out servant, Har stood quietly leaning against the wall. He tried to remember the exact words. Normally he was pretty good at listening, but what he picked up didn't fit much of anything that made sense. Why would a field hand mention the words, flashing, or kid? And just as importantly, why would The Commissioner care?

It wasn't much, but he had a feeling it was important. Replacing the worn-out broom, Har walked slowly through the house in his normal, stilted walk. At least it was normal when he worked here. Nobody paid attention to an almost crippled old man.

Picking up two glasses and a pitcher of sun tea from the kitchen, he made his way to the office. Walking with a stooped back and his creaky gait, he knocked once and opened the door.

"Mr. Commissioner sir, I thought you and your guest might enjoy a bit of sun tea." With a quick glance, Har noted the young workman, and continued hobbling to the desk where he set the glasses.

"Can't you see I'm busy here?" The Commissioner complained, not at all pleased by the intrusion.

Har shivered slightly, setting easily into his role as a worn-out domestic lackey. "Sir?"

"Just get out."

"Certainly, sir. I'm sorry to disturb you. Would you like me to remove the tea also?" Har was stalling for time, and scanned the room for any additional information. His alert senses could tell there was something out of place here.

He began reaching for the glasses and pitcher but was stopped by The Commissioner. "Just leave the tea and get out. No more interruptions. Do I make myself clear?"

His harsh voice did indeed make itself clear. The Commissioner held a heavy hand when it came to his working staff, and nobody dared challenge him.

Har dipped his head several more times as though in fear, and began backing toward the door, managing to bump into a chair, and the hired hand, before finding the doorway and slipping out. He had gotten a good view of the young man and would pass on the information. Maybe someone would know something more.

The rest of the day went by slowly with no further developments, and nothing had been said about the previous evening. Maybe they had gotten away with the attempt. Too bad it had only been an attempt.

The tavern was just as empty as the previous evening. Nobody had extra money to spend on lavish settings like the town's tavern. Or better said, it was a lavish expense when you had nothing. But Har had a job. It was only minimum pay, but at least he had steady work. His stop at the tavern made him pretty much a regular. Maybe the only regular.

"Howdy, Mack. How's business?"

"You ask me that every time you come in. Does my answer ever change?"

Mack was nothing if not pragmatic. His version of life was, if it can go wrong, it probably will, and he was seldom disappointed. Life was predictable, and if that meant crummy, well what did you expect?

"There's always a chance," Har said glibly. He was a believer. If there was a possibility, then let's try. And while it might not work, it just might.

Entering the low light of the low-ceilinged room, Har set himself at a corner table and re-ran the events of the afternoon. He had a feeling, and wanted to pass on the information.

As soon as Mack brought over a full mug, Har gave a small signal, then picked up the mug and took a sip. It was an old game between the two. It wasn't difficult to pass on information. The tough part was not getting caught doing it.

After downing the mug, Harold got up and made a show of stretching his hunched back, adding a few guttural grumps to go with it. No subtlety there. Everyone knew he was almost crippled. All he had to do was prove them right. With a nod to Mack and a quick good night to the only other customer, Har left the run-down building and hobbled off. He would return later when the shop was closed.

⁕

"I don't know, Mack. Something's going on. The Commissioner doesn't meet with hired help. It just doesn't happen. So, what was so important? I gave you a description of the guy, but they all look alike as far as I'm concerned. Still, maybe somebody will hear something. Remember, he said something about a kid, and the word flash."

Mack cut him off with a wave. "I heard you the first time. My guess is it was probably some kid up and flashed the Mrs. or something." He chortled at the thought of Mrs. Dodge's reaction to some fine young meat on the hoof. Could be interesting, but that was not his concern. "But I hear ya. I'll keep an ear open. Anything more about the other?" It was a thinly veiled request about the previous evening.

"Not a thing. Looks like it slipped past okay."

It was an important trade secret. Never mention an activity, at any time. You never, ever knew who was listening. Not even at a closed business in the middle of the night.

"Okay, Mack, I'd better get some sleep. I'll plan on dropping by after work."

"You take care, Har, and be safe."

The two separated and Har quietly disappeared into the darkness of the night.

Without something solid to go on, Harold could only keep to his daily norm. Sweep, straighten, and assist with the kitchen work, which never ended, then make sure the plants were watered, so they didn't dry up and blow away. The garden was an important part of the household and kept them with a good supply of berries and vegetables for the table. The Commissioner was not interested in paying for something he could have for free, and since he was already paying the hired help, he expected them to deal with the garden. If it died, they would pay. It went without saying as to what, a tooth for a tooth, really meant. Not to The Commissioner.

At least The Commissioner didn't appear suspicious. When Har offered an apology for not having ice the night before, he had been summarily dismissed from the room with the comment, "Then get out there and find some. I don't expect to go the entire season without ice." It was enough.

Harold's, "Yes, sir. I'll see to it," wasn't even heard, as he backed forlornly out of the room.

At least The Commissioner's headache seemed to have passed, forgotten, as just one of those things. Now, Har's concern was to find out what the clandestine meeting in the office had been about. The Commissioner's 'behind the scene' workings, was the reason Harold was here. Timely knowledge of imminent happenings tended to save people's lives, and this community needed his service. There had been multiple losses already, and more would occur as long as The Commissioner stayed in power.

But the thought of yesterday's meeting kept returning to Har, which meant it had some importance. He just didn't know what. His memory of the field hand was of a tall and gaunt young man, which covered most of the field hands in the area. None of them had enough food to actually gain weight, so gaunt was the outcome. This young man hadn't been much older than a teen, but most young men were just kids to him. That's what happens when you keep adding on the years. Everyone else just looks younger.

He considered how much longer was he going to do this kind of work. He would have to stop someday, but right now, he was curious. The question was, why was one kid bringing information about another? And why would The Commissioner be interested in anything to do with teens?

He couldn't come up with anything. Maybe he had heard wrong. And what in the world did a 'flash' have to do with anything? Mack's concept might have been funny, but Har didn't believe it for a minute. Still, if the Mrs. did get a hankering for some young meat, The Commissioner just might want to hear about it.

Shoot, maybe it did make sense, but he couldn't afford to guess wrong. Making a decision without the correct knowledge could lead to disaster.

With a timid knock, Harold stuck his head into the office doorway. "Would you be caring for anything else before I head out? I believe I am done for the day."

Every minute in The Commissioner's presence had a two-fold potential consequence. One, he might hear or see something of value, but two, it was dangerous. The Commissioner was not one to trifle with. Those who didn't take him seriously paid the price, one way or another.

The Commissioner's deep voice answered with total disinterest. "Ask the Mrs. She might have something. And close the damn door on your way out."

The gruff reply was nothing more than he had expected. It was the norm.

"Will do, sir, and a good evening."

Giving the finely appointed room another quick look, Har slowly closed the heavy slab door, hearing the solid thunk and click as it latched. Other than the pile of papers on the desk, it was clean, and those would be locked up in the cabinet tonight. The Commissioner was circumspect to the point of meticulous, dealing with those kinds of things himself. He trusted no one.

⚬———— ﷲ ————⚬

"Mack, have you heard anything? I've come up empty."

Harold and Mack sat on stools at the deserted counter of the Tavern. Mack had closed early tonight. There hadn't been any customers after the few trickled in on their way home from work. The only way he made an income at all was because he did all the work himself. But at least he wasn't breaking his back in the fields all summer and freezing to death in the winter. The tavern may be old, but it was warm and dry, which was a blessing. Even a few customers were better than none.

"Well...." Mack drew the word into a sentence of its own. "There was one odd thing that might fit. I overheard one of my customers talking. Mentioned his work partner whacked his head on a tree limb. Ran straight into it, the guy said. Then the friend tried blaming it on a blurry spot in front of his eyes. Said he couldn't see good, 'cause he almost got blinded by a light the other day. Of course, the customer didn't believe it. Said the guy must have been drinking, and got so plastered he lay staring at the sun too long. I've got to admit, it makes more sense."

Har set his glass on the highly polished wood of the bar top. "Too convenient to be a miss. Any idea who he was talking about?"

"Nope, but I might be able to find out. Do you really think this is something? It sounds pretty far-fetched to me. Blinding lights and Commissioner Dodge? Other than this meeting you keep goin' on about, why would there be a connection?"

"I haven't the foggiest," Har agreed, "but the kid in the office thought it was something The Commissioner should hear about. Waves a big flag as far as I'm concerned."

"I don't know. A guy whacks his head, so The Commissioner is instantly connected." Mack shook his head wearily. "Bad as he is, I hate to go blaming everything that happens on the guy. Maybe I'm just too old for this stuff. Anyway, I thought I'd pass it on. Good hunting, Har. I'm done for the day." He got up and started picking up the glasses, carrying them back to wash.

Harold climbed wearily to his own feet, scooted his stool in neatly, then slapped the countertop. "There's got to be something there, Mack. I feel it. You find out who it was that thumped his head, and I'll do some more poking around. Thanks for the beer, and the info. I'll keep in touch."

With that, he headed to the door and slipped out, his hobble instantly dropping back into place. He was good at his job.

If he could find Mack's customer, he might be able to find where the guy worked, and hopefully, who his partner was. It was a long stretch, but it sounded like the guy with the bad eyes might be the one they were looking for.

A pathway of discovery began to open in his thinking, and a plan was developing. Har smiled for the first time in days. The job was almost fun, when things were going right.

CHAPTER 8

Aundrea and the Government

The Council met at the most inopportune times. Aundrea wondered again if that was intentional, to keep the opposition on their toes and as unbalanced as possible. It was an understandable, non-confrontational, method of aggression, and it worked. If the opposing party couldn't keep up, they were left behind, playing with issues that were outdated, instead of those on the front of the people's minds.

She knew the public had short memories. They swayed with whatever politics happened to catch their attention at the moment. So the best method of changing the public's interest was to create new situations to divert the public's attention. It was an old tactic and worked surprisingly well. She was constantly amazed at the gullibility of the public and their willingness to be led by the nose from one construct to another.

Her job was to mitigate the prevalent situations and assist the redirecting of public emotion. It sounded easy, but with the constant interference of not only the opposing party, but some in her own core, it was an almost impossible task. The odd meetings didn't help either, making her own scheduling difficult to maintain. It came with the title though, and she knew what she was getting into before she had accepted the position. Public Recrimination Officer meant she was at the front of every issue the public wanted to bang heads with. Some issues were definitely valid and needed a rewrite of the government's methodology. Other issues were simply made up, hoping to gain notoriety and fame for taking on the establishment. Both needed review and handling, and both met tough legislation regarding any attempt to make change. It was odd, but the world seemed to enjoy solidarity against any change it was asking for.

Ask and be denied. It was the one common element. It was also her job.

While politics occurred mostly at The Capital Stronghold, it affected the dealings of the entire country. Commissioners were delegated to oversee the various sections and assist the people in bringing about abundant commerce and affluence to their people. Mostly it worked. But there were, without a doubt, problem spots. Rumors abounded of corruption and heavy-handedness, and her office took the brunt of the public outcries. She did what she could, but the distances involved made her job difficult. By the time she received news of a problem, it was mostly past her ability to influence the outcome. That was where her network came in. Her budget included a category for her discretionary use, and she had made sure it included salaries for her 'behind the scenes' personnel.

Right now, she had people out in four different locations, attempting to discover the exact cause of the disturbances. Unfortunately, they had not been very effective in their recent efforts, and the outcries continued unabated. Whenever she brought up the issues with the council, she was emphatically told, it was her job to take care of the problem. The threat was implicit, and she was forced to step back without assistance to her concerns.

One of the biggest problems was with the rank of The Commissioners. While there were superb leaders in the group, there were others she wouldn't have allowed to babysit the neighbor's children. But it was not in her power to control those pieces of the puzzle. The council chose them, and it was rumored that the old brotherhood controlled the council. The round-about flow of power was unmistakable, but again, ran beyond her level of government to affect. She dealt with the people, not the powers that be. Keep the people happy and controlled, and the government was happy.

Climbing the time-worn steps, she entered through the heavy door into her conveniently placed office. She had worked hard to get it moved to the Capital Stronghold itself. The closer to the governmental officers she worked with, the less time was wasted on transportation to and from. There was no time to waste in her work, and with her constant interaction with the powers that be, it saved immeasurable amounts of her workday.

Aundrea slid her lithe and fit form into the seat of her one prized possession. The chair's hand-carved seat and back were fitted to her like a glove on her hand. It made the long hours at her desk almost a pleasure. And if not exactly pleasurable, then at least do-able.

Settling in, she drew a sheaf of papers from the shallow box where they had been deposited and began scanning their contents.

Troubles in Courtney. Problems in Galley Prime. Public discord in Farrow. Extreme poverty in Skragmoore and famine threatening in Harrow. Having read them so many times this week, she knew them by memory.

Setting down the last sheet, she sighed and placed her chin on her braced hands, elbows on the desktop. There were just too many major issues occurring at one time. Three was to be expected. Everyone knew bad things came in threes, but five? Something, or someone, was behind the problems.

Now if there was a true problem, say, with the weather or other natural situation, The Commissioners should have asked for assistance. Those things happened. Drought, floods, insect infestations, or whatever nature could throw at them. No commissioner could be expected to overcome everything by themselves. That was what the government was for. But her budding suspicion said there was something further behind the problems, and it wasn't new. It was why she had cast her net.

She smiled, thinking of the term. It was appropriate. She cast her people out into the maelstrom to see what they caught. They had been an even more effective asset than she had hoped, and the main reason she still had her position. She, and they, were effective.

The next stack of papers were letters from her net. She sat back, relaxing into the seat as she read through their reports. The more she read, the more unease she felt. Things were getting worse, and Skragmoore led the way. Her reports showed failed commerce in the region, failed public affluency, and failed inter-zonal commerce. All in all, the place was heading the list for one of the worst places to live. That did not bode well for the government. As soon as the information got out, the opposition's griping would grow. They were always looking for a soft spot in which to anchor their predatory teeth.

She read back through Harold's newest report. He was a wonder in the field and had given her more than one win over her opposition.

He had a nose for things and knew where to poke for information. This report didn't have much real data, but definitely led her to an understanding of the problems. The people of Skragmoore were almost to the point of failure. When that happened, there would be a revolt. She would need to read up on Commissioner Dodge, but she already knew enough to worry. While he wasn't much of a problem himself, he was backed by the very powerful organization of The Brotherhood. Or so she believed, and that was worth worrying about. The Brotherhood wasn't advertised, but they were a behind-the-scenes influence on everything doing with power. No one knew exactly who they were, but their position in the creation and distribution of positions and titles kept them in the superior position of influencing anything that made a difference in the country. If they were real.

She needed more information and set about sending requests to her various connections. She would send the obvious notices through the normal channels and protocols, but there would also be the encrypted versions, sent by other means.

Aundrea rubbed her eyes as she considered the situation. Who was entrenched in a position to gain from the failures of the troubled zones? That information would be a good start. Always, follow the flow of power.

Ringing for her aide, Aundrea gathered the documents and placed her seal on each, securing them against general perusal. A knowledgeable opponent could get past the obstruction, or may simply not care, but for general purposes, it worked well. The other documents, she folded tightly and sealed in their own waxed folders. These would be carried by hand and distributed in secret to the select few.

Bran stood patiently waiting for his directions. He was used to the scene and knew the convoluted methods she required for safe transmittal of her missives. He too, was good at his job.

Finally, she was ready. "Bran, Please take these and see to their dispersal. You know the routine. This batch by general dispatch, and the others for our personal couriers." She showed him the two sets of dispatches and gave him a smile. "See these gone and take the rest of the day off. I won't need you any further today."

Bran gave a respectful nod. "I'll see it done, and thank you, ma'am. I was planning on stopping by the flower shop on the way home. This will let me get there before they're all gone." He paused and cautiously asked, "Ma'am, Is there going to be trouble?"

Her smile deepened as she shrugged casually. "There's always going to be trouble. It is merely a matter of when and where. Maybe we will get some information back from these that will help us through this one more easily."

"I'll see to them right away then."

He gave her another deeper nod of acknowledgment, before picking up the dispatches and making his way out of the simple but elegant office.

Aundrea rolled her shoulders and arched her back until it cracked, relieving at least some of the ache from sitting at the desk for so many hours. Now she would change clothes and go for a run through the country. Most of the people around thought it very strange that she ran when she could have ridden, but it didn't bother her. She worked hard to keep in shape. Her hours at the desk did not promote a physically fit body, and she was proud of herself for maintaining her slight form. Most did not, and it showed. She could also pull a good bow, but that, she didn't advertise. Besides, her use of a cross-bow almost made it a negligible skill. Then there were the other weapons.

But her running not only kept her fit, it allowed her to see the people where they worked. They would shout as she passed by, joking amongst themselves at the antelope they had for a Public Recrimination Officer. It was good fun and didn't hurt her title with the people. They trusted her, and therefore her office.

She also knew attracting attention this way would distract her opponents from the real situations. As long as they were watching her and her actions, they wouldn't be watching her people as closely. That knowledge kept her at the road for long distances, when it would have been easy to call it a day. Occasionally, she would even catch glimpses of her political tails, as they attempted to stay obscure while following her around the countryside. Such were the games she played, even on her time off.

Her work was an intricate overlay of machinations, as she attempted to gain an accurate view of the events affecting the country. With her net spread across the entire government, her knowledge of the comings and goings of the powerful was probably better than almost anyone in the council. She knew there were others with their own informers. There always were, but hers were special. Her people did their jobs because they believed in what she did, willingly giving of themselves to promote the common good. Certainly not for the meager funds she was able to filter their way. She loved them for their service, and worried about every single one of them. They weren't just employees. They were her family.

The run did her good, not only burning off the excess stress of the day but burning into the muscles themselves, strengthening them.

At least she hoped that was what it did. Either way, it felt good after being imprisoned in the office all day.

The soft moccasins she wore had been specially made for her, wrapping up her ankles for extra support and extra layers in the soles for protection from the rocks. She ran with a freeness that brought looks of appraisal from both men and women. The men appreciated the view of muscular legs showing alluringly under her knee-length skirts and often allowing fleeting glimpses of the fitted leggings on her upper thighs. The women looked wistfully at her fleeing form, wondering what it would be like to be so fit and free. There was no jealousy in something so far out of reach, and they waved as she passed, her hair flowing wildly with a mind of its own. She would be sorry later when she had to work the tangles from its masses, but today, she hadn't felt like wearing it in the intricate braids she normally wore when she ran. She hoped its freedom would help her think.

What was going on in Skragmoore, and who would be behind it? She had a lot to worry about.

CHAPTER 9

Meanwhile, Back at the Farm

"Okay, try it now."

Rhone stood across the clearing from where Stone lay, still in his collar setting. Furrowing his brow, Rhone strained his hearing, closing his eyes to better concentrate. Try as he might, he heard nothing but the buzz of grasshopper wings, as one jumped and flew over the dry ground.

"I don't hear anything," he called, frustrated that the plan hadn't worked.

He started to cross back to Stone when a clear, solid note rang through the warm air.

"Did you do that?" he called out excitedly. "I can hear that perfectly." Running to Stone, he picked up the collar and secured it around his neck. "That was great! I heard it clear as a bell."

I did, Stone answered smugly. *I am glad you are excited by this simple experiment, but it is a long way from coming to a reliable conclusion. On the first attempt, I held back. I wished to see if you would falsely relay information you wanted to occur, but created in your own imagination. Then I struck the correct frequency, activating the sympathetic vibration of the rock I lay on, thus creating the tone you heard. Between the two actions, I believe we have a consensus and an accurate outcome.*

Stone was always looking farther down the pathway than the simple steps they had gotten so far.

"Okay great, but it worked. I heard you."

You can always hear me, Stone answered, as though trying to burst Rhone's excited bubble. *What you heard was a tone I struck with my vibrations. Everything has a frequency at which it will vibrate. If that frequency is struck with enough energy, it will cause a vibration to occur, sympathetically, in said item. So you did not hear me. You heard the sympathetic vibration on the stone upon which I sat.*

Rhone squinted into the bright sun, thinking through the long explanation. Finally shaking his head, he acknowledged Stone's explanation. "Whatever. It may not have been your voice, but it was still from you."

Well, yes. I did cause the vibration.

"Good enough," Rhone stated jubilantly. It wasn't often he actually won one of these conversations. "So now we know you can make noise others could hear."

It was an exciting concept, but Stone wouldn't accept the praise.

We *already knew that possibility,* he replied. *What I did not do, was 'speak' so that another could hear. Noise and speech are two entirely different things.*

Rhone knew he was right, but having Stone make a noise was still a big step in understanding his limitations. At least part of their experimentation was to find what he could do, and what was beyond his abilities.

"I get your point," Rhone conceded, "but I like the thought that if you needed to, you could make a noise someone could hear. That tone had good volume. Far better than when it was just you."

It did, Stone agreed. *The boulder has more spatial volume I could affect, producing greater amounts of resonance, or sound.*

Rhone didn't mind the little bits of information Stone kept adding to the discussions. He was learning at an astounding rate. Sometimes it felt like his mind was actually swelling from the amount of thinking he was doing.

There is, however, a limit to the size of the item I can affect, Stone continued. *If it is too large, it would take too much of my energy to accomplish. You saw how tired I got when we were attempting new things. I don't know what would happen if I used too much of my reserves. It takes time for them to regenerate. Even for my crystalline construction.*

Something in the discussion tickled a thought in Rhone's head. Grimacing in a comical squint, he tried hunting down the flickering idea. He finally gave up, catching only a vague shadow of what he had felt. "Maybe someday, we'll figure out how to change the tones so you could fake the sounds of speech."

Did you come up with that on your own? Stone asked in wonder.

"I think so. I was just thinking, if you could make one tone, maybe you could make others."

Yes, I see. And if I put the tones together, it might make sounds like words. That was very good thinking Rhone, but the answer is no. The rock vibrated, but it only has one frequency it will vibrate to. That particular note is why it has a sympathetic response and begins to vibrate along with me. If I resonated on a different note, the tonal vibration would not occur at all.

Rhone accepted the answer but was a little disappointed. "Okay. I was just thinking."

Do not take the answer as a reason to stop thinking, Stone said clearly in Rhone's mind. *It was an excellent question. Maybe someday, one of your questions will actually work.*

Rhone knew Stone meant it as a compliment, even if it didn't sound that way. Deciding to skip the issue he brought up his next question. "What are we going to do to find the We? I know you've been working on the idea, but I don't have a clue. I could wade up a lot of rivers without finding another We. It was just luck."

I agree, and I have been thinking about it.

Rhone stopped in the shade of a tree so whipped by the constant wind, that the few remaining leaves were mostly tattered sails. It still gave more shade than none, and he gratefully settled himself against the rough trunk. "Okay, what's the plan?"

Quite simple really. We grid off the land into equal sections and at each intersection, we will call out, then listen for a response. If a We is in the area, they will undoubtedly answer my call.

Stone projected great enthusiasm for his plan, but Rhone wasn't nearly as impressed.

"How big a grid are you talking about? It would take us more than my entire lifetime to cover that much area. I've never gone any farther than town, and that only a couple of times. Do you have any idea how big the world is?"

The more he talked, the more dubious he became.

You do not like my plan, Stone said in a deflated voice.

Rhone felt somewhere between an apology for disappointing his friend, and absolute surprise at even the need to answer.

"I think it's a great start, but maybe we need a few more days to think it over."

Perhaps, in my excitement, I did get a little ahead of myself, Stone murmured in his own apology. *A perfect plan is a work of art, and should not be thrown into place like mud.*

Rhone rested against the rough trunk thinking through Stone's latest words of wisdom. It was unique, but it was one way of saying it. Mostly, he was relieved at how quickly Stone had accepted his response.

Stone plowed on with his thought not noticing their effect on Rhone. *With the understanding of the distance sound waves travel, and keeping those distances in mind, we could judge the area required for a complete coverage. My grid leaves very few gaps and little double coverage. I decided to leave out the consideration of changing rock densities in any given area. Too much data would confuse the process.* Pausing in his dissertation, Stone asked, *Are you following this, Rhone?*

"Yes, I'm listening, but how about if we start out by trying it first."

Yes, that would indeed give us better data to work with. When do you wish to start?

Rhone couldn't help but smile. While he was totally behind the idea, he would feel more comfortable knowing what he was getting into.

"About your plan. Is there anything I need to do, or is it all you?"

It is pretty much just me, Stone admitted. *My contact projections will work best if you place me on solid rock, but I already understand there may not be rock everywhere. We will simply have to see what is available and correct the grid from there.*

"Any idea what you're going to say?" Rhone asked, still digging for details. "And do the We even talk like people do? The more I know, the more I realize how little I really know."

That is true for all of us, Rhone. It is when we realize our lack of knowledge, that we can make our greatest growth. But to your question. No, We do not form words as humans do, and yes, we do have understanding through the variation of energy waves. It is the patterns. Remember how we spoke of the energy patterns affecting your eardrum? It is something akin to that. Different of course, but similar.

Rhone chuckled, remembering other, 'similar but different', conversations. It seemed like there were a lot of things, different yet similar.

As to, what am I going to say? That is a question I have been asking myself.

"How about, Hey, I'm over here!" Rhone jokingly suggested.

I believe that will work, Stone said, taking it as a real possibility.

"Really?" Rhone questioned. "Honestly, I was just kidding."

There does not need to be any additional information. If there are We within our range, they will recognize the contact and will respond.

"If you say so. Maybe we'll get lucky."

CHAPTER 10

Flash in the Fire

"And you'd better listen good."

The almost quiet warning locked the poor man into a stiff-spined posture. But The Commissioner wasn't done. His volume grew until the final words were almost a shout, the sound echoing through the halls.

"If I tell you to sit on a rattlesnake, I expect you to go find a really big one and plop down on it. I don't want your excuses or your ideas. I'm here because The Council put me in charge, and decisions are made by me. Now get out of here, and see what you can find. If you come back empty-handed, you had better have a really good reason, or you may find some parts missing. Do I make myself clear?"

A visibly shaken foreman edged his way out, with Commissioner Dodge slamming the door behind his departing figure. Everyone within hearing took themselves farther away, lest they be unwittingly connected to the day's newest underdog.

The Commissioner was not in a good mood today. Businesses in town had shown a loss again, for the umpteenth month in a row.

Soon The Council would hear about it, and someone would come asking for an explanation. He would have to find a way to cover himself. Someone to blame. That wouldn't be difficult. There was always someone he could blame, and if not, he would see that there was a good reason, even if he had to create a reason himself. He had learned from a good instructor and knew the ways around most problems. But this was only minor.

The thing that had him on edge wasn't the failing businesses. He could see that with his own two eyes. It was the odd report from the other day. The more he thought about it, the more it bothered him. At first, he had scoffed at the young man coming for a reward. It was common knowledge that, as commissioner, he paid for information regarding the comings and goings of people and products. It only made sense. A commissioner needed information to run the place well, and if the town's residents could make extra coin from hearing or seeing something that might be of interest, well, why not?

So it wasn't that the guy had brought information. It was the information itself. He had laughed at the time. Some stupid, handed-down story the guy hoped would earn a reward. He hadn't gotten any, of course, and was lucky he left walking. Stupid and untrue stories still got what they deserved, but it wasn't coin.

The problem was, the more he thought on the story, the more it disturbed him. If it was true, then there was something out there he wanted. He had heard stories of items that could carry light. Not just a torch or a lantern, but a bright light that would throw a beam out into the dark. How could you throw light? He had always thought they were made up magics by people who needed an untruth to find a reason to keep on going, but maybe not. The kid had been serious, and stuck to his story, but it had only been a repeated story.

Second-hand stories were always flawed. Everyone expanded on the truth. That's what made a good story. But what if? There were lots of strange things in the world. He had the rock in his study to prove it. How could old bones be embedded in solid rock? It was a mystery, but it was still true.

Then his foreman had come in and made the mistake of questioning him about orders. He was lucky to be walking out. When would they learn? Nobody questions his orders. Nobody.

The Commissioner sat back in the heavy leather seat, pondering the problem. If someone out there had found a relic of some kind, he wanted it. He would purchase it for a reasonable price, or...he would find another way to have it. There was still room in the safe, and he would see it filled before he got reassigned.

The stonework of the Town Hall had been quarried long ago from the rocky escarpment at the edge of the town. After this many years, the building looked almost as old as the hills surrounding it. The stone had been mortared together in a rough semblance of good masonry, but the years had done more than sunburn the rock. It had weathered the mortar away until it hardly held the stone in place. Several pieces had fallen in the last few years, and people were beginning to walk on the other side of the street, keeping a safe distance from the walls of the ancient structure. With no money in the town's coffers to rebuild, they would just have to live with it. The town was visibly failing, and if the Town Hall fell, it would simply signal the end that much sooner. When anyone complained, The

Commissioner simply answered that it wasn't his fault. He couldn't fight Mother Nature.

The other buildings in town weren't much different. With so much rock around, stone was the basic building material, although some of the buildings were made of brick. But the old kiln that had baked them burned to the ground years ago and had never been rebuilt. It was simply too much work to dig the clay, work the clay, and bake the clay into bricks, when the rock was there for the taking.

The wooden buildings didn't fare much better. The weather was too hard on the lumber, causing it to dry and warp in the hot summer sun, and shrink in the frigid winters. They were costly to build too and needed to be constantly repaired and repainted in order to last any length of time. All of that cost money. Even though the wooden buildings might possibly be warmer in the cold winters, few had even tried. The few that still stood had been built when there was still money in the town.

M ack put on his biggest smile of the day. "Mr. Commissioner, sir. So glad you could drop in."

At least The Commissioner paid in coin, unlike most of his other customers. Trading for goods wasn't bad, but it didn't pay the bills. Like the town's doctor, Mack often took items or services in trade for his brew, and since he made the beer himself, it was a fairly inexpensive product. And another reason he could still stay in business.

"Just a mug, Mack, and I hope it's cold."

"Yes sir, Mr Commissioner. Found a bit of ice buried deep in the storage. I had to dig it out the other day, but I knew you liked your beer that way. Most of my customers just drink it warm, since they can't afford the surcharge."

Mack rambled on about nothing while skillfully serving up the beer in a cold mug he kept in the cooler.

After a long draw, Commissioner Dodge slapped a coin on the counter, then carried the mug to a well-worn table and slumped his big body onto the even more worn bench.

"It's been a long day, Mack. Stupid people and stupid problems." The Commissioner rubbed his forehead, feeling the beginnings of another headache. "Don't even know why I stay on in this backwater place. Maybe I should just pull up stakes and tell The Council to place me somewhere worth being." He took another sip of the cool liquid and visibly relaxed. "Mack, have you heard anything about someone with an artifact? You know I collect such things. I caught a rumor there was someone with some kind of a light. I thought perhaps you might have heard something. You being the center of activity around here."

Har had been right.

Mack scratched his head before answering, thinking of ways to get more information and still stay out of harm's way. "Haven't heard anything, but you bet I'll keep an ear tuned, now that I know you're interested." Picking up an already clean mug, he vigorously re-polished it.

Commissioner Dodge shifted, tightening his gaze on Mack. "By the way, I think I got some bad brew last week. I had a headache like it was going to kill me. I suggest you check your stock, or I'll have to check it for you."

That got Mack's attention. "Bad brew? From here? Dang, I don't know, sir. I haven't heard anything from anyone else, but you can bet I'll check everything I've got. Wouldn't want that to happen. You understand how bad that would be for business."

"You do that." The Commissioner's grim stare seemed to bore a hole right through Mack. "This whole town's going to hell, and yours is the only place I can trust."

"You got it, sir, and thanks for letting me know. It's as good as done." Mack's knees were all but knocking as he faced The Commissioner. "I'll even close up early, so I can check it out tonight. You've got my word on it, sir."

The Commissioner's mumble wasn't really words, but it accepted Mack's promise.

"Time I got on home to the Mrs. You take care, Mack." He got wearily to his feet and dropped his odd hat back onto his head. "See you Friday."

The front door squeaked its protest as The Commissioner pushed it open and stalked away up the street.

Mack slumped onto one of the bar stools, letting his forehead bang lightly on the counter. So, The Commissioner did suspect the brew. At least he had suspected a bad batch and not that it was poisoned.

Dang that Harold! He had been right again. There was something going on, and he didn't believe for one minute The Commissioner just wanted to buy a trinket. He would indeed listen to his customers' conversations. Somebody would know something. But right now, he would go check his stock. If Commissioner Dodge said he would send someone to check his goods, he would. Mack needed to get it done first. And as soon as Har came by, he would hand off the information.

Herding the other two customers out, Mack flipped the open sign to closed and headed to the storeroom. There were kegs to check.

He was sure all traces of the poison were gone, but this incident was too close. If it wasn't for Har still working on the project, he would seriously think of moving on himself. The Commissioner had been right. This town was dying, and he didn't plan on being here when it happened.

Their plan of getting rid of the main problem in town hadn't worked as hoped. So on to plan two. Find the places Commissioner Dodge was squeezing, and build a case to use with The Council. The Commissioner enjoyed his power, using it indiscriminately for his own gain. It wouldn't be so bad, if the people gained with him, but when it meant he got the lion's share, and those doing the work got none, it became usury, leveraging high rates for inferior service. It was simply wrong, and the town was dying because of it. The Commissioner was strangling an already dying body and didn't seem to care.

The next problem was, while they might indeed get him moved, it would just move him to a different location where he would start his problem-making all over again. Har was keeping Aundrea aware of everything they found, but they honestly hadn't found much. The Commissioner was very good at keeping his secrets. They had been briefed before being sent out on this wild goose chase, but knowing a piece of a person's past was not at all like finding their secrets.

It had taken a lot of time for them to set up in a new location and they had each come separately, months apart. Luckily, it took so long to get anywhere, no one questioned anything. It was simply inconceivable that someone would take the energy to get here if they didn't need to. To the isolated people of Skragmoore, everywhere was just as bad. Since no one moved in, no one had better information.

It really was a backwater.

Harold hobbled into the tavern after another difficult day at the Dodge residence. His back ached from the work of scrubbing the floors and digging in the garden. The fact that he hobbled everywhere didn't make it any easier. It took effort to hold to the lie he did so well, and now it was past time for a little liquid elixir to ease his way into the night. This whole recent gamut was becoming a muddled affair, with very few leads to know where to look.

"Evening, Mack. How's business?" It really had become a ritual.

Mack looked up from his never-ending wipe-down of the counter. Seeing Har, he broke into a very un-natural smile. Un-natural for Mack's normally expressionless face.

The unique sight intruded past Har's aches like an unexpected rain in the desert. Instantly covering his own expression, Har raised an eyebrow in a quiet question. "Got a table for me tonight? I don't think I can sit at the bar. I need a bench to slump into."

Tonight his aches were for real, and slouching into a worn bench sounded just about the best thing he could think of, right after a cool beer. "Put it in a chilled mug, Mack. I could use it."

Mack's face creased in concern. "You okay, Har? You look a bit worn around the edges. Tough day?"

Harold's tired nod answered eloquently enough. He didn't need to fake the stiff pace of his hobble as he made his way to his corner.

Mack headed over with the cold mug. "Why don't you just sit for a while? I'll be back with a bowl of stew I was making up for dinner. Looks like you could use some."

Har sighed and slid onto the bench. "That would be awfully nice, Mack. I'd appreciate it more than you can imagine." With a flicked glance, Har gave the little signal, requesting a verification of information.

Mack gave another of his un-Mack-like smiles and a short nod. "I'll be back with the stew. Gotta check on the other customers." Still smiling, Mack turned to the bar and the two customers sitting there. "You guys need a refill?"

Harold sat quietly staring at his old friend. *That was interesting.* He couldn't fathom Mack leaving the tradecraft so obviously, not that he was worried, but it certainly wasn't normal.

Har had almost finished his brew by the time Mack brought the stew. It smelled more than wonderful, as the steam rose from the large hunks of potatoes and carrots breaking the surface of the thick brown gravy. If he was lucky, there might even be some meat in it. Maybe rabbit, or venison, although probably not beef. It was too expensive for a stew. Har's mouth was already watering as he realized just how hungry he was. He had burned through a lot of calories today, and Commissioner Dodge was far too tight-fisted to provide lunch for his staff.

"Thank you, Mack. It smells fabulous."

"Better try it before you give compliments," Mack warned. "I made it myself you know. Unlike The Commissioner, I don't have house staff to do my work."

Har gave a chuckle. "You do just fine." Then, dropping out of trade-craft as Mack had, asked, "Should I drop by later?"

Mack showed his surprise at Har's lapse. With nervous eyes quickly scanning the room, he finally caught on and swept into the new routine. "Yeah, come on by after I close up. Maybe we'll play some cards."

"Sounds good, but I'm getting tired of the same old game. A new game would be fun."

Beginning to enjoy the interplay of puns, Mack added one of his own. "Good, 'cause I've got a new twist to an old game you just might like."

Har chuckled. "Hope it's as good as this stew looks, now go see to your other customers and let a guy eat."

Mack gave the little signal of acknowledgment and wiped a speck off the clean tabletop. "Eat well, Har, and don't worry. I'll put it on your tab."

Instead of making a rude comment, Harold picked up his spoon and dug in.

CHAPTER 11

New Light on an Old Subject

The gangly older teen knew he was in trouble. He just didn't know why. He hadn't done anything recently to cause problems, but these guys didn't look like they cared much about that minor issue. They were The Commissioner's men. He knew, because of the black vests they wore, like their uniform of office. Some people said the vests were because The Commissioner was too pinch-pennied to actually pay for real uniforms, and at this point, it didn't really matter. The men were wearing the vests, and they had him pretty much surrounded. Since he couldn't outrun them, he stood his ground.

"Hey, kid. We want to talk to you." The man in charge spoke nice enough, but there was a warning tone that said more than the words.

"Wha'd ya want me for? I didn't do anything." The young man's worried eyes swung between the men, looking for a way out.

"Just a question. No need to get all worked up."

Cautiously, the teen mumbled, "I don't know anything." Which made the man snicker.

109

"That much I believe. But my boss, The Commissioner, told me to find out about some things he heard. And what I hear is, you know somebody I do want to talk to."

That seemed to confuse the kid. "I don't get it."

The man raised his eyebrows suggestively. "Let's say, if you knew someone who told you a story, and you thought you could make a buck by telling it to our Commissioner, well, maybe it could. Does that help?"

The kid squinted, trying to work out the string of words. "I think so."

"You think so? You think you understand, or you think you might know a story you could sell?"

Even his men were beginning to get confused at this point.

"Ah... I think I understand. You want to hear the story I told The Commissioner?"

"Yep. That's exactly right, and I have a buck right here in my pocket. If we like the story as much as The Commissioner did, maybe you can have it."

The men snickered at that. They might just get to hear a story, and have a beer. The kid would undoubtedly end up with nothing, which was fine with them. They were, after all, The Commissioner's men, so they deserved a drink.

The kid relaxed a little. He could tell them what he had told The Commissioner. At least he might not get beat up. Careful not to move too fast, he swept his dark shaggy hair out of his eyes and started in. "Okay, It's pretty simple. One of the guys I work with said he almost got blinded out in one of the dry gullies. I thought Commissioner Dodge might be interested in hearing about something like that. Everybody knows he pays for information."

The foreman snorted derisively. "Why would The Commissioner care about somebody 'almost' being blinded? The guy probably got dust blown in his eyes. You know the winds out there can do that."

The kid wasn't brave, but he stood his ground. "I know what I heard. He said it was a light. I don't know much more than that, and neither did he. Just that he ended up with a big red spot in front of his eyes, and it lasted for a whole day. Said he only made it home by feeling along the edge of the road, walking like a blind man. That's pretty much it." He shrugged his shoulders as evidence.

"That's it? Somebody was staggerin' around? Dang, even my guys do that," the foreman said, chortling at his own joke. "He was probably drunk."

"I don't think so," the kid answered with a shake of his head. "I saw him myself, and he was scared. Thought he might be blind forever, but he was better the next day."

The foreman thought about it. "So he was blinded by a light. That's it? What kind of light, and where? We gotta know more, or no mulla. Got it?"

That got the kid thinking. He could use some money. "Okay, Let me think. He said he was outside of town in the valleys. It couldn't be very far, or he wouldn't have made it back. That's when he ran into the limb."

"A limb? Okay. Keep going." The foreman hadn't expected anything at all and only came because the commissioner was so fired up, but maybe there was a light at the end of the tunnel.

Unfortunately, the kid didn't have anything more and was getting edgy. With a shrug, he said, "So that's about it. Like I told The Commissioner, this guy I work with almost got blinded by a kid with some kind of light. I don't know anymore."

Sticking his hand deep into his pocket, the foreman brought out the big coin, letting it flash in the sunlight. "See this? It's yours, if you find out where, and who. Otherwise, I'll flip it over to my boys, and they'll get to have a drink, on you."

The teen scratched at his unruly hair as he contemplated his options. "Okay, I'll see what I can do." Then rubbing his dirty nose with an even dirtier hand, he asked, "When do I get the money?"

The foreman cracked an unsavory smile, and leaned forward slightly, saying, "When you give me the information. And… I find out it's good. The Commissioner doesn't pay for bad information. If you come up with something, just drop a note by The Commissioner's house, and I'll get back to you. Good enough?"

The nervous shake of the kid's head was enough acknowledgment.

"All right then. You have a great night."

As a parting gift, he slapped the kid on the back good-naturedly, almost knocking him off his feet. His guys snickered and turned to follow their departing foreman.

The young man gathered himself, and without another word, left in the other direction. He rubbed his shoulder where it stung, but felt lucky at having successfully evaded a real mugging. Tomorrow, he would have a long talk with his friend.

⚜

The tavern had filled tonight, but it was Friday after all. The Commissioner was doing his duty, hanging with the locals, and the place was almost festive for a spot as drab as Skragmoore. Jeers and cat-calls rang back and forth between the men, most of whom wore black vests, but there were others. Most of those wore the rough home-spun overalls of farm workers, but a few wore somewhat finer garb, as though to prove their position in the little town's hierarchy. All were well into their cups, apparently enjoying the evening. The more they drank, the louder they got. The only exception was at the large table where The Commissioner sat with his cronies. While their attitude may have been more subdued, it was easy to see they weren't feeling any pain either.

Mack was busy filling mugs with beer and working at the old bartender's trick of toasting up seasoned bread slices. Make them thirsty and they drink more, whetting the appetite for even more brew. Tonight, he had more than enough work to keep him hopping.

"Mack, we need a refill!" The Commissioner's deep baritone could easily be heard above the general noise of the room.

Mack quickly grabbed a pitcher and headed to the table as requested. Filling the empty mugs, he emptied the pitcher and wiped at the table between the customers, listening inconspicuously to the ongoing conversation.

"The kid's knees were knockin' like they were crackin' nuts," the foreman said with a laugh, reminiscing about his recent activities.

Another wan-na-be chortled, "He probably pissed his pants too. You guys do make a pretty believable threat to most people, let alone a poor kid. Too bad he doesn't know what a pussycat you really are."

Peals of laughter broke out from everyone but the foreman. He snarled grumpily and responded, "Heck, I'd have broken him if he gave us any problem."

Nobody doubted the claim, but they also didn't want to give him satisfaction.

"Sure you would. More likely you'd let your boys play while you watched."

Unexpectedly, The Commissioner stepped in at that point. "He does a good enough job, and he was on a mission."

The fact that The Commissioner had stepped in was enough to spark interest in the group, let alone the fact that there had been a mission.

With whetted appetites, and less caution than might have been normal, or wise, one of them asked, "What's up? Anything good?" It was an unwarranted question, considering they knew The Commissioner was in on it.

Without thinking, the foreman spoke out bluntly, supporting his position. "Some dumb guy nearly got blinded by a light. We wanted to know who and why."

The gruff throat-clearing sound from The Commissioner instantly stopped him from going further.

"Just a normal search for answers," Commissioner Dodge said calmly. "Always on the lookout for trouble. That's my job and nothing you need to worry about. I worry plenty enough for all of us." His seemingly genuine smile defrayed the tension, and luckily, everyone knew enough to drift away from the topic.

Mack finished a last swipe of the table and looked up at The Commissioner questioningly. "You need anything more, Mister Commissioner? I'll be happy to get it."

"No. I think we're just about done for the night. Mrs. Dodge will be waiting, and I expect the rest of you are in about the same boat."

The general murmurs of agreement filtered through the group, and they began gathering their wits, as well as their hats. The Commissioner had called it an evening. Saying their goodbyes to the guys the group dispersed, making their way to the door.

Less than a half hour later, Mack closed the front door and dropped the latch bolt. Har should be here soon and he had a tale to pass on.

The backdoor had no more than closed before Har spun to face Mack. "What's up? I saw your signal and got here as soon as it was clear."

"Dad-gummit, Har. I hate it when you're right. Now I owe you a beer."

Harold squinted in Mack's direction, trying to read his face in the dark. "Well, of course you do. I'm not out here for the good of my health."

They both knew why they were out here in the middle of nowhere, and it certainly had nothing to do with their health.

"Let's just lay it on Aundrea's doorstep and charge her for the bill, but you were right. There's something afoot. Come on in and I'll grab some glasses. We can at least be civilized while we talk."

Leading the way into the front of the building Mack began filling glasses in the candle's dim light. Har settled himself at a table, while Mack brought the glasses over, offering one to his friend.

"Okay, what gives?" Har asked. "I don't mind winning, but I'd like to know how I won."

Mack tipped his head obligingly and broke the news. "The Commissioner just happens to be lookin' for a guy with a light. Sent out his crew to hunt him down, but from what I could tell, they just found the kid you saw at The Commissioner's."

"We already suspected him, so..." Har wasn't going to be dragged down a rocky road without a reason.

"So...when his foreman started to mouth off about what was goin' on, The Commissioner covered for him. Did a pretty good job too. If

I hadn't already been listening for it, I probably would have missed it. Called it a mission of some kind. Not only that, he actually talked to me about it the other day. Almost forgot about it with all this going on. He asked me to keep an ear open for anything about an artifact. Said he had heard someone had found one and that he collected such things and might be interested."

"An artifact? Hmmm." Har rubbed his chin while he thought. "Let's see....A light. A flash. An artifact, and somebody blinded. It actually makes a pretty straightforward story. Might even be true."

"Yeah, maybe, and he does collect strange things. But why send out his henchmen? That's just searching for trouble, 'cause trouble always happens when they go out. That's just general knowledge."

Har had to agree. He had heard the stories too, and more. "So he wants it kept secret. That's my read on it. If somebody went blind..."

"Nope. Not totally blind I guess," Mack corrected, "but at least for a while."

"Okay, a brilliant flash that temporarily blinded someone." Har looked over to see if Mack approved of the correction.

"Yeah. That's my guess."

"What could do that? I haven't heard of any such artifact, and I've seen a few. Some rusty old gadgets and gears, but nothing that worked."

The two sat sipping their brew while they thought through their dilemma. How did all this tie in with the reason they were here, or did it?

With his beer finished, Har pushed back from the table. "Very interesting. I'm doing what I can from the residence. You keep an ear to the ground. There might be more happenings, but I have no idea what those might be. Maybe elves dancing in the moonlight, or posies poisoning the water troughs? I don't know, but there'll be more. I can feel it."

"Almost arcane isn't it?" Mack said, raising his eyebrows theatrically. "You take care, Har. You're not particularly safe at the residence."

"Yeah, now you tell me." Har nodded, making his way to the back door. He would be careful, but something was going to happen. He could feel it.

CHAPTER 12

'Till Death do us Part

I am here. Please respond. Stone sent the message through the surrounding stonework of the rocky cliff.

Rhone watched as Stone lay against the surface of a rocky cliff. He couldn't hear anything, but there might have been a light buzzing sensation from the rock. Stone was working, and he didn't want to intrude with silly questions, but he hadn't had contact for quite some time. As far as he knew, it could be a couple more hours, or maybe days. He should have asked, but for now, he relaxed against the rock as best he could. Pulling a jug of water from his pack, he lay back watching the fluffs of clouds drifting past in the steel blue sky.

It was interesting, but even though there were clouds, they never seemed to drop rain. He didn't know why, but it never rained this time of year. The rains would come later, in sheets of water that sluiced off the roof and the rocky slopes, filling the shallow rivers to overflowing. When that happened, it wasn't uncommon for raging floods to take bridges and homes with them. This was not a very hospitable environment, but it was home. The only one he knew.

But today wasn't so bad. He had gotten good at sitting around, watching things happen. Mom had taught him a lot about the plants in the area and their uses. Some were good for food, or to spice up their simple meals. Other plants had medicinal qualities that helped keep them healthy. Almost everything had some use if you knew what you were doing. He had watched and learned. Today was just another lesson.

Stone lay on the rock, not moving. Not that he expected Stone to move. He had almost drifted asleep in the warm sun when Stone's voice cut through his wandering thoughts.

Failure I am afraid. Not that I was expecting a response. Still, it could have come.

"Sorry," Rhone replied automatically. "I know you were hoping."

Hoping, yes, but not expecting. It will undoubtedly take many attempts, and many miles, before fruition. Do not worry on my account. I am used to waiting.

Stone was philosophical at recognizing their chances, and it all made sense, but Rhone thought it was more like faith than data. But what else did he have to do with his life? They had a goal, and a lifetime to do it in.

"Where next?" he asked, getting to his feet.

You pick the direction. I'm just a passenger, Stone answered smugly.

Rhone squinted up at the bright sunlight and refastened the collar around his neck, before slinging the bulky pack over his shoulders. "I guess we're ready. There's no need to go by the house again, so I figure we'll head to the road and away from town. There's no reason to go through it."

Sounds like a very informed decision. I place myself entirely in your control.

Rhone smiled at that. He was the one walking, and Stone was attached around his neck. They were going together, or Stone wasn't going at all.

"Sounds good. So, Tally ho, and off we go!" he shouted cheerfully, full of youthful excitement, until Stone effectively brought him back to reality.

Are you going to continue shouting everything? A quiet hum would be quite sufficient.

Rhone made a wry face, but it didn't last. They were on a quest, and he was feeling good. "No problem," he said charitably. "How far do we go before you try again?"

I am not certain, Stone replied quietly. *At some point, we will have the needed data for effective spacing, but I am afraid it will be trial and error for a while.*

The answer was just about what he had expected. Stone didn't know but didn't want it to sound that way.

Rhone shrugged his acceptance and really couldn't care less. They were moving, and he had a direction. The rest would come in its time.

⁂

They had only been gone a few hours when a group of black vested men rode up the rocky road, following a buckboard toward the house.

"Is this the place?" The foreman held a skinny older teen at arm's length as he questioned him.

Ahead, a rickety, two-story house stood looking like it would blow over at the first gust of wind. It had once been a nice place, but that time was long past. Beside it lay a neat garden and a great old apple tree.

"I don't know. I never saw the place."

The foreman held the young man by the arm, pushing him toward the edge of the wagon as though the extra couple of inches would improve his vision.

"I told you, I was near the main road, not way back here. I've never seen this place before," said the kid carefully.

"So you say, but why should I believe you? It's a pretty crazy story."

The foreman knew enough to let his detainees squirm a bit. A lot of information could be gained without the need to squeeze.

"I know. It sounds crazy, but it's the truth. When I told the guy to empty his pouch, something flashed. It was so bright I was blind for hours. Look, I've got scrapes all over my hands from when I couldn't see and kept tripping."

He had told them the same thing at least a half dozen times, and it hadn't made any difference. They wanted something he couldn't tell them. But if he couldn't give them more, he was afraid they were going to hurt him.

"What do you want me to do? I don't know anything else."

"That makes you pretty worthless then, doesn't it? We already figured out you're a thief, so I guess you got what was coming to you. You know The Commissioner doesn't like thieves in his town." Thinking a moment, the foreman put a plan together. "Here's something you can do. Walk up to the house and see who's home. We'll be waiting."

It didn't leave the kid many options, but at least he would be out of this guy's grasp for a few minutes. "Yeah, I guess I could do that."

Climbing down from the rig, he gave the place a long worried look before slowly making his way up the scarred dirt that could hardly be called a road. The closer he got to the old house, the slower he walked.

"Get on up there! We aren't going to wait all day," the foreman called, tired of the whole affair. "If I have to come drag you, you'll wish you walked on your own two feet."

The other guys waited without interest. They got paid no matter the outcome. It was just another worn-out house, no better, and not much worse, than the others this side of town.

Cautiously, the kid walked toward the rundown place. Nothing moved around the old home. It seemed totally empty. No animals or people to fill the space. The desolation itself was almost scary, but it was broad daylight, and the group of men behind him leveraged the gangly teen forward. A gust of wind blew the dry leaves of the big apple tree, making a light rustling sound, showing the still-green apples growing along the limbs. He was almost tempted to grab one as he walked past, until he saw the large stone standing upright in the hard soil. Only one thing looked like that. A tombstone, and it was totally fitting for this place.

As an icy shiver ran down his overheated body, he wanted nothing more than to turn and run.

"Hey, Get in there! We're tired of waiting." The rough call was as sharp as the wind.

With a quick glance at the flat rock, the youth took a deep breath and began moving his feet across the yard toward the sunburned house.

Suddenly the wind died. Not a breath of air moved. Even the insects seemed to have found a good reason to stop moving. In the deathly quiet, the only sound was his own soft footsteps plopping into the thick dust. The unexpected stillness only made his nerves jumpier, but he finally made it around to the front porch. Slowly inching forward, his fear grew, until he could hardly hear past the pounding of his heart, and cold sweat began trickling down his already sweaty back. Putting a foot up on the first of the few steps, he started up.

The loud creak of rusty nails complaining against the dry warped wood, caused him to freeze where he stood, as more cold sweat oozed like glue from his armpits. How could he be sweating when his heart was frozen in him? But when seconds passed and nothing happened, he shuddered, forcing himself to take another step. Then, step by step, he worked his way up to the porch.

Feeling better now, he grinned self-consciously, knowing he had let his fear overcome his reason, until a sudden gust flipped the screen door open, slamming it back against the peeling paint of the old wall. Flinching violently at the sudden noise, his over-quick action caused the sun-dried decking to crack loudly under his feet. Then the screen door slammed back into place with a loud bang. Nerves already at their edge, he reflexively jumped back ready to bolt, but the overstressed decking broke beneath his feet and he fell, only catching himself when his palms slapped against the warped decking. Without regaining his feet, the kid clambered madly on hands and knees off the deck, then launched himself into a dead run, headed up the valley, away from the house and the guys waiting for him.

Angry shouts followed, but he wasn't stopping for anyone or anything. He had never known fear like this, and it drove him up the craggy hills as fast as his feet could take him. There was nothing for him in Skragmoore, and he had no intention of returning.

"Damn!"

The word exploded from the foreman. Now what was he going to do? His hide was as good as flayed. It had been his job to get the goods on this dumb kid. Now he had nothing.

He watched the quickly settling dust as the kid scrambled up the rough incline and out of sight. The horses didn't like riding up banks that steep, and there was no way his guys would be able to outrun the fleeing teen. They were just hired hands, and certainly not trackers. The kid would be into the next county before he could get anyone back here, and even then it would be a worthless search.

In anger, he slapped the closest man's arm. "What are you waiting for? Get in there and check the place."

"Me? Why me? I didn't lose the kid."

"No, you didn't lose the kid, but unless you want to lose something else, you'd better start moving." The foreman's tight-lipped scowl made the threat real. "All of you guys. Get up there and check the place. I don't know what made the kid run like that, but don't think you're going to get away with it. Now git!"

While their foreman sat trying to figure out what he was going to say to The Commissioner, his group of sullen men started their slow walk toward the worn home.

"It's empty."

The bleak report was no worse than he had expected. "Nobody home?" he called.

"Yep, no one home. In fact, it's cleared out and empty. I mean, there's still some furniture, but it's all packed up nice and tight, like they weren't expecting to be back soon."

The foreman shook his head wearily. "Damn." It was worth just about that much energy. "All right, let's get ourselves back. The trouble will only grow if we're slow."

It was a weary bunch that made their way back to town. The hot, dry wind, blew incessantly, but at least that was normal. It was a crummy place to live.

"Honest, Mr. Commissioner, I've never seen anybody high-tail it faster than that kid. He was gone before I even knew he was movin'. I don't know what set him off. He was doing okay up until then."

Manny, the foreman, saw The Commissioner's look and correctly interpreted the meaning. "Honest boss. I never touched him. Well...I held his arm, so I touched him, but I never used any force, and neither did the guys. I kept an eye on 'em."

"So he just ran away, and you let him go." It was not a question.

The Commissioner did not like questions. He liked answers. Ask a question and you might get an answer you didn't want to hear. If you had all the answers, you didn't have to ask questions. It was a simple outline.

"Well, yes, sir." Manny had to agree. "The kid was clear up on the porch, then all of a sudden, he was fallin' down and running like the devil himself was after him. I'm serious, sir."

The Commissioner didn't waste energy on theatrics. He sat in his office chair and steepled his fingers, elbows resting on the desktop. "So he got spooked. I suppose he had some right. He was the one who got blinded. Probably scared it would happen again." With a pointed stare, he said, "You should have thought of that and had someone up there with him."

The foreman could feel the weight of the judgment, but expected no less. "Yes, sir. I've thought a bunch on it since. It was a bad call."

He knew how to take his licks, and was one reason he was still around.

The Commissioner gave a derisive snort before asking, "So what are your plans to correct it? Got any?"

Manny nodded shallowly, looking not at all so sure. "I was thinking', somebody probably knows who lived in the place."

"Probably," The Commissioner granted. "But we don't even know if the kid you were looking for lived there. Remember? Maybe he was just in the area. You know absolutely nothing. The only thing you do know is, the one you let get away was a thief. Thieves tell lies to cover up what they did, so you know absolutely nothing!" The Commissioner's words were hard and brittle, as his meaty hand hit the desktop with a slam that resounded off the paneled walls. "Think! That's why you have a head. Now, use that brain you've got crammed in your skull, and figure out what's going on. I want to know who, and what they have. Can you manage that?"

Sagging under The Commissioner's glare, Manny gave a, "Yes sir. I'll try." But at the teeth-grinding growl from Commissioner Dodge, he rethought his words. "Yes, sir. I'll get right on it."

"Get it done," came the growl. "I need to work on things around here or The Council is going to show up. That's something I do not need. We have enough problems without having outsiders looking into everything."

He was already back to his work by the time his foreman made it out the door.

Manny made his way to the tavern and pushed open the door to the semi-dark interior. Walking up to the well-used counter, he plopped down on a stool.

"Make it a cold one, Mack. I've had too much heat today."

"You got it, Manny. Tough day, as usual?"

Mack was used to the guys dropping in after their rounds. The black vests of The Commissioner's men made some kind of a statement in his place, but mostly it wasn't good. They were usually local guys, possibly a step up from the common labor that worked the farms and ranches. The step up being in their own eyes. Most people tended to look away when they were around, especially if there was a group of them. They were The Commissioner's men, and that was enough to keep them separate. For Mack though, they were a source of paying customers, and he didn't have enough of those.

"If you only knew." Manny sighed.

He was The Commissioner's foreman, and he took the brunt of whatever The Commissioner was dealing out for the day.

"You wouldn't believe what happened today. Can't tell you, of course, being The Commissioner's stuff, but dang it, Mack, it gets so frustrating. Now I'm supposed to think."

Mack was used to their normal grumbles. It was part of the job. He would have made a good counselor, had he gone into a different profession. He smiled to himself, hearing Manny's complaint. He was good at getting information. Particularly by not paying attention and letting the guys talk. Just nod, and a glance to show he had heard, then stick to the wiping.

"Can you believe it? The Commissioner about had a fit, and told me to think. What does he think I am, a professor or something?"

Mack turned to face him, one eye raised, and a chuckle hidden on his lined face. "You're supposed to think? Thinking's pretty overrated as far as I'm concerned." He then went back to his work.

"Dang right it is. I did what I thought was good, but it turned sour. Now I've got to come up with a way to fix it. Damn!...." He glanced at Mack and dipped his head, acknowledging the error. "Sorry about that slip, Mack."

Mack had a rule. No swearing in the tavern. It was funny, but it actually seemed to work. The place had almost become a church to these guys. A sanctuary of sorts. A place of refuge from a rough day.

With a nod, Mack twitched a cheek, saying he understood. "So what are you gonna do? I've found it isn't easy to fix past problems. It's much easier to figure out what to do ahead of time."

"You got that right. And how do you find a kid that you don't even know exists when the only guy that knew skipped town?"

The story was beginning to come out, and Mack hadn't said more than a word or two. Raising his shoulders in appreciation of the problem, he began washing a glass over again.

Manny was in heavy straights and sighed as he worked on his beer. "Tell me, Mack, you've been around. What kind of thing could flash bright enough to blind someone? Well, temporarily blinded. I can understand walking out into the sun after being in here for a while. It takes time for my eyes to get readjusted to the light, but for someone to get 'flashed'? I think that was the word he used. What could do that?"

Mack was surprised, hearing so much from the normally quiet foreman. He stopped his constant wiping and scanned the shadowed ceiling as though in thought. "Could be some gadget from the past. What do they call them...artifacts? I can't think of anything we have nowadays that would do that sorta thing. Nothing comes to mind anyway, unless it was a mirror." Picking up the broom, Mack began sweeping behind the counter with purposeful motions, as though he had no interest.

"Yeah, that's what I was thinking too," Manny agreed with a squinted frown. "The Commissioner wants whoever it was, but they're as good as gone. Damn kid today took off like he saw a ghost. Honest, Mack, he all but flew to get away." Manny was so far gone now he didn't even notice his swear word.

Mack couldn't help himself and turned to look at Manny. "Get away? From where? There's nowhere to go?"

"Couldn't agree with you more, but he headed up the hills at a dead run, and we weren't even chasing him. I don't know. But he's gone."

"The hills? You mean, up in the draws. The dry gullies?"

"Yeah, but you never heard it from me. Besides, we didn't find anything. Just an old, worn-out framed house. But nobody's there anymore. Looks like they got smart and moved on."

With a nod, Mack went back to his sweeping.

"Mack, If you could top this off, I'll finish up and get out of here. I've gotta head back and start thinkin'."

Mack refilled the now-warm glass and asked his clincher. "What are you going to do, Manny? I'd hate to see you get in trouble."

After a couple of deep swallows, Manny wiped the suds from his mouth, ending with a decisive nod. "First, I'm going to see if I can find who owns the house. There just aren't that many people out there, so somebody will know something. But something that flashes? I have no idea." With a final swallow, Manny slipped off the stool and laid a coin on the counter. "Thanks, Mack. You'd have made a good priest."

Mack shouted at the departing form. "You better get out of here! You say things like that and I may not let you back in." Then he chuckled to himself. Why go out hunting, when the game just walks in the door?

So Commissioner Dodge really was into the game. That made things so much more interesting. Information was gathering, but he had no idea where it was leading.

CHAPTER 13

Trials and Tribulations

"**A**re you sure we should go this far? It seems like a long way to me."

Rhone wasn't complaining, a mile was a mile, but they had gone several already and hadn't repeated the call.

You worry too much. We are close, and if you would prefer, we can attempt it here. There is no particular reason why we cannot. Overlaying projection patterns does produce better coverage.

Rhone shrugged his acceptance. "Fine. Whatever. I was just wondering."

If he was going to spend the rest of his life searching for Stone's kin, here was as good as there. It made no difference to him, particularly since the day was nice. With the sun out but not too hot yet, a nap wouldn't be all that bad.

Then we shall do it, Stone agreed, with more excitement than Rhone had heard yet. *This could be the one.*

"I suppose it could," Rhone said, mimicking Stone's tone, and taking his part as the knowledgeable control entity, while Stone took the excited youth position. It was gratifying in a strange way. "Can you see the area? Where do you want to be?"

I can see fine, thank you. Shall we try the gully up ahead? There are bound to be areas of rock showing.

"Areas of rock, and a few miles apart," Rhone repeated, compiling a list of requirements. He would watch for those, and it would give him something to do, other than simply being a pack mule to carry the load.

I do not consider you a mule, Stone interjected into Rhone's wandering thoughts. *For one, mules are said to have large hairy ears, which does not fit your description at all. Their stubborn attitude, however, does make it a possibility.*

Rhone exaggerated his eye roll, and pointedly asked, "So except for my ears, I'm like a mule?"

Oh come now. Do not get peevish over little things. There is a game afoot, and we need to concentrate.

Rhone scowled, but there wasn't much he could say. Instead, he gave a conniving grin, and let out a loud, braying, "Heee Hawww," then broke into a spontaneous laugh at Stone's instant reaction.

I have no idea what you are doing, but it is seriously worrying me. Are you feeling all right?

Rhone's laughter died in a sigh, and he shrugged. "Never mind. It's a people thing."

A people thing? You humans make very little sense sometimes.

Rhone gave up. "Never mind. Now, are you ready? I'm going to set you on this rock." Unfastening the collar, he set it face-first against the rocky embankment.

Yes. Thank you. This will do nicely. But in a quieter corner of his mind, Rhone was pretty sure he heard, *I believe I will need more study on these 'people things'.*

Rhone smiled sadly. "Really, it's okay. I suppose I am sort of mule-like, and you see right through me."

Of course, I can see through you, Stone commented, *but mostly I do not. It gets quite confusing to see all the squishy things of your internal being.*

Rhone dropped his head in defeat.

After another try at contact, and another, not totally unexpected disappointment, they still had no contact.

"Don't worry, Stone. There's a big world out there, and we just started."

Thank you, Rhone, but I am fine. A little disappointed, yes, but it is all worked out in the feasibility equations. It would have been extraordinary to have made a contact so soon. Far beyond the realm of expectation.

It may have been true, but it didn't cover the feel escaping Stone's solidness. He had hoped.

The evening brought a chill with the darkness, and Rhone was trying, ineffectively, to start a fire.

I could do that for you. Stone said, breaking into Rhone's fuming thoughts. *I was cautious about mentioning it, since it is one of your evening routines. I hope you are not offended.*

Surprised by the comment, Rhone dropped back on his heels and cocked his head questioningly. "You can start a fire? Why didn't you tell me? You knew I was trying to figure out everything you could do."

Well, yes, but your request was regarding things for protection. This is not for protection. I honestly did not consider it as pertinent.

Already short-tempered, Rhone scowled, considering how to answer tactfully. "I recognize that, 'technically', starting a fire may not be for protection, but it is certainly a useful thing I should have known."

I can see that now. I am sorry. I never considered it like that. To crystalline constructs, fire is of no matter, and since we have no use for its heat, we never consider it of any usefulness. Heat is simply another reaction of focused energy and friction. As I have learned here, in an atmosphere containing oxygen, heat something enough, and it flames. The heat breaks down the structural binding of the compounds, converting them to gases. Remember, energy is never lost, it simply changes form. In this case, from a solid to gas and the gas ignites when oxygen is present to sustain... anyway, it is all very simple.

Surprisingly, Rhone had followed the explanation, almost, and had to ask. "You just said, 'as I learned here.' What did that mean?"

Here on earth, Stone said, which actually surprised them both. With growing excitement, he hurriedly continued. *In space, there is no oxygen, so it was never a consideration. Rhone! Another sign, I came from space!*

"Wow. That's totally cool. You really are from space."

Contemplating Rhone's response, Stone questioned, *Did you not believe so? I do not understand. If you did not believe, why have you been assisting me to find the We?*

The question hung in the air as though it had been spoken aloud, and Rhone didn't know what to say.

"I ahh... I didn't really have any reason not to believe you I guess, and it sounded like more fun than staying at home. You said you wanted to go find your friends, or those of your kind. I just wanted to help. I know what it's like not to have a family. My own mom isn't here anymore. She died, and…now I have you. What kind of a friend would I be if I didn't help?"

It had been a long time since Rhone had cried, but the weight of his loss suddenly hit him. Sagging back onto the rough ground, tears he had never shed began to fall. Without Stone, he would be entirely alone. Then the whole total strangeness of it hit him and he began to chuckle through his tears, thinking about having his own pet rock. Life was so weird it was downright stupid sometimes. And he still didn't have a fire.

Stone had been quiet but now spoke. *Thank you, Rhone. It is difficult to see things through another's eyes. I am sorry.*

With a hand cupping the stone in his collar, Rhone held his unique friend in his own version of a hug. "Right back at you, Stone. I am here."

Life was indeed strange.

CHAPTER 14

The Skrag you say

"Get your acts together," Manny shouted at his men. "The Commissioner is not going to be happy if we don't get this done, and if I find out you're not doing your part, it's going to be your hide nailed to the side of the barn, not mine. I'll see to it myself."

As foreman, it was Manny's job to keep everything under control, which sounded a lot easier than it actually was. When it was simply the day-to-day issues to deal with, it wasn't all that difficult, but things had gotten somewhere beyond that now.

It was supposedly a simple job. Find somebody who wasn't known, who had something, that also wasn't known, then beg, buy, borrow, or steal it. And, The Commissioner wasn't happy. Now his option was, do it, or fail and get fired. Or worse. But his men, hardened to the problems of life, weren't impressed with his personal problems. Besides, if he was gone, there would be one more step available on the ladder.

He had been attempting to get the men moving, but their task was so vague, it made it difficult for them to focus on the situation. The fact was, they could ride all day and do nothing, and the outcome would be the same. As far as they were concerned, it was a bogus job, whether The Commissioner wanted it done or not.

A jeering call came from somewhere among the men, "So, what was it we're supposed to do?"

Manny gritted his teeth but accepted it as a real question. "All right. Once more, you idiots. The Commissioner said to find this character and get the artifact, or whatever it is. If he wants it, that's good enough. Since we don't know who this guy is, and our information said it was a young guy, I expect you to find a young guy. If that means you check out every young guy in the county, then you check every young guy in the county, just don't cause any more damage than you need. If reports come back that end up costing The Commissioner time or money, you'll hear about it. Which goes just the same if you come back empty-handed. You got it?"

He had said all this before and was more than frustrated at needing to repeat it. They were wasting time.

The thought crossed his mind that maybe he should just check out, and quietly find another job.

But too late, the men were moving. In ones and twos, they chose a direction and headed out of town. Not in a hurry, but at least they were going.

Manny shook his head slowly, knowing the odds were against him.

With almost twenty men to cover the few roads and farms scattered throughout the county, it shouldn't have been a difficult task, but considering the lack of upward thinking in the group, it would be a miracle if they actually fulfilled their quest.

Unfortunately, and as luck would have it, two of the men stumbled into Rhone and Stone within the day.

"**W**hat's he doing?"

The voice was thin and wavering, like it had somehow gotten stuck in the question mode. The speaker, the shorter of the two men, shaded his eyes with a hand, hoping to see better. The second, broad-shouldered and darker-skinned, with long black hair showing under his sweat-stained hat, sat atop his even sweatier horse, scanning the base of the rocky-faced cliff just ahead of them. Both men wore the black vests of The Commissioner's men, but the taller wore his over a bare chest of coarse, curly black hair. He had listened to the smaller man's gripe for so long that he hardly heard them anymore, but at least, this time, it was a valid question.

"Haven't you got eyes? So why is it I have to tell you everything?" Regardless, the taller man started in with the information. "Looks like a kid for sure, and I think he's talking to himself. I don't see anyone else."

The short guy smiled as he stood tiptoe, but even that additional elevation didn't allow him to see over the brush. "I wonder what The Commissioner's going to pay us, I mean, if we bring the thing back?"

"You idiot! You must be if you think The Commissioner is going to pay us extra for anything. He's already paying us to be out here searching. So you can damn well be sure he ain't gonna pay us anymore." He dropped his gaze to his partner and made a sour face. "Dang it, Will. Do you ever bathe? You stink."

But Will wasn't fazed, as he made his own derogatory comment. "Well, you smell like your horse, so I don't see it's much different."

They both scowled, but a noise from the cliff brought them back to watchfulness.

"What's goin' on?"

"Dang it, Will. Shut up at let me find out. If I'm talkin' to you all the time, I can't keep an eye on him."

Will grumbled, but kept silent, again peering through the coarse brush.

Juan, the taller of the two, wasn't satisfied with his position, and whispered to Will, "Let's get in closer. I don't see anyone else. Maybe we can get a jump on him."

Will's nod said he accepted the suggestion, and the taller man swung down from his horse ready to advance on foot.

Rhone, there are two men approaching.

Startled, Rhone quickly finished fastening the collar and cautiously turned toward the two incoming men. "Hi, can I help you?" He didn't know what else to do.

The two men walked toward him casually enough, but an instinct kept him wary. That, and the fact they wore black vests. Even he knew of the black vests.

The taller of the two, with his sunburned neck and shoulders, accepted the invitation to talk. "Howdy, kid. What are you doing way out here by yourself? Is your momma around? You should know it's not safe bein' out here alone."

Rhone knew enough to stand his ground, besides, there was nowhere to run. "I'm just fine. What about you guys? This is a long way from town."

Both men's eyes locked on the collar around Rhone's neck. When the taller of the two spoke, it was in an overly sweet voice that didn't leave a doubt of their intent. "Very nice. That's pretty fancy for a kid. Is it your momma's?"

The short guy laughed at that. "Yeah, Pretty rock you got there."

"No, it was not my mother's," Rhone said gruffly, "and yes it is nice. I found the rock in the river."

"In the river? Did you hear that, Will? His necklace just washed up onto the bank."

Rhone could feel the tall man's disdain, and it made him angry. "Guess it doesn't matter, does it?"

It probably wasn't the best approach, but wasn't the place to back down either. It would simply give them an excuse to walk over him. Perhaps literally.

Surprisingly, Stone hadn't said a word.

The tall guy wasn't impressed with Rhone's bluff but did back off a bit.

"Maybe true. Maybe not. It's just, that we keep our eyes open, 'cause our boss is always interested in nice pieces. He might even be interested in buying yours," he said, scratching his rough chin speculatively. "So I was thinking, you might be able to earn a bundle, and seriously," he said squinting at Rhone with disapproval, "it looks like you could use it."

This guy was pretty good, and Rhone even believed a piece of it. Their boss probably would like Stone's collar. It was beautiful, but there was no way he would sell, and it didn't matter how much was offered.

"Thanks for thinking about me, but I'm not interested, and I'm doing just fine." Deciding it was time to have them move on, he bent to gather firewood, hoping they would get the hint and leave. But he was bound for disappointment. When they didn't move to leave, he straightened and took a deep breath. "Just tell The Commissioner, no thanks. I presume that's who you meant."

The tall man raised his eyebrows in mock surprise. "Smart kid, Will. He figured that out all by himself. Too bad he isn't smart enough to realize, The Commissioner doesn't take it well when he gets no for an answer."

Will chuckled nastily. "You got that right, Juan. I can hardly wait to tell him."

Rhone knew trouble was coming. The two men showed their hand easily enough he didn't need to be a card shark to read it. The tall man's fists opened and shut impatiently, while the short man, Will, wrinkled his nose, working himself up to face an opponent, both younger and taller than he was.

Rhone saw the tells and knew what they meant. There had to be another way. "Hey guys, just go tell The Commissioner no, and see what he says. Who knows? Maybe I'll reconsider."

Juan had been ready to jump in and take the bauble but now looked confused. The foreman's words of caution, and the attached list of do-nots, had been pretty specific. While his initial thoughts had been to snuff this stupid kid and take the thing, he now worried what would The Commissioner say if they could simply have bought it, and the situation ended up coming back on him, as bodies tended to do.

Juan looked at Will, who just shrugged. With their fire doused, their heat quickly dissipated.

Rhone was more than relieved, and held his calm long enough for one more comment. "Okay then. Let's see what he comes back with. Until then, I keep the rock."

The undignified nod from Will finished the game, and the two made a strong showing of their departure.

Juan made their gruff farewells. "I wouldn't take his offer lightly, kid, and make sure we can find you when we return. I'd hate to have to track you down, but you can bet we will."

Rhone nodded his understanding and watched as they left, working their way back through the scraggy brush.

That was incredible, Stone whispered in awe.

"And where were you?" Rhone snapped back, still tense over the exchange. "I could have been killed, and that's when you decide to go quiet?"

Had anyone been watching, it would have appeared as though Rhone had gone mad, stomping around the little clearing, kicking rocks, and raving to himself.

I was with you, Stone said cautiously. *You did an amazing job and you were not even beat up. In fact, I do not understand why you are upset. Although they did mention telling The Commissioner. Was that a threat?*

In exasperation, Rhone kicked at another rock but made the error of choosing a large one that hurt his toe. With a yelp and growl, he dropped to the ground, grumbling, "I had to do that all by myself, and you just sat there. What if they had grabbed you? They could have ripped you right off my neck, and probably wouldn't care if my neck broke while doing it. Those are not nice guys, Stone. They work for The Commissioner. Didn't you see their vests?"

Vests? What about their vest? And why would they want to hurt you? They said they were interested in me, because their boss liked unique pieces. I am a unique piece, am I not?

Rhone grimaced in frustration at trying to explain human things to a rock. "Listen Stone…" he started, then paused, allowing a couple more breaths to clear the jumpiness from his system. "Those guys wore the black vest of The Commissioner's men. They're… bad guys. They do whatever he wants."

You were thinking the words, 'heavy-handed', but you said something different. Yet your hands are as big as theirs. If you would like a percentage breakdown of the size difference, I could calculate it in a short time.

Rhone tried not to think, as he squeezed his eyes shut. It took another deep breath before he could answer safely. "Heavy-handed means, they don't mind hurting people if that's what it takes. Some might even enjoy it."

Oh my, Stone said, taking a moment to process the information. *But why? They said they would pay.*

In disbelief, Rhone asked, "Were you paying attention at all, or just watching the show?"

Carefully, Stone answered, *I was observing.*

"And did you notice the tall guy getting ready to hit me?" Rhone said in irritation.

Hit you? I thought he was signaling his desire to buy me.

"What he was signaling was his intention to pound me to a pulp and take you! If I hadn't messed up their plan by saying they needed to talk to their boss, you would be theirs right now, and I would be lying in the ditch. I don't know how to fight, and these were two grown men."

A wave of fatigue washed over Rhone and he flopped to his back, attempting to settle his emotions. The bright sunburned blue of the late afternoon sky was so deep it felt like he was floating, spinning slowly with the motion of the tall weeds beside the clearing. He let himself drift until a very quiet whisper filled his mind.

I am sorry, Rhone. I really had no idea you were in trouble. You handled the entire situation as completely as any person, or We, could have asked for. I am very disappointed in myself for not doing a better job of protecting you. I will strive to do better.

Rhone smiled wearily. Rolling to his side he propped on an elbow. "I did do okay, didn't I? I honestly didn't think I had it in me, but Mom always said I had to stand up for what was right. She said, Things may still go wrong, but the right thing is to do what's right."

Minutes of silence passed as the afternoon sun moved across the silver blue dome of the sky, and while the hot rocky surface was uncomfortable, he wasn't interested enough to move. His mind kept returning to the encounter, and the one question. What would happen now?

A silent whisper finally broke into Rhone's silence. *If what you say is true, they will be back. Are you planning to sell me? I might be quite valuable, and it might save your life. Also, if you did, you would have money to work your property. You might be very good at it if you had sufficient funds.*

Rhone frowned and sat up, unfastening the collar. With the stone in hand, he looked carefully at the beautiful piece flashing in the sunlight. "What would you do if you were locked away for years? People don't normally wear things like you, even if you are pretty. I really doubt The Commissioner would. He would lock you away in a vault somewhere with the rest of his treasure. Mom told me what people say about him, that he takes a cut from every business around. He's not a good man. Besides, I'm not going to sell you."

After a moment's pause, Stone said, *Thank you. I am quite certain I would not enjoy it, but if you do not sell me, what are you going to do?*

Now that was a good question. Within a day or two, The Commissioner would be looking for him, or his hide. He wouldn't be interested in a deal either. He would want it all.

It was time to run.

CHAPTER 15

True Colors

The two men stood side by side in the closed office. It was not a place they were comfortable in, being far more used to the inhospitable outdoors than the plush, wood-paneled walls and fancy furniture of The Commissioner's office.

In quiet undertones, the shorter one whispered, "I knew it was a bad idea. As soon as he said it. I knew it."

"Shut up, Will. You practically jumped at the chance to get out of there. I know how you are. You're like the scum on the water trough. You just lay around and go with the flow, but you ain't good for nothin'. In fact, you were practically peeing your pants, seeing he was taller than you."

Will's eyes drooped at his partner's words. He couldn't help that he was short. He'd lived with that problem his entire life, but it didn't make him worthless. Not exactly. He managed. Some things were just more difficult than others, and fighting was one of those things. Irritably, he wiped at his nose with the back of his hand, thinking of telling his partner to try fighting with his own legs cut off at the knees and see how well he fought then. But he thought better of it. He was in enough trouble as it was.

He was saved from further concerns on the subject as The Commissioner walked into the office, his 6'6" barrel-chested frame barely making it through the doorway. Even then he had to remove his dumb-looking hat before he entered. Their foreman followed and stood across the room from the two. Whether as a witness, or a character reference, they weren't sure.

Sweat began to run down both their backs and an odd smell was coming from Will. Juan glanced at his little partner and hoped the smell wasn't what he thought it might be. Things were bad enough now, but that would only make it worse.

Hoping to be proactive, Juan stepped forward and addressed The Commissioner. "Mr. Commissioner, sir. I believe we found the item you were searching for."

The Commissioner stopped and glared at the two, then dropped heavily into his leather-covered desk chair. "So I heard. My foreman gave a quick run-down on your story, but I do not see a young man or an item. Therefore, I must interpret it to mean, you stole the item and are looking for some sort of bribery to gain more funds. I see no other alternative."

The Commissioner's face could have been a poorly carved statue, a golem, with features etched into deep lines like the gullies around the town. It wasn't a pleasant face, especially to the two standing in judgment. It could become their final judgment, and they knew it.

"No, sir!" Juan responded in terror. "No way. We work for you and already get paid. We wouldn't do anything like that."

Will was in so much fear that he couldn't even move to respond. He stood rigidly, rooted to the spot, as the smell got stronger.

Juan looked to their foreman for help. They had told him the entire story, and he knew they hadn't done anything like that, but Manny didn't say a word. He stood with arms crossed, refusing to meet Juan's eyes.

The creak of the heavy chair brought Juan's attention snapping back to the seated figure of The Commissioner, now leaning forward with fists clenched on the tabletop.

"If I wanted your lies, I would ask you to talk. Since I don't want to hear your yaps, shut...up."

Juan's head was shaking so hard it was difficult to tell he was actually nodding.

But The Commissioner wasn't done. "So you found our friend, and his toy, then you let him go, because he wanted more money? I find that very difficult to believe. It's far more likely you wanted more money and made a deal with him. Do you really believe I would willingly make a deal with some dumb, country bumpkin kid, just because he didn't want to give away his momma's jewelry? And you say he wanted to deal. What damned kind of deal? You didn't say how much he wanted, because you didn't ask!" The Commissioner had been hot before but was now trembling with rage. "I am not going to let some stupid kid tell me how much he'll sell for, because I am not buying. I am going to take! Do... you... understand!" He was standing now, his fist hitting the table with each word as he slammed his point into the solid surface.

The foreman looked at his two men and shook his head sadly, but he wasn't going to interfere. There was no way he was stepping up for these guys. There were plenty more where they came from. They weren't bad guys. They just weren't worth his life.

Will's quavering voice squeaked as he tried to speak. "W...we know where to find him."

"I should hope so," The Commissioner said with a deep snarl, dropping into his chair so hard the wood groaned as it took up his weight. Amazingly, it didn't shatter into a hundred pieces. "Manny!" He swung to look at his foreman with eyes that could bore a hole through rock. "Sharpen your knives. I'm gonna have some new skins on the wall if these two don't bring that kid back."

Manny nodded, arms still crossed over his chest.

"Take ten men and follow these guys. Bring the kid, the necklace thing, and these two back with you. And one more thing. If they don't find him, I really don't care what condition these two are in when you get here. They can hang on the wall either way."

Tipping his head, Manny answered, "Yes sir, Mr. Commissioner. We're right on it."

Disgusted with them all, The Commissioner rose and shouted, "Now get out of here!"

The men fled the room, foreman included.

They were halfway down the hall when Manny grinned and addressed the other two. "That went pretty well I think. You both have your heads and a chance to live another day. Could be worse."

Manny got a sidelong glare from the two as they headed for the door as fast as their legs would take them.

Thirteen men sat on horseback, looking at the dry clearing at the base of a rocky cliff. No one said a thing, but the little guy up front kept turning his head back and forth, as though his first look didn't tell him all there was to see. There was no kid. Nothing but dry scraggly brush growing from drier rocky ground.

With evident fear in his voice, Will whispered. "Where'd he go? We left him right here."

Juan just shook his head and swung down to see what he could find. A few minutes wandering around, stooping here and there to scan the ground, he walked over to the foreman, once again shaking his head negative. "Not a single print. It's like he was a ghost or something."

Closing his eyes in a silent curse, Manny nodded, acknowledging the report. "Mount up boys. We'll split up and cover everything from here to tomorrow, before I tell him we've got nothing. I suggest every one of you better use both of your eyes, or you may not have them much longer."

He didn't wait for a response. Turning his horse, he shouted for their attention. "I want you in twos. Search every crack and cranny, every rock and gully. If we don't find him, I doubt any one of us will enjoy our homecoming. You know The Commissioner, and I don't need to say more. The kid was right here yesterday, so let's get it done."

The group began to break up, heading in different directions, when Manny called, "Juan, you and Will are with me. I'm not letting you out of my sight." He wasn't going to take any chances on losing these two.

As they watched the other teams drift away, Manny drew his two in closer with a hand signal. "Now listen up. Unless you have some strange desire to hang on a wall, I suggest you put your mind to it and let's figure out where this kid went. I want you to go over this area on your hands and knees and find something to help us."

Their slow nods said enough. Dismounting, they tied their horses to the scrub brush. As they started their slow search, Manny sat his horse and tried to figure what he would have done if he were the kid. An hour later, they had no more than they started with, and Manny chose to enlighten the two on his plan.

"We're going to continue away from town. The kid knows we'll be looking for him, so he'll make himself scarce. Now, I don't know where he's going, but if he's smart, and he's at least smarter than you two, he won't head to where anybody might know him. That means the badlands."

"But there's nothing out there," Will whined, not much in favor of heading anywhere called the badlands. They were, after all, named for a reason.

"You got a better idea?" Manny asked, giving Will a look that didn't expect much. "If so, I'd like to hear it. If not, then shut up and follow. And keep your eyes open. Falling asleep in the saddle will be the last 'nice thing' to happen to you."

Juan glanced sourly at his short partner and rolled his eyes in disgust. They had found nothing, and things were not looking good.

It took a while to find a cut in the cliff face that allowed the horses to climb, and the three slowly made their way up to the flats above. It was as though a giant knife had sliced through the land and squished one section down a hundred feet. The land here looked just like the land below, except it was higher, and if anything, dryer. Short scrubby brush and coarse patches of dry grasses covered the low rolling hills as far as they could see, and other than a few minor cuts of dry washes in the distance, it all looked the same. This might be God's country, but it had to be an angry god to leave it in this condition. This was not going to be easy.

"We'll ride side by side, about a hundred feet apart. We'll cover a lot more ground that way. Just keep your eyes open, or you might as well keep on going until your horses go down under you."

No response was required, and with the foreman in the center, they headed away from the cut and across, into the highland flats.

Hours of heat, dust, wind, and sun wore away into boredom until there was nothing but sun-dried ground and the occasional glimpse of antelope cutting across the far country. The animals were so elusive, you couldn't get close enough to hunt them. As soon as they saw movement on the open plains, they were gone, crossing into another drainage.

"How much farther?" Will complained.

They had become more frequent as the day wore on, and the other two gritted their teeth as his complaining made their day that much worse. But as the sun slowly made its way toward the hilltops, the foreman finally called a halt.

His dry voice cracked as he called out, "Enough is enough. There's a wash over there. Let's call it a day."

The three turned toward the shallow rocky slope showing above the monotonous flat ground, grateful for the shade of the low cut.

Climbing wearily out of the saddle, Juan swung down and almost fell to his rump, legs complaining as loudly as Will had. With a stumbling step, Juan dropped to a knee, bracing himself, and stared in disbelief at a footprint in the dusty soil. "Damn, and double damn," he whispered hoarsely, then called, "You sure know your stuff, Manny."

The three men stood gazing at the footprint until Manny broke the trance. "Juan, see where they head. We don't want to mess up any tracks by camping right in the middle of them. Get the direction and we'll finish this up tomorrow. Will, get a fire going. We don't have much, but I want something hot. I'm going to climb the cut and see what I can see."

As the other two followed his orders, Manny rode up the short slope and stared into the distance.

Maybe a mile away, rocky outcroppings began to show above the smoother flow of the dry flatlands. Their coarse, weather-abused sides rose sharply, almost stately, making fantastic shapes against the skyline.

The true badlands. It was an area nobody traveled. Nobody with sense. Bad water and bad rock made the place bad enough, but it was the bad winds raging through the standing pillars, making sounds reverberate from every rocky face, that made it a place so inhospitable to humans. Even looking at it from a distance brought a shiver to Manny's back. He knew where they were headed, and once again, it wasn't good.

CHAPTER 16

And You Thought You had it Bad

Without water, the trek across the flatlands was almost unbearable. Rhone started out just before dark, but with the sliver of moonlight, decided to travel all night.

He didn't know how long it would take for the two commissioner's men to get back to town and report in, but he suspected Commissioner Dodge wouldn't take more than an hour to send them back out. With their travel in both directions, he had a head start, but not much. They had horses.

After climbing the cliff, he headed out across the flat brushland. He didn't know where he was going, but at the moment, anywhere was better than staying put.

Stone remained uncharacteristically quiet, but Rhone figured it was because he didn't have any experience with traveling cross country, therefore had nothing to offer. That suited him fine. With Stone's lack of help the previous day, he was pretty put out. It would take a while before things improved between them. Still, it felt empty without the ongoing chatter.

As the evening dragged by, so did the miles. Rhone was glad he wasn't doing this in the middle of the day with the sun blazing down on them. It was bad enough in the relative cool of the night, but the lack of water truly worried him. Stone wouldn't need any of course, and probably hadn't even thought about Rhone's need, but it was just one more issue he was building against his collar-mate.

The word brought a twitch to Rhone's otherwise grim face. Collar-mate wasn't a bad way to look at it. Friend yes, but you could have lots of friends. There could only be one collar-mate, and he had his.

I like the term, Stone murmured, speaking his first sentence in hours. *We are more than just friends. We have become partners.* His mental words died off expectantly, with a feeling of hope.

Rhone gave an eloquent shrug, shaking off the tension that had built from his confrontation with the two men. "Yeah, I like it too," he said with relief. "But are you really okay with it? I don't want to use the term if you don't agree."

I believe it is a perfect blend of the actual and the metaphor. I could not think of a better term myself.

Rhone blushed at the casual compliment and reached up to rub the stone thoughtfully. "So we're collar-mates. I like it."

Good. And now my collar-mate, what is our plan? I noticed we are no longer on the road. Is there a reason, and is it to assist with locating the We?

Rhone was instantly embarrassed. With yesterday's trauma, he had totally forgotten Stone's search.

"Stone, I need to explain. The guys that left yesterday? They're going to be back, and this time, they won't be alone. The Commissioner will hunt us down, mostly because he wants you, but also because I managed to get away."

He wants me? But I do not even know him.

"I know. It is a bit strange, but that is exactly what I think. I think they were out here looking for us, but they didn't know what to look for.

Then they will be back, and that is why we left so quickly. You do not normally move around much at night. I recognized that.

Rhone smiled to himself. His friend was learning, but there was a long way to go.

"Yes, I am running away, and maybe they won't be able to find us. I've never been this far from home, but we have to keep going. I hope we can get far enough The Commissioner won't follow. Maybe we'll be outside his jurisdiction."

And how far is that?

"I don't know, and since he doesn't seem to follow rules very well, it may not make much difference to him."

That does make it difficult. Let me think about it. Perhaps we can come up with a way to stay out of sight.

Rhone grinned at his friend's words. "Thanks, Stone. I don't like doing it all by myself."

No problem. We are collar-mates, remember.

Topping another low ridge in the seemingly flat planes, Rhone stopped and stared. In the distance, the moonlight's glow showed tall rocky chunks sticking up above the surrounding low brushland. The stark shadows cast by the moonlight stretched across the dry ground like fingers from a giant hand reaching out to grab him. He shuddered involuntarily, and Stone immediately picked up the emotion.

What is wrong? I do not sense danger, yet your system registered a definite response.

"It's nothing, just a feeling like having someone walk over your grave."

But you are not dead.... Is this another of those odd sayings you seem to have a penchant for?

Rhone thought that one over for a moment. "Probably. It was just a feeling when I saw the rock shapes up there. I'm not sure I'll like them, but it might be a good place to hide."

Yes, if you do not like it, maybe others will not either. A place to 'hang low', as I believe the saying is.

"Exactly, so I guess I'm game if you are," Rhone said lamely.

Game? Oh, I believe I understand, Stone said, with a feeling of satisfaction at having worked it out by himself. *We are game, like a hunted animal is game.*

"Close enough," Rhone said, not having the heart to say the explanation wasn't quite correct. On the other hand, maybe it was.

Hoping he was doing the right thing, Rhone started across the highlands toward the tall sections of rock. As they progressed, the sun rose, and the formations became even stranger. A thin layer of dirt crowned the pillars jutting from the nearly level ground, the slight cap of soil allowing scant footing for the few hearty plants that somehow managed to live on the rocky tops. There were literally hundreds, more probably thousands of the stones, all sizes and heights, jumbled into a massive maze miles wide. Rhone shuddered, thinking how easy it would be to get lost in there.

"I don't know, Stone. The more I look at it, the worse I think the idea is. We could get totally lost, and maybe never find our way out."

If your concern is about getting lost, do not fear. I have the ability to track our journey. I will know exactly where we have been and how to retrace our steps. I cannot, however, determine our initial route. That, you will have to do.

Rhone stood staring at the foreboding stoneworks but didn't have a better plan. They needed a place to hide, and soon.

"Well, here goes nothing."

Before he had even taken a step, he heard Stone's exasperated voice echo in his mind, *I truly do not understand most of what you say.*

There was no straight path through the stone pillars, as segments became clusters, and clusters became large sections, turning into full cliff faces running to the next corner. Between the stoneworks, the ground was fairly level, with the rocky soil sprouting hardy mounds of brush here and there. Even a few grassy patches managed a footing along the edges of the rocky faces.

Shade from the tall rocks made the air slightly cooler than it had been in the brushy flats, but the walls also tended to block the air movement, making it feel stuffy and still. All in all, it was totally unique, and with the view blocked by rock walls every few dozen feet, it was not what he would call fun.

Rhone slowly made his way another mile into the maze of tall stone before he felt secure enough to call a stop. His muscles ached from the long walk of the previous day, all night and most of today, and all with very little water. He hadn't brought much with him and what he had was almost gone. Rhone pulled the jug from his pack and sloshed it around, feeling how much was left. He would love to drink it but decided to save it for later. He would need it for tomorrow's walk. Hopefully, he would find some in the maze.

It was a big hope.

As bad as it was, the maze wasn't just rock. Clumps of old dead brush showed it had managed to find a hold on the rocky soil and enough water to grow. Now their skeletons stood as stark reminders that all things come to an end. But at least he would have a fire. There were even a few stunted trees growing from the tops of some of the larger stones. If he needed a bigger fire some night, he could try scrambling up and find some wood, but for now, a tiny fire would be more than enough. Without water, he wouldn't be cooking anyway.

Would you like me to start the fire? Stone asked, attempting to be discreet in his inquiry and not wanting to build any hard feelings now that they had smoothed out their problems.

But Rhone wasn't grumpy anymore, just tired. "You know what? I think I would like to do it myself today, but thanks. I like building a fire. It's comforting somehow, and I don't have anything else to do."

Stone accepted the words graciously, and Rhone laid out the sticks according to size, allowing him to easily grab the exact piece he wanted when the flames grew. The pouch had what he needed, and soon a spark caught in the dry tinder. He worked at it with little puffs, slowly building the lint pile around the tiny smoldering bundle until a tendril of lazy smoke began to rise. He smiled, as he always did when it worked. It was almost like magic. Adding the thinnest pieces of broken branches to the tiny flames, they grew hungrily, eating everything he fed them. In no time, the small campfire blazed merrily against the rough stone of the rocky wall. Rhone closed his eyes, feeling the fire's heat ease away the day's struggles. It wasn't fully night yet, but he was asleep almost as soon as his eyes closed.

The fire burned through the small branches quickly, leaving a small pile of soft grey ash on the ground and a smudge on the rocky face of the standing stone. As the flames died away into nothingness, Rhone slumped farther down onto the hard grass-tufted floor, tucked away among the maze of stone walls.

With a twitch of her long whiskers, the little grey mouse scurried from one place of cover to the next, moving intently toward the bundle of intriguing new scents in the middle of her self-chosen section of rocky ground. Rhone's pack lay close, inviting her curiosity, and she watched warily before approaching, stopping under a tall stalk of grass. With a quick movement, she sat on her hind feet and stretched upward, reaching for the ripe cluster of seeds hanging over her head. Pulling the bowing grass stalk down, she quickly stuffed the entire cluster into her cheeks, releasing the stem to spring upward, now less the weight of the seeds. With that distraction dealt with, she quickly resumed her trek, climbing through the loop of the leather arm strap and heading toward the cavernous opening full of wonderful smells.

She was almost inside when she stopped abruptly, her ears standing upright and quivering as they panned back and forth, listening intently to the night sounds. Her whiskers felt for the vibration that warned of danger. With a flip of her long tail, she moved almost faster than an eye could follow, and was gone, streaking back to the crack in the rock she called home.

If anyone had been looking, they would have seen Rhone stretched out on the dry ground, a warm, golden glow at the base of his neck. His face changed to a gentle smile as he tucked his chin down, curling his arms around himself. Snuggling into the warmth, he fell into an even deeper, restful sleep, oblivious to the little creatures of the night.

CHAPTER 17

The Roundup isn't Round

Asingle footprint. The only indication a human had ever crossed this particular piece of ground since it had risen from the primordial ooze. The land had been drying out ever since.

One single track, but they had found it. What chance could have brought that about? It must have been preordained since no one could have planned it as coincidence.

Juan had combed the area looking for more, but there was only the one. Luckily, one was all they needed since it was heading toward the badlands, exactly as Manny predicted. They had pulled a long day, and Will was worried their foreman would want them to keep going but was quickly relieved when Manny swung down from his worn saddle.

"We'll camp in here tonight. With the bank to keep the fire out of sight, we won't give him any warning we're comin' up on him. Better get some rest. You'll need it tomorrow."

With that, he efficiently stripped down his horse, dropped his saddle on the ground, and lay down, using it as a pillow. The hat drooping over his eyes made an effective screen, blocking them from his view.

Will and Juan simply stood looking at each other, until Juan shrugged and started unsaddling his own horse.

Early the next morning, with the sun barely breaking over the shallow ridge, they were back on the trail. Actually, there was no trail. Even the single print had worn away with the night's wind, but Manny knew where to go.

They had hardly started before the sun's heat began to build. The nearer they got to the odd stone pillars standing starkly above the dry ground, the wider Will's eyes grew. Neither he nor Juan had ever seen anything like them before, and the odd, whispered stories heard around the tavern suddenly held more meaning.

The day's heat made a good excuse for the sweat that began to run down Will's sides. Even his palms were sweaty, which made the reins slippery in his clammy grasp.

Juan seemed indifferent until he jumped at the sudden flutter of a little bush bird flushing from the scraggly brush.

The foreman turned in his saddle and scanned the countryside, verifying the disturbance was nothing of import. "Keep it together, boys. He's in here somewhere. Our job is to find him, so don't go all screwy on me." He gave them each a hard look and turned back to the stones. "Stick close. I don't want either of you wandering off."

With that, they began winding their way between the stones and deeper into the strange setting. The farther they went, the stranger the rocks became. Instead of the single stones at the entrance, there were now clumps of stones, grouped into multifaceted pillars. Some groupings were so large they became walls, directing their travel into new headings. If it weren't for the horses' hoof prints, they might not be able to find their way back out. Deep shadows cut across their path, made even more shaded by the scraggly plant life growing on their tops and hanging down. It was a good thing the ground was mostly level since they spent so much time looking up at the odd walls.

Manny attempted to remain aimed in one direction, which was difficult with all the twists and turns the stones forced them to take. If it wasn't for the sunlight coming from the east, they would have already gotten lost.

"How far we gonna go, Manny?" Will wasn't much of an adventurer, and this was far beyond his comfort zone.

"Don't you worry about it. You just sit your saddle and don't lose sight of us."

"Not me," Will said with a shudder. "I'm not leavin' your side."

Juan shook his head in disgust, pretending he didn't know his little partner.

Manny had just about run out of patience with both of them. "Are you guys watching for tracks, or are you so involved in your little sightseeing tour, you forgot why we're here?" He was turning surly as the morning sun bore down on them.

The other two looked guilty but didn't say anything.

He growled as they started off again, deeper into the badlands. "And try watching the ground, not the sky."

Maybe an hour later, Will broke the monotonous sound of echoing hooves. "Hey, guys. Is that something?"

The other two swung to see Will pointing at a smudged spot on the rocky wall.

Manny climbed down and led his horse to the mark. Bending stiffly from sitting so long, he carefully looked over the area, then ran his finger across the dark smudge. A dry grin cracked his rugged features as he dropped to a knee. A fine grey dust had settled between the rocks from what had been a small ash pile. He stood and did a quick scan of the area, looking for any other sign. Then without a word, he nodded to their right and remounted.

It may have been the correct direction, but it was just more dismal corridors of rocky ground and dry dirty brush. No sign of their quarry. It wasn't long before the energy of finding evidence had given way to heat and tiredness. Even Manny was looking worn.

Without warning the wind picked up, beginning to blow fine sand down the passages with stinging force. As the men hunched forward in the saddle, reducing the surface area the sand would hit, the walls began reverberating with the sound of the wind. Like voices you couldn't quite understand, the sound made them all tense, and it didn't matter which way they went in the convoluted maze, the wind seemed to follow.

Raising a hand, Manny finally called a halt. Squinting to keep sand out of his eyes, he shouted into the gritty wind. "We've got to get some shelter or we'll end up being skinned alive. This wind is flowing down the passages like water in a river, so get behind this outcropping and bring the horses up between us and the wind. It'll be better than standing here in the middle, getting flayed."

The men could hardly hear him over the sound of the wind echoing off the walls. Juan's arms were already red from the stinging sand, and Will was going to make some comment about the cursed place, but quickly closed his mouth, as sand found the cavity inviting. Clambering stiffly out of the saddle, they drew their horses behind the convenient wall of rock jutting out from the corner. When their foreman unsaddled, Will and Juan did likewise. They knew enough to follow his lead.

With the horses lined up, rumps to the wind, the men stood their saddles on end and squatted behind them, draping their saddle blankets against their backs like a screen. The poor horses stood with their heads hanging low, snorting occasionally to keep the sand out of their noses. It was far from comfortable, but as good as they were going to get. Sitting hunched over, with the saddles and blankets protecting their backs and necks, the three men waited for the wind to die. It was a long wait.

Hours later, long after dark, the air cooled somewhat and the wind lost its force, finally dying away to nothing.

It was a long tiring night before the three climbed wearily out of the low drift of dry sand, dusted off their clothes and shook out their hair, dislodging even more of the clinging grains. They would be finding sand in their gear for weeks, but the worst was past.

Manny was all business as he asked, "How much water do you guys have? We're close, and I would really, really," he articulated the word heavily, "prefer not going back empty handed."

The other two understood his meaning, merely nodding as they dug into their saddlebags, drawing out their canteens.

Nobody went out of town without a canteen. There were rivers of course, but not necessarily in the direction you were headed.

Shaking his, Will glanced uneasily at their foreman. "I ah... Mine's about gone."

The foreman slowly shook his head in disbelief, although he did believe it. He was working with idiots.

"I drank it," Will said with a pathetic look, and tried to explain his reasoning. "I was thirsty."

Embarrassed by Will's comment, Juan stepped in. "I've got half."

Manny calculated the distance back to water and knew they didn't have a lot of time to spend walking in circles.

"Saddle up, boys. We've got to get this done in a hurry. There won't be any tracks to worry about because of the wind, so just keep your eyes open. We could run into him around any one of these corners."

It didn't take much to break camp since they really didn't have a camp to break down, but the horses would need water today, and that was more important than water for the men. No horses meant a long walk home, and losing one would cost more money than any one of them had on hand.

Taking care to shake out, and brush off, as much sand as they could, they saddled and mounted.

Rhone, we are being followed.

Stone gave the information without inflection or emotion, like he was dealing cards. He lay against the rock face, still in his collar setting, while Rhone wiped at his neck, trying to get as much sand off as possible. They had weathered the wind in a little rocky alcove that at least kept the sand from blasting them to a skinned carcass, but Stone's information galvanized Rhone into action. "Are you sure?" he asked, spinning around as though expecting to be jumped. He saw they were alone and puffed a breath in relief. But he was a little shaken. "How far away?"

Yes, *I can feel them, but it is difficult to determine distance due to the twists and turns of the passageways. As to how. I can feel the vibrations of the horses.*

Rhone looked about worriedly, wondering how to escape. He had no desire to meet those men again.

The segments of rock pillars jutted skyward in disarrayed jumbles, capped with their hats of dry grey vegetation. This particular section was broader than most and had more plants hanging over the rim and down the sides. With a sudden inspiration, Rhone grabbed Stone, quickly fastening the collar before grabbing his stuff and frantically searching for a way to the top. A quick glance to check for the men brought him to a sudden halt. A look of horror crossed his face as he saw his own footprints showing clearly in the coarse sand of the passage floor.

"Nooooo!" he cried in panic. "I'm leaving footprints all over the place."

Can you remove them? Stone asked seriously, but Rhone was in no mood to listen.

"What am I going to do? They're on horses and we won't have a chance."

Rhone, settle down. Panic will solve nothing. Stone's calm voice flowed through Rhone's mind, breaking through the quickly forming panic.

"Okay, yeah, I'll try," he said breathlessly, almost panting as he worked to calm his jumpy nerves. "But I left footprints and they'll see them."

What is the surface like? It does not resonate like rock.

"No, it's mostly dirt and small rocks, but it's covered with sand from the storm. There's even some grass and a few shrubs." He was learning to be specific.

I presume then, the imprints are in the sandy portion.

"Yeah, between the rocks." He began breathing more normally after his near panic.

Are you able to step on the rocky portions and brush away your prints from the sand? The calmness in the question gave Rhone the strength to consider the suggestion.

"Maybe. I can try I guess."

Then do so. I cannot feel their presence from up here, but I would prefer you did not take the collar off right now. If you could be quick about it, we may still have a chance.

Rhone didn't take time to answer as he began brushing away tracks, then blowing on the sand, trying to remove the lingering telltale prints. It wasn't perfect, but it was all he had time for. Careful to stay on the larger rocks, he made it around the bend, searching frantically for a place to climb the wall.

At last, he found a section rough enough that the plants extending over the wall had rooted into the little cracks and crevices. Using these for additional support, he crammed his fingers into the cracks and managed to drag himself to the top. Then bending low, so as not to show himself above the edge, he scurried deeper into the growth, away from the cliff edge. The segment wasn't more than fifty feet wide before coming to another abrupt edge, but at least he was safe for the moment. Now that he had a refuge, Rhone crept back the way he had come.

Coming back to the edge, he lay on his belly and inched forward, working his way quietly through the plants, careful not to rattle their dry leaves.

It wasn't five minutes before he heard the echoing clops of three horses coming around the bend.

"This place gives me the creeps," Will stated under his breath.

"Shoot, everything gives you the creeps, you creep. Now keep your mouth shut." Juan wasn't feeling particularly friendly this morning.

"I'm not a creep, and it is creepy. You heard the voices last night. It ain't natural. It was like ghosts were talkin'. You've heard the stories. They say dead men walk through these passages. People have seen 'em."

Juan rolled his eyes. "Will, you're an idiot."

"Both of you shut up," Manny groused irritably. "You two are enough to scare off the devil himself. How are we supposed to sneak up on anybody when you two are jabberin' away like jaybirds? Now snap 'em shut and listen up. We're going to have to turn around before long because we just don't have enough water. So hold it together." Wearily, he settled back into his saddle and mumbled, "It's like havin' two kids tagging along." He was just about done with these two.

Will and Juan looked a bit sheepish at being called kids. Having their foreman grumpy at them didn't bode well for their future.

Rhone held his breath, willing them to pass on by. They hadn't noticed his tracks, but he remembered these two, and knew they were looking for him, but hearing they would be leaving soon allowed him to start breathing again. As the horses continued on past, Rhone finally relaxed.

He had done it.

CHAPTER 18

Just When you Thought it was Safe

As the men vanished around the bend, Rhone jumped to his feet and ran to the far edge of the dirt-capped stonework. Below was another passage, no different from the one he had been in, but away from the riders. He studied the intricate design of passageways meandering across the landscape. Looking back the way he had come, he saw more of the same, but he could also see the far edge, where the pillars thinned and finally died away, leaving only dry brushland beyond. He had come a long way from the flatlands, but not nearly as far as he thought. The twists and turns of the passages didn't go in straight lines.

Where he stood was just one piece of the giant broken puzzle. He studied the terrain as best he could, plotting a direction he thought would give the best options. Since he had no idea where he was headed anyway, anywhere would probably do. He looked for the men again, but the pillars were too tall to see down into the passages at any distance. They were gone, and he had to go too. At least to the east, the rock sections became larger, like small plateaus with canyons between them. Perhaps they would be slightly more hospitable than where he was now. It was at least somewhere to head.

Carefully sliding over the edge, Rhone managed to scramble down far enough that he could drop the last few feet.

Are we safe yet? Stone queried, having felt the sudden drop and shock of landing.

"For the moment. It looks like we're clear, but those guys are still out here somewhere. We're going to try heading east. It looked like the land changes out that way."

Stone seemed very agreeable with the plan. *I too noted the subtle change in pattern. Would you like the shortest route, or are you planning a meandering course to confuse them?*

"You can do that?" Rhone asked, surprised by this new confession.

Of course. I noted the pattern, and now have a mental picture to work from.

"Very cool," Rhone said, happily impressed. "Straightest line, please. Let's not waste any time."

In that case, you had better turn around. You are facing the wrong direction.

So much for Rhone's directional smarts, but he accepted Stone's hint and began the next phase of their trek, winding through yet more of the passages.

T

he scant shade from the scraggly overhead plants was better than none. Manny called a stop to share out the water that was now getting scarce.

"I really hate to say it, but we've gotta call it quits. We'll just end up dying out here, and no one would ever find us. You can just bet, our good commissioner won't be sending out a search party."

Manny wiped the sweat from his forehead and took a small mouthful, savoring the swallow of warm water. As long as he was still sweating, things weren't too bad. It was when the sweating stopped that he would be in trouble. Without sweat to help the body cool, he would overheat until his brains cooked.

He checked the other two, making sure they were okay.

"Backtracking won't do us any good since the windstorm erased our tracks, but don't worry, I kept to an easterly route on the way in, so we'll just have to head west. Sooner or later, we should find our way out."

Juan looked almost comfortable, slouching casually in his saddle. He was used to the heat. It was the rocky passages and their unending labyrinth that had him on edge. He didn't like the feel of not knowing what was around the next corner."

Will had gone silent, a fact the other two found a blessing, but ever since the sandstorm his wild eyes had constantly flicked between nothings, as though expecting a ghost to drop in on him.

Manny was just mounting, ready to begin the homeward journey when Will screamed. The gut-wrenching sound caused Manny to haul his horse's head around, not knowing what to expect. "What the...!" Furious at Will, he swung around, locking eyes with a horrified teenager who stumbled to a stop as he rounded the corner.

"It's him!" Juan shouted, putting heels to his horse and bolting into an instant gallop. His cutting horse was trained to quick action take-offs and stops, and played it like a game. While this wasn't a steer, it was a target, and the horse launched forward at a dead run, ready to play.

Manny began his own advance, shouting, "Get him!" as he too kicked his horse's flanks.

Will was almost in a faint, certain he had just witnessed the ghost he was expecting.

With no warning from Stone, Rhone stood petrified, rooted to the spot as the two men on horseback raced toward him. Finally reacting, he turned to flee, which was also the moment Stone finally made a comment.

You are aware, that I cannot flash them effectively if you are facing the wrong direction.

The disconnect between the comment and his need to run caused Rhone to stall mid-stride. "What? You want me to stand here?" In his confused state of uncertainty, Rhone again stumbled to a stop.

It was that precise moment the horses went wild, snorting and screaming in fear.

A quick glance over his shoulder was enough for Rhone to see all three horses going crazy, bucking in earnest as they leapt skyward, twisting like bullwhips. Their wide eyes showed stark white around the dark irises, and their nostrils flared widely, blowing steaming hot blasts with their fearful snorts.

The short man had lost his seat first bounce, and lay on the ground in a daze. The other two fought valiantly to stay in the saddle.

Run you fool! came the shout in Rhone's mind.

That much he could do, and started running as fast as his pack would allow.

Unfortunately, in evading the crazed horses, his path took him past Will who had climbed back to his feet and dove in determination at Rhone's legs.

Will may have been short, but Rhone had the weight of the pack throwing him off balance. Tripped by Will's tackle, Rhone fell flat on his face, hitting hard and scraping his cheek on the dry packed dirt. He was down, but not out. Rolling to his side, pack still pulling him off balance, Rhone struggled to get his legs back under him. The air was filled with dust from flailing horse hooves, as Rhone clambered wildly, hands and feet churning in the gravelly rock of the passage floor. He was almost clear, when a hand grabbed the pack, wrenching him sideways and off balance again.

"No!" Rhone screamed in frustration. It simply wasn't fair!

Then a voice cried out in his mind, *Close your eyes! which* took less than a moment for him to understand.

The instant Rhone squeezed his eyes shut, a blinding flash showed him the red lines in his eyelids, and he vaguely heard the sound of a scream echo through the narrow passage. A moment later, a sharp pain turned everything dark.

* * *

"Leave him. We have the damn necklace. I don't want to worry about hauling him all the way back, and he won't last long anyway."

The foreman stood looking down at Rhone's still form, awkwardly crumpled against the wall of the rocky passage.

"Sounds good to me," Juan said indignantly. "I bruised my damn knuckles on him, but it's Will I'm worried about."

Will lay curled on his side, whimpering in little gusts of child-like anguish. His dirty hands covered his eyes as tears streamed in rivulets, washing streaks across his dusty face. "I'm blind, Juan," he whimpered. "I can't see anything but red."

"Ahhh, you'll get over it. Remember that other kid? He said he was blinded. You're just like him."

Juan's voice was kinder than Manny had ever heard from the man. It just goes to show, you never know about a person.

"Yeah, Don't you worry, Will," Manny agreed. "We're not going to leave you out here. I'll tie you to the saddle if I need to, but you're coming with us."

The foreman meant his words as supportive, but they may have had a threatening quality too. Will would be coming, whether he wanted to or not. He needed Will's story to back up his own, and The Commissioner would want to know everything.

The collar was wrapped securely in the bedroll strapped behind Manny's cantle. Whatever had happened, Manny hoped it wouldn't happen again. The collar thing was a treasure for sure and, as with every treasure, it came with consequences. Maybe it would be safe, bundled up and out of sight, but he still wanted it gone as soon as possible.

"Juan, help Will into his saddle. Let's get back before something else happens."

"You got it, boss. You gonna carry that thing?" He was referring to the thing in the bedroll.

"Yep. I don't rightly know what happened, but this piece is going back with us. I think it'll be safe bundled up like that, and if it was the kid that did something, well, he won't be doin' much for long."

The foreman was happy the way things had turned out. As luck would have it, they had found what they had come for, and he would be buying the drinks when they got back.

"Let's get moving. We got a long way to go."

Rhone came to with a start and a blinding headache. The afternoon sun shone piercingly through the coarse branches high above, directly into his eyes, but squinting simply made it hurt worse. Pain was all his mind could recognize for a minute or two, but gradually, Rhone came to the conclusion he was lying hunched in the dirt of the passageway.

Groaning with every move, he rolled to a sitting position, cradling his head to ease the pounding. His exploring fingers quickly found the pain of the swollen jaw that hurt more than anywhere else. Stretching his neck slowly, he found the limits of acceptable motion and took a slow, painful breath to clear his thoughts.

As the memory of a flash drifted through his thick fog, Rhone slapped a hand to his neck, then slid into total dejection. Stone was gone.

"Stone?" he shouted dryly. "Stone!" His now panicked voice got harsher as he searched frantically for the collar that wasn't there. But he knew where it went. The men had come for it, and he had let them take it. He had failed. Failed himself, and his friend. Now they were both alone.

The pain of his head, and the pain of his failure, buried him in guilt, as the weight of his error crushed him. Why hadn't he paid more attention, and why hadn't Stone warned him?

The question was meaningless since it had already happened. But what would he do now? He was no good without Stone. He had been nothing before, and he would be nothing without him. His entire recent life had centered around his friend, and he honestly didn't want anything else. Who would possibly want to be a farmer, when they had Stone and a life's goal? He lay back onto the rocky ground and wept tears that rolled into little puddles, refusing to be drawn into the dry dust of the passage.

What went wrong?

The words echoed round and round in his head, but no answers came back to him.

Eventually, the sun dropped over the lip of the cliff, and Rhone managed to climb painfully to his feet, beginning to wander blindly through the pathways, turning first one way, then the other. He had no idea where he was going but forward was at least away from the tracks the men left. He wanted as far away from them as he could get, but his head still hurt, making thinking difficult. When he tried to chew pieces of the dry meat he had left, the pain became excruciating, but maybe that was partially mental. The pain somehow reminded him that he was alone and that he had failed.

Surprisingly, he had found his pack tossed against the rocky wall with his stuff still in it. Obviously, they hadn't wanted to carry any more than they needed to, and the pack had no value. The only thing missing was his water jug. Which was a big thing indeed. Without water, he wouldn't last long. No wonder they hadn't worried about him. Nature would do it for them.

He could only agree. He wasn't worth anything. Not without Stone.

The words, *I let him down*, kept circling through his mind, echoing hollowly where Stone's knowledgeable voice should have been. But another day of this, and he wouldn't have to worry any longer. First, he would start to stumble, then he would begin seeing things that weren't there. Soon he would go down and wouldn't get back up. The desert had its own ways of taking care of things. Then he would be free.

He would be free, but Stone wasn't.

The words rang emptily through his stalling mind. He knew he was dying of thirst, but that's what he deserved. Anyone who fails a friend doesn't deserve to live. He was thirsty.

Bouncing off yet another wall of stone, Rhone's head struck solidly, cracking against the rocky face. He felt dazed by the blow, but the pain was slow to come, almost dull. Vaguely he knew he was failing, but it didn't bother him. Sooner would be better. But poor Stone, his friend. He would be locked away in the dark of The Commissioner's vault, never to be seen again.

He had failed his best friend.

Stumbling now with every step, Rhone followed the rock-strewn path that never ended.

His mind still dreamed of walking, as step after step he slowly moved up the endless stone passageways, failing to recognize he had hit the ground. His body kept moving in small, disconnected motions, until finally, even that action stopped, and he lay calmly at the base of a rocky pillared wall, next to a scraggly thorn bush. The large flattened stone his head lay on made a good pillow, but it wasn't his Stone. It was just a rock. A dead rock for a dead man.

CHAPTER 19

All is Lost

Rhone groaned weakly, eyelids scraping across his dry bleary eyes in a slow, stiff blink. They didn't want to move, but something had interrupted his bone-weary rest.

A light spatter of rain caused him to blink involuntarily and, still too groggy to make sense of it, lay stiffly on the rocky ground, face to the cloudy sky. It was important somehow, and the thought slowly worked its way into his stalled mind.

Annoyingly, another drop struck him, landing on his dry cracked lips that instantly soaked up the moisture, then wanted more.

And more fell. Rolling his aching head, Rhone angled it to a better position, allowing even more of the precious drops to land on his face. Soon there were so many he didn't have to worry about reaching for them, but more about drowning in them. His dehydrated body wasn't ready for this kind of treatment, unable to respond to draw himself out of the quickly forming puddles.

Rhone cracked open his dry mouth, trying to capture the wonderful sweetness of the wet drops pouring down on him. He was alive.

Very slowly, his mind began to work again, which meant he wasn't dying. Not anymore.

He blinked again and rolled to his side, attempting to sip from the quickly growing puddle. He was alive and had to drink. As the rain refilled the empty puddle beside his head, his sips refilled the reservoirs of his body and his mind slowly began to work. Even the few sips had made a difference. Water, drink water.

His breathing became stronger, but his muscles began to burn, letting him know they were trying, but were stuck, without the moisture they needed to help them move. Sip, swallow, sip, swallow, wait for the little puddle to refill, and sip again. It wasn't long before he managed an elbow, then a knee, and from there, to drink like a man, bending to sip from the puddle, not belly-down in the mud like an animal.

And there was mud. As the drops hit the powder-dry dirt, the rainwater mixed with the pulverized soil, instantly blending it into runny mud. The light rain soon became a torrent, falling from the sky in sheets. There was nowhere to hide from the downpour, and the wind was picking up, pushed as much by the drops themselves as from any other source.

Rhone dragged himself to his feet and crawled to the wall, using it for support as well as for the minor protection the overhanging plants managed to give. It wasn't much, but they were better than nothing.

The continuing rain filled the low spots of the passage, and the puddles grew. Rhone continued to work his way along, not sure where he was headed, but it seemed the reasonable thing to do. Even his slow brain knew it wasn't manly to simply sit in the rain and wait until he drowned. But even his slow realization said it might be the outcome anyway. The desert was well known for flash floods. The poor soil could only hold so much rain coming down so quickly, then the water would begin to flow to wherever was lower. Water simply followed the rules of gravity.

The thought instantly brought a pang of guilt. He wouldn't have considered gravity before Stone had taught him. He had learned so much. Stone taught him so much, and he had let his friend down. Now he would drown, and Stone would be left alone, again.

As Rhone stumbled along, splashing through the growing puddles, his mind slowly began to work at putting things back in order. Survival was good and something his body wanted. His moving forward was an example of that. He could have laid there and drowned, but he didn't. He had struggled to get up, then he had staggered along the cliff face, trying to find a way out of the rain. Now he was trying to stay alive. But why? There had to be a reasonable answer. Questions were the quest of life.

The answer hit like a sledgehammer's blow, stopping him in his tracks. Stone had taught him to think, and thought had power. He needed to find Stone. Stone needed help as much as he did, and Stone was unable to help himself. *He relies on me.*

He had failed Stone, and he might not be able to do much, but he could still try. He might not even succeed, but he could do his best. Without his help, Stone had no future. He would be locked in a dark box forever, without help.

The power of hope flared like an elixir, giving him strength.

Rhone picked up his feet and began to run through the ankle-deep water. He still didn't know where he was going, but it would be out of here. He would find Stone, and he would save his friend.

It was a heroic thought and one that should have been given a chance. All the gods should have been aware of Rhone's fervor as he plowed through the deepening water.

The water's flow was gaining direction now and would soon become a river, rushing headlong to nowhere. With the current assisting him, Rhone found it was far easier to keep going forward than trying to work his way back up the torrent. Besides, he had just come from that direction, and it wasn't where he wanted to be.

As the water continued to rise, Rhone's feet found it harder and harder to keep their footing. Calf deep. Knee deep. Thigh deep, and the water kept rising. He was seriously beginning to worry. It wasn't difficult to continue, but continuing to walk was a different matter.

When the muddy water reached his waist and the rain hadn't subsided, Rhone knew it was past time to find a way out. The current had continued to build as the water rose and rushed past at an amazing speed, attempting to carry him with it. Debris and odd pieces of driftwood floated past, soon to disappear around the next bend, but the rock walls stood tall against the flow. They had seen similar floods many times and had proven their strength. Any weaker sections had long ago given way, and the remaining walls stood strong.

Rhone tried unsuccessfully to get a handhold on the smooth rock, but his energy was nearly gone. His uncoordinated fingers slid along the face, only managing to rub themselves raw and bleeding. Staggering forward, fighting for footing, he finally saw what he was looking for. A heavy root hung down from the top edge, and he reached out to grab it.

Grasping at the gnarly root in one cold hand, he reached up with his other, struggling to get a better grip on the now slippery wood, but try as he might, his fingers couldn't hold. Sliding back down its length, he dropped back into the rushing water. Instantly he surged up, ready for another attempt, but his luck was up. A long dead tree from parts unknown had been caught up with the flowing current. Its massive weight struck him in the back, knocking him off his feet and under the muddy water.

Not having slowed in the least, the log followed the pull of the flowing water, continuing its tortuous path through the labyrinth. When stubs of its long-gone roots caught against the bottom and wall, the log twisted, forcing its way back into the current's center.

Face bumping hard against the bottom, Rhone clawed madly for something to grab, but the cursed log kept pace, sitting on his back and holding him under the surface. His lungs began to scream, letting him know they required air. He had already been working hard, sloshing through the rising water, and his body hadn't recovered yet from his near-death by dehydration scenario. Now he was dying from too much water. Such was his recent luck, and suddenly, he was simply too tired to fight.

Without air, and without hope, Rhone slipped quietly into unconsciousness. His last thoughts were of his friend.

I'm sorry, Stone. I tried. I honestly tried!

Silently and alone, Rhone drowned in the desert.

When the gnarled snag of old root caught again at the edge of rock, it pivoted the log, rolling as it turned. As it rolled, a stub caught on the strap of the pack the body still wore, drawing the limp form out of the water. A slow trickle drained sluggishly from his mouth, returning to the now roiling muddy river.

The swollen current continued following gravity's pull, drawing the log through the tortured channeling of the passageway. With each roll, more water drained from Rhone's open mouth, the gentle rocking motion moving slight bits of air into, and out of his lungs.

***

A gag reflex woke Rhone and he gasped for air, feeling like his body was being torn apart. His back ached intolerably as he hung head down, draped over the log, stretched nearly to the breaking point. Coughing violently, spitting up bile and dirty water, he gagged again as the vile liquid ran back into his throat.

Can't breathe! his mind screamed.

Switching to automatic, his body reacted in a panic, rolling to his side where he could retch more effectively. Totally exhausted and breathing with difficulty, he lay draped over the log like a wet rug. His face lay pressed uncomfortably into the section of rough bark that remained on the weathered surface, but he hardly noticed in the haze of his other pains.

Through burning red eyes, Rhone studied the picture for several minutes before his mind caught up and he realized what he was looking at. The fact that the ground was ground, and not flowing water, finally struck him. Struggling, he tried to pull himself up into a sitting position, but the waterlogged pack held him firmly in place. With bleary eyes and raw stiff fingers, he managed to unhook the strap, sliding it off his shoulder and onto the wet ground.

Ahead of him lay the shallows of a small lake with low muddy mounds poking wetly from the surface. Tall canyon walls rose high above, hemming it in with the same pillar-like faces he had been walking through prior to the rain. But there was a big difference. There was water here, and there was greenery on the cliff tops, with more growing along the faces. Even the tops of the low islands showed green, with the points of new grass showing through the mud. This was not the rocky, sandy dirt of the past few days. It was beautiful, and he was more than comfortable just sitting and gawking as he stretched the ache from his cramping back.

A final coughing fit shook him, and Rhone lurched over, spitting bad-tasting mud from his mouth. Bracing himself, he rose to stand on shaky legs. He had survived, again. How, he wasn't sure. The last thing he remembered was drowning, caught and dragged underwater, pressed uncaringly into the murky bottom. But it was undeniable, he was alive. The aching joints and burning lungs proved it. But muscle cramps and upset stomach he could live with.

His life had changed in so many ways in the past few weeks, it was difficult to keep everything straight. Then the memory of Stone came rushing back, and Rhone closed his eyes, feeling for his friend's presence. But there was only emptiness. Stone was gone.

The vast emptiness brought a heart-rending sob from his abused lungs. He was alone, and Stone would have to wait. His first move was to survive, then to find out where he was. Later, he could plan how to get to wherever Stone was. He could only take one step at a time.

On unsteady feet, Rhone slid and stumbled through the mud, exploring his new whereabouts. The water was already beginning to drain away into the loose ground, lowering considerably even in the short time since his waking. But the greenery proved that the water table was shallow here, and the soil itself looked fertile instead of simply rock. The valleys around Skragmoore had been like that too. One would be fertile and productive, the next rocky and barren. This was obviously a fertile valley, set snuggly in the middle of the badlands. He wondered if anyone had ever been here before. It would take a stalwart soul to wander through the stony corridors to get here. Even then, they would have to find their way back out. He felt a quiet satisfaction at perhaps being the only human to ever see it.

Then the sudden realization hit him. This wouldn't be of any value if he couldn't find his way out.

The water continued to lower until finally Rhone was able to wade to the cliff wall and began the arduous climb to the top. It wasn't terribly difficult, but his body had been through a lot recently and complained at every move. The stretch of climbing made his back hurt worse, and the sun made his head ache. His still-dry muscles told him they weren't happy either.

Shutting his mind to their complaints as he would to Stone's constant chatter, he climbed the near-vertical cliff. The seams in the rocky face made it somewhat less dangerous than it might look, but any slip would still be a damaging fall, and any injury this far from civilization wouldn't be good. Still, it was what he needed to do. Wandering around, hoping to find a way out, was a sure way to fail.

Remembering his last climb to the top, Rhone knew he would be able to see a lot of the tangled maze. Maybe he could even trace a path out. Stone had been able to do it, but that was Stone. He wasn't so sure he would be able to.

With the help of a thick clump of fern, Rhone pulled himself over the top edge and crawled forward until he was sure of the footing. Standing, he surveyed his surroundings. Other than the rocky segments being larger, his view was very similar to what he had seen before. The crazed pattern was the same. Zig-zagging passages crossed back and forth as their towering rocky cliffs dominated the countryside, but far into the west, with the heat-haze making it difficult to be sure, he thought he could see their end. Turning eastward, the segments continued to grow in size until finally becoming almost normal ground. He was in the middle, or somewhere close to it. No matter which way he went, it was going to be a long way out.

Dropping exhaustedly to the ground, Rhone slumped into the shade of a small scraggly tree rooted deep into the rocky surface. He remembered the log earlier, and it made sense that there would be trees around. Nature always finds a way, and if nature could, he could.

If he went directly westward, it should take him back toward where he had come. Undoubtedly, that was the direction Stone had gone, but just following along didn't seem to be a great plan. What would he do when he got there? Go up to The Commissioner and demand Stone back? Unlikely. More than likely, it would get him thrown into jail, or worse. Even he had heard about the dealings of The Commissioner. Whatever the outcome, it wouldn't be healthy. But what alternative did he have?

Unsure, Rhone continued to study the jigsaw puzzled pieces of the landscape.

Stone had mentioned being able to follow the landscape's layout by memory. He wondered if he could do the same. Staring intently at the scene, Rhone attempted memorizing the picture. Not the individual sections, or the winding pathways that separated them. Just the picture of the landscape. If he could see the picture in his head, the way Stone did, then he would always know where he was. It was worth a try.

After studying the view, Rhone closed his eyes and tried to see it in his mind. When the picture faded or distorted in his thoughts, he would look up again, re-visualizing the scene. All afternoon he continued, attempting to remember the picture. When the sun finally dropped so low he could no longer see past his squint, he stopped, but the afterimage of the picture seemed burned into his vision. It also made the climb down that much more difficult.

Even his few hours on the bluff had been time enough for the water to lower considerably, seeping away into the porous ground. How could the land drink up so much water and still be dry desert? It was definitely a strange world.

Walking along the edge of the lake, Rhone noticed the slight ripple of a current showing in the water's depth. It wasn't much, but he was sure it was moving. Like all water, it was trying to find its own level. Rhone quickened his pace and began running along the gravelly shore, following the flow.

It wasn't a wide lake, but it was long, and the lowering water had exposed a narrow gravel swath along the cliff base. Rhone followed nature's trail until it was blocked by a rocky pillar jutting sharply from the cliff face. Working his way carefully over and around the obstacle, he could see the end of the lake butting up against the rocky cliff. Where the water met the cliff, the lake ran directly into the low mouth of a cave, disappearing into its dark interior.

CHAPTER 20

The Hunt is on

Commissioner Dodge stoically listened to the three men as they attempted to tell him of their troubles. Manny had mentioned the item was a gemstone set in a collar, not the artifact they had expected, but The Commissioner wasn't disappointed, and the item lay wrapped in a bedroll taking up the middle of his desk.

But the men were obviously disrupting his thoughts as they tried to explain. Unfortunately, his totally unconcerned look said, Who cared? He most certainly did not. He didn't care if the kid was left out in the badlands, and he didn't care if one of his men was blind. He simply didn't care. He had his necklace. Any other information was superfluous.

When a smile of satisfaction crept across the commissioner's face, Manny saw the look and realized his boss wasn't paying the least bit of attention. As Will continued to whine about his being blind and needing help, Manny made a subtle gesture to Juan.

Placing a hand on Will's shoulder, Juan quietly said, "Come on, Will, we're done here. I'll help you get home. Maybe tomorrow you'll be able to see again."

Will started to object, but the foreman's quiet hiss stopped him, and he let Juan guide him from the room.

Manny stayed behind, closing the heavy door and turning to see The Commissioner greedily eyeing the bundle. The avarice in The Commissioner's hungry gaze made a chill run down Manny's spine, and he scrunched his shoulders unconsciously, trying to ease their suddenly jumpy muscles.

Finally noting the other two had gone, Commissioner Dodge looked up and smiled. "Good job, and I'll see you get a bonus. But I must say, I wasn't so sure when you left. Thought I might have to come up with some other...incentive, to get things done." His smile may have deepened, but the eyes never changed.

It was not easy working for this man. The odds were always stacked against you. The Commissioner not only held the key, but the scorecard.

Manny accepted the seldom-heard praise with a nod, but knew The Commissioner's threats were a far better gauge of things. "It wasn't easy, sir. The kid was smart and did things I'd never expect. To be truthful, I'm not sure if it was the kid, or that thing." He pointed to the bundle warily.

"Don't be so dramatic, Foreman. He was just a dumb kid for goodness sakes."

Manny made note of the 'was' comment. It didn't seem to disturb his boss at all.

The Commissioner shrugged noncommittally. "You said there was a flash. That other kid said something similar. I didn't believe him of course, but there are strange things. Now, seeing Will's condition, I suppose it's even true." He paused, deliberating, then made up his mind. "I'll be honest myself. I don't know why your man can't see, and I don't care. I was expecting an artifact of some kind, but you brought me a necklace. Whatever. You said it's a beauty. A single large stone? Sounds nice." He harrumphed noncommittally. "Interesting anyway. Where would a young man get a large gemstone?"

Manny had an answer to that. "The guys made mention from their first encounter, sir. Apparently, the kid said he found it in a river, but I don't know. More than likely, he stole it from somewhere. I've never seen him before, so he could be new to town."

The Commissioner chortled evilly. "New? Nobody comes here, new." But he chewed his lip as he rethought the words. "But if he did steal it, maybe he was forced to run. You know, find a place out of the way. That does make sense, and this is about as 'out of the way' as you can get."

"Sounds about right, sir. Far more than finding it in the river, but it doesn't explain about the horses."

The Commissioner tore his gaze from the bundle and glared at him. "What about the damn horses? Horses are always problematic. Maybe there was a cougar around." Pointedly, he nodded to his mountain lion skull on the wall.

Manny had to admit the possibility, but the timing had been so...perfect. They had almost lost the kid in the fight to keep the horses in control.

"Yes, sir. That's probably it." Manny said, shuffling his feet, but discontented with the answer. He let it go. "Guess I got caught up in Will's craziness."

He knew it was best to go along with The Commissioner, no matter what his own feelings were on the subject. Besides, the kid was gone by now, so it probably didn't make much difference. Even with their horses, he and the boys had barely gotten back. The badlands were a bad place to be. He could still feel that first drop of rain, as they finally managed to find their way out. Rain? It had poured buckets and barrels. And of course, they didn't have their rain gear. Not this time of year. Just more bad luck, from a very unlucky place. Unconsciously, he shook his head, glad to be home.

The Commissioner wasn't paying any attention. Lifting the bundle, he felt the weight, shifting it back and forth between his hands. He hadn't unwrapped it yet, more like he was building suspense to make it more enjoyable.

To Manny, it was almost scary.

Realizing his foreman was watching, Commissioner Dodge set the bundle gently back on the desk and again said, "Good job," as though forgetting he had already told him that. "You can go for now, but I'll have another job for you tomorrow." Instantly he forgot Manny as he turned back to his prize.

It was a welcome release after the tension of trying to explain their journey. With a quick unnoticed nod, Manny left without further delay. Not only had his recent task been an extreme hardship, it was unique in untold ways. Untold ways that needed telling. There were just too many ill-fitting pieces to the story, and his itch to work them out needed more help than simply repeating them to himself.

He headed to the tavern for a cold glass. He had earned a cold one, even if it did cost more. While he drank, he would mention an item or two to Mack. Mack was a good listener.

"Honest, Mack, it was the weirdest thing you ever saw. The horses went crazy, and I mean totally mad. I've had plenty of horses get jittery around wild animals. You know what I mean. Bears and cats, that sort of thing. Shucks, the worst I ever saw was over a dumb curled horn sheep from up on the high rocks. Dang'est thing, but the horses went nuts over it, but this was different. I'm tellin' you, they went mad. And I mean crazy mad. Snortin' and bucking, practically flipped inside out, and over nothing. It's got to be the kid. Then there was that flash. It was just like what that other kid said."

Mack hadn't responded, simply kept wiping glasses and stacking them in an intricate pyramid that was far too artful for this place. But it made him feel good and reminded him that he had come from somewhere else.

When Mack didn't respond, Manny spoke more loudly than he intended. "Damn it, Mack. It's not just coincidence."

Luckily, it was a tavern, and nobody paid him any attention. After a quick scan of the room, and a notice of Mack's lifted eyebrow, he continued, in a quieter voice. "Honestly, Mack. It was weird. I was busy trying to stay in the saddle, not looking at the kid, like poor Will. I think he might just end up blind. Said he can't see anything but blood red."

Mack shook his head in his prophetic way, and Manny came right back to topic.

"So I was thinking. Is the kid a wizard or something, or was it something to do with that necklace thing? I wasn't sure, so I wrapped it up in my bedroll just in case. No more flashes, so maybe it worked."

Manny hadn't mentioned bringing the kid in, and Mack recognized the lack. Looking up from his wiping, he tipped his head, acknowledging Manny's woes. "Sounds like you did good then. The Commissioner must be happy." He was getting more information here than he had for months.

"The Commissioner?" Manny sputtered, almost spraying his beer. "When is our Commissioner ever happy?"

Manny hadn't been fooled by The Commissioner's careless demeanor. He had only been happy because he had a new treasure. That didn't make him a happy man.

"But didn't he like the gift?" Mack asked, trying to stretch the conversation a bit further.

Manny gave a shrug before saying, "I don't know. He had me leave before he opened it. But truthfully, I'm just as glad. I didn't want to be around it any longer than I needed to. I don't know what it is, and I don't really care. It's done, and The Commissioner has his toy. I'm sure it's locked away in his secret vault by now. Right along with the rest of his stuff."

"Secret vault," Mack said with a quiet guffaw, grabbing another glass to start polishing with his ever-present towel. His motions showed total disinterest in the topic. Just another story, from another patron.

Manny sat back with a guilty look, realizing he had said too much.

Finally, Mack set the glass down and leaned forward, resting on his forearms. "You can have the cold one on me today. Sounds like you had a rough time."

Manny looked up, surprised, but Mack gave a tilt of his head. "I gotta take care of my good customers. There aren't too many of those." Then he picked up the glass again, absently stacking it on top of the others.

Manny's sheepish grin told him he had done right. Mack had just made a new confidant, and quietly wondered how much information he would be able to get.

"But a wizard? Really, Manny, and you're a grown man." The humor made his comment a simple effort to make a friend happy.

Manny accepted it with an embarrassed grin. It may have looked out of place on the rough man, but everybody feels dumb once in a while. "Yeah, I know. Sounds dumb to me too. It really was weird, but it's done, and The Commissioner says he has something new for me tomorrow. Guess I'm not going to get a break."

Mack gave him a wise nod. "Shoot, you're too good for him to let go, and he knows it. But you take care out there. I hear there's magic afoot." He bobbed his eyebrows comically, and Manny gave a short laugh, appreciating the jest. Climbing to his feet, he said, "I've gotta go, Mack, and... thanks."

Once Manny had left, Mack started his rounds of the other two customers. When he reached the one at the corner table, he made a small, simple gesture, and passed on by.

Within the hour, he closed up for the night and waited for Har's return. He had a story to tell.

Mack heard the single light tap on the back door and made sure the room was dark before opening it a crack. Seeing it was Harold, he opened it further and quickly searched the area for anyone else.

"Come on in, Har. It's too late for you to be out standing around in the dark."

It was a simple statement, but one that wouldn't sound odd if anyone happened to overhear.

"Don't mind if I do," Har said agreeably. "I've been scrubbing floors all afternoon. With all his money, you would think The Commissioner could afford some young women to come work for him."

Har limped through the doorway and gratefully made his way to a table, gently easing himself into a comfortable position.

Mack's face was full of smiles as he re-lit a lamp. "You know good and well, it would be Mrs. Dodge that won't allow it. She knows her husband quite well, and is not one to put candy in front of a child." He chortled at his own jest, which made Harold grimace in distaste. The mere thought of The Commissioner with any young lady was enough to turn his stomach.

"You're right, but it doesn't do my back any good. Can't wait until this is done and we're gone. This place only gets worse, and I'm tired of it." He really hadn't had a good day, and even thinking of The Commissioner was more than he wanted to do. "Have you got a cold one around? I know I was here earlier, but that was work."

Mack nodded affirmatively. "You bet, Har. Another sip would do you good. Almost as much as a little story I have for you."

With that tidbit hanging in the air, he dug out a cold mug and filled it until the thick froth foamed over the top, almost hypnotically sliding down the sides. The brew coiled and spun in the glass, as beautiful as any woman.

Harold's suspicious look made the free drink worth the effort, and Mack settled himself in the chair before saying more.

But Har beat him to it. "What kind of story? Ain't nothing happened around here, except some kid getting lost in the flats. At least, that's all I've heard."

Mack grinned and waited just a bit longer, until Harold leaned forward, almost threateningly.

"No need to get your pants in a wad. I'll tell you," but he still let it drag on as long as possible. When Har grumbled something under his breath, Mack finally gave in. "Seems I've got a new contact at The Commissioner's. His foreman. You probably know Manny. Anyway, he just came in from a short trip. Stopped in for some brew and asked for my thoughts." He raised his eyebrows suggestively at his status as a counselor. At Har's reluctant nod, he continued. "Yep, He asked my opinion on a few things that happened on the trip."

Har was tired and not in the mood for finesse. "All right, spit it out. I haven't got all night."

With no further hesitation, Mack spilled his information. "The Commissioner sent his boys out to search for an ar-ti-fact." He spread the syllables, stretching the word for emphasis.

That got Har's attention. "An artifact? Do tell."

"Yep, except they didn't find one. What they found was a kid with a unique collar. Then their horses went crazy, and one of the guys got blinded by a flash. In the end, The Commissioner has a new bauble. Apparently, the collar the kid wore had a large stone set in it."

"The kid?" Har wanted everything now.

"Yep, but Manny didn't say much more. I presume they did him in and left him in the badlands to rot. You know how The Commissioner works."

"They killed a kid and stole his necklace? That sounds pretty bad, even for Commissioner Dodge. You sure?"

Mack mentally ran through his story before answering. "Pretty close to it. But the kid part wasn't what bothered him."

"Killing a kid didn't bother him?" Even though Har knew The Commissioner, and Manny, it still surprised him.

"Didn't seem to."

Har sipped at his cold beer, thinking. "I don't get it, Mack. If it didn't bother him, why did he need your words of wisdom?"

"Ahh, now's the good part. He was worried the kid might be a wizard or something."

But his words didn't get the response he had expected.

"Had been, you mean," Har mumbled. "Even if he 'had been', the kid's dead, so why would it matter?"

"That's a good question. So I'm thinkin', they may not have killed him outright. Maybe they just left him there and figured he wouldn't make it. You know the stories about the badlands."

Harold took another sip before bringing up a comment. "An odd collar, even with a rock in it, doesn't make the kid a wizard."

"No, it was other things," Mack said with a frown. "When they jumped the kid, Manny said the horses went mad. Started stomping and bucking, all kinds of crazy. I tend to believe him on that since he's been riding all his life."

With Har's nod of acceptance, he went on.

"Then there's the flash thing. You were the one who told me about The Commissioner being interested in an artifact that flashed. Something like that. What if it was the kid that made it happen? Maybe he has a protection spell or something. I don't know, but the way things are starting to gather, I'd believe just about anything."

Har sipped his brew slowly as his mind turned at a furious pace. "Thanks, Mack. I think we've got enough here to send a report at least. I have no idea what it all means, but maybe someone at the office knows something more." He drained the last of the beer and watched intently as the thin film of suds slid back to the bottom. "Keep your ears open, Mack."

Mack started to object, but Har raised a hand, stilling him. "I know. You always do, but I've got a feeling we're on to something. Something big." He climbed from the table with more energy than he had arrived with. "Wizards, artifacts, the Badlands, and wild horses. Shucks, Mack, this is starting to sound like fun."

CHAPTER 21

Building a Case

Aundrea kicked back in her favorite chair and reread Har's letter. *He can't really mean it. Wizards?* The rest was all explainable and she easily followed the possibilities, but a wizard? Seriously? Maybe Har had been in the field too long.

But the mention of a large stone tweaked her interest. Something... Some memory. A comment, or text maybe. There was something, and it tickled the back of her mind invitingly. She finally gave up. It would come when it came, and playing mental games, trying to dislodge it, would only build frustration. At least she had heard from Har and Mack, and that was important.

So Commissioner Dodge was up to something. That wasn't a surprise. They had everything but the proof of his running fingers through the town's profits. But stealing from kids? Honestly, it wasn't any worse than taking candy from a baby, and she was sure he wouldn't hesitate, as long as no one actually saw him do it.

Then there was the issue of artifacts. Artifacts were an interesting item of themselves. There had been some very interesting pieces come to the surface. Some even worked, or so she had heard, but a flashing light? And one that was bright enough to blind? Still, it was entirely possible. A large lantern perhaps? If it had proper optics. She had seen one in use at the ocean cliffs, but that was huge, and she tossed the idea as being impractical.

But what had happened to the boy? Definitely a thing to check on. If he was still out there somewhere, maybe he could be found. It would certainly build her case against Mr. Dodge and his poor ability as a commissioner.

The more she thought on it, the better she liked it. It was well within her jurisdiction. She even had available staff.

Determined, she began listing her agenda. She had extensive experience in matters like this, and her life in the streets finally came to good use.

"Bran, do you have a moment?" He would be perfect for the lead, and he could use the experience. Knowing the office routine was good, but there was far more to the job than knowing your way around town. Bran would be going on a quest, and she would get some answers.

***

"But why can't we find a more dignified way to travel?" MaryEllen asked as the group listened to Aundrea's rundown of the coming event.

Aundrea kept her scowl hidden, thinking perhaps she had chosen wrong. MaryEllen would be a good fit for her part, but she did ask questions, constantly, which tended to wear on every team leader she had ever worked with.

"I do not want our insertion to be noted," Aundrea explained, emphasizing her words to make her point. "If you went by normal transport, I'm afraid you would catch the attention we don't want."

She didn't have to say that MaryEllen tended to catch the eye of most men, in most places she went, but everyone else understood. When her bright red hair caught the sun, it absolutely radiated its brilliance. She would work perfectly when it came time, but her insertion too soon would cause unneeded trouble.

"Are you saying I can't be discreet?" Again, MaryEllen questioned the reasoning, and Aundrea was truly beginning to rethink her choice. Bran didn't need this kind of pressure on his first assignment as lead.

But Bran had picked up on the discussion. "Emmy, it has nothing to do with your being discreet," he said with feeling.

He was sitting with his feet up on the hearth, taking the entire meeting casually, and had been extremely happy since the announcement of the project and his position.

"You are simply too eye-catching. Why, every man in town would be snooping around, trying to find out who you are, and why you're there. Remember, this is a small town. They haven't seen someone like you since...well... ever. Give them a break, girl." He chuckled at MaryEllen's look of embarrassment.

No, it wasn't her fault, but they did need to work as a team.

"I'm sorry, Bran. I should have thought," MaryEllen said, dropping her head in embarrassment, not used to being called on her good looks.

Bran gave a noble nod. "It just means you're ready and quite willing. I like that."

"Thank you, Bran," Aundrea granted approvingly, surprised by his smooth managing of the situation. Focusing on the other team members she asked, "Are there any other questions?" She searched every face, but they appeared ready. "Take what you need from the storehouse, and please be careful. We know Commissioner Dodge is crafty, greedy, and plays by his own rules, which does not make a good combination for you. But it's what we have, and a good part of why you're going. Your job is to find this young man and bring him here so we can use what he knows. We need it to build a case against Commissioner Dodge.

Now, if the young man does turn out to be a wizard of some kind, and I find that questionable at best, then work with him. Not against him. We want him on our side. So, do what you can, and I give you some leeway in making an offer. Since I don't know what that will entail, I leave it to you. Once you return, I will do my best to see that it is fulfilled. But please, make it something reasonable. We do not have a large budget, and I do not intend to spread this around by asking for more. And, Bran, I've already notified the stables. They have mounts ready."

"Excellent," Bran acknowledged. "Once we're away, we'll be splitting up. I plan on meeting at the rendezvous four days from now. I don't want a large group seen heading that way, and from what I understand, anything over two is a large group in Skragmoore."

That got a snicker, but it was also true. Anyone new in a little town would draw attention, but a group would draw trouble.

Aundrea released a sharp breath, signaling her acceptance of his plans. "Good hunting to you all."

The room cleared without further delay and Aundrea returned to her office. She had paperwork to finish up.

Aundrea worked her way through the never-ending pile of letters, but the thought of the gem kept returning to her, until she found herself with the pen between her lips, eyes staring blankly into space. A single large gemstone. There was something about it.

The itch was growing, heightening her sensitivity to the problem, and one of those things she had learned to be aware of. Large gems were simply not something common in most people's lives, and this one was unique in many ways. So how did a young man come to have this one? Maybe the files had something tucked away in their depths. If so, it was time to go visit their Keeper of Histories. If there was something there, Maynard would know.

The storehouse for The Keeper of Histories was on the far side of the complex, buried in the lower levels of the stronghold. The walls had been tarred a hundred years ago, keeping the hundred cabinets and their contents dry and safe from the mildew that would damage them. Maynard was the old master and had an innate knowledge of the place, knowing what, and where, anything could be found in the labyrinth of shelves and cabinetry that filled the space. It was actually rumored he had designed the entire place, but that was silly since it would mean he was over a hundred himself.

As she pushed open the heavy wooden door to The Histories, the particular aroma of old documents filled her nostrils. Its pungent scent was unmistakable to anyone who had worked with them before, and she smiled, thinking back to the hours she had spent here in the years following her stepping away from the streets. In fact, it was Maynard who had first seen her bright mind and drew her into the almost sacred halls of the building. He had allowed her to wander through the complex, awed by the masses of knowledge around her. Even as a street urchin, she had gone to school, but it was here where she had learned to expand her horizons and her knowledge of the workings of the government. Later, with a written note from Maynard, she had managed to enter employment at The Office for Public Recriminations. The work had intrigued her, and she flourished. As her aptitude expanded, so had her position. She was a natural, and now the boss, but The Histories was where she had started.

For a moment, she reveled in the memories the scent brought, but breaking through their pleasant haze, she entered the main office. She had no doubt Maynard would be there. He was always to be found somewhere in the rows of cabinets, digging into the secrets buried in their depths, but the foyer was empty, which suited her fine. Maynard was the only person she was interested in seeing right now. Anyone else would simply be a distraction. She wandered her way into the back where the entry to the enormous storage rooms was. Then on into the vast space beyond. The cool air was another trigger to her memories, but she held herself to the task and began a row-by-row search for her old mentor.

She found him, ankle-deep in a stack of parchments rolling around in the aisle, his head deep inside the cavernous cabinet.

"What are you looking for?" It was an innocent question and one she had asked many times.

"What? Who's that?"

Maynard's almost white head of hair pulled out of the recess, and blinking several times behind his thick round glasses, attempted to refocus in the light of the lantern sitting on the shelving behind him.

These lanterns were designed especially for The Histories, their wide bases making them virtually tip-proof, their doubled glass making them fireproof. They were as safe as could be made. Fire was the one enemy that could destroy the entire collection in a blink.

Maynard looked squinty-eyed at the tall figure in the aisle, before recognizing Aundrea. "My girl. I am so pleased you came by. It has been too long."

She grinned at his obvious warmth. "It has indeed. I'm sorry I haven't come sooner. I just get so busy in the office, I can't seem to find the time to come see my best boss ever." She stepped carefully over the errant parchments and gave him a solid squeeze, wrapping the old man firmly in her arms.

He gave a happy chortle at getting a woman's hug and grinned awkwardly. "All right now, the truth of it. You didn't just happen to drop by on a whim. You have a task. Am I right?"

Aundrea pursed her lips, wishing she could avoid the question. "Yes, I do have another reason for coming, but it's still been too long, and you know I love it here." Her forehead wrinkled at the need to acknowledge her lack of connection.

She needn't have worried, as Maynard grinned too. "Then I am even more pleased to be of service. I do love being of use, and so much of what I do is simply holding information that nobody has any use of. Now what can I do for you?"

Without answering, Aundrea began picking up the scattered manuscripts and handing them to Maynard. He gave her a nod as he accepted the papers, stacking them carefully back in the cabinet. The simple work brought a moment of de ja vu, as she remembered doing this exact thing, handing papers and books to him as he arranged them correctly on the shelves. While it was a nice feeling, she wasn't going to waste his time by beating around the bush.

"I have an interesting case going and was wondering if the histories mention anything about single, large gemstones. I've been racking my memory, but I can't come up with anything. Still…" she trailed off suggestively.

Like a guppy waiting to be fed, Maynard took the bait, as she knew he would. "Well, let me see. Gemstones… Sounds like an interesting case." His eyes took on a canny look as he began a recitation of building interest. "Hmmm, Maybe someone was burgled, or perhaps they were waylaid and killed for the gem. Oh, so many exciting things happen in the world, and I am stuck down here in the basement."

"Perhaps," Aundrea conceded, "but not that I'm aware of. At least, not yet. One of my men sent a report that mentions a single large stone. In this particular case, it was set in a collar or necklace. I don't know if that is important or not, but the stone itself might be."

She watched his face, looking for any signs of recognition. Maynard merely rocked between heels and toes, with his finger to his chin, thinking.

She knew the moment something triggered in that old white-haired head.

Maynard's eyes lit up expressively but remained in question "Yes, there is something, but it is old. So long ago, I'm not certain it would still be valid."

They had finished repacking the cabinet, and Aundrea closed it before slipping her arm in his. "Let's go have dinner. I would love to spend some real time with you, and you can tell me about it as we go. Sound good?"

Maynard was all smiles. Even at his age, the thought of dinner with a beautiful woman brought a thrill of anticipation. "Absolutely, my girl. I haven't been out of the office for so long, I am not even sure where the door is."

Of course, he was joking, but the humor was simply him, and one of the things she loved about him. Things were only serious when it was serious. The rest was simply happiness to be alive, even in his basement.

They sat across from each other at the polished table, waiting for their food, when Aundrea finally brought up the subject again. "So, what did you remember? I'm always awed by your mind and the things you have stored up there."

She wasn't complimenting him to get his information, it was true. He had the most refined memory she had ever met. He could reproduce almost any record he had ever studied. Not necessarily everything he read, but once studied, it was there, buried in his mind. It was probably the reason he held his office. As Historian, he would need to remember what had happened, when, and by whom. Having the verifying documents only supported his statements.

"Oh yes. It is so nice to be dining with you, I almost forgot there was an underlying reason."

Reaching out, she patted his hand laying on the table. "This is nice and don't think it's only because of my search. I am thoroughly enjoying our time. Sometimes I really miss the old days. You saved me you know. I would probably be on the streets right now if you hadn't helped me."

Maynard swung his head in a negative gesture, denying the thought. "No. I do not believe that is true. You were already on your way up. I just caught your hand and assisted your climb. The rest you did all by yourself." He smiled at her like a doting grandfather acknowledging his paternal love.

Aundrea squeezed his hand and shrugged. "Maybe, but I still want to thank you. You made my life better."

Clearing his throat, he slapped the table lightly and changed the subject. "All right, back to business. The gem." He stopped speaking and leaned forward, resting his forearms on the tabletop. Aundrea was surprised when he glanced at the neighboring tables and spoke in a lower tone. "The gemstones mentioned in The Histories is an interesting story. But you might expect that of large gems. They do seem to gather stories like dust. But perhaps this is important. It is one of the only records I have ever seen with a connection to the actual Brotherhood."

At Aundrea's startled twitch, he gripped her hand still lying on his, and spoke quietly. "Calm please, and listen."

Using her training, she feigned a motion of disquiet. Brushing back her hair as though it was misbehaving, she gave a casual nod. What had she stumbled into? The Brotherhood? They were only a myth, or at least, probably a myth. She put an easy smile on her face and leaned forward as though he had said something enticing, which in reality, he had.

Their eyes met, and she saw he was playing his own part, acting as though he were patronizing her. "My dear girl," he said in a voice that could be overheard if any were paying attention, "that is exactly what I meant." He raised his eyes suggestively, which considering his age, was not quite believable.

She held her snicker at the unexpectedness of the comment but managed to maintain her part. "I don't believe it. How can that be true?"

Dropping his voice back to a quieter level, he spoke sincerely. "My dear Aundrea. This may be dangerous. The only specific mention of gems that comes to memory was in connection to what was to become known as The Brotherhood. It was in an old record and not of general distribution. A police record mentioning stones as part of a situation where the officers involved reported strange things. It appears the gems were in the possession of a group attempting to take government documents dealing with elections. Therefore, the entire situation should have been reviewed and the data distributed expansively for protection and oversight, but instead, it seems the situation went black."

Aundrea drew back slowly before clutching her hands in her lap. She looked at the old man with interest, then asked, "Did the police take the stones, or were they left at the scene?"

"Let me see," Maynard mumbled, making a face as he re-ran the report through his memory. "It appears the stones were set into rings the men wore, and apparently, they glowed, which was why the officers thought they might be the cause of the problems they mentioned. Very interesting, if I do say so."

"Rings? The stones couldn't have been very large then."

"Large enough to catch their attention," Maynard said with a chuckle.

"And they glowed." Aundrea wrinkled her nose unconsciously as she thought. "So why would that make a connection with the, you know who?" She wasn't sure why she shouldn't mention them by name, but discretion seemed prudent.

"That would be further along in the report. Apparently, they were never apprehended. There was a mention of the name, as I said, and suspiciously, government actions began changing shortly after. The only connection that I can truly attach, is that the name began to circulate after that. It wasn't until several years later, and quite a few unexpected changes in The Council, that the name eventually went quiet. I remember that much myself. A surprising number of changes. I hadn't actually put it all together until you brought this up. Now, after so many years, I see a pattern I hadn't noticed earlier." He stopped talking and let the information settle.

Aundrea was uncomfortable with this kind of information. The Brotherhood had always been a myth, yet myths had a strange way of coming from bits of unrecognized truth. If The Brotherhood had a nefarious connection, and she didn't doubt it at all, not if they had the power she suspected, then what was the connection to a strange gemstone in the Badlands? It was baffling.

"You say the officers reported the stones as having odd powers? Did they say what kind?" Again, she cased the room casually, noting everything.

"The report does not say, but that might be from the officers not wanting to sound ridiculous. It would be bad enough to have to make the report, but stating they were scared off because of a ring would make them a laughingstock in the office."

She could only agree. She was having a difficult time believing it even now, and she had already heard of a stone that may have done something odd. It was a big 'may', but at this point, it was definitely worth looking into.

Aundrea put a hand to her cheek and spoke just loudly enough that anyone listening in could hear. "Thank you, Maynard. It has been a fabulous evening, but tonight, I believe I need to be alone." It was a perfect performance.

"Certainly, certainly, I understand, but you can't blame a man for inquiring. Might I see you out?" The twinkle in his eye had more than one meaning.

Gracefully, she accepted his offer, and the two rose from their seats, winding their way through the other diners.

CHAPTER 22

I'm not Dead Yet

R hone leaned a shoulder against the dusty cliff wall and stuck his head inside the cavern's dark mouth. He could only see a few feet, but it was about what he expected. It was dark. The lake water ran farther than he could see, but the light sound of drips told him it continued for quite a ways. Other than that, it was silent. The cool air felt good after the heat of the sun, the gravelly sward continuing its way along the wall, working around the water that quickly turned dark with the low light and probable depth.

As with most young men, he wanted to explore.

The cavern mouth hung low, with a gentle arch spanning the entire width of the lake. Vegetation hung down from the top edge, not quite reaching the water, and he couldn't decide if it was beautiful, or creepy. It would probably depend on your mood when you saw it.

If Stone had been with him, exploring wouldn't be a problem. Stone's glow would have lit the space, and they could have explored at will, but he didn't have Stone. He had lost his friend.

221

With a suddenly heavy heart, Rhone turned back into the bright sunlight and began searching for a stick. It didn't take long. Even in this desert environment there was brush and a few scraggly trees that tended to be stubby things, but made them perfect for what he wanted. The heavy sap content built into their wooden structure, helped them survive the heat and cold, as nature's way to assist in their survival. The good point for him was that the thick sap stayed in the wood long after the tree was dead, making it perfect for starting fires.

What he needed was a torch. Gathering a few pieces of the weathered wood, Rhone began binding them to the end of a long stick using a piece of the leather cording from his pouch. It didn't make him happy. There was only so much cord in his gear, and now there was less, but he really wanted a look in the cave. He would need cover if he was going to be stuck in this maze for long.

Once the torch was ready, Rhone looked for something to take a spark. When he found a badly decayed stump, he had what he needed. Scraping at the old wood with a rock, he built a small pile of the dust, then once again dug into his pouch, pulling out the fire starter kit. It had gotten thoroughly soaked in his float down the river, and he took time to dutifully replace the soggy tinder. You never knew when you would want a fire, and tinder was one of the needed elements to get one going easily.

With his flint and striker, Rhone began to throw sparks. It wasn't a perfect art, but he had practiced for years and had become pretty good at it. It was all in knowing the angle of the strike and where the spark would land. When enough hot sparks landed in the correctly piled dry tinder, it began to smolder. He cupped the powder-dry pile between his hands, gently gathering it and hoping he wouldn't smother the newly growing heat. A soft breath helped, and finally, a tiny flame flicked between his hands. Very carefully, Rhone added a few slivers of wood to the tiny flame, then grass stems and twigs. He didn't need much of a fire since he only wanted to start his torch.

Once again, he thought of how much he missed Stone.

When the little fire was stable, he gently thrust the newly made torch into the small flames. Almost instantly, the dried sap caught, greedily bursting into a yellow-orange flame that licked at the bundle. When a dark tendril of greasy smoke rose from the torch, Rhone kicked the small fire apart. He wouldn't need it anymore. At least not until evening, when the unburnt pieces would be ready to use on a new fire, but now it was time to explore.

With the torch in hand, Rhone again entered the dark cavern.

The flickering light of the smoky flame caused immense shadows to flutter across the high rocky ceiling. Even in the poor light, Rhone could see roots protruding from what seemed solid rock, but they quickly lessened as he moved forward, finally becoming only a few hair-like tendrils hanging from the high ceiling. Dew drops of moisture sparkled along them like stars in the black sky. As his torch sputtered and the light swayed, Rhone stood wide-eyed in wonder. The air was heavy with dampness, not at all like the clean outdoors on a summer night. He drew in a testing lungful with some distaste but continued around the wall.

When he was almost directly across from the cavern's mouth, the blackness of another opening swallowed the light from his torch, drawing him like iron to a magnet. His torch easily showed the ground at his feet but gave off no reflection from beyond. Stepping cautiously into the opening, Rhone gasped, as a thousand glittering sparkles sprang awake at his approach. The golden glow of his torch reflected a thousand-fold from the thousand faces of the drooping stalactites hanging in the cavernous space. The gravelly floor was almost level, just above the height of the lake he had been circling. The lake must have been higher at some point in the past, allowing the gravel to wash in, but for now, it was dry.

It was a perfect place to hole up, and he quickly made plans. Plans for helping Stone would just have to wait. First, he had to get himself safely settled, then he could work on the future.

Jamming his torch into the loose gravel, Rhone began gathering larger stones for a fire pit. He would need firewood, but that thought didn't bother him. There was enough around for tonight's fire. After that, he would just have to search a little farther.

Finding a particularly soft-looking spot, Rhone rolled out his bedroll and lay down for a trial run. Scooching and squirming, he molded a slight depression in the gravel to fit his body. Finally satisfied he stretched out, tucking his hands behind his head. With elbows wide, he stared at the ceiling high above him. The glow from the flickering torchlight was almost hypnotic, as they shimmered and sparkled on the hanging rock formations.

Stone should see this, Rhone thought to himself. But Stone wasn't here.

When his body felt the chill, and the need for firewood came to mind, he noted his torch was sputtering and almost gone. Disappointed with himself, he got up and made his way back outside.

With a place to call home, Rhone worked on his memory game. Every morning, he climbed the cliff and attempted to memorize the picture of the twists and turns, learning the layout of the jigsaw-puzzled badlands. He was getting better at it. The picture became more solid with every practice, and he was beginning to feel the urge to try it out.

The water level had stopped dropping after a couple of days, and there were fish in the lake, which meant it never dried up entirely. The weathered wear lines around the lake's edge showed where the water level most often sat. The graveled edge also made a decent trail around the lake, and he followed the cliff's shadows, keeping himself to the cooler sections during the heat of the day.

The cavern was always cool. But whenever he went inside, he needed to burn more of the precious wood just to see. Every day, he wandered farther, collecting dried sticks. The effort would only become more exhausting as time went on, needing to go farther and farther to find new sources. In one of his searches, he found tall trees totally filling a narrow canyon, their tips almost reaching the height of the surrounding walls. He could hardly believe his find, knowing he might need them if winter caught him here. They added a new perspective to his growing plans.

With one more trip to the canyon's top, Rhone scanned the badlands before him. The crazed gullies wound around and around, with enough crisscrossing pathways to make even a thatcher see double. Left, left, right, right, right, left, right...the pattern ran through his memory.

"I think I'm ready," he crowed to himself. "It's time, and Stone is waiting." He had talked to Stone so much that he did it almost unconsciously now.

Climbing down the treacherous rock, Rhone gathered up his things. Making sure his water jug was full, he settled the pack on his shoulders and was ready.

Looking back at the cavern mouth, he gave a nod of respect to the dark opening. "I want to thank you," he said to the rock wall. "Without your help, I wouldn't have made it. I'm leaving now, but I'll be back, and I'll bring a friend. I think you'll like him. He's stone, just like you." Rhone laughed at himself, realizing he was talking to yet more rocks. Then turning on his heel, started up the flat draw into the maze.

Walking the winding passageways in the stifling heat was certainly more difficult than simply seeing them from above. His mind tended to wander in the time it took to get from one turn to the next, and after a turn or two, he would forget where he was on his mental map.

It was difficult, but it also made it a safe place, and knowing the ins and outs of the badlands meant it would be hard to get trapped. Occasionally, he would turn around and look at his route from the other direction, working his mind back through the turns he had taken. Back through the tortured paths to his lake.

His lake. He liked that. Not only did he have a place, he had land. He was rich. The only thing he didn't have, was Stone.

After hours of walking, he finally got to where the tall stones thinned and the flatlands began. Stopping tiredly, he set up for the night. The hot air of the flats hit him like a heavy blanket, and he instantly missed the relative cool of the shaded canyon lands.

He camped just inside the canyon walls and made sure his small fire couldn't be seen by anyone who happened to be looking his way. It was a slim chance, but why take the chance at all?

With plenty of the scrubby brush scattered around, he soon had enough fuel for his fire. The dry brush burned hot and fast, but he didn't need a big fire. Just enough to cook his dried fish into a brothy soup. Tomorrow, he would rise early and head across the plains. He wanted to get as far as he could before the heat became a problem. Two or three days' walk should bring him to Skragmoore. Then another day to survey the town and figure out where Stone would be. Beyond that, he didn't know yet. He still had a long way to go.

Into Danger

Rhone nestled between two large weathered rocks as he looked down into the little town. The rough slab of the rocky escarpment stood above him, starkly streaked with varying colors of grey and ocher. Below him, the talus slope of broken rock and dirt gradually dropped to the flats of town. He sat just below the sheer face of the broken cliff, at the top of the talus slope, where the cliff had fallen in a thousand pieces, over a thousand years. Bit by bit, time gradually moved the cliff back, as the face continued to slough off like a layer of old dead skin. It was a bit dangerous sitting at the base of the cliff, but he doubted anything would fall this particular minute. More likely, it would happen with the winter's freeze, when the water expanded in the cracks, pushing the slabs free.

The sun still glowed white hot on the escarpment, but down in the streets of the town, shadows were already extending into long parodies of their normal dimensions. Rhone had watched as the workers left at the end of their day, but he hadn't seen The Commissioner, so he had waited. He still didn't have a plan on how to find Stone, but finding The Commissioner seemed a good place to start.

This might have been his town, but Rhone had never actually been to the town before. Mom had never let him go, saying it was too dangerous. At least the tavern was easy to spot. The hand-painted sign reading Mack's Place made it an easy guess. It wasn't a large town. Tiny, old, or rundown would be a better description, but it might have been considered bigger if the derelict buildings had been used in the count. But those businesses had closed long ago, and no one had bothered to open anything new. Few customers meant poor business and not a good way to start out.

As he watched, a large man came out of the big building in the center of town. He wore the signature squat hat of The Commissioner, and Rhone watched as he moved down the quiet street. The man moved hesitantly, and after a block, stopped and looked around, then moved on again. Rhone wasn't used to spying on anyone, but the odd travel caught his attention.

Distracted by an ant climbing up his arm, Rhone vigorously brushed it off, quickly checking to be sure there were no more. When he looked back to the town, the man was gone.

Rhone searched the empty streets twice, but they remained empty. The man had disappeared.

It wasn't much of a task to memorize the small town's layout, and he was soon climbing down from his perch. The dry and rocky slope constantly moved under his feet, and his pack wasn't helping, as it tried to throw him off balance at every move, but he was used to the weight and counter-balanced effectively, staying on his feet. Once at the bottom, he made short work of the run toward the edge of town, the derelict buildings making it easy to hide his approach.

Even in the relatively short time it took to get down from his watching post, the streets had darkened considerably. Rhone stayed in the growing shadows, making his way along the empty streets to where he had lost sight of the man he hoped was The Commissioner.

Trying to appear casual, Rhone slowly worked his way along the unfamiliar streets, knowing that any stranger would be noticed. Hearing the solid clunk of a door, he quickly dodged into the darker shadow of a pillared block building and held his breath. He wasn't used to sneaking, and just the thought of being caught made his underarms begin to sweat.

He had no experience with this kind of thing. He wasn't even used to people, let alone powerful people, but Stone needed him.

Heart racing, and barely breathing, Rhone steeled himself to peek around the corner.

The streets were empty, but heat still radiated from the rock walls, making the cooling air of the shade sultry and stale tasting. He had found his way to where the man had been when he had lost track of him, and looking back up the hill, tried to find where he had been sitting. But it all looked the same from here. Just a re-run mix of cliff face, broken rock, and scraggly brush. One piece looked much the same as another.

Rhone felt exposed on the vacant street and crept forward, checking every building and trying every doorknob, but they were all locked. Some doors were even nailed shut with weather-worn boards crossing over them. But the moment he saw it, he knew what he was looking for.

As silently as a lizard, he slid along the wall, moving forward until he stood directly before the new door. The heavy wood stood out in sharp relief, compared to the old dry wood of the other doors he had passed. Large strap hinges stretched across the planks binding the door, and the heavy hasp that would have held the lock was thrown back, but the padlock was missing. Although unlocked, it was obvious the place held something that wasn't for the eyes of casual observers and was important enough to install a new door to keep it secure. It might not be Stone, but it was definitely worth investigating.

Rhone stepped closer and put one hand on the warm wood. His other hand reached for the decorative and very worn knob. Slowly turning the intricate mechanism, he felt the smooth motion of a latch that, surprisingly, didn't complain about being used. Then with a click, the bolt slid free.

Rhone leaned forward and pushed ever so gently, then harder, as the weight of the heavy door took more muscle to move than he had expected. He only wanted a peek, but as he leaned close, the door suddenly released from the snug hold of the jam and swung wide. Rhone made a panicked grab at the wildly swinging door, catching it just before it slammed against the wall, then almost toppling from his quick motion, awkwardly stepped into the dark room.

Having already announced his presence, Rhone readied to make some dumb explanation.

Luckily, the room was empty, and he released a relieved breath. The greying light of the cliff's shadow gave poor illumination to see by, but there was enough to see the cobweb's ghostly latticework liberally scattered from ceiling to wall, and countertop to broom closet. The entire place appeared totally abandoned and unused. The dirt-encrusted window with its fly-covered sill matched the filth piled in the corners.

The room was vacant.

It made no sense. Why the new door and heavy hardware if there was nothing here? There were plenty of old buildings in town. He had seen that on his short trip into the place, and many of those buildings had been vacant, some even boarded up, so why was this one different?

Since he was already inside, Rhone closed the door carefully and walked around the large space. A few odds and ends lay stacked below the countertops, as though waiting to be used. Only the thick layer of dust showed they had been waiting a very long time. A quick search of the cabinets brought the same results.

The last of the day's light barely made its way through the dirty glass of the window, and dust motes danced eerily in the single golden beam that washed a stripe across the wooden floorboards.

In the dimming light, Rhone continued his way around the room, almost tripping on a broom propped lazily against the side of the broom closet. The door stood partly open, and Rhone was about to close it, when his quick glance noted it was a very deep closet. Curiously, he opened the door farther, surprised to see the back wall sat at an odd angle. It didn't take but a moment for him to recognize it was a door, and it was partially open. The darkness beyond called to him, but his sense of danger screamed even louder.

If Commissioner Dodge was down there, there was no way he wanted to be down there too. He did have some sense of intelligence, or at least self-preservation. Quickly, and much more quietly, he tiptoed across the room to one of the old cabinets. It was a tight fit, and he had to remove his pack, stuffing it into a different shelf, but he managed to tuck himself in, pulling the cabinet door closed with his fingertips.

Breathing in shallow breaths, he waited and tried to calm his racing nerves. If The Commissioner found him, he had no doubts as to his outcome. He would be considered a trespasser and a thief, and would quickly be brought up on charges. If he made it that far. From the stories his mother had told him, he had no doubt The Commissioner would see his hanging as a benefit to the community. He could build a case any way he wanted, personally seeing to its finality. Removing a thief would prove how well he did his job and would only improve his standing with the townsfolk. Worse, since no one in town knew him, there would be no one to stand up for him. Besides, it was true. He was here to steal Stone back. It didn't matter if Stone had been his, or not. Stone was now the property of The Commissioner, and no one would say differently.

It was not a good position to be in, and Rhone began to sweat, not only from the fear that was growing but from the heat building in the closed cabinet. The tight confines made the rancid smell of his own body remind him of how long it had been since he had bathed. Surely, anyone would be able to find him by simply following their nose.

Rhone was ready to climb out of the cabinet and make a run for it, when he heard a heavy metallic thud, and instinctively resettled himself, drawing the doors even tighter.

Holding his breath, he listened for more sounds.

Almost immediately, the muffled scuff of heavy footfalls could be heard echoing hollowly into the darkened room. Shuffling steps, a solid clank of metal, and the softer sounds of wood on wood brought a vivid picture to Rhone's mind. The old story from his childhood, of a giant setting his big axe on the floor and rubbing his hands together gleefully, made Rhone's stomach churn. He almost yelped in fear, as another lighter thunk and a click sounded loudly in the quietness of the empty room.

With his heart pounding like a drum, he lay paralyzed in fear, expecting the cabinet doors to be yanked wide and himself pulled awkwardly from his poor hiding place. He almost fainted when the heavy steps approached, then unbelievably continued past. The sound of the exterior door closing solidly into its jamb sent echoes ringing through the room.

Rhone almost wept in relief when he heard the unmistakable click of the lock as it latched securely. He lay there for several more minutes, letting his pulse slow and his breathing returned to normal. Finally, he pushed open the cabinet and crawled weakly onto the floor.

He hadn't been found.

Climbing stiffly to his feet, Rhone snuck to the front door and put his ear to the wood. All was still. The room was dull and dark, with a slightly lighter grey coming through the dirty glass of the one window. Time moved quickly when your life was at stake. Evening had come, barely illuminating the building's interior.

With a deep breath, Rhone considered his options. He was already where he wanted to be, and now knew where to look. With just enough light to see shadows, he used his hands to help feel his way and slowly worked across the room. It wasn't hard to find the broom closet, and now the sounds he had heard made sense. The Commissioner had come through the back wall of the closet, closed it, then closed the door. Feeling smug, Rhone opened it and, with one hand in front, slipped in, reaching for the back wall.

Rhone stopped dead in his tracks as shooting stars of pain suddenly burst into his head. He had walked straight into something running at nose level across the closet.

"Dad-gummit!" His curse burst out involuntarily, his eyes instantly beginning to water. Rubbing the bridge of his skinned nose, he suddenly realized the volume of his shout, and paused, listening fearfully for some response in return. But all remained quiet. Leaning shakily against the door jam, he took a long breath to ease some of the sting. It was time to rethink his approach. If Stone had been here, he wouldn't be running into things. He would have all the light he needed.

But once again, no Stone.

The need to find his friend grew, and he reached forward more carefully, feeling for whatever he had run into. It wasn't hard to find, and he quickly removed the pole, setting it aside before reaching in farther, feeling for the back wall. He wasn't sure what he was looking for, but the rough wood of the wall felt solid under his fingers. He swept them back and forth knowing it was a door, and searching for a handle or latch of some kind. It had been open earlier. He had seen it, but now it was simply a wall. There had to be a release of some kind, but it was so dark in the tiny closet that he could only sweep his hands back and forth, searching, until he jabbed a splinter deep into the soft part of his hand.

Rhone jerked back with an "Owww! Why does everything I do end up getting me hurt?" He didn't expect an answer, and it simply added to his frustration. He was trying to save Stone, and not only was he locked inside the stone building, he couldn't even find his way into a closet.

Slamming the wall in growing frustration, he felt the boards give slightly, which gave him an idea. Mumbling to himself, he started wrenching roughly at the old boards. "I'll pull it down piece by piece if I have to." But try as he might, they were simply set too tightly, and he couldn't get a good hold on them. Peeved at being thwarted at even this simple task, he kicked at the wall, and the base of a board shifted inward. It must have been the release mechanism as, without a sound, the board's top pivoted out toward him.

"Now that's better," he praised himself, instantly forgetting his pain. Placing his hand against the wall he pushed, swinging it back several inches. He had done it. With real joy, he called, "I'm coming, Stone. Hang on."

He had only opened the door a couple of inches, so using his shoulder, Rhone gave an aggressive shove, swinging the door back on its hinges. His body blocked what little light might have shown in, and while the broom closet was dark, the space in front of him was even darker. Feeling a rush of excitement, Rhone eagerly stepped into the dark opening.

But without a light, Rhone missed the fact that there was no floor, and his misstep pitched him headlong into the darkness of the unseen stairwell. Instinctively, his hands flew out to catch himself as he crashed heavily onto the stone steps leading downwards into the black abyss.

Arms and shoulder took the brunt of the first hit, before he tumbled, thumped, and bumped down several more steps, bruising most of his body and banging his knee so badly it had to be bleeding. Rhone had experienced tumbling down several rocky slopes in his life and now fought to keep from landing face first, protecting his head from cracking on any of the steps.

He finally came to a stop, piled in a tangled mass against a stone wall. He lay in a huddle, taking a moment to verify he was alive, and another moment to lose the spinning in his head. His body, scraped and bruised, ached from one end to the other, but he was lucky. Amazingly, he seemed to be in one piece and hadn't broken his neck, or any other bone.

Slowly Rhone worked to right himself, getting the pack untangled and his legs under him. It wasn't an easy task in the blackness of the basement. His lack of sight was disorienting, and with no point of reference, he found it hard to balance. This rescue thing was becoming a very dangerous endeavor.

He wanted to stand but thought better of it. Feeling around in the dark, he first located the wall, then the end of the stone stairway. It was a good place to start.

Dragging himself onto the step, Rhone managed to sit, then used his hands to help crawl his way up the wall to a standing position. With one hand out to evade another nose bump, his other slid along the stones of the wall, working his way forward in the total blackness.

When he finally found a corner, he congratulated himself, having done it without running face-first into it. Maybe things were looking better, even if he couldn't see. With a feeling of hope, he stepped forward again, almost tripping on something piled against the wall. He could imagine all kinds of things in the dark, but honestly, didn't want to know. Having a pattern going now, he carefully slid his feet around the obstruction. The space was cool and smelled musty, but by the sound, it wasn't very large.

Rhone hurt from practically every square inch of his body, but he had come this far. He wasn't going to quit now. His eyes were useless in the blackness, and he closed them, feeling his way along the wall until his hand touched cool metal. The cold smoothness sent shivers through his tight shoulders.

Now using both hands, he felt along the surface, investigating further. The flat heavy metal sat flush with the wall, and he ran his hands exploringly over the face, feeling an odd assortment of metal pieces and bars projecting from the otherwise smooth exterior. This had to be what he was looking for. A safe.

In relief, Rhone laid his forehead against its cool metal and took a thankful breath.

It is about time you got here, rang through his pain-filled head.

The words were buffered and dull, but hearing Stone's caustic rejoinder, sparked Rhone's mind back to life.

"Stone! You're here!" Rhone called excitedly, hardly able to contain his joy, as he pressed his forehead tighter against the metal. "How do I get you out? You're locked in a really strong safe, and it's pitch black in here."

Of course, it is locked. That is why it is called a safe!

Stone was all Stone, and his true-to-form comment brought a huge grin to Rhone's smudged and bruised face.

"That doesn't help me get you out," Rhone commented easily. Now that he had found Stone, the world was better.

It should be no problem whatsoever if you can follow directions.

"Seriously? Okay, what should I do?"

There will be a mechanism of some kind on the door. I felt The Commissioner open it, and I believe I will be able to feel its movements. Can you see it?

Rhone chuckled quietly. It was darker than midnight down here and he literally couldn't see his hand in front of his face.

"I can't see a thing, but I can feel." He ran his hands over the cool metal again, searching. "Okay yes, there are some gears...and a couple of flat bars. Wait, here's something. I think I found it. A dial maybe? It's round and I can feel marks on the edge."

It was amazing how much his fingers could 'see' with his eyes closed. He tried to visualize the mechanism.

Very good. Now, if you will attempt to turn it.

"Okay, here goes." Rhone gripped the large knob and gave it a spin.

No, no, no! Gently, and slowly, came Stone's exasperated response. *Treat it as you would an egg.*

Rhone was embarrassed by his awkward approach to thievery. "Sorry. I've never done this before." He was getting nervous too. Breaking into a vacant building was one thing, but breaking into a safe was totally different. Still, Stone was in there, and he had only come this far because he had to save his friend.

It is all right, Rhone. Just turn the dial gently. Stone understood his friend's unease. This was a long way from his normal home life. Things had changed dramatically.

Rhone tried again, turning the dial with exaggerated slowness.

Good, You are doing fine, but be ready to stop.

Rhone turned the dial even slower until Stone sang out.

Stop! Now reverse the direction.

Again, Rhone slowly began turning the dial. And again, at Stone's signal, he stopped. "Now what?" The slow work was making him jittery.

Very good. Only one more time. Now, turn it back in the direction you were going the first time.

Rhone's nerves were beginning to fray, and he snapped a comment to Stone. "Is that it, or do I need to do something else?"

When we are finished with the dial, you will need to turn a crank to operate the release bolts. There must be one. I very distinctly felt the mechanism grinding before it opened.

"Got it," Rhone mumbled. "Turn the dial, wait for your signal, find the handle, and crank until it opens." The excitement had worn off, and now his body was aching all over. "I guess I'm ready."

You may begin.

And he began again. Slowly turning the dial, he waited for Stone's signal.

Stop.

Which he did. His mental picture of the door was pretty good by now, and it wasn't difficult to find the handle. Getting a grip on it, he began to crank. He could hear the gears on the door's front beginning to move, but the motion was far heavier than he expected. There must be more gears inside. He felt when the release bolts pulled out of their stops. The door was heavy, but as he pulled the handle, it smoothly swung free, opening the safe. He truly was a thief now. He had just broken into a safe.

They had. He certainly couldn't have done it without Stone.

CHAPTER 24

To the Rescue

Manny sat, belly to the bar, a tired expression on his sun-burned face.

"What's up, Manny? You look like your best friend just died." It was Mack's attempt at making a jest.

Manny stared at his beer and replied without energy, "And they probably will."

"Who will? Somebody's going to die?" Mack asked, in worried surprise.

"Yeah, my guys. Somebody's gonna end up dying, and I just know it. That damn commissioner is gonna get us all killed."

Mack nodded, trying to agree with Manny, but disagreeing with the dying part. "Can't be that bad. There are always bad days, but things get better."

Manny's eyes already showed the effects of his one glass of beer. That in itself said something. Manny could hold his drink. This was stress in action.

Mack gave a midline answer. "So Commissioner Dodge finally got caught, and somebody is going to pay the price." It was all he could come up with, and also very reasonable. It was part of why he and Har were here in the first place.

"Nope," Manny said, shaking his head sadly. "That I could understand."

He didn't say any more, and Mack leaned on the counter, resting his weight on his hands. "Then I don't get it. What's with somebody dying?"

With a sour chuckle, Manny said, "It's gonna happen 'cuz somebody stole his loot."

"No kidding," Mack whispered, eyebrows raised in an arc of surprise. "So he's got somebody locked up, and they're going to hang." It was more like a benediction than a question.

But again, Manny shook his head. "Nope. They got away clean. And now his 'High and Mighty' is gonna hunt them down, and it's gonna get us all killed."

"Who?"

It was a simple question. Who had managed to break into The Commissioner's place and steal something? They had to be gutsy, and it must have been something valuable, or The Commissioner would simply put up a reward. There were always men willing to go on a hunt, for real cash.

"Can you keep a secret?" Manny whispered conspiratorially.

Mack glanced around the room and slid closer.

"Remember the kid we hunted down a while back?" At Mack's questioning nod, he continued. "Well, we got the artifact thing the kid had, and now it's gone." He looked up into Mack's startled eyes. "Yep, Somebody broke into The Commissioner's private vault and took it, along with some other stuff. He's gone totally insane, and he's building an army to go hunting. So I asked him, where are we going to go? We don't even know who it was. But he's determined. He's gathering a few dozen guys and we're heading to the badlands." He looked up again in disgust. "The badlands! I never want to go back there, and I told him so. I told him it was dangerous, and we could all get killed. I'm telling you, Mack, the place is haunted." Manny was past caring who heard now and was almost raving to himself. "I know it sounds crazy. I'd think so too, but I was just there. Damn horses went berserk. A freaking storm all but drowned us, and we barely got back without dying of thirst. I'm telling you, somebody is going to die this time."

With that said, Manny drained his mug and sagged even farther on the stool.

Mack straightened up and considered it all, then grabbed his towel and started wiping. Manny was The Commissioner's foreman and rose up through the ranks to get there. Even so, he was a good man. A good man to have on your side.

So someone had the gall to steal from The Commissioner himself and took one of his personal treasures to boot. He had to admit, that took guts. But who could do it? It had to be someone who knew how to crack a safe. That limited an already slim list.

Mack put that aside and considered the other information. The strange kid had come up again, and he wondered what had really happened out there. Maybe the kid really was a wizard of some kind. It might give an explanation as to how the safe had been opened. Everybody knew wizards could do all kinds of strange things. But why? Was the trinket from the badlands that important? If so, Har needed to know. Aundrea too. This would be top priority.

"You going to be okay, Manny? I'm a little worried about you." Mack was concerned. When a guy was this far gone, they could do anything.

With a snort, Manny shook his head. "Yeah, I'm good. Wouldn't do to get myself killed before The Commissioner got around to it. But thanks, Mack. You're the best." He slapped a coin onto the counter and made his way to the door, hinges complaining as he pushed it open. He turned, speaking over his shoulder. "If I don't come back, it's okay. I'm about finished workin' for him anyway. Too dang crazy for my taste," and the door slammed shut.

"Har, I'm telling you, this is important!" Mack's expression verified his concern.

He had closed the tavern early, and Har was again sitting across from him. The room was dim with the lights out, except for one small candle lantern on the counter.

"I don't doubt it, but what do you want me to do? We can't go running around the country, chasing down every kid we hear about. Besides, The Commissioner's already done that."

Mack shook his head in disgust. "We have to do something. Did you send the dispatch yet? Aundrea needs to know about this. It might be just the thing she's looking for."

"Of course I did," Har responded more gruffly than he intended. "Her reply said she was sending a crew to work over the area. She wants to find the kid and bring him in, dead or alive."

At Mack's surprised look, he explained.

"If they find the kid, and he knows something, she might be able to build a case from it. If they only find the body, then she has a different case. But if The Commissioner's out running around with all his guys, there is going to be trouble in paradise. The badlands are big, but not that big, and somebody's nose is going to get bent."

"Or somebody's gonna die," Mack said under his breath. He had heard those words already. "You know we've got to warn them." He wasn't going to let it go. They had to do something to help. "Do you know where they'll rendezvous? Maybe we could amble out there and talk to them."

"We might, but what can we possibly use for a cover story? I work for the guy. If he finds me running around in his field, well... he's smart enough to put two and two together. I won't have legs for very long."

Mack chuckled lightly. "That's pretty good, Har. I didn't know you had a lighter side."

"Whatever," Har grumped. He had been serious.

Mack thought it over for a moment and asked, "When is Mr. Commissioner headed out? Have you heard anything from the house end?"

"Surprisingly, yes," Har said with a nod. "I heard him talking to the Mrs. He wants every man he can grab, so he's willing to wait for another day or two. Personally, I don't think he knows where to look, but since the news is out, he has to save face and uncover every rock from here to The Council."

"That'll take a while," Mack said to himself, then turned back to Harold. "Manny mentioned the badlands, but that may only be a starting place. There's a lot of country out there and lots of places to hide."

Har picked up on the idea and ran with it. "What if we create a diversion? Get them headed in another direction. While they're out running around, we can slip out the back and meet up with our own boys." Har raised his shaggy grey eyebrows and waited for Mack's endorsement.

It didn't take long.

"Dang it, Har. You're good at this stuff." He got to his feet and took the empty mugs. "I know you've got a lot of planning to do, so I'd best get this stuff tucked away." He grinned at his friend. "Shucks, Har, you're okay for an old guy."

Harold looked longingly at the mug being carried to the sink, but Mack was right. He did have some planning to do. Getting stiffly to his feet, he wondered what he would come up with.

A thunderous boom exploded from the draw, and a second later, a blindingly brilliant flash first lit the cliffs along the pass, then filled them with dusty smoke. The skinny little guy in torn and dusty overalls laughed like a loon, partially because he couldn't hear anything at the moment, and partially because he was a little goofy to begin with. The titanic boom made his ears ring crazily, and he danced around in child-like glee at having been the creator of such a fine display.

The explosion was easily bright enough to be seen from Skragmoore, and had been built specifically for the bright flash. The boom had simply been the catalyst but was also to catch their attention. In actuality, the boom had gone off first, since sound traveled so much slower than light, and he wanted to catch their attention in time to see the flash. This way, if people hadn't seen it, they might as well be blind.

Realizing the show was over, the little man glanced around suspiciously, and quickly gathered up his stuff. Har's words had been, "Get out like a shadow."

Slinking along in the thinning smoke, he made his way up the scree bank of the steep slope. Nobody could track you through the scree. It moved under your feet, covering the footprints you just made. He was good at his particular trade and knew what he was doing.

A few minutes later, he glanced back and smiled, disappearing across the ridge top. Har always paid top dollar, and the money in his threadbare pocket would see him through the winter.

"I've got reports from twenty people saying there was a brilliant flash near the pass west of town." Commissioner Dodge paced back and forth across his office, lecturing a very humble foreman. "You and your boys were ready to head off to the badlands, and I got a report of a flash west of town, not east. Why would that be? I pay you good money to be where you're needed, not to go traipsing off into nowhere on one of your hunches."

Manny knew better than to say anything. The Commissioner had no desire to be reminded, he was the one who chose their search area. His old dad had a saying, 'You pays your money, and you takes your chances'. The truth of it came to him as seriously as church doctrine.

But The Commissioner wasn't done. "Thank the gods you hadn't left yet. At least I don't have to go hunting around, looking for you too. Now get your men up to the pass and find my gem. I want it back!" He stomped around the office a bit longer, and when he looked up, his eyes were almost bloodshot in his growing rage. "You better get me that rock. Do you hear? If that damn thing can flash, then I want it. Can you imagine the power I would have? With that 'thing' in my hand, nobody could challenge us. Not even The Council!" His voice rose as he continued to rave, and Manny was getting worried this might not be the place to be right now. The Commissioner was not a gentle man when he got riled. And while Manny knew he might, possibly, be able to take him, nobody fought The Commissioner and got away scot-free. They would be lucky if they got away with their life, and they weren't just stories.

"Yes, sir. I'll get right to it. We'll be out of town within the hour."

"Make it twenty minutes, and you might see some pay when you get back. If not, I'll start counting the coins backward, until either you, or the coins, are gone. You got it?"

Manny dipped his head in understanding and made a quick retreat from the room. There was no place he would rather be right now than out of this town. Pay or no pay.

Ten minutes later, the foreman was shouting at his men. "Let's go, guys! If you're not in your saddles and behind me by the time I get to the edge of town, you might as well keep right on going. The Commissioner is steamin' hot, and we're not hangin' around. Now let's go!"

Manny was already mounted, bedroll and pack tied behind his saddle, and itching to be gone. A trip through the corrugated county west of Skragmoore may not be a picnic, but it was far better than a trip out to the badlands. Once they were away from town, they would head into the hills and take the trail up toward the pass. He wasn't exactly sure where the flash had come from, but he had a lot of men. They would find whatever there was to find.

The men knew things were tight, and five minutes later, all were headed out of town.

Manny was thinking about the flash people had reported. If it had been seen from here, it had to be unbelievably bright. On the other hand, he personally had seen the flash that had almost blinded Will. The poor guy could see now, but it had taken time, and he still had problems. How could he fight something like that? His only consolation was knowing he still had to find the thing. Until he did, he wouldn't have to worry about it. Maybe retirement wouldn't be so bad.

Mack leaned against the frame of the tavern's open doorway, watching as the line of horsemen made their way out of town. It would be a quiet couple of days while the guys were out, but he had to smile as he snapped the end of the towel at a fly lazily buzzing around. He was also thinking about what a genius Har was.

It had been a great plan. All The Commissioner's men were now headed West, up into the hills, and in another hour, he would be headed East, out to the badlands. He had at least a day, maybe two before he would be missed. It would be plenty of time. If he rode hard and got lucky.

Waving a casual hand at the men, Mack slid back into the dark interior. His pack was already made up and ready to throw onto his wiry little mountain pony. His small brown mare wasn't really a pony, just smaller than most of the big, rawboned nags here in the outer reaches, but she was a sure-footed beast, and he could trust her to keep them on the trail.

CHAPTER 25

From the Mouths of Babes

Apparently, they had taken a couple of wrong turns, but Rhone was pretty sure he was back on track. Much of the badlands looked the same once you got into it a ways, and now, retracing his steps, he began counting the corners as he pictured the map in his head. Stone wasn't any help this time. He hadn't been with Rhone on the way out and didn't have the same picture to work from. Not only that, he was deep in conversation with his new friend. It had been quite a surprise when there had been another We in The Commissioner's vault.

At present, Stone's task was to bring the other We out of its apathy. It had been locked away for months at a time with no outside connection. A veritable solitary confinement for a thinking entity. When the commissioner did choose to view his treasures, the We would find itself fumbled with, and invaded by the hard psyche of The Commissioner. Under the tremendous stress and with no way to understand the onslaught of the strange energy, it had lost all hope, sinking into the oblivion of depression.

Finding the We in such a depleted state, Stone had literally sent shock waves of energy into his new companion, stimulating it into electrical activity again. Then came the training. To be truly useful in their new environment, the We would need to understand the human mind. The twists and kinks of the human psyche were so different from their own crystalline workings, that it would take considerable time to accomplish. Certainly not an overnight transition. It was still a bit of touch and go, but things were looking up.

"When can I meet your new friend?" Rhone asked, excited by the idea.

He had grabbed the piece of rock from the vault's shelf, but only after Stone's refusal to leave without it. All Rhone could see was more trouble, taking something that truly didn't belong to him. Stone, of course, had been his to begin with, and he was only reclaiming what was already his. Taking another item would simply be stealing. But Stone had been adamant. They were not leaving without it.

We have been searching for We, and leaving it would be no better than slavery, allowing The Commissioner to keep what he does not understand.

Rhone wasn't sure he agreed exactly, but when Stone added, *And by my calculations, The Commissioner will be out for your life, whether the We is taken or not,* Rhone could only agree. If he was going to die for being here, he might as well take the high road, and do something right.

Dumping the gem into his pouch, Rhone held Stone's collar in his hand, using it like a torch to light his way.

Now they were deep into the badlands. If he could manage to find his way, they had a place to hide out.

Playing to Stone's good nature, Rhone tried to explain. "You'll be amazed. It's really cool. There's water and a big cave, and it's so far into the maze, they'll never find us. Once we get there, I can meet your friend."

There is no need for that, Stone said archly. *The We does not need your input to cloud the training process. In fact, the poor thing will not be complete until it has its own partner to host with. And that will not be you!*

Rhone was a little hurt by the tone, but Stone didn't seem to notice as he continued his rant.

As to the cavern. Well, I am certain it will suffice. It seems you not only managed to survive, but were quite enjoying yourself, playing in the water while I was incarcerated.

"It wasn't quite like that," Rhone sputtered defensively, surprised at Stone's abruptness. "I practically died. In fact, it was only by accident that I didn't. Then where would you be? I'll tell you where. You would still be in that stupid safe. Locked away in the dark for the rest of your life. That's where you'd be."

This was not going well, and they both closed the connection so recently reunited.

In a huff, Rhone stomped along, following the rocky channel deeper into the badlands. He hadn't touched the new We since he had stuffed it into his pouch, but now it seemed to burn a hole into his leg where it rested against him. Stone's collar was back on his neck, and that sensation too seemed to burn with a cold connection.

What had gone wrong? He had done everything he could to find Stone, and it had been a miracle that he had actually accomplished it. But they weren't happy. Stone had hardly said a thing since they managed to escape through the window, and he had no doubt they were being hunted even now. Speed was what he needed. They had a good head start, but The Commissioner's men had horses. It was a race, and although he hadn't seen anyone yet, it only made it worse on his nerves. He had run into The Commissioner's men once before without realizing they were there. He did not want to do it again.

The track seemed endless, with the twists and turns of the rock walls all looking the same. Only by keeping a mental tab on their passage was Rhone pretty sure they were headed the right way. It would only take one wrong corner to send them on a path that missed their cavern entirely. He had eventually given up on worrying about meeting The Commissioner's men out here. Even if they had gotten to the badlands already, they would be going slowly now, as they searched for him.

Finally, Rhone broke the ongoing silence. "We're almost there."

Not only did his mental map say so, but he saw the change in the plant life as it turned greener and more lush.

It is about time. You do not travel very quickly, you know. The Commissioner's men were much faster.

It wasn't a compliment, but it was Stone.

Rhone wasn't going to be badgered and responded bluntly, "I suspect they were. They had horses, remember?"

And you do not. Why is that? The animals seemed quite prevalent on my journey. Everyone had one.

"All three of them," Rhone reminded him crossly. "Mom and I never had horses. I guess we couldn't afford one, but I'm not sure. We just didn't. We probably didn't need one, since we never went anywhere."

It was just an observation, Stone commented archly. *I am merely saying, you would travel much more quickly if you had one. That is all.*

Stone may have been grumpy, but the simple act of speaking with him made Rhone happy again and he didn't want the conversation to end. "Hey, when those guys found us last time, what happened? I thought for sure I was dead, then their horses went crazy, and I...well, I'm not sure what happened, but when I woke up, all of you were gone."

Stone was quiet for a moment, then spoke in a very different tone. *I am sorry, Rhone. It was my fault. I was thinking about the calculations needed for contacting the We and did not notice their presence. I am afraid it was entirely my fault.*

It was Rhone's turn to be quiet, as he felt his own guilt slip away. But it really had been his fault. He was the one who knew what they were doing. How could Stone know? He was only a rock, thing, with very little knowledge of the human world.

The thought made him smile, bringing back their first day together. They would be okay.

"I think we both goofed up," Rhone admitted. "But we're back together now."

Yes, we did, and we are, came Stone's uncharacteristically subdued reply.

"I missed you, you know. It was so empty without you there to tell me what to do, I just had to find you, and knowing you were in The Commissioner's hands kept me moving. You couldn't do it yourself, so it had to be me, and I'm sorry it took so long."

A comfortable quiet stretched on as Rhone continued forward and around the final corner. Stopping, he swept his arm across the panorama before them. "This is our new home. What do you think?"

There was a pause before Stone spoke. *It is much more open than I had expected. You mentioned it was enclosed, but this is open to the sky. I can feel the sun.*

"It's not the cave yet, but this is where I ended up, when I almost drowned," he added unnecessarily, but reminding Stone he had been through his own troubles. "The cavern is at the other end."

Ahh yes. I can sense the opening, Stone said with interest. *It is not a very large lake. Quite different from the river I was in.*

Rhone smiled. He had missed the ongoing exchange between them.

"It was a lot bigger after the storm, but most of it has drained away. The lake continues on into the cavern." After a moment, Rhone felt the need to make sure things were all right. "Stone, are we okay now? I don't like it when we get grumpy. I really did miss you."

Stone almost purred with a soft, warm vibration coming through the collar. *Yes, We are good. And thank you for coming to my rescue. I am afraid I panicked a little, seeing what could happen to me in The Commissioner's hands. I am embarrassed now, as we speak of it, but it is true. I missed, and need your friendship. It has become...comfortable, and I enjoy it.*

Rhone didn't need anything more.

"Hey, let me show you the cave. It's really awesome."

Hurrying along the edge of the small lake, he ducked into their new home.

Bran's team appeared in singles and doubles throughout the day, each having taken separate routes and methods to this outlying section of the country. Their singular thought was, *Why in the world are we worried about this place? There is nothing here worth worrying about.* But they were here to do a job, and they were up to the task. Each had been discovered and cultivated. Each with their own specialty, and each with a personal reason to work at holding the country together despite itself.

Bran had arrived first and found a suitable location for their camp headquarters, far enough from town, and out of the way enough, to have a very low potential of being spotted. Here was where they would work to discover what was going on in this backwater part of the earth. If Aundrea was concerned enough to send them, it was important.

"Keep your tents below the hillocks. I don't want them standing out for some passer-by to notice. Although I haven't got a clue why they would be out here in the first place. It's downright depressing."

Emmy happened to be walking by and gave her agreement with raised eyebrows and a sassy grimace that put little creases at the corner of her pretty blue eyes. "That is a vast understatement. If I die out here, would you please make sure I don't get buried here? Would you do that much for me?"

"You got it, MaryEllen. Let me make a note, and I'll add my name, just in case I go down."

He grinned, but she shook her head, disavowing his affability.

"All right, boss man," she said in resignation, "but when can we get started? I don't want to be here any longer than we have to."

He perked up at the prospect of starting the project. His very first run at lead. "As soon as everyone's here we'll do a quick gather, then we'll get to work. By the way, I'm saving you for my backup plan."

She raised a curious eyebrow at that. "A backup plan already? You must expect this to go bad."

"Always. My training says, it always goes bad, so my plan has a backup plan already ready."

"And that's me." She didn't question its validity, only verifying that she knew where she stood.

"Yep. That, my sweets, is you. If Commissioner Dodge needs dealing with, you are the one to do it." Bran wasn't just priming the pump. He meant every word.

"I'll be ready then," she said without a trace of a smile. She turned to leave but swung back to face him. "Bran, I want to thank you for your trust. Not everyone would."

"No problem," Bran said with an understanding smile. "I know there is a lot more to you than just great looks, which you have in spades. I also know looks can sometimes be a real problem. It can make it hard to be fully appreciated for what you can do. I did my research when I was building the team. I know what you can do, and I'm glad to have you along."

Her smile couldn't hold still. The corners of her mouth twitched, the red of her lips almost matching the color of her hair, showing her thanks in living color.

Bran appraised his agent as she walked away, hips swinging seductively. It wasn't a put-on, it was simply how she was. She was quite a girl, and there was nothing more to say.

It was almost magic the way the camp grew. Within a few hours, the entire team had arrived. Tents were set, and all had made their appearances before Bran.

Only MaryEllen had come by wagon. It was a pretty little thing. Almost dainty. But the horse was anything but dainty. He was a giant beast and seemed almost to carry the little wagon instead of pulling it. If you didn't know better, you would swear he was part devil, the way he threw his head and stamped, shivering with unexpended energy. It took a brave man to walk close by, and even then, every man watched to be sure he wasn't within reach of the massive jaws, knowing he could lose a hunk of flesh to that bite.

To those who knew better, he was as docile as a lamb, unless he didn't like you. But since no one was sure, they all left him alone. To MaryEllen, he was her baby.

While she didn't have a tent, it only took a matter of minutes for the little wagon to be made up with a fly and side walls, giving her security, privacy, and a mattress. The little carpet bag she traveled with held an assortment of clothes, lady things, tools of the trade, and miscellaneous items she had found useful on previous missions. She did indeed make quite a package.

Emmy was glad Bran had told her of her part. It would give her time to set up her stage. If the time came when she was needed, she would put on a real show. If not, she would just have fun. The setting wasn't much, but she was doing her job, and getting paid to do it. In a few days, she would be back home.

CHAPTER 26

Bacon, Bacon, Who's got the Bacon

Manny stood in his stirrups, looking down the mountain back toward Skragmoore. What was he doing here? They had found exactly nothing, and there probably wasn't anything to find. He checked their location as best he could, but from this angle, he just couldn't be sure. The whole town had seen the flash, but who knew if this was the right hillside? There were a lot of slopes that could be seen from town.

While his position on the rutted road gave a good view of the area, nobody said the flash had come from a road, and how would they know? It had been almost dark when the flash occurred. Even he had heard the boom, but he had been in the tavern at the time, and everyone had run outside, looking for the source of the noise. While everyone else had looked to the west, he had expected the worst, and instinctively ran to the corner and looked east, toward the badlands. That's where he had expected any problem to occur, but he had guessed wrong and had missed the flash. Once again Will had been right. The place had been bad luck from the start.

Now there was nothing to do but continue the search. The Commissioner had been in a state of near apoplexy since the theft of his treasures, and Manny was more than happy to be away from town, and his boss. Bad things happened when The Commissioner was unhappy, and he had never seen him this mad.

So being away from town was good, but it would be even better if he found the gem, or at least the thief. The problem was, he had no idea who could have done it. It certainly wouldn't have been the kid. The kid was just a kid, and most probably dead. Besides, safe cracking took a mastermind, and that took training. Any of his men could have blown the safe, but it had been picked. That took a special person, and one with guts.

Manny almost wished he could meet such a person. Not to drag him back to The Commissioner, but to actually meet, like a brother worthy of friendship, but he knew better than to think those thoughts. He had a job to do. And right now, he had men scattered all over hell and gone, looking for...whatever they could find. The collar. The thief. Even the site of the flash would be something. He needed something. The Commissioner would be expecting it.

Manny Cluck to his horse, settling back into his saddle like he had been molded into the heavy leather. The heat was rising already, and it was going to be a long day.

With Bran's final directions, the team began putting the finishing pieces together, ready to head out to the badlands, when a small mountain pony crossed the hillock and descended into camp. The unexpectedness of the arrival had everyone reaching for weapons, but no one made an outcry. They were too well trained for that. If the approaching person had bad intentions, they wouldn't leave alive. It wasn't even a question, but the happy cry from the lone horseman wasn't something they had expected.

"All hail to The Council," came the call, as he waved merrily to Bran sitting stoically on a boulder.

Boot knife ready at hand, Bran looked up in disbelief and squinted to be sure. "Mack, is that you? Dang it, man. Are you trying to get yourself killed?"

"Like you could," came the happy reply. "I'd probably have to fall on my own knife to make that happen. Just look at all those guys," he said, waving a hand airily toward the group, "and I just walked right in. You should be happy as a clam it was me and not some ruthless broken-down cowpuncher or snake oil salesman. You guys gotta keep on your toes."

It was all said in fun, and when Mack dismounted, the two slapped hugs to each other. The rest gathered, unsure of this newcomer.

Bran circled his hand overhead, gathering the gang. "All right, you guys, this is Mack. He's one of the real old-timers, and you probably heard at least a dozen tall tales of some of his exploits. His partner is Har, and I know you've heard of him. He's practically a demigod all by himself, but he's about ready for pasture, so he's got a partner this time around. Ain't that right, Mack?"

Mack gave a huff. "Close enough, kid, but Har doesn't need anybody. He's a whole troop all by himself. I'm just there for company."

Mack's easy way made everyone comfortable now. They did indeed know the names, if not the faces. A couple had even been lucky enough to have worked with one or the other before. They were both honest-to-goodness heroes.

But this was business, and Bran stepped right in with his questions. "So what brings you out here? We got Har's message, of course. That's why we're here. But what brings you out? We were just heading to search the badlands. Are you coming along?"

Bran would love to have Mack along, but this was not the plan he expected.

"Nope, and I'm glad I caught you before you all left. I would have had to try finding you out there, and that's not easy. I know. I've been through some of it before. It's a crazy place, and you'll lose someone if you are not careful, and I do mean, every one of you needs to be careful. It's a bad place. Far too easy to get lost, and no way to find your way back out. It all looks the same once you're in it, and I'm not kidding. Go in unaware, and you won't come out." He turned slowly, looking at each one, making eye contact to be sure they were listening.

Bran picked up from there. "That's good to know but doesn't explain why you're here. What's up?"

He knew Mack hadn't left town just to drop by. There must be new information they needed to hear.

"Yeah, Let's get to it." Mack settled himself on a boulder and waved them in where they could all hear what he had to say. He could see their tension, worrying about the upcoming news, and smiled disarmingly. "All righty, ease up a tad. I was just pulling your leg, sorta. There was an imminent situation, but thanks to Har's quick handling, you have a wee bit of time to get things ready."

He looked very pleased with himself as the looks flew between the team members. Finally, one of the team, a pretty red-head, held up her hand requesting his attention.

"Are you going to explain further, or are you just getting your kicks at rustling our feathers?"

Bran shot him an apologetic glance and broke in, covering for her. "Mack, I'd like to introduce you to MaryEllen. She's our backup specialist on this mission, and pretty darn good at it too." He didn't want any questions as to her abilities.

"Works for me," Mack said with a nod to the both of them. "Glad for the company miss....MaryEllen." His nod was to let her know he considered her both as a newbie, and he respected her for being here. She was part of the team.

Bran introduced each of the others, giving names and a short dossier, explaining their specialties.

"Looks like a good team, Bran. Tell Aundrea I approve. Now, down to business. As I said, you do have some time, but not much. I expect Commissioner Dodge's dudes will be headed this way in another day. Which may give you two, since Har sent them all the other direction on his diversion. That's not a lot of time out here. There's a lot of ground to cover, and there may be someone else out there, or maybe just a body. I'm not sure. Seems The Commissioner's foreman ran across a kid. The one with the artifact, or whatever it was. I talked with Manny myself. He's the foreman, so it's good intel, but he was not all that certain the kid made it. They just left him at the scene, without water. Like I said, it's a bad place, so be sure you head in there with full canteens, or you won't make it back out."

Bran was thinking over the new data. "So, Har sent The Commissioner's men running off in the other direction. How'd he do that? The Commissioner seems pretty sharp to me."

Mack grinned like a catfish. "Remember the note about this thing giving off a brilliant flash? Well, Har had one of his contacts create an explosion of some kind. It was really something. Practically everybody in town saw it. It was good work. Even I was pretty impressed." Mack gave a far-off squint, thinking it through. "Timing. It's all in the timing."

Bran nodded his understanding. "So they headed out in the wrong direction, but there's nothing to find." It was a thoughtful statement. "Commissioner Dodge is going to be pretty pissed off when they come back empty-handed. Hope they don't just grab somebody for a scapegoat, trying to cover their loss."

Mack agreed. "Could happen, but Manny's not a bad guy, even if he does work for The Commissioner."

MaryEllen raised her hand again but didn't wait for acknowledgment before speaking. "So what's with the kid? Is he important, or just a bystander?"

"Good question," Mack allowed easily. "I'm not sure myself. Manny said something about the kid possibly being a mage or something like that. He said their horses went absolutely crazy, and he would know. He's been around the barn a couple of times. It's not easy to get him riled up, but he was sure worked up when they got back from that trek, and I mean really spooked, so I believe him. There are strange things out there, and a kid being a mage isn't all that difficult to believe. Just another reason to be wary."

"A magician, really? I'm surprised you'd even consider it."

The question came from one of the men on the team, but Mack made short work of the comment.

"I said a mage, not a magician. Magicians do tricks. A mage does magic. Real magic, with real power." He looked them over again. "If you plan on working to get this situation under control, or possibly to side with us, you had better have an open mind. Besides, with the dry passages of the badlands, the echoes, voices, windstorms, flash floods, and getting so lost you can't find your way out, this place will play with your brain. So don't go out there if you can't handle it. Get your heads on straight, and I mean right now." His intensity made his point even better than his words.

Bran turned to his team and spoke seriously. "I expect you all to listen. Mack knows what he's talking about, and he came all the way out here to let us know before we end up dead. So get your stuff together. We're out of here as soon as Mack and I are done talking." He switched his attention back to Mack, expecting his team to do what was needed. "Is it really that bad out there? Aundrea looked up all the references she had in the archives, but there wasn't much. Seems most people just leave the place alone. The ones that don't, well, I'm not sure they come back at all. There just aren't many reports, and you know how far back the reports go. A zillion years or something. Maynard runs the place and you know how old he is."

Mack chuckled. He did know Maynard, and no, he didn't know how old he was, but considering he was in charge long before Mack himself was even in the system, he was old. "Well Bran, I did my best. When you go in, be sure you come out. Then write a book about it. It would be a best seller for sure. Bran and the Badlands, Book One."

They both laughed at that, but Bran knew he was lucky if he got his reports in on time, let alone extra time to write.

"Whatever," he said. Cutting off the idea before it went any further. "Now, what do you suggest we do for our first pass? Map the place as we go, or spread out and cover as much distance as possible, hoping we find whatever we're looking for before we get interrupted?"

Mack considered it and shrugged. "Whatever you do, go carefully and be sure you know how to get back out. Don't leave marks on the walls though. It'll just lead them to you."

"Makes sense. I guess we'll map as we go."

Mack gave a nod. "You're the boss here. I'm just an observer."

"Yeah right," Bran retorted. "I'm pretty sure you wrote the class."

"Naw. I'm just a field agent. Har's the one that wrote the book. Make sure you come out and you can ask him yourself."

They sat a moment longer before Bran felt the itch to get going. He had a project to oversee and the time for camaraderie was done.

"Gotta head out, Mack. Thanks for the intel. We might just make it out alive thanks to you two. Also, Aundrea sends her greeting." He almost blushed as he reconsidered. "Okay, Aundrea sends her love." He shook his head at the notion of sending love to an agent, and got up to leave.

But Mack just took it in stride. "You got it, kid. That's a good woman. You keep on her good side and you just might make something of yourself."

Bran gave a short nod, accepting the wise words, and left to find his horse.

Time was marching on, and they had a lot to do.

R hone stood just inside the cavern's overhang, looking up at the rocky ceiling crisscrossed with roots and mosses.

"What do you think? Pretty cool isn't it?"

It is very interesting. I can feel the rock supporting the roof exposure. There is very small chance of its collapse during our entry.

"Thanks, Stone. I'm sure I needed to hear that," Rhone complained, wanting to glare at Stone, but Stone was securely fastened at his neck.

Stone noted the sarcasm in Rhone's words and apologized. *Did I say something wrong? I was merely giving you the data as I perceive it.*

"No, it's fine. I was just thinking how beautiful the place is, not its potential for collapse."

Oh yes, the visual, I see the difference. I will have to make notes on such things. Humans do not enjoy the sense of imminent failure, even if they logically realize all things fail sooner or later.

"Yeah. I suppose that's it," Rhone muttered. "But right now, I just want to show you the place." He turned in a slow circle, allowing Stone to survey the cavern. "We can walk around the lake, and in the back..."

Stone's instructional voice overrode his own. *In the center back is an opening, presumably the entrance to a secondary cavern complex. It is quite a remarkable find.*

Rhone held his aggravation and soothed himself, allowing it to dissipate. Stone could be irritating, but it had been far worse when he wasn't there. Maybe all partnerships were this way. He allowed a warm feeling to flood his mind, thankful he had Stone back. "I keep forgetting how much you can see. The second cave is where I plan on staying whenever we're here. Want to go see your new home?"

Absolutely, Rhone. Lead on. I am in your care.

Rhone smiled ruefully, thinking how poorly that had gone. "I only promise to do my best, but come on."

They headed around the lake to the far side, where even with the daylight reflecting off the water, it was almost dark.

"Here it is. I'll need to start a light now. I made up some torches before I left, so it won't take long."

A light? Would you desire me to light the way? I am quite capable.

Rhone was stunned by his own forgetfulness. He had been so proud of his ability to make torches that he had forgotten Stone could do it. "Sure."

A glow began to light the area in front of them. Stone adjusted the brightness to illuminate but not blind. *Will that be sufficient?*

"Wow, that's great!" Rhone said ecstatically.

With Stone's light, he was able to see across the entire cavernous room. Something he hadn't been able to do with just a torch. Wherever he turned, the light pointed directly in front of him. It really was like magic.

"This is perfect. Thanks, Stone."

Glad I could be of assistance. And one more thing. I am sorry about earlier. I am afraid to say, I did not do so well being in the vault. I would not have expected such difficulty with separation, but it is true. I was terrified.

"But you had the other We with you. Didn't that help?"

To be honest, it did not. Your human input has been most stimulating, and the We has been woefully treated. Being locked away without outside stimulation was very hard on the poor thing. I have been making progress, but it will still take a while before it is ready for the outside world.

"It's that bad? I was hoping..."

As was I. Perhaps my search was not the best-laid plan. I was simply unaware of the possibilities.

Rhone thought for a moment, trying to find good in the situation. "You did find one though, and it may have some problems, but I believe in you. You'll get it back in working order. I'm sure of it."

Stone's glow shifted until the cavern took on a golden hue. To Rhone, the color meant warmth, Stone's attempt to show his love for his friend.

Rhone's rough and worn fingers smoothed across the polished stone in his collar, and he mumbled, "You're okay, Stone, thanks."

CHAPTER 27

Breaker Breaker One Nine

Manny was pretty sure the spot had been blasted. He had seen plenty of explosions in his time with The Commissioner, and a few prior to that. Now the question was, why would someone want to do any blasting here? There was no mining close by, and the rock wasn't worth the cost of the explosive it would have taken. When he added in the fact it was at the base of a scree slope, it didn't add up to a hill of beans. At least you could eat the beans. This would have been worthless.

He spoke to Will, who he kept pretty close since their return from the badlands. "What do you think? Was this an explosion, or just a slip of the hillside?"

Will squinted like an old professor, casually scanning the site. It was a mannerism that had become typical since his near blinding. "Well, Manny. I just don't know for sure. A slip could have brought down a new slide, but a blast would too. Your guess is as good as mine."

"You're not much help, Will. I already figured out that much. Remind me why I keep you around?"

Will harrumphed, then shrugged. "Guess you just like me. Can't think of any other reason."

Manny almost chuckled at the response. He could almost like the guy. Well, maybe not that much, but at least he was a constant, and that had its good side.

"Makes me worry," Manny replied. "If somebody was blasting the hillside, what are they after? We came out here looking for a flash, and ultimately the artifact, but we ended up on a blank hillside looking at nothing but broken rock. What are we missing?"

Will wasn't sharp enough to realize Manny was asking a rhetorical question. But he did have an answer. "Well, I guess we're missing the point. Either that flashy thing is under the rock or it isn't. If not, maybe it's somewhere else."

Manny closed his eyes as he shook his head. Why did he keep this guy around? But the words kept rotating through his mind. *Somewhere else. Not here. Why are we here? To find the flashy thing. An artifact that got itself stolen from The Commissioner, by a brilliant-minded thief.*

All at once, the gestalt came together and he understood. This was a diversion. With everyone running around looking for whatever had flashed, nobody was looking anywhere else. It was perfect.

Manny appreciated the skill of the thief, who had not only stolen from The Commissioner, but had gotten away. He, or maybe she, was a genius.

"Will, you're a genius," Manny said, slapping the shoulder of his bewildered co-worker. Then he shouted across the slope to the men searching the hillside. "Gather 'em up. We have places to go, and double time it!"

✦

Mack and MaryEllen watched as the group rode over the hillock toward the badlands. She was back-up, and wouldn't be needed, unless things went badly. Hopefully.

"Would you care for some refreshment? I believe I have some sun tea I could pour."

The, "Sorry, Ma'am," came with Mack's nod. It certainly wouldn't go against his morals to have tea with a beautiful woman, but he was running on a timeframe, and time was about out.

"Ma'am, really?" MaryEllen gave him a brow-wrinkling frown of disapproval.

Looking slightly abashed, he shrugged. "Just didn't seem proper to go using your given name right off."

"Well, it's MaryEllen, and I don't see anyone else around to worry about."

Mack dipped his head, accepting the allowance, then raised a finger and cocked his head with a squint. "MaryEllen, didn't Bran call you Emmy? Wait... MaryEllen..., M...E..., Emm...Eee, Emmy. Dang, I'm getting old. Should have had that an hour ago." He gave another shrug. "Sorry, just one of those things. See, almost everything with a nickname has a reason, so I just gotta figure it out. Been that way all my life."

Since he was rambling on non-stop, she didn't see a need to interrupt by agreeing, or disagreeing. It was kind of cute, but he had hit it. "You got it right, and Bran is the only one to call me that." Smiling enticingly, she decided to go for it, and raised an eyebrow, adding to the dimple at the corner of her pretty mouth. "You can call me that too if you want. I have no problem with it."

"Well, MaryEllen is definitely nice, but it sounds pretty formal for a guy like me, so Emmy it is. Unfortunately, I've got to be riding. I've got a shop in town that needs seeing to, and I haven't got it trained well enough to run itself."

MaryEllen gave him a sweet pout of disappointment. "Who knows, maybe I'll drop by sometime. Skragmoore is it?"

"Yep, there's only one, and there's only one place in town called Mack's Place. Should be able to find it."

She brushed back the red hair that had slipped down to cascade over her shoulder and watched as he mounted his sturdy mountain pony.

"Good luck, Emmy. And I sure hope you won't be needing it, but The Commissioner's a hard man, and thorough. It won't take long for them to figure out the flash was a fake, then they'll be all over this place like ants at a picnic. So I don't mean to be skipping out on you, and I'll probably be kickin' myself for weeks, but I do need to be getting back. I'll keep my ears open and do what I can, but do stay safe. If you need me, you know where to find me."

He gave a final nod and a tip of his hat, then the soft kick to his pony's flank got them moving. The last she saw of him was his silhouette dropping over the top of the shallow hillock.

Taking a breath of hot air, MaryEllen squared her shoulders and turned back to her wagon. She would be ready. Hopefully, they wouldn't need her at all, but Mack's warning lay heavy on her soul.

It would work. It had to. If not, they might all die out here, and she would end up buried in this desolate place. Determined, she hitched up the wagon, moving it closer to the road.

The Commissioner's massive fist slammed against the desk, creating a mild earthquake and toppling the neatly stacked paperwork. His lips were drawn back in an animal rage, and his teeth were gritted so tightly that Manny expected to hear them shatter. The Commissioner wasn't spitting mad, but only because his teeth were clenched, making it impossible to spit. When he finally did manage words, it came out as a strangled roar.

"Damn your stinking leather hide! If you were any good, I would have someone else's hide to hang on the wall, but it looks like it's going to be yours. How in the world could you let yourself be deceived by a dumb safe cracker? You're worthless! Now get out of my sight, before I have you skinned where you stand."

His foreman complied, hurriedly slipping from The Commissioner's office at the Dodge residence. In his worried haste, he collided with the old butler-type servant passing by the door, almost dumping him to the ground.

As the two teetered in an arm-lock hold, attempting to remain upright, the old man began to apologize.

"Excuse me, sir. I am terribly sorry. I was simply not quick enough to evade you, and you are obviously in a hurry. Again, I ask your pardon."

"Darn it all," Manny said in irritation, finally managing to get his feet back under him. "I ran into you. I should be the one apologizing." Finally gathering himself, he held the old man's arm until he too seemed stable. "You okay? We almost had a tumble, that's for sure."

"Thank you, sir, but be assured, I am fine." Harold stood straighter, adjusting his jacket to hang at the correct angle. "See, no dents." His bright, wrinkled smile removed all doubts. "Might I ask why the hurry? There may be some way I can assist," Harold asked in all innocence.

"Thanks, but no," Manny replied, still wishing to be gone as quickly as possible. If The Commissioner chose this moment to leave his office, this would not be a good place to be standing. "I've got to be going." Under his breath he mumbled, "And the sooner the better." It was not meant for anyone to hear, just a mumbled thought to get himself moving.

"Ah…The Commissioner," Harold said, giving a solemn nod of understanding. "Perhaps you would prefer the back door and through the garden? It is a bit more circumspect."

Manny thought for the briefest of moments. "I don't need to sneak out, but I wouldn't mind just slipping away. You know the saying. Out of sight, Out of mind."

"Indeed I do. I also work for the man, and it is not always pleasant." His knowing eyes and arched brow spoke volumes, saying, 'What can you do'.

Manny could only agree. His wry smile came with an excepting nod.

Harold led the way down the hall, through the kitchen, and to the back door. "If ever I can be of further assistance, do not consider it a task. I am most always here, and quite willing to help, wherever I can."

Manny was actually impressed. This old man was okay, even if he worked for the Dodge family. He was also far more cultured than anyone he had ever met. On an impulse, Manny thrust out his hand. "I'm Manny, foreman for The Commissioner. Thanks, and I'm glad we met."

Harold looked at the proffered hand as though he had never seen one before, then reached out and took it in a firm grip. "If you ever need, just ask for Har. That's what my friends call me."

A single firm shake and they released.

With an uncharacteristic grin, Manny gave a quick scan of the yard and moved along the pathway to the gate.

So that was Manny. Mack was right. He is a good man.

Aundrea paced her office, wearing out her boots, if not the wooden plank floor. The information she had from Maynard gave her goosebumps. Who were these men, and what did gemstones have to do with anything but jewelry? The more she pondered, the more the information bothered her. More and more of her time was being spent trying to unravel ancient documents, looking for some obscure note that might, or might not, shine a light on what was becoming an obsession. Mage kids, gemstones, The Brotherhood, and of course, Commissioner Dodge. He may be the small potato in the sack, but he was still a loose end.

Har and Mack had been at the Skragmoore site for a long time now. Their search had been to find evidence of improper tampering with Skragmoore's funds and heavy-handedness among the people. Those kinds of things were far too prevalent in the far-out areas, where commissioners had an open book as to their management methods. But some things were just wrong, and it was her job to correct what she could, alerting the population to the need for corrective actions. From there, her information would go to The Council, and it was their job to see that the corrections got accomplished. All in all, it worked pretty well. Most of the time.

Squatting in the aisle, Aundrea sat back on her heels as she checked out paperwork from a hundred years ago. It was more work than it sounded, and her back hurt. This was the old section and hardly ever used anymore. No one seemed to need old documents of things that had happened so long ago.

Repositioning, she leaned back against the bookshelves lining the wall, and eased her sore knees. Whoever said being a file clerk was easy work? Not! It took work to bend over that far, dozens of times a day, arms full of books and documents. It really did wear on the body. Stretching her aching back, she opened the next police report she had just pulled from the cabinet. Perhaps this one would give some information the last fifty hadn't.

She was specifically delving into the robberies of the past. Particularly the big ones. If she was looking for information on large gemstones, or government documents, it would probably be considered a big heist. But other than the one mentioned in the report Maynard had shown her, the files were blank. No further comments at all. That itself was suspicious. If it had been big, there should have been more to the investigation, and notes of the attempts to find the culprit, or culprits. Even the reporting officer's own actions looked as though it might have been reworked. But it was so long ago, who knew how things had been done?

Now it was time to make up her mind. Either there was something worth acting on, or put it away. But Maynard's reaction to her simple request said, he obviously believed it. So much so that he had warned her, and activated his own 'old school' agent protocols. Nobody knew more about the old stuff than he did. That left her with one certainty, there was something to it.

Now what could she do about it?

As her thoughts spun round and round, she took each and checked them off her mental list. Gemstones that had power of some kind. But what kind of power? The possibility of mage power had been mentioned, but... Then there was the kid. Commissioner Dodge's own foreman had explained him as a mage, which was a bit of a stretch, but he hadn't been found and was presumed dead... although that may not be true either. It was one of the things Bran's crew was supposed to check out. Was there a body, or not? Either way, it didn't mean he was a mage. She knew just enough of the badlands to know strange things happened there, and had, ever since the records had started, but none of it had any connection with Maynard's story of the early gem encounter. That record said a stone had been on a ring and had glowed. But there had been no comment about the man wearing it being a mage. Still, if the kid could be, why not the man? It was worth thinking about.

There was a lot to think about.

So what did she have? Stones, gemstones apparently, and elements of stories that are mentioned in conjunction with light. In both stories, they were carried by people who, possibly, used them for some purpose. And, in both cases, they had disappeared. The old one, in the shadows of history, and the other, apparently stolen from The Commissioner's vault.

She had nothing.

Maybe Bran would find something, and that thought brought an itch to be part of the scene. Instead, she was stuck here, digging in dusty old files for information that was so old, it couldn't even be trusted. But the itch was there. She couldn't deny it. The field action was where her heart was, and she wasn't there.

CHAPTER 28

With Understanding Comes Freedom

*O*ur friend is doing better, Stone mentioned casually, *but it will be some time before it is back to a normal state.*

Stone's words had broken into Rhone's mind as he lay listening to the cavern's silence. He sat up, looking to where the two stones lay side by side. "How long before I get to meet it?" he asked with interest.

But Stone's growling vibration quickly changed his question. "What I mean is, you understand other people, but you can only talk to me. So, will it ever understand what I'm saying, or is it just a...rock thing?"

He couldn't decide how to say what he was feeling, or how he could talk about a...rock thing, without being discriminatory. But if it couldn't talk, move, or react, what did it matter?

Stone felt his concerns. *Do not worry. I am working with our new friend, exchanging information and teaching it about humans and your foibles. It is a great deal of information to take in, and even more effort to understand, but before long, we will be able to expand its capabilities. You will see. It may not be able to communicate directly into your mind as I do, but it will be able to show its understanding in other ways.*

Rhone was about to ask how, but Stone stalled his question. *You will just have to wait. It is not ready. Give it time to heal.*

Rhone resisted the urge to roll his eyes. He was bored. Every time Stone wanted to do more training with his new friend, Rhone would have to take off the collar and place the two rocks together, allowing their vibrations to transfer better. It also left Rhone with his own thoughts for company. While this place was nice and had begun to feel like home, it was boring too. He couldn't even explore farther into the cavern without Stone's light, and the sticks he used for the torches were now used for firewood. So most often, he sat outside in the sun, waiting for Stone to do whatever he was doing.

Rhone spent long hours swimming naked in the warm shallow water of the lake, but once he was under the cavern's overhang, the water deepened and got chilly in a hurry. The rest of the time he fished, and for once he was in luck. His pouch still had a hook and a line. It only took one fish for dinner, and while there were more, it just didn't seem right to catch them and let them go. He knew he didn't like to get stuck by the hook. So why would they?

Beyond those simple chores, he was warm, fed, and bored.

Are you awake?

Stone was nothing if not polite. He knew perfectly well whether Rhone was asleep or not, but asked anyway.

"I'm awake, now," Rhone answered, sitting up and yawning. "What's up?"

If you are interested, our new friend is ready to attempt a... he paused, *I hope you will not consider it undignified if I say... a trick.*

Rhone was instantly intrigued. "No, that would be cool. What's it going to do?" He could think of several interesting things, and his mind went back to his vision of hot rocks jumping around.

I am not going to spoil the show. So just sit and watch.

"Okay. I guess I'm ready."

There was no fanfare, no drum roll, and no circus master, but as Rhone watched, the little stone began to glow. Then the color quickly changed from a dull gold to a bright pink, then a soft white, before slowly returning to the original golden pink of the smooth shiny gem.

"That's great!" Rhone burst out in a surprised exclamation.

It is only a start, but I thought it was very well done.

"Absolutely. So it's all better?" Rhone asked hopeful. Maybe they could move on to other things now.

Oh no. It is some better, but as I said before, it will need a partner to help it return to normal function. I say normal, but that is not quite correct either. This is not the normal state in which the We function, but it is what we have now.

Rhone considered it. "It must be very different, but is it difficult?"

To some extent, yes. It took time for me to understand, but in the process, I have gained knowledge of how to assist another. I have also learned more of my own past.

"That's right," Rhone said, remembering their first days together. "You mentioned something about coming apart or being incomplete. Something like that."

Correct. And now I understand why, or at least more of why.

"Your friend knew?" With a sudden feeling of unease, Rhone wasn't sure he wanted to know more. What had Stone learned, and how would it change their relationship?

My new friend was able to show part, yes. Part of Me.

Rhone's mind went still. Stone had said Me, not We. With more than a little fear, he fought for a footing on this new ground, knowing Stone had once been part of this new We. Would he want to go back and connect to it again? If so, what would that mean?

Rhone tried to push his thoughts into some coherent strand, but a heavy sluggishness now slowed his thinking. It was as though his brain had changed from icy cold creek water to a thick mud pudding. It didn't want to work right, and he didn't know what to say. He felt a cold streak work its way down his back, wondering if Stone was going to abandon him.

If Stone's new friend had been part of him from before, it made sense. Rhone was the newcomer here, not this new We. The two rocks actually belonged together. He was the surrogate.

Rhone's heart matched pace with his mental slowdown, and he felt a sinking in his chest. Everything had been going so well. He had rescued Stone, not only getting away safely but finding another We. Now this. It was almost more than he could take.

Are you not feeling well? Stone asked, feeling Rhone's panic and helplessness, but not understanding why. *I sense a radical change in your heart rate. I am scanning, but I do not feel any danger about.*

Rhone couldn't talk about the real problem, and held his mental block in place. If Stone wanted to be with the new rock, he had every right to. It even made sense, but it didn't mean he liked the idea.

In an attempt to make things right, Rhone mumbled a reply. "I was just thinking of how good it must be to meet one of your own kind again. You must have been lonely."

It only took a moment's pause for Stone to process the words. *I believe those are half-truths. Meaning, I am certain they are spoken with truth, but there is more behind them than you are letting me hear. Is that not true?*

Now Rhone was stuck. It was hard enough being friends with a rock, but having it lecture you on truth wasn't helping. The worst part was, Stone was right, but so was he, even if it was a half-truth.

Rhone decided it was safer to change the subject. "Hey, I thought the demonstration was really great. It even changed colors. You're a good teacher, but I already knew that."

Thank you, Stone said, obviously proud. *Our new friend did do well. It is learning how this world's energy is transmitted and used. It will need to know these things in order to assist us, and to match with a partner.*

"A partner? You two are going to connect somehow?" *Here it comes,* he thought sadly.

Aware as always, Stone almost purred in self-congratulations. There was more to the truth than Rhone had admitted. *Did you expect me to leave you, just because there is another We?*

The question caught Rhone flatfooted, though he had been thinking that very thing. Immediately embarrassed, he felt the blood rush to his face as he tried to answer honestly. "Maybe. But if you needed to, I would understand. I'm not one of your own kind, and if it was the other way around, I might choose another human. I don't know. Anyway, I thought, maybe..." Still embarrassed, he let it drop.

Yes, I see, Stone said calmly, the words echoing through Rhone's thoughts like a boulder rolling downhill. *Let me explain a bit more, if that would be all right?*

A small snort slipped from Rhone. Since when did Stone need approval before he gave information? But he recovered quickly, giving a curt reply. "Of course you can. I'm right here."

Yes, you are, but I think your mind is running away with itself. I feel a separation, as though you have almost left me. But I am not certain why.

Because you're going to leave me! The silent accusation shrieked behind Rhone's block. Instead, he shrugged noncommittally.

I see. But before we get into that, let me explain some of what I learned. You might find it of interest.

Glad for the diversion, Rhone gave a nod, accepting the invitation.

As you know, I have been working with our new friend to assist it into this world of human connection. When I first came into your possession, I had plenty of time to do so. You carried me in your pouch, giving me ample time to assimilate the data and find the patterns. At this point, I must say, perhaps not all of my kind would have done similarly. Perhaps some would simply have lost faith and became... rocks. Earth is so very different than where We are from.

Rhone was intrigued despite himself and had to ask, "Where did you come from?"

As I said, We, come from far away. So far, in fact, I do not believe there is any We that could tell you. The thing you need to understand is, We are from beyond this earth.

Rhone didn't respond. While it was unbelievable, he had already come to that conclusion but still had a question. "But I found you in a river. So how did you get there?"

I honestly did not know when we last spoke of it. Only that I felt...separated. Not whole. Now I understand... better.

Rhone was not in th mood to be played. "Are you going to tell me, or are you just making me wait?" This was serious, and he wanted information.

Stone's vibrating chuckle was somehow reassuring. *I learned from the We. When we put our knowledge together, we each had gaps. Some were filled with my knowledge; such as how humans work, and some with our friend's knowledge; such as what happened and why the We are here.*

"Really? You can do that. You can share knowledge?"

Of course, silly. You and I share knowledge, do we not? We just go about it in a slightly different way. With the We, the knowledge is...traveled through, in our mind's structure. To us, the pathways make sense. Your human minds are not structured the same. Each pattern is very different, as well as your methods of storing the information. It is the main reason that one We cannot easily understand a different human's mind. Two human patterns are simply too different to make a translation workable. Truly, you do not realize how complicated your brains are.

Rhone shook his head as though to clear it. "Okay, whatever. But if you say so, I believe it."

Good, Now back to your original problem. And yes, it is a problem. Stone was very firm on that distinction.

"Which one?" Rhone replied meekly. "I seem to have quite a few."

Joking is good, Stone said with his normal lack of humor. *Now, would you like to tell me the problem, or shall I bumble about and try guessing, as you seem so prone to do?*

Rhone puffed out a breath while considering his options, but knew the truth was best. "I didn't want you to go." Quickly he continued with his reasoning. "You have every right to. You do. You're free. I don't own you, but you are my friend, and I don't have any other friends, so...I would miss you." The words came to an empty stop, not having come out quite as he had intended. Quietly, he sat waiting.

Rhone felt the contemplative head shake as if Stone actually had one. *It is much as I thought. If I may explain something to you, it may help.* Then he continued, without waiting for a reply. *When the We were not on Earth, we were in space. An asteroid, I believe you would call us. We were a crystalline construct that apparently evolved on our own, much as you seem to have done here on Earth. Small bits of energy floating through our internal crystal structure began connecting this thing to that. It is not so very different from the electrical currents running through your own bodies.*

Rhone nodded his vague understanding.

We were all one. The We. It was a group of individual crystalline structures, bound together as one large crystalline group. We were each separate, yet all one. Each touching the next, making a large, interconnected community. Together, we drifted through the vastness of space. We knew this, because of the astronomical bodies we swung around and were diverted by, yet we were a free body, belonging to none.

I now remember some of this. Now that I have a reference to attach it to. As I said, I am old. So old, I don't even remember what I remember, but in all that time, there was never a moment when I have had so very much newness to contemplate. Never so much new information and mind-stimulating thoughts and feelings. Consider, space is called space, because there is so much of it, and very little to attend to. We could not change our direction or speed, we simply thought. We are very good at computing and contemplating, but not so good at reacting to stimuli. Change was difficult for us. Then you came along.

"Wait," Rhone cut in. "How did I come along if you were in space? It doesn't make sense."

Stone chuckled like an old grandpa, happy the kids were listening to his story. *Ahh, how? Yes, that is important. As I said, the We floated through space, affected by the celestial bodies we encountered. It seems we drifted too close to Earth and were caught in its gravitational pull. And being caught, we were drawn to Earth.*

"But you said you were a big asteroid, all clumped together?"

You were paying attention. Good. And that is exactly right, but falling to Earth is not a gentle act. Perhaps you can imagine running to the edge of the escarpment and jumping off. Now think of jumping from a cloud.

Rhone's pinched look said he could imagine, and it wasn't good.

You are correct again. Now add a fire so hot, it eats you alive. Falling to earth is something like that, and then We hit. The We that had not been burnt up on entry were broken into tiny fragments and scattered far across the country. The explosion was enormous, throwing rocks and ground far into the air. When it settled, it became part of the new land, and for the We, a new life.

Rhone was awed by the story, his vivid imagination viewing the incident, watching the asteroid disintegrate into thousands of pieces, scattering to the ends of the earth. "But you made it. You're still here." His quizzical expression wanted to believe, but still had questions. "I've never heard of anything happening like that. Not around here. People would have seen it for sure."

Yes, that is true, Stone said un-fazed. *I said it was long ago. Not multiple eons, but long enough for no one to remember. For a long time, I was on a mountain, but after a time, the snow and rains washed me free. I slid and rolled down with the water until I washed into the river. Later, I came to where you found me. It was a long time. I learned to understand the animals that came by and the fish in the river. Of course, I did not know what you called them, but I knew them. There was nothing else in my life, and they were alive. I could sense their simple lives and enjoyed their company. But then, you came along. I sensed you coming. You have a very engaging energy and I...attracted your attention.*

"A flash!" Rhone blurted. "You gave a flash. I remember a flash catching my attention, and I looked for it. I thought it was a reflection. Maybe from an artifact or something, but it was you." Rhone was almost worshipful as he thought back to the hot day, walking in the river. "I'm glad I found you."

I believe we found each other.

CHAPTER 29

The Show Must Go On

Manny drove his men hard, riding toward the badlands like The Commissioner himself was on their tails, which might even be true. It was another good reason to keep them going far longer than they would normally ride at those speeds. Their horses were showing the miles, and if they didn't stop soon, one or more would begin to falter. In this rough country, it could mean the rider's life.

Finally, Manny raised his hand and shouted, "Hold up guys! Let's take a break." As his tired horse slowed to a frothy-mouthed stop, his very willing troop came to a dusty halt, bunching up around their foreman.

"It's far enough for this leg. Tomorrow we'll hit the badlands themselves, but you probably guessed that already. See to your horses and get a good rest. There's no water beyond this point, so drink your fill here."

He was referring to the small wet spot that could hardly be considered a watering hole, but when it's all there is, you become very thankful it's there.

As everyone began to move off, Manny shouted again, his tone announcing its importance. "And don't muddy the water!"

There were mumbles, but whether in support or simply complaining, didn't really matter. It was important. Nobody liked drinking muddy water, but if that was all there was, it was amazing how quickly the finicky attitude dropped away.

Manny held his own grumbles. While he didn't want to be here at all, it was his job. But the more he thought on it, the more he considered moving on. Even good pay couldn't be spent if you were dead.

<hr>

Bran delegated a map keeper in each group, as he explained, "You won't make it back if you don't know 'how' to get back."

Each unit was to map their own route, working through the torturous twists and turns of the badlands as they looked for information, a body, or a kid. They knew there was little time, but not knowing how long kept them on edge. It was hot and dry, and the sun reflected mercilessly off the rocky walls, only to be absorbed by the stone, then released back at the wandering invaders.

"What's the chance we find anything?"

It was the question on everyone's mind, but having it stated out loud seemed to make their own thoughts less offensive.

Being upbeat about the whole affair, Bran gave his favorable opinion. "Actually, I think we have a pretty good chance. Har's report said, once they got what they wanted, the guys left in a big hurry. They were scared to death and didn't want to stay any longer than it took to grab the collar and run. Apparently, they thought the place was haunted, and a ghost had spooked the horses.

"Now, just so you know," he continued lightly, "I don't believe in ghosts. So if their horses went crazy, and I do believe that much, there must have been a good reason. Could it have been the kid? Could have been, and maybe the kid was a mage or wizard or whatever. Again, we don't know. Shucks, maybe it was the collar itself, or something else entirely. Maybe the horse backed up on a cactus. We don't know, but whatever it was, I want to find out. It will undoubtedly be important data, so we want a report on it."

The wise-cracker that made the original comment popped out another. "So no ghosts? What about goblins?"

The laugh from the team actually seemed to settle them down a bit.

"Just keep your eyes open," Bran admonished. "You never know what you might find."

"Does an old campfire count?"

Bran turned to see who was asking and saw the soot mark on the stone wall. "Good job. We don't know who made it or when, but it shows that someone has been in this direction. It's a good start."

As Bran and his small team wound through the aimless passageways, the mapper had a difficult time trying to keep his work on the page. The day was hot, and the dry foliage overhanging the tops acted like a lid, effectively keeping in the heat. One would think the shade would offer cooling, but it didn't seem to. The heat felt as heavy as a blanket, layering their bodies with sticky sweat, as oppressive exhaustion began to wear on their minds.

Bran mumbled morosely to himself as his horse caught the toe of its hoof on a rocky outcropping, almost stumbling to its knees.

"No wonder those guys wanted out so badly. This place is Hell."

He kept his seat but was ready to vault clear if the horse went down.

"All right, crew. These critters are having enough problems on their own. I think it's time to walk. Everybody down."

There were no complaints. They all knew, if the horses went down, it would be a long walk to town. Taking care of your mount was a top priority to anyone in the field.

"Let's go ahead and take a break. I'm going to climb up to the top and have a look around."

He was already scaling the rock, beginning to work his way along the far too-smooth surface. Only the few cracks between the unique pillars gave any secure hold, and his feet didn't fit those.

"Hey, somebody catch me if I fall," he shouted over his shoulder.

But an unsupportive jest echoed off the stone. "Not to worry, boss. The gravel looks pretty soft."

Bran glowered at the wall but didn't give the speaker the satisfaction of a reply. He finally made it to the top and wondered why he hadn't carried a rope up with him. Now he would need to climb down too. So much for being lead. He was going to have to learn to delegate.

Before him lay the length and width of the badlands. It ran in all directions, cutting jagged pathways through the desert landscape as it crisscrossed and zig-zagged its torturous route, only to return to itself on another pass. No wonder no one came out here. This was crazy.

He shouted down to their mapper, "How's the map doing? Can you get us back the way we came?" It was important information.

"Got it," came the reply. "It isn't pretty, but I think we can get back."

"You think?" Even with the sticky sweat, the little hairs on the backs of Bran's arms stood up. Mack wasn't kidding when he said there would be no return if they got lost. Calling back down, Bran said, "I hope you mean, Why absolutely, sir. I could do it with my eyes closed."

The strained laugh answered cautiously, "Why absolutely, sir. I'm pretty sure I wouldn't want to try with my eyes closed."

"Yeah, yak it up, but you should see this place. I will repeat, we do not want to get lost out here. Got that?"

"Ah, got it, but I think we're okay."

Bran nodded his answer, although no one could see him up here. Standing away from the edge, he looked at the jigsaw-puzzled land-scape, trying to figure where he would be if he actually wanted to be in here. It was an easy decision. He wouldn't want to be here at all.

Will struggled for breath as Commissioner Dodge held him up against the wall by his shirt front, causing the old buttons to strain against the worn fabric.

"But, Mister Commissioner," Will whimpered in strangled words, "I don't see so good anymore. I'm not sure I'm the best man for the job."

Almost peeing himself in fear, Will tried hard to hold it together. Having pee running down his leg would not make it go any better.

"I didn't ask what you think, and if you're able to ride a horse without falling off, I'm taking you with me. You might not see well, but you were there, and you just might remember something."

With a last hard push to Will's chest, The Commissioner let the little man drop to the floor.

Will moaned as he slumped against the wall. He had never been brave, and he certainly wasn't a fighter, but going back into the badlands was almost more than he could bear. Left with no options, he accepted his defeat. "I guess I can try."

"Good enough. Now get your stuff together. We're leaving within the hour."

With that said, The Commissioner strode out of the bunkhouse and slammed the door.

With his eyes clenched, Will sat banging his forehead against his knees. He really, really, did not want to go back there. He had been lucky to get out alive the first time. Going back would just give Mother Nature all the ammunition she needed to see that he got killed.

The door swung wide as The Commissioner strode forcefully into his residence, bellowing to whoever would be listening.

"Get my stuff ready. I'm going to see this problem gets fixed, if I have to do it myself, which is exactly what I am going to do. Mavis! Where are you?"

He wasn't in a good mood, but there was nothing new about that. Even hollering for his wife wasn't special, but using her first name, loudly, and in semi-public, was not normal.

Making his way to the office, he found Mrs. Dodge, leaning casually against his door, waiting for her husband to find her. She was not smiling. She was making a point. She, Mrs. Dodge, wife of

The Commissioner, was not a house servant to be ordered around like chattel. She was Mavis Dodge, and he would remember that, or she would have her father take back the dowry he had delivered at their wedding. But unbeknownst to her husband, the dowry had been in her name. Not his. Dad had never trusted this man, but the marriage was a good maneuver for the both of them. Her father and her husband. Not necessarily herself. Even so, she had tried. It was expected of her.

But this was too much.

When The Commissioner finally stomped his way to his office, she merely smiled, and in her sweetest voice said, "You called, dear?"

He glared at her. "You heard me. I need my things packed. I'm going to get that guy if I have to rip that collar from his cold...dead... hands! Nobody else seems to be able to get anything done around here."

Mavis didn't flinch at his building heat. She had seen it before and wasn't impressed. "Well, I suppose you should go pack then. It wouldn't be good to head out without a change of under-things." With that said, she turned, ignoring his incredulous look, and headed toward the kitchen.

"Where are you going?" he called roughly to her retreating back.

She simply waggled fingers over her departing shoulder and smiled grimly to herself. A cup of tea would be nice.

Being alerted by The Commissioner's bellows, Harold heard most of the conversation and was in the process of preparing a cup for the Mrs. He had a good sense of the situation, having maneuvered into a position as confidant for Mrs. Dodge.

As she came walking crisply into the kitchen, Har gave a small nod of acknowledgment and pulled out a chair from the small sitting table by the window.

"May I be of assistance, ma'am? And would a cup of tea be acceptable?"

Mrs. Dodge nodded briefly, accepting the offered chair. She sat, heaving a heavy and dramatic sigh. "Tea would be wonderful, Harold. Thank you."

"Of course, ma'am. That is why I am here."

She almost twittered at that and gave him the smallest of smiles. "I am afraid we treat you terribly, but you must understand. It is so difficult out here in the wilds of nowhere. You seem to be the only person in a hundred leagues that has any culture at all. I just want you to know...well, that I appreciate it." Her eyes misted slightly, as she considered her position.

Her words surprised Har so much that he almost forgot to look away, as a proper servant would.

"Why...Thank you, ma'am. I am most heartened to hear that my service has been adequate. I do try."

Actually, he was flabbergasted by her words. He had never heard her say anything, to anyone, including Mr. Dodge, in that kindly manner. His sense of concern began to grow. What was her game?

With a shallow bow, he handed her the tiny teacup and stepped back a pace. "Will there be anything more?"

"Oh, do sit for a moment. I am afraid The Commissioner is leaving on very important business and is not in a good mood just now. The tea will help, but having someone at hand may help steady my nerves."

This was the very reason he had manipulated his position away from The Commissioner, to the Mrs. She was a fount of information. All he had to do was listen.

"Of course, ma'am. Whatever you wish." Har pulled a second delicate chair a ways from the table and sat. It would not be correct for him to actually be seated at the same table as his employer. "It has not been a good day?" he coaxed apologetically.

Mrs. Dodge sat holding the tiny cup, but without drinking the tea. Her neatly coiffed hair was done to perfection, as always, even if she was only staying at the house for the day. She released another, smaller sigh, and theatrically made a sad frowny face. She was not a very good actress.

"The Commissioner and I are having some difficulties I'm afraid. It is sad, and I have tried, but he is tangled up in some devious plot, threatening people. I'm even afraid to say it, but he's not doing his job very well. This other thing is taking all of his time, and I simply do not know what to do." She lowered the cup, resting her wrists on the edge of the table. "I am only a woman, not a commissioner, but it doesn't seem right." Again she sighed, and very quietly asked, "What can I do?" Her words drifted off.

Always a gentleman, Har responded correctly. "Would you care for some more tea, ma'am?"

Seeming startled at the question, Mrs. Dodge sat upright and smiled briefly. "That would be wonderful. Thank you, Harold."

Aundrea would rather be riding, but in her position, a buggy was more appropriate. Women were allowed to drive cute little buggies, but riding off alone, across the country, would definitely bring a chorus of complaints from 'caring citizens'. All in all, the buggy was all right, since it gave her a lot more room to carry things. Especially with the false bottom in the rig. If she was going into potential trouble, she was not going empty-handed.

Aundrea flicked the reins, giving Pasha plenty of lead for the climb up the slope. He wasn't a very large gelding, but the beautifully deep red-brown of his bay coat made him worthy of his name. The trip was almost like a holiday, except, she was headed for the badlands.

Luckily, she knew where she was going. In fact, it was the only reason she would actually allow herself to go. New data and new questions. When Maynard had dropped by with a discovery of a very old document, his old, but still perky voice had said, "This may be part of the answer, my girl. This old traced map is even older than me. Still, I don't think the land will have changed much. After our discussion, I thought I would do a bit more research, and managed to come up with this. It is a map of a place simply called The Badlands. I didn't even know there was such a thing, but it seems to fit all the parameters."

A quick view of the old parchment was enough. She had to go, although she hoped she wouldn't run into Bran and his group. That would raise questions about her trusting his leadership, which she did. No, this was something different. Something she needed to do.

Maynard saw her decision and, with regretful eyes said, "I wish I was young enough to go with you, but I would simply be in the way." Then he patted her hand gently. "Please go carefully."

MaryEllen lay against the fabric of her wagon home, soaking in the morning sun. She loved the warmth in the early morning, but by midday, it would be far too hot to be lying out like a lizard. With her skirts hiked up to her thighs and her bodice open, she was showing far more skin than was decent, had anyone been around to witness, but it didn't bother her. She was free for the moment.

When the distant clatter of hooves caused her to sit up straight, exposing even more chest, she quickly gathered herself, laced, and hopped down to stand casually next to the wagon wheel. Dervish, her horse, gave a snort, and stood alert, ears forward, signaling that someone was coming.

"Take it easy, boy. We were expecting someone. We just didn't know when they would get here."

The horse seemed to understand, beginning to graze in the dried, sunburnt grasses but kept his watchful eyes on those approaching.

Two men rode up, bringing a cloud of fine dust swirling with them. Their horses' nostrils flared wide at the scent of Dervish standing in his proud regal posture, poised still as a statue. They knew a threat when they saw one.

The two men were as different as could possibly be. The really big man sat his horse like it was a rock, and it must have been to hold his weight without stumbling. They may not have been traveling hard, but they had put in miles. The lathered sweat on the neck and flanks of his horse showed its stress as easily as the heavy blowing of hot moist air from its widely flared nostrils.

The second man was much smaller, distinctly showing the incongruity of their sizes. MaryEllen could see the man's timidity in the way he slouched in his saddle, making it more than obvious, he did not want to be riding with the big man. He kept as far away as he could, without appearing rude, and there was fear in him. His eyes shifted constantly, as though he was waiting for something to jump out and grab him. She almost felt sorry for him, but the big man was more on her mind, and definitely the one to watch out for.

The big man sat his steaming mount, surveying her and her encampment with interest. She could see the wheels turning in his not-so-obscure review. She was both game, and a challenge. He liked both.

Part of MaryEllen's useful abilities was reading people, understanding what they were about by their actions and postures, and she was good at her game. Intuitively, she did not like this man. He not only stank of sweat but of guilt and...power. Maybe strength was a better term, but stink of it he did.

He hadn't said anything yet, and she raised an eyebrow questioningly. "Good day, gentlemen. How may I be of assistance?" It was a good enough way to start. "See anything you like, or just shopping?" The words may have been nice enough, but her slight frown let him know she wasn't interested in anything he might be selling.

"Just passing through." His big voice rang out, thickened by the dust that was beginning to settle. "This is pretty far out for a lady such as yourself. Camping here? Why would that be?"

MaryEllen gave him a cautious look, with eyes narrowing in defiance. "And who's asking? Unless you own this land, I can pretty well camp wherever I want. Besides, this was as far as I got last night, and I decided to stay a couple of days and let my horse have a rest. Is that all right with you?" She stared him down with no smile at all.

The big man gave a nod, allowing her the rightness of her words, then dropped his winning hand with a disarming smile. At least he thought it was disarming. To her, it was more of a predator's snarl. One that was sure of its kill, before it had even struck.

"My error, miss. I am Commissioner Dodge of the Skragmoore region, granted so by The Council of Government, and you are in my lands. No, I do not own them, but I do oversee the economic growth and civil order of things here, and that places you directly in my jurisdiction." His big cat smile carried a look of self-satisfaction, expecting her to fawn at his feet with awe.

He was bound for disappointment, however, because she couldn't have cared less.

"Do tell." It wasn't given as a question. It was a put-down, in tone and manner. She shrugged lightly and turned to the smaller man. "And you? You look like you could use a cup of tea. Would you care for a quick cup? The pot's still warm."

She was pushing the big man, this Commissioner Dodge person, acknowledging his small companion over him, but it was worth it. She could almost feel the heat build inside him. One thing he did not like was being ignored.

Will was totally taken aback, managing to stutter, "Ah... yeah," hardly able to comprehend that she was talking to him. But as The Commissioner's head swung around, staring death at the smaller man, Will's quick rebuttal of, "Or... maybe no. I don't think we have the time right now, but thank you."

With his budding hope canceled, Will almost shrank into his own clothes under the weight of The Commissioner's silent snarl.

Miraculously, the snarl suddenly converted to a politician's smile as The Commissioner returned his attention to the young lady. "It is obvious, you are not from around here. May I ask, what brings you to Skragmoore?"

There must be a good reason for this young lady to be out here, and being the predator he was, he could feel...something wasn't all up and up. What, he couldn't fathom. Skragmoore was simply not a place on any local 'tour of sights' where anyone wanted to go. He continued his verbal grilling as his eyes took in her obvious delights.

"I only ask, because it is my duty to know. Important guests need to be seen to, and such."

It was a simple ploy to gain information. Information was his glue to money, and he had sticky fingers. If she had information, he wanted it. She wouldn't be a bad morsel either. He liked his toys.

As he looked her up and down appreciatively, her stomach turned. He was disgusting, but she wasn't overly worried yet. A pig, yes, but she'd had bacon on many a morning.

"Commissioner Dodge, you say? That wouldn't be, The Commissioner Dodge, of Skragmoore? Sorry, I haven't heard of you."

The smile that had started to form, changed abruptly. It had been a slap to his self-prestige, but he took it stoically. This woman was an enigma. A rose in the desert, and she was in his way.

"As much as I was looking forward to making your acquaintance, miss, I have important business to attend to." Gathering the reins, he readied to set his horse into motion.

Anticipating his intentions, MaryEllen shifted her hand up to her hair and fluffed it, bringing it sliding back down to her long trailing earring, almost petting her lobe.

The change in The Commissioner's attitude was automatic. His eyes swept to her ear, now visible from beneath her red curling hair. The male part of him was powerless to change the ages-old reaction to feminine charms, and he instinctively sat back, absorbing as much of her glow as possible.

She beamed a shy grin at her obvious error. "I may have been a bit hasty, Mr. Commissioner. A woman has to be careful out here in the wilds. You never know who, or what vile man might show up and be a threat." The smooth drawl she put to the words was alluring to almost any ear.

The Commissioner raised an eyebrow at the comment. "Are you suggesting something?" He was no fool. He knew a guise when he saw one, or thought he did, but he couldn't quite tell about this female.

MaryEllen didn't so much as blink. "You never said where you were headed in such a hurry. Surely there isn't much going on in this backwater place that wouldn't hold for a cup of tea?"

Her main thought, after his initial threat, was to protect her team. This was The Commissioner, and if he was headed toward the badlands in a full charge, it put her people in danger. Her job was to keep it from getting to them.

The Commissioner was caught in an obvious state of indecision. He wanted to stay, but his plans were important, at least to him. His gem, and the collar, were out there somewhere, along with the thief that took them. He wanted revenge and the piece, but it wouldn't take long to indulge this girl, and whatever else he could get.

But the moment passed, his game being more important than hers. The thought that this sweetmeat would still be around when he was done, gave him the hand.

MaryEllen saw his decision as he made it, making her own with the same clarity.

With a quick pull, the earring's long crystalline dangle separated from the holder. A lightning-quick flick of her wrist sent it flying through the air, striking Commissioner Dodge in the throat.

His look of surprise would have been quite comical, except for the animal rage that instantly took its place. His roar of affronted dignity surprised her as much as it did Will, stoically sitting as though awaiting execution.

Will almost fell from the saddle, as his horse skittered in fear from the animal sounds coming from the big man. Grabbing at his reins, Will jerked the horse to the side, only managing to run the poor animal into The Commissioner's horse. The bigger steed spun, trying to evade the unexpected attack of the smaller animal, almost unseating The Commissioner.

But the dart had struck well. The nerve agent in the crystalline vial injected as designed, pumping the liquid directly into his system. Almost immediately, The Commissioner's body stopped working correctly.

Barely able to move, the big man fought valiantly to stay in the saddle, managing to kick the horse firmly in his attempt to get away. With meaty hands clenched to the saddle horn, his vise-like grip helped him stay seated, but his horse only managed three or four ground-eating strides before his massive body slid off, hitting the ground hard, his limp form rolling into a crumpled pile of non-functioning body parts. Surprisingly, he wasn't out, but his body wasn't working either. Watching through disbelieving eyes, he followed the beautiful redhead as she gracefully walked across the small clearing to his side.

Seeing The Commissioner go down, Will screamed at his horse, wildly kicking it into a savage run. His addled brain only knew, the badlands were going to kill them all. The ghosts would be after him next.

MaryEllen didn't worry about the little man. If he became a problem, it would be taken care of. The man she had been tasked to stop was lying at her feet. Unbelievably, he was trying to get up. How much drug did it take to put down a man like this? She would work on that problem later. Right now, she had to take care of bigger issues.

Unable to move, The Commissioner watched with disbelief as the young redhead swung the shovel. The sudden blackness was another thing he couldn't avoid.

CHAPTER 30

Clowns to the Left of me

"Hey, Bran. How long are we going to wander around in here? Won't The Commissioner's men show up soon?"

It was a good question, but Bran didn't like the idea of giving up. With a shrug, he answered, "Until we find something. I want out of here as much as you, but we can't give up yet. We need a body at least." *If there is one.* But he didn't vocalize the thought. "Let's give it the whole day. Tomorrow morning we'll head out. Leaving will go faster, now that we know which way to head."

It was true. By the map, which now took up three pages, they would be able to track themselves back out of the maze, but they were still empty-handed. Maybe one of the other units would have found something. Anything. It would be hard to write up an action report with nothing to put in it, and 'Failure to complete mission' wouldn't look good for his first lead effort. He sighed, thinking of the words stamped across his file, but he had tried.

"Let's give it a good day. We'll head out tomorrow." He re-said the words, hoping duplication would give a sense of strength to his case.

Just then a call rang out, "Bran, over here. What do you think of this?"

Too concerned with his own commiseration, he hadn't noticed the area of dry ground covered in scarred hoof marks. Tracks and scrapes gouged the thin dirt between the bigger rocks, while other areas looked like they had been trampled by a passing parade, or maybe a Saturday night square dance.

"I think we found something," Bran said coyly, nodding to the disturbed area. "Be careful not to walk over it, but let's get a survey done and see if we can plot movements and numbers. Come on. This is what we came to do."

The sudden increase in the noise level showed the unit was behind his directions. Digging into their saddlebags, they began pulling out tools and notepads. Investigate and find answers, is what they were trained to do, and within minutes, the place was virtually a scene of industry. With the number of people and the relatively small area to survey, it didn't take long. Before the sun had set, Bran had the data he was looking for.

Stories normally grow, and at a much faster rate than the parson's sermon would decree, but unexpectedly, and far from the norm, the data seemed to agree with their original story. Let's just say, that having the data prove the story was an interesting turn of events.

"All right, settle down." Bran was giving an overview of the data they had just collected and was working on the timing of the events. "It appears there were three horses. Their tracks are everywhere, which proves they weren't just standing around eating hay. So here's a question," he asked of no one in particular. "There are four sets of footprints, but only three horses. So, who was walking...and why? It's a long way from nowhere, and a long way back. So riddle me that." He waited for an answer.

One of the crew gave a tentative answer, hoping it didn't sound stupid. "You said there was supposed to be a kid, so maybe this proves it?"

"Good point, but did he ride in with them, and out? Or was he already here, and maybe still here? I only ask because there's no body around that I see."

But no one wanted to hazard a guess, or perhaps they were simply too tired after their long day.

"Well, here's what I think. I think the stories were all true. All of them. That in itself is pretty suspicious, but when all else fails, try the obvious.

But let's call it a day. First thing in the morning, I want to take a wider look from up top. Now that we found something, we might just want to stay a bit longer."

There were groans, but no mutiny. They were definitely too tired for that.

• • •

Aundrea followed the old map, driving far out into the rough countryside. She had left the road long ago and could now see the badlands with the odd statuesque columns rising ahead of her. They stretched for miles, starting as single pillars rising up from the dry flatlands, growing larger and closer together until they created walls of rock with passageways running haphazardly through them. This would not be a good place to get lost. Luckily, she had a map. A very old map, but as Maynard had said, the land didn't change much. Not in a lifetime anyway, and the map wasn't older than that. Probably.

Double-checking her position she drove on toward the pillars. She would have to leave the buggy, which wouldn't be bad. It had been a rough trip overland, and the buggy hadn't been built for cross country. It was more of a citified rig, but it had gotten her this far. From here on, her trek would be on horseback. She had no idea how far it would be, but she wasn't going to leave her horse to fend for itself while she walked. She may be a runner, but she was smart enough to ride when it was available.

Looking at the map again, she got it correctly oriented and plotted her course ahead. She was in the right place. At least the open pathways corresponded with the picture on the map. It was now or never. Unhitching the buggy, she saddled her beautiful bay, threw the saddlebags on, and gathered the rest of her things, strapping them behind the saddle's cantle. The big canteen was the last item. Never leave home without it. Not in this country.

Mounting, she clucked to Pasha and started the next leg of her journey. Somewhere out there was Bran's team, and somewhere out there, according to her map, was...something. But it didn't say what.

⚜

Commissioner Dodge lay so well hog-tied, he could hardly breathe. Actually, MaryEllen was surprised he was breathing at all. The dose she had given him was so big, it would have put down a buffalo, but he was still breathing. He was a sturdy man, as anyone could see, but in the end, he had gone down like any other man. Well, not quite, but he wasn't going anywhere. He could simply lay there and rot in his own…. She wasn't going there either, but he was a foul man and would get even more foul as time went on.

Thinking of that, she hoped Bran wouldn't take too long. She didn't actually want to kill The Commissioner… accidentally. Sometimes it happened in a fight, but just having him lying there made it a much less interesting game.

Of course, it really wasn't a game, but it was easier to think of it that way. She was here to do a job, fighting for her country and community, and if this man made problems, it was her job to take care of them.

Giving a gentle push with her foot, she accepted his responding movement as a sign that he was okay. Then working hard, she managed to roll his big body under her wagon and dropped the canvas sides all the way to the ground. For the moment he was safe from casual eyes. She would check on him again in a few hours. Until then, she had some sunning to do.

The horse worked hard to keep its hooves under it, with flecks of foamy spume marking the widely flared nostrils. Will's heels pounded the poor creature's sweating side, trying to force it to go even faster, but it wouldn't be able to go much farther, not at this pace.

With no other place to go, he was headed back toward town, but even with his horse faltering, he didn't plan on stopping. He was leaving. He had seen The Commissioner drop from his saddle, and he was sure he had seen the glint of disembodied teeth shining at his throat. He had tried to warn everyone the place was haunted, but

The Commissioner wouldn't listen. No one ever listened to him. His only regret was the poor girl he had left at the scene. She had been nice to him, which wasn't something he was used to, but he wasn't going to turn around for any reason. He would find the road out of town and be away from here. After this, the only thing the people of Skragmoore would see of him would be his footprints.

Juan called to Manny as they worked their way into the intricate maze of the badlands. "Do you have a plan, or are we just gettin' lost so The Commissioner can't find us?"

"Shut up, Juan. Why are you always asking questions?"

Manny was already irritated after his run-in with The Commissioner and had been for two days now. There was nothing out here, and they had already proven it, but he would be dead if he came back without something. Having anyone griping only made it worse.

Manny turned to face his men and shouted grumpily, "We are going to find whoever it was that took The Commissioner's goods, and if not, you might as well look for a new job. So spread out and look. Juan, take one of these guys and head up that passage over there. Check it and keep your eyes open. I don't know who it was, but I'll bet they're here somewhere. Everybody seems to be heading to the badlands all of a sudden."

With a grunt, Juan swung his horse to the side, flagging one of the guys to follow. Manny had been in a bad mood for days now and it would be good to be away from him for a while.

"And don't fall asleep while you're out there," Manny shouted needlessly. "The rest of you guys, keep an eye on the tops of these things. I don't plan on getting jumped by anything, and that goes for big cats, or a person." He pointed to the next two guys. "You two, take the next offshoot. We're going to cover this place like a rug. Nothing gets past us. Got it?"

No one seemed overly worried at their foreman's manner. They were The Commissioner's men after all, and used to being hollered at.

At each new branch, two more men broke away, heading deeper into the maze, and Manny was beginning to feel pretty good about his plan. It might even work.

The brilliant white flash caused a strobe-like effect on Rhone's eyes, leaving only the solid black of the cavern's interior when the light finally dissipated

"Perfect!" Rhone cheered, as Stone's glow began to absorb the blackness, coming to a gentle light much easier on the eyes.

"Great job, Stone, and tell our friend so too. It was perfect."

It had been another test, using a variation of the first to test the capabilities of their We-in-training. It was learning fast, even beginning to understand some of what Rhone was saying. The new We's ability to travel the neural networks of Stone's core had increased its speed of learning dramatically.

Stone explained some of his methods. *It is similar to what it was like in the We construct. We pass on information in this manner, from one We to the next. It may seem time-consuming, only connecting with one We at a time, but if you consider our time-to-action requirements, you will see that without frequent need of action, speed becomes quite irrelevant. We think, we do not often react.*

Rhone closed his eyes, attempting to feel himself in a similar process. His inability brought up other questions. "But you said you were drifting through space. Isn't that moving?"

It is, but not quite what I meant. Think of placing a large group of humans into a wagon, sitting them so closely together that they could not move. The people would be inactive, yet the wagon could be moving very quickly down the road.

"Got it," Rhone said happily. "And since you were just riding, you weren't affecting your direction or speed." He was getting smarter, which made their dialogue even more fun. "So your new friend is learning our language too. That will be handy."

It does not change the rules however, Stone said firmly. *You may not make contact.*

Rhone didn't truly understand why, but accepted Stone's decree.

Feeling Rhone's dissatisfaction, Stone thought it was a good time to explain. *It is not ready for contact. Soon, but not yet, and I would prefer it was not you.*

But Rhone was frustrated by Stone's words, taking it as a lack of trust.

No, Rhone. It has nothing to do with not trusting you. The We needs its own partner. It needs someone to make that connection, and you already have me.

Rhone sighed expressively. "I do have you, and honestly, one of you is enough."

He grinned at his quip, until Stone archly replied, *And you are complaining? You should try it from my side.*

Stone didn't take teasing very well and Rhone quickly gave in.

"Anyway, It was a great trick and it is learning fast. So what now?"

Seeming mollified, Stone said, *We are considering the most effective method of communication between ourselves. It is quite simple when we are connected, but at a distance, it is more difficult.*

"Come up with anything?" Rhone asked, knowing it was beyond him.

Perhaps. We are working on a system of wavelengths that would transmit through the air. It is a bit more complicated with the curvature of the earth, but it will work for line-of-sight distances.

"And you could still use the ground sound thing for longer-range stuff," Rhone added supportively.

Yes, that is a possibility. We are working over the parameters and returns, but to change the subject, what are you doing? Do you have plans?

Rhone had tried to skirt his boredom issue. "I don't know. Maybe I'll do some fishing and swim for a bit. It's going to be pretty nice out there this morning."

And...?

Caught, he squirmed, trying to think fast. "Maybe I'll climb to the top and have a look around. I should review my picture of the place and make sure I've still got it. One of these days, we'll need to leave here, and it would be nice to be able to find our way out."

Mmm hmm, so you're bored.

It didn't take a genius to tell he was tired of sitting around. Even a rock could see it.

Rhone's embarrassment brought color to his cheeks, and he responded vaguely, "A little maybe, but I know you're doing good stuff. I'm going up top. You two have fun."

Rhone felt the bareness of his neck as he scrambled up the cliff. It reminded him of being alone, and his boredom. Finally clambering over the top, he draped spread-eagled in the bright sun, absorbing its rays after the cool of the cavern. It was nice, but he had climbed up here for a reason. Repositioning for a clear view of the countryside, he closed his eyes and brought up the mental picture. Once the picture was firmly in his mind's eye, he opened his own and re-examined the scene. When the view was an exact copy of the picture in his mind, he instantly felt more secure. He was pretty sure he could find the way now, no matter which way he went. It was much better than only having one way in and out.

Then a movement caught his eye, and he stared into the distant heatwaves already beginning to form as the day warmed. There it was again. The shimmering distortion made it difficult to determine what it was, but there had been motion down one of the longer pathways in the far distance. With all the twists and turns, he wasn't able to track it for long, but it was there. Now what? His heart raced as he thought through his few options. Should he stay here and hide, or should they run?

CHAPTER 31

All Roads Lead to Stone

Aundrea carefully followed the intricate map, pushing her bay deeper into the labyrinth's passageways. She wasn't going fast, but she was making steady progress. It was amazing just how far you could go and not seem to get anywhere when every turn was a close copy of the one before and all passages looked much alike. She shuddered involuntarily, glad she had a map.

It was no wonder there were so few stories about the place. Few would ever go in very far, and even fewer would come back out, but according to the map, her end was near. Hopefully, the little spot of dark blue showing enticingly on the map wasn't just a drop of misplaced ink, dripped accidentally from the mapmaker's pen.

Aundrea spoke calmly to Pasha as he shied at nothing, flicking his ears forward and back, unsure if he was being followed. She had to admit, it was a bit spooky in here. The clip-clop of horse's hooves echoed hollowly down the walled passages, then returned as echoes, coming back from around the corner, or even behind her if that was where the corridor happened to connect. It was truly unique in her experience. Luckily, the map showed it wasn't much farther. Only then she would know whether her use of company time had been a waste. While her target destination may not be a treasure, she hoped it was something worth searching for. Of course, a true treasure wouldn't be so bad either.

From early morning to late afternoon she had followed the tortuous pathway, working her way through the desolate labyrinth, until rounding another corner, a big log lay crossing much of the path. The log was well-weathered and must have been carried here by some long-ago flood to get so far into this desolate place. At least it would be as good a place as any to call a rest. She was tired of sitting in the saddle. The buggy had been bad enough, but at least it had springs.

Using the log for a bench, Aundrea looked over the map and decided she was very close indeed, almost on top of the blue dot. With sudden energy she jumped up, ready to get it done. Brushing off the back of her riding skirt, she smoothed the pleats then straightened her fitted vest, a very essential part of the proper woman's wear. The puffy-sleeved blouse was dusty and smudged, not as easily fixed, but it would have to do. She was a professional and had a reputation to uphold, even if this was not the place to worry about such things.

"Come on, baby," she cooed to the bay. "Just a wee bit more. But I'll walk this time. It's not far."

Leading Pasha carefully around the end of the log, she turned the rocky corner and stopped short.

A vision of blue water and eye-soothing greenery lay before her. The scene was so unexpected in this trackless labyrinth, she stood open-mouthed, gawking like a kid at the circus. The azure water reflected the cloudless sky like a perfect mirror, as birds flitted in and out of the drooping foliage.

Pasha pawed the ground and butted her with his head, telling her he was more than willing to keep going.

"All right, I get the picture. Let's get a drink, and maybe a bath, if you don't get the place too muddied."

Pasha shook his head, snorting and spraying her with a less-than-desirable muddy mist. He was ready, and started to push past her, but Aundrea was already moving, leading him to the edge of the narrow lake. Slipping the bit from his mouth, she let him step out into the shallow water, then giggled like a girl as the sound of his long slurps echoed off the walls.

"Okay. That's enough for now. You have to leave some for me."

In obvious disagreement, Pasha shook his head wildly, again showering her with a cool mist. She led him from the water and quickly tied him off around a boulder, then without further thought, stripped off her outerwear. In frilly undergarments, Aundrea trotted to the water's edge, sticking one toe daintily into the mirrored image. It was perfect. Closing her eyes with a sigh, she balanced like a tightrope walker and waded out into the water. Only when it reached her thighs did she drop straight into the cool depths with a plop, dunking completely under the surface. She rose majestically, throwing her hair back and out of her face. The cool water ran off her skin like butter on a hot skillet, which wasn't far from the truth.

Staying in the shallows, she sat, splashing water over her head in an almost comic attempt to wash her hair free of the trail grime. The scrubbing continued as she worked her way to her face, neck, arms, and finally, her feet. How long had it been since she had a bath as good as this? Once washed, she floated on her back, hair spreading in a brown fan around her head. No wonder there had been a map.

It truly was a treasure, and once found in this maze, anyone would want to find their way back.

The thought brought her head up with a snap, scanning the surrounding lakeside. If there was a map, then someone else knew of this place, and someone could be here even now. Her freedom was over. Trying to appear casual, she cautiously waded back to the shore. Maybe it was a silly fear since it was just as possible she was the only person in a hundred years to have come here, but she was no longer comfortable walking around in wet underthings that stuck to her with far too much familiarity. It certainly wasn't something she was accustomed to, especially knowing they must be practically see-through.

Without waiting for them to dry, she quickly climbed back into her outerwear and cinched up the laces, putting herself back into a more confident and appropriate apparel. At least the damp underthings would keep her cool for a while.

Pasha looked on without comment. The fact that he wasn't concerned gave her confidence a boost. It had been a silly worry.

She took the time to run her fingers through her wet hair, separating it into long strands. When it dried she would try braiding them into something more decent, although she certainly didn't need her hair coiffed for this outing. The one thing she didn't neglect was checking her weapons, making certain they were handy, just in case.

Rhone simply couldn't keep from watching as the woman stripped from her clothing and walked out into the water. He was embarrassed by his impropriety, knowing he was spying on her, but he honestly hadn't planned on her being here. It was her fault, not his. He couldn't very well stand up and wave his arms, saying, 'Hey I'm watching you.' That would be worse for both of them. Besides, he had no idea how to talk to a woman about such things. He had certainly never talked to his mom about anything even close to the subject, even though he had seen her in her underthings on several occasions, but again, that was very different. This woman was amazing. Beyond anything he could put a mind to. He couldn't help but watch as she floated on the blue water.

He was almost relieved when she quickly dressed but felt disappointed too. He also knew Stone would have something to say about it, and there was no way he could defend himself, but for now, he put it aside. He would have to search for a way down where she wouldn't see him. That would be too embarrassing.

Rhone backed from the edge before feeling comfortable enough to stand and even then walked to the far side of the cavern's opening before attempting to climb down. She hadn't noticed the cavern yet, and he needed to get there first. Stone needed to know too. Maybe not everything, but at least that there was company.

The entry cavern was dim, lit only by the sun's reflection off the water, patterning the rough ceiling in shivering glimmers and glints. The shifting light made it difficult to focus, and without a torch, he would need to be careful. Rhone entered the inner cave hurriedly and crept along the wall. It was pitch black this far inside and only the fact that he knew where he was going, and that there was nothing to run into, allowed him to shuffle forward without panicking.

He whispered loudly, not wanting to make a noise someone might hear outside. "Stone. Where are you?"

Speed seemed to be of the essence here, and he needed Stone's counsel.

We are to your right, approximately five paces. Rhone, why are you acting strangely, and where is your light? Stone was ever perceptive, but usually when Rhone didn't want him to be.

"Never mind that. We have company. What are we going to do?" Shuffling in the indicated direction he stopped, reaching to feel in front of him.

One more step and lower.

Having directions piped directly into your head did have its benefits, but Rhone was beyond caring. After stubbing his toe, then scraping a knuckle as he reacted to catch himself, he managed to find the boulder where Stone lay.

Unfazed by Rhone's clumsiness, Stone continued as though he hadn't witnessed the young man bumbling around in the dark. *Company? Indeed,* then he seemed to ponder the information. *Obviously we need to determine who it is and what their intentions are. At that point, we will have better data to determine our own actions.*

Frustrated with his inability to see, and still upset with the situation, Rhone spoke tersely, letting it all out. "All right, it's a woman, and she's by herself, except for her horse. I mean, she's got a horse, so she isn't totally alone." He felt himself stammering as the picture of her swimming came vividly to his mind. He quickly clamped down on the thought, hoping Stone hadn't caught it. "Anyway, she's here. So what do we do?"

Stone noted the growing panic and the elevated heart rate. *Hmmm, First, as it does not appear we are in immediate danger, you need to settle down. You say this woman is alone. Is she preparing to stay, or simply passing by?*

"How do I know?" Rhone said, throwing his hands up in a wild gesture of annoyance. She just went for a swim!" The words just slipped out.

Oh rats, he thought behind his mental shield. *Now what do I do?*

He was worried, and all Stone wanted to do was think, which wasn't much of a plan as far as he was concerned. Now Stone would have more questions, particularly ones he didn't want to answer, and he would have to explain, but it felt just a little too personal right now.

I see... Stone held the word until he felt Rhone squirm. *A woman and a horse, and she went swimming. I must say, this does not sound very threatening.*

"Maybe not," Rhone shot back, "but I thought you would want to know, so I came right here." Which was almost true.

But you had time to see her swimming.

Rhone felt himself flush to a bright red, and although it was still dark, wondered if Stone could tell. "I had to make sure she wasn't going to find us right away. Then I came."

And what is your opinion? Will she be staying, or is she leaving soon?

Rhone felt trapped, as though Stone was playing with him. But taking a cleansing breath like Mom had taught him, he thought through the implications and surprisingly, came up with an answer. "I think she'll stay for a while. If so, she might see my tracks and the wood cuttings, and will probably find the cave." His thoughts whirled in a dance, data pieces falling together in a pretty detailed picture. "So, I think she'll find us."

Rhone could have sworn Stone smiled, which was, of course, impossible.

Stone's answer was warm. *I am impressed. You did that all by yourself, which is not a put-down. You did amazingly well, and without any direction on my part. That leaves one final question to solve. What are you going to do about it?*

"Me?" Rhone sputtered in surprise. "I figured you'd tell me what we should do. I'm no good at this."

Stone gave a deep rumbling, somehow soothing vibration, before responding. *You may not have been, but you are learning, and growing. You may be young, but I believe you are beginning to think like a man. Give it a try. Now, what should we do about this woman at our door?* The emphasis was on the word 'we'. They were a team.

In total darkness, Rhone reached for the collar. Beside it, lay the second gemstone.

With Stone around his neck and the gem safely in his pouch, he was ready. Stone's warm glow lit their way as the three walked into the outer cavern and on into the daylight.

Abruptly, Aundrea sat upright as something caught her attention. She had been lying on her bedroll, indiscreetly lounging in the sun. Her vest was off and her long riding skirts hiked up to her thighs, both allowing them some sun, and to keep from baking. Unhurriedly she smoothed out the skirts. Her hair had finally dried and was almost ready to be braided back out of her face, but that would have to wait. Quickly buttoning the rest of her blouse, she glanced at the vest, but it would take too long. If not fashionable, she was at least modest. Standing now, she watched as a young man approached from around the lake. If he hadn't been alone, and young, she would have been concerned, but she knew she could handle herself against one boy.

Pasha had also noticed the intruder, and stood proudly, neck arched and ears at the alert. Even for a gelding, he had pride of ownership, and knew to protect his mistress. He stomped one hoof and snorted his annoyance of the stranger.

The young man was walking, which told her he was either without, or within walking distance of support. Nobody was out here on their own if they could help it. Except for her of course. Maybe she should reconsider her position, but he was almost here.

With a cheerful tone, the young man called, "Hello," slowing his progress, but not stopping. "I saw you over here and decided I should say hi."

"Hello yourself," Aundrea replied casually, "and what brings you out into the badlands alone?" It was both a statement and a query, wondering if he was really alone. Giving a quick glance to the ridge line, she was relieved not to see anyone.

Rhone stopped a discreet distance from her and smiled. "I could ask the same thing. I was watching you come in, so you must have a good reason."

She was as pretty as he had thought, but that was secondary. This was his place and he needed to know more.

For Aundrea, the thought that someone had been watching made her jumpy, especially when she realized what she had been doing a short time before. She decided to play her hand. "Just how long have you been watching?"

His reaction was answer enough. This young man was really just a kid, and his blush could have heated dinner.

"I wasn't spying on you," he said defensively. "I saw you coming from way down the passages, and you came straight in. Nobody knows about this place, but it seems you do. So why are you here? Did The Commissioner send you?"

She had to admit he was playing a fair hand. He had taken his lumps and was ready for more, but... what was around his neck?

Trying to appear as though she hadn't noticed, she asked, "The Commissioner? No, I followed a map, and as you said, nobody knows about this. So, maybe I should ask, how did you get here?" With questioning eyebrows, she swept her hand toward the lake.

She had him, and now he had to up the ante or show his hand. And since she had a map, she was the one with a valid reason for being here. He had just stumbled in, almost drowning in the process.

Only pausing a moment, Rhone decided in her favor. "If you have a minute or two, I could explain. Can I come in?"

His mother had made sure he had basic manners at least, which Aundrea instantly recognized. It said a lot. After all, louts didn't have manners. They made demands.

"Come on in. I can't offer much in the way of hospitality, but you're welcome to a rock. It seems we have plenty of those."

She drew him in with a flourish of her arm, and Rhone marveled at how such a simple gesture could be so elegant.

Feeling foolish now, and hardly knowing what to say, he managed, "Thank you, ma'am."

Aundrea spoke with an easy smile that she hoped wouldn't frighten him. "Do have a seat, and we can talk for a while."

This was what he had asked for, but he felt like a fish out of water, and hoped he wasn't acting like one, with his mouth open gasping for air.

She found a seat too, and tried not to stare at the choker-type neckpiece he wore. The large stone shone in the sunlight, reflecting golden hues of brilliance. It was breathtaking. No wonder Commissioner

Dodge wanted it, and was willing to kill this young man for it. She had no doubt this was the piece taken from the vault.

Choosing a handy boulder, Rhone sat before clearing his throat. Stone hadn't given any hints on how to go about this, and it was all new to him. Feeling like the lost teen he was, he stumbled his way into a conversation.

"Well, ma'am, I ah...I thought it would be best if I dropped in and said hello. We being in the same vicinity and all."

He fumbled for words, trying to make a coherent thought. It wasn't going the way he had planned. He had no idea how to talk to a woman. Even her glance sent his heart leaping, so how was he supposed to come up with a conversation?

Aundrea became acutely aware of his problem. This was an innocent soul lost in the badlands. After his run-in with The Commissioner, she was surprised he would come to talk with her at all.

Holding out her hand, she stretched to reach across the intervening space. "I'm Aundrea, and I am glad to make your acquaintance. May I ask your name?" She spoke with no hint of intrigue or flirtation. He wouldn't be up to that.

His return smile was almost comic in its relief. "Hi, Aundrea. I'm Rhone. I grew up outside of Skragmoore, but this is my home now."

His answer surprised her, and she spoke without thinking. "You live here? But, there's nothing here."

"I'm doing okay," Rhone spoke up in his own support. "And there's fish in the lake." He realized how vague this sounded, but she raised a hand, stopping him before he could say more.

"I apologize," she said with real feeling. "Here I invade your home, and then demand to know why you're here. It is not very neighborly of me, so no need to explain further. I'm the one who should explain. Would that be all right?"

He could hardly complain. Besides, she was so nice, that he simply wanted to agree. "Sure, that would be fine. Besides, this isn't really my place. I just found it." But as soon as he said the words, he wished he hadn't.

Noting his chagrin, Aundrea smiled knowingly. "Don't worry about it. It was honest, and I won't tell. In fact, if I explained further, it might make you feel better. Or maybe not. I won't judge one way or the other, but let me start, and you can tell me if I should stop." Her raised eyebrows framed her blue eyes in a query that was almost hypnotic to the poor kid. "Is that okay?"

He nodded and tried answering. "I'll listen, but I can't imagine why I would worry." And of course, as soon as he said it, his mind came up with a dozen reasons. The thought even crossed his mind that he might be falling under a spell. He had never met this woman before, and here he was ready to dump his entire life into her lap.

Stone's calm voice broke into his thoughts, smoothing his worries. *You are doing fine. We will learn as much from her as she learns from us. It is good.*

With a mental nod, Rhone relaxed and as his tension eased, he settled himself to listen.

Noticing both the buildup and the relaxing, Aundrea wondered what secrets he was trying to hold back. Even without the collar, this was an interesting young man. Smoothing her skirts, she clasped her hands in her lap and began her explanation.

"First off, I came here on purpose. I told you I followed a map, but I have never been here before. I must say, you have quite a place here. I had no idea there was anything but the badlands. But beyond that,

I also happen to be head of The Office of Public Recrimination, and I am here on business."

The lack of understanding clearly showed in Rhone's eyes. And while he didn't have a clue of what it all meant, he didn't ask.

"It all has to do with you I should think." Her raised eyebrows wrapped the simple statement in intrigue.

But, as the saying goes, her words fell on deaf ears. Rhone sat quietly, listening to her beautiful female voice. She didn't talk like his mom had, but it had the same feel. Something he could only describe as feminine, and it drew him.

Until Stone's sharp words snapped him back to awareness. *Rhone, keep your mind on track!*

Aundrea paused with a worried look. "Everything okay?" He certainly wasn't acting as she would have expected.

Having been caught daydreaming, Rhone blushed again. "Sorry, ma'am. Of course, I'm fine. You said something about your job?"

"Yes. I work for The Council, in the Office of Public Recrimination."

A glint of recognition came to Rhone's eyes, but he remained quiet.

This place was so far from anywhere, it was no wonder the young man's only recognition was to The Council. But this much she could handle. "I was saying, I believe you are the reason I came all this way."

"Me? Why me?" Near panic reached for Rhone. All he could think was that the Commissioner had sent her. He was caught with Stone around his neck, and he was the thief.

Surging to his feet, Rhone was ready to run, when Stone's shout rang clearly through his head.

Stop! She is not a threat!

"Not a threat? But she knows!" he shouted in panic, his words echoing off the rocky walls.

Well, That was certainly subtle, Stone said calmly.

Realizing what he had just done, Rhone turned to face a startled Aundrea.

She too had risen to her feet, a bewildered expression on her face. "Did I say something wrong?"

Rhone closed his suddenly tired eyes, letting his head droop. Once again, he had blown it. Now he had to face the music.

Lifting his head, he simply said, "No, It's just me."

"I don't think I understand," she said carefully, "but you were correct. I am not a threat. I came here to find you, but only to talk."

Rhone eyed her suspiciously, trying to decide what to do. He was embarrassed by his outburst, but Stone hadn't given any further directions. Once again, he was on his own and nodded his acceptance. "I have this...problem," he began.

Aundrea raised her hand, stopping him. "You have a very good reason to be careful. I know Commissioner Dodge is looking for you. I have an entire team out trying to find you and to delay The Commissioner's men, who are also trying to find you. So for me to run straight into you must be a good omen. Anyway, as I said, I am head of the Office of Public Recrimination."

Again the blank stare. He had no idea what she was talking about.

"Which of course, you know nothing about." She took a deep breath, trying to come up with a way to explain government politics, but gave up. "And why would you? I doubt Commissioner Dodge has explained much to the town about our governing body, except that he was granted placement by them."

"Mom told me about that," Rhone said proudly, wanting her to know he wasn't a total dummy.

"Your mother?"

The look on his face told her enough.

"So it's just you, or is your father still here?"

Rhone shook his head. "Never had one. Well, of course, I had one, but Mom never mentioned him." It was a futile effort to contain his dignity, and somehow in admitting it, he felt smaller, briefly wondering why it had never concerned him.

"So you're on your own."

Aundrea's gentle look was almost more than he could take, and he suddenly felt very alone.

When Stone's equally gentle voice whispered, *I am here*, Rhone choked back a sudden emotional breath. A moment later, Stone's voice came again. *Tell her. It may help.*

It was time to come clean.

With a shallow nod, Rhone began. "I took the collar from The Commissioner's safe, but he stole it from me first." He looked imploringly at Aundrea, willing her to understand. "Stone is my friend. I couldn't let him be locked away in a vault for the rest of time. It just wasn't right."

The words ran from Rhone like water over a dam. Luckily, Aundrea knew when to listen. Her words would come later.

Rhone reached up to his collar and gripped the stone protectively. "This is mine. I found him, and then I rescued him." He was serious, letting her know he would protect his collar from all takers.

She nodded, not quite understanding, but knowing it was important.

At her nod, Rhone relaxed a bit, letting his eyes drift down to his belt pouch. "I did take his other We, but he had it locked away, and it was sick. It needed help."

Aundrea knew she was missing something important. His words weren't making sense. Squinting, she tried to understand what he was trying to get across.

"I see your... collar, as you called it, and I see the stone. It's absolutely beautiful by the way. I can understand why you wanted it back, but I think I got lost after that." She let the words drift off, hoping he would fill in.

He nodded and dropped the hand holding his collar. "This is Stone. He's my friend."

Thoughtfully, Aundrea pursed her lips as she stared at the stone. Maybe this young man needed more help than she had anticipated.

Seeing her disbelief, Rhone quickly covered. "No, really. I found him in the river and, after a long time, we started talking to each other."

Now it was obvious. Aundrea squared her shoulders, ready to help as she could. This young man was in a delirium. Possibly from isolation, or losing his mother, or even guilt for the theft. It would probably wreak havoc on any young person's life, and this one had simply cracked under the strain.

Rhone saw her critique coalesce. He could read it on her face. But it was wrong. "Wait, there's more," he blurted. Then spoke aloud to Stone. "Would you make a small light please?"

A good plan, Rhone. And Stone began to glow.

Aundrea gasped, covering her mouth as the stone began to pulse in a beautiful pinkish-golden light. "It obeys you?"

"Not really," Rhone said with a shrug. "Stone listens, then sorta does what he wants."

I do not! came the sharp retort only Rhone could hear. *I listen and determine the best response.*

Exactly, Rhone replied silently, feeling justified.

Aundrea saw the momentary unfocus of Rhone's attention and asked, "Not really?"

Refocusing with a lopsided smile of apology, Rhone said, "It's a weird thing, but Stone is alive."

Tight ridges furrowed Aundrea's normally smooth brow until she remembered Har's words and she whispered, "You're a wizard. That's how the stone glows." It was at least as possible, and far easier to believe than a rock being alive.

"A wizard? Why would I be a wizard? They aren't real." Then silently asked Stone, *Are they?*

I can only say, from the information I have.... Stone began.

But Rhone cut in, saying, "Not now, Stone, and if you could turn off the light, please. She's seen enough." He spoke aloud, so she could hear.

Well, Yes, of course, and the light dimmed.

Without thinking, Aundrea reached to touch Stone. "It's alive? But how?"

Rhone gave a shallow shrug. "I call him Stone, and he could tell you himself, but you can't hear him. It has something to do with energy and the vibrational paths. Thoughts are energy you know. He taught me that."

In awe, Aundrea continued to stare at the stone. "It's a boy?"

She had a hundred questions.

Unfortunately, it was a question Rhone didn't have an answer for. His nose scrunched thoughtfully as he chewed on his dry lip. Mentally, he asked Stone. *She has a good question and I'm sorry I never asked, but are you a guy?*

Stone answered with a feeling of satisfied amusement. *Let us say, I accepted your assignment of sex, although We do not have such things, so one was as good as the other. Or as bad, since we do not need either.*

Rhone felt himself blush. "Really? I just assumed."

Aundrea watched as the conversation went back and forth between them. She could almost feel the words, but it was his facial changes that gave her most of the data. She was good at reading people by their body language, so when he spoke the last words out loud, she had a pretty good idea of what they were going to be.

With the blush still on his cheeks, Rhone focused back on her. "Stone says the We are neither, but since I decided what he was, it will work. I honestly never knew."

She smiled at that, recognizing the possible reason for the blush. "If you would tell Stone..." She tried to think of the rock as a being. "Well, tell him I'm sorry I caused a problem. It was not intentional."

"Oh, I don't have to tell him. He can hear you. It's just that you can't hear him." He smiled in a very boyish way that explained it all.

"He can hear me?" She was enthralled by the idea. "Can I talk to him then, or maybe I should talk to you? I'm not sure what protocol to use."

Rhone thought about it. "If it's just you and me, you can talk to either of us. But no one else knows. I think it's best that way."

"Of course. I should have thought of that myself. Then let me ask...Stone. It's a perfect name by the way."

Rhone smiled as Stone spoke to him. "Stone says thank you. He likes it too."

Smiling brightly, Aundrea said. "I'm talking to a...well, I was going to say rock, but what would be the correct term? I don't want to make a bad first impression."

"They call themselves the We, because they're a collective entity. He wasn't a single being until... Well, until they crashed into earth. That's when they broke apart."

Aundrea's eyes grew wide as she considered the information. "From space? He's a Martian?"

Rhone's quizzical look showed his confusion, until Stone spoke to him. Aundrea could tell by the change of expression.

"Oh, I should have figured it out," Rhone said, rolling his eyes. "Stone just told me that Mars is a planet, and people think space people would come from there, so they would be Martians. It makes sense I guess, but I never heard of them before."

She tried not to smile too broadly. "My error, but he is from space?"

Rhone nodded his agreement. "They weren't from Mars, but they did drift through space. There are others. We were looking for them when The Commissioner's men found us."

"There are more? Where?" And why hadn't she heard of this?

Rhone shrugged. "I only found the one, in The Commissioner's vault, but it wasn't doing well so we've been helping it."

Rhone felt words quietly entering his mind. *Why don't you show her? She may make a good partner for our new friend. It would be up to the We of course, but it really does need a partner.*

Rhone blinked in surprise. *Are you sure? We hardly know her.* With Aundrea standing so close, he was having difficulty trying to think the words to Stone.

Aundrea could tell they were communicating and let her gaze drift elsewhere so as not to intimidate the young man.

Resigned, Rhone gave a half-hearted smile. "Ah, ma'am? Would you like to see the other We? Stone's been working with it, and he thinks it's ready."

"Can I?" Aundrea asked carefully, a catch in her breath. "Would it be okay?"

Rhone understood her sudden hopeful look. Meeting a We would make anyone excited.

He nodded. "Stone said it would be okay, but you need to understand, it's had a tough time. It was locked up in the dark for a long time and hasn't had time to learn as Stone did, so it's a little messed up."

His look was apologetic at his choice of words, but it was true. He just didn't know how to explain it better.

"Is it safe? It's not crazy, is it?"

"No, It's fine. I've been carrying it since we left Skragmoore. Stone's been helping it learn. Here, I'll show you."

Rhone! Do not touch it.

Rhone had reached for his pouch but stopped instantly at Stone's warning.

Be careful. I do not want to confuse it with two signatures.

Relieved, Rhone carefully removed the leather bag, upending it to tumble the mixed contents into the dirt.

Like a tiny flame, the little gem flashed in the sunlight.

Aundrea drew close in amazement. "It's beautiful!" she gushed. "It's the most gorgeous thing I've ever seen." Forgetting Rhone was even there, she bent closer, looking deeply into the tangled facets and swirling clouds of the pink-gold stone, unconsciously drawn into its core.

Hello? Came the tiny, soft, and musical voice.

Aundrea was hardly aware as it tickled her mind. She simply existed, with it inside herself, and in the stone at the same time.

"Hello? Are you the We?" She said the words aloud, unsure how to communicate with this tiny being.

In response, the little stone began to glow, first golden, then pink, and finally a brilliant white, which held for several heartbeats, before lessening to a soft, gentle glow.

"Ohhh my," she breathed. "You are absolutely precious, my little jewel. I think I'm in love." Without thinking, she scooped up the little We and held it reverently in her two palms. "I will call you Jewel. Would that be all right?"

The gem's glow pulsed with her heartbeat, and all was good.

I believe they have partnered. Stone whispered to Rhone. *Jewel fits her well and will obviously be female from here on.*

Rhone's startled expression showed he hadn't caught much of what had just happened. "A girl? Is that okay?"

It is fine, and most expedient right now. Jewel can now learn how to communicate with a human. It is a very important quality she has not been able to do so far. Her training will advance rapidly now.

Nodding absently, Rhone watched as Aundrea held her new friend, remembering back to his own first day with Stone.

CHAPTER 32

Twists and Turns

Bran squirmed in his saddle, staring across the rock-sided corridor at Manny and his two men. Behind Bran, his team waited uncomfortably. So far, there hadn't been any violence. So far. Although all parties had their hackles up. Anything unexpected would bring on the action. But really, it was simply too hot. Nobody wanted to put out that much energy, and for what? There was nothing here but more of what they had just come through.

Moving slowly, Bran raised a hand. "Afternoon, guys. Unless I miss my guess, you belong to Commissioner Dodge."

Manny gave a snort and answered, "Now why would you think that? Just because it's his territory, and we're wearing his outfits?"

"Sounds about right," Bran said, giving a shallow nod. "Besides, I guess pretty good. In fact, I figure you must be Manny."

Manny glowered, eyebrows gathered in a tight knot. "How'd you know that? I don't recall seeing you before." He carefully scanned the men before him, noting their readiness to get this over. But the odds weren't good. In fact, this entire event was about as bad as everything else about the place.

On both sides, a multitude of weapons were ready at hand. None aimed as yet, but everyone sat warily watching, wondering if this would be their day. It didn't matter if you were hit by a knife, stick, crossbow bolt or bullet, it wouldn't be a good day, and the narrow passage meant it wouldn't take much in the way of aiming to hit something.

After a moment, Bran stretched casually, straightening in his saddle and producing a smile that confused Manny. "A friend of mine told me you might be wandering around out here. Do you know Mack? He owns the tavern in Skragmoore."

"Of course, I know him," Manny grunted caustically. "I come from there. It is called Mack's Place after all, but that doesn't make you a friend." He was cautious. Too many odd things had happened around here to let a name weaken his position. "And since my boss ordered me out to this stupid place, I'm going to have to ask why you're here. I can't find any good reason that comes to mind." He glared at Bran's still-smiling face.

Bran gave a nod, recognizing Manny's right to ask. "Well, I suppose, we're here for the same reason then." His eyebrows raised in a 'what do you think of that' kind of look.

This was not what the foreman had been expecting, and it threw him for a loop.

"You're out here because The Commissioner told you to?"

It was confusing, but only because The Commissioner hadn't mentioned a thing about it. Maybe he had called in some new guys while they were out at the pass.

Bran made a sour face and shook his head. "Nope, wrong guess, but a good one." He smiled brightly again, throwing the whole conversation off-key. "We're here to find the kid. The one you killed."

Suddenly, all the weapons were moving. Not pointing necessarily, but shifting. Unsure of what to do.

"I didn't kill any kid," Manny shouted angrily. "Yeah, I left him there, but he wasn't dead, just knocked out." Then his expression changed to suspicion. "How'd you know about that? I never told anyone."

He was angry the information had gotten out. The Commissioner wasn't going to like this.

"Really," Bran asked innocently. "I thought everyone knew. I'm sorry if I'm spreading false rumors. I consider myself to be a gentleman."

Manny continued to glare. The guy didn't look very sorry, although he did look like a gentleman. His fancy duds and boots were a whole batch nicer than his own worn-out and threadbare things. The Commissioner wasn't known for handing out quantities of money to his workers. It just wasn't done, and right now, he was feeling pretty shabby.

Settling back in his saddle, Manny made a motion for his men to ease off on their weapons. "So you're out here looking for a kid. It doesn't look like you found him, or anyone else." He left the comment open, hoping for an answer to the unasked question.

"Too true, my friend. We haven't found a thing. What about you?"

Manny's face drooped, unable to keep his expression from giving away the answer. "Nope. It was a dumb idea to begin with, and it hasn't gotten any better stompin' around in this horrid place."

"You've got that right," Bran agreed, carefully using a hand to lift his hat and wipe sweat from his forehead. "This is not an easy place to deal with, but maybe..." He pantomimed thinking, his brow crinkling and a hand to his chin. "Tell you what. How about, you and I ...and the boys, head out of here and grab a drink at the tavern. I'll bet Mack's got some on ice, and I know I could certainly use one."

Manny paused, almost able to feel the cold liquid wash down his throat. It had been so dry, for so long, he could hardly swallow his own spit.

Bran saw he had hit the mark and tipped his head to the side with a wide grin. "In fact, I'll buy. I'll just charge it to the company. That'll show them what for, sending us out here on a wild goose chase."

Manny's eyebrows rose at that. "You're buying?"

He glanced back at his men. They looked like a pack of starving dogs watching free steaks being handed out. "Hmmm, well I don't think it would be polite, not to accept a drink from a gentleman." But what he was thinking was, he would be mobbed if he said no. Besides, right was right, and a free round of drinks could make up for a lot of things. "I think I could persuade my boys to allow that. It being gentlemanly and all."

Manny's men were practically salivating as they nodded wisely to each other.

Bran's men sat with a look of wonder at the perfection of their leader's wisdom. Not a shot or bolt fired, and a drink to boot. Not bad for their first-time lead.

Bran dipped his head, gesturing toward the pathway out. "Why don't you lead the way, Manny? I've never been in here before."

With a sideways look, Manny thought better of saying anything. He didn't want to lose the possibility of a free, ice-cold drink. Not today.

⚜

When MaryEllen kicked the smelly bundle again, it moved and gave a muffled groan. That was good enough. It was alive. She didn't want to give it the credit of calling it a man. He was scum.

Glancing at the dial of her fancy calendorium, she considered distances and expected travel time, then began unpacking the back of her wagon. A heavy chain, block and tackle, and a couple of heavy hooks piled onto the ground beside the bundled lump of Commissioner Dodge. Then she kicked him again just to hear him squawk. Grinning, she clambered up on the wagon and began setting up a three-legged hoist. There was no way she could lift the giant man unaided, so using a bit of ingenuity, she got to work. He would hardly feel a thing.

A half-hour later, she dropped the sides of her tarp and tied them off, making sure they fit tightly. With no gaps showing the interior, it was time to move on. She had a gift for The Council.

⚜

As Mrs. Mavis Dodge stood, Har pulled her chair back and nodded in deference. "If there is anything further I can do, ma'am."

It was a simple statement, from a butler to the woman of the house, but she took it as a true request and swung around to search his face.

"Harold, I know you have not been with us for overly long. What has it been? A year? Two?"

"A little over a year, ma'am." *A very long, trying year*, but he didn't let that slip out.

"Yes, and you have been an immense help. This house runs like a watch. I just thought I would tell you since you probably do not get much thanks from The Commissioner. He is not a very gentle man I'm afraid."

That was an overstatement. Har had never heard a single word of appreciation from the man. Quite the contrary. Most days, if he was spoken to at all, it would be a comment about the lack of good help, or, if he could only find competent employees. But it went with the job, and it was only temporary employment, lasting only until he could help put the man away. The longer he was here, the worse he thought of The Great Commissioner Dodge.

Mrs. Dodge was rambling on, her words finally cutting through his thoughts. "I am afraid that one of these days, he is not going to come back. He is a hard man, and he deals with other hard men. My father warned me of such before we were married. But it was a good move for the family. That's how things work in the upper levels of society, although you wouldn't know about that. It is a difficult part of a young lady's upbringing, to give herself to a man she isn't truly in love with, but again, it is expected."

Har almost felt sorry for her. Honestly, he hadn't thought much on the subject. The upper class did their own things, for their own reasons, and he had never worried about them.

"Ma'am, as I said, if there is anything I can do to assist, just ask. It would be my pleasure."

"Thank you, Harold. I was just thinking, if The Commissioner did not return, I wouldn't have the foggiest idea of how to run this town, and maybe I should look into it. It can't be all that difficult. He is not an overly intelligent man. So if he can, I could." With that statement, Mrs. Dodge stood a little straighter and tossed her hair. "Yes, I am certain that I could." Having made up her mind, she took a deep breath, that threatened to burst the bone buttons on her bodice. "Come with me, Harold. We are going to the office. It is time I looked into the affairs of my husband."

A very startled Har followed the flouncing form of Mrs. Dodge through the house.

CHAPTER 33

The Brotherhood you Say?

The tavern was full as men used cool beer to wash the last of the dust from their dry throats. The ladies in the team had thought it a better idea to find somewhere to clean up from the same dusty road. They would find their own refreshment once they were in a better state to enjoy it. At the moment, the dirt and body odor was more than the women found acceptable, although it didn't seem to affect the men in the same way.

Mack had his hands full, trying to keep up with the demands of the place. Men in worn black vests sat beside men in starkly newer gear, clapping each other on the back and joking in the dusky, low-ceilinged building, telling stories of the badlands. Most were about as real as Christmas trees in July, but nobody seemed to mind. They matched each other drink for drink, with all parties glad to be out of the badlands.

"Wonder what happened to the kid?" Bran asked casually.

He and Manny had taken up a table for themselves, and Manny shook his head, considering the problem. "Honestly, I don't know. Never saw him again, but The Commissioner sure was pissed. Thought he was gonna have a seizure when I told him. It's downright scary the way he can get worked up. I've worked for him for a long time, but I've been thinkin' about movin' on. I'm afraid this place is going to kill me if I stick around." His inner voice said it would be the man, not the place, that did the killing, but he didn't voice the thought.

Even though the two were talking, everything had been pretty vague so far, and Bran decided to try getting more information from the tight-lipped foreman.

"I heard something about the kid being a wizard or some such thing. Sounds mighty strange to me. Don't believe in them myself."

Manny shook his head in short rapid beats. "I don't know, but it was weird. Really weird. A damn flash about got Will blinded, and our horses went crazy, and I mean totally crazy. It just makes you wonder, ya know?"

Bran nodded as expected. "Does sound weird, but we didn't find him, even with both our groups out looking, so we may never know."

Manny took another sip and signaled Mack for a refill. "Can you top these off for us? I got mighty dry out there." A thought crossed his mind. "Hey, Mack, this guy says he knows you. Is that right?"

Mack stepped over and refilled their glasses with an affirmative nod. "Sure enough. It was before I came this direction, so it's been a while." He set the pitcher down, and a subtle dip of the head said he would play whatever game Bran was up to. "How are you doing, Bran?"

Bran acknowledged the ploy and took the discussion. "We were just talking about the kid at the Badlands. Manny says he thought the kid might be a wizard or something." Then before Mack could make a comment, Bran denied the entire concept. "I told him there aren't any such things, so what's your take, Mack? You've been around."

Mack rubbed his chin, as though considering the subject. "Well, wizards I'm not sure about, but a mage, now there's something that just might fit. You see, mage is a derivative of Magi, like the wise men in The Good Book. So it goes to say, if it was good enough for The Good Book, it's good enough for me. Now I'd think a mage could have lots of powers, and I don't see why he couldn't bring up some kind of light, or spook horses. It only sounds reasonable. Especially if he was being threatened." He slid a look over to Manny, checking for a reaction.

Manny's face had taken on a yellowish tint, as though he was going to be sick. "You really think so, Mac? You think I took on a mage?" His voice wasn't sounding so good. He was thinking that leaving the kid's body lying in the desert passageway might not have been such a good idea. If the kid was still alive, would he be looking for revenge?

With a swallow to clear a suddenly drying throat, Manny began thinking that his moving on might be sooner than he had planned.

Mack noted Manny's look and cautiously asked, "You okay, fella? You don't look so good." He always took care of his customers. It was more than just part of the job. He actually cared about people.

"A mage?" Manny replied uneasily, as though trying out the words. He didn't say anything more, but it had certainly affected his evening. Setting down the glass, he looked around at the men. "I didn't kill him, Mack, but I did leave him there." It was an acknowledgment of the deed, and equally obvious, he was worried.

Bran could see where this was going, and with calculated effect, agreed. "And we didn't find a body."

Unexpectedly, Mack broke in. "Now hold on, Manny. You're The Commissioner's foreman. You can't just up and leave. He'll hunt you down. Then he'll deal with, well, with what he would consider treason. I'd guess you know enough of his operations to get him hanged. He won't wait for that."

Manny's face changed to an even greener hue, as Mack quietly started looking for a bucket.

They barely heard Manny's voice as he said, "What am I going to do, Mack? I didn't sign up for this. I can't have both of them huntin' me."

Bran shook his head in understanding. "Let me work on it. I may be able to come up with something."

Manny's look would have been comic on someone else. His eyes were hollow, and the travels of the past couple of weeks were wearing heavily on him. "Would you?"

Mack put a hand on Manny's shoulder and gave a nod of reassurance. "Bran's a good man. Let him see what he can do."

"Okay, sounds good," Manny said hollowly, "but I'd better go for now. I don't feel so good." Climbing unsteadily from the bench, he placed a coin on the tabletop. "Thanks, guys. Let me know if you come up with something, okay?"

The two nodded silently and Manny made his way out to the dusty street.

Bran was practically cheerful as the front door slammed shut. "That was awesome, Mack. Dang, but you're good at this."

But Mack's eyes flashed, and he frowned. "That's a good man. Not a church goer maybe, but he's good in his own way. What are you up to, other than getting him away from here?"

Bran was surprised at Mack's outburst. "I just thought, the less of The Commissioner's men around, the better."

"Yeah, maybe. But I hate to leave a man in that condition." He looked around the room, then commented, "I've got work to do. We'll talk later." With a quick nod, he picked up the empty pitcher, then turned back with a last comment. "Drop by tomorrow," and left to deal with the other customers.

✳

Mrs. Dodge stood before the big double doors of The Commissioner's private office. The large key ring in her hands had come from her bottom drawer. Fumbling with the mass, she finally slid a heavy key into the brass mechanism, turning until even Harold heard the click of the tumblers. She pushed the doors open with a dramatic gesture and stood looking at the fancy desk with all its various drawers and slots. "Do you have any idea where I should start?" she asked, glancing over her shoulder at a nervous Har.

"Well, ma'am, I would probably look in the lower drawers. That's where I would put the more important papers. The everyday things would be on top, where he can get to it more readily."

Actually, he had no idea how Commissioner Dodge set up his desk, but it was at least reasonable.

"Very good then. You start on that side and I will start here." She attempted to pull open the bottom drawer, but it was locked too. "Oh ragweed!" she fumed, then looked at Har with a guilty expression. "I'm sorry. I don't usually use those kinds of words."

"Under the circumstances, ma'am, I can understand," Har said, holding back a smile. "Perhaps there will be another key to fit the desk."

The idea brightened her pouting disposition. "Of course. I should have thought of that." She almost giggled as she selected a much smaller key from the ring and inserted it into the tiny keyhole in the drawer. "This is quite exciting."

Har wasn't at all so sure. It was exceptionally handy, but far more dangerous than exciting.

The drawer slid open, exposing a neat row of files, each filled with papers. The Commissioner was tidy, he could say that about him.

"There are so many," she said, somewhat dismayed. "You had better help me with these. I won't be able to look through them all."

Each took a folder and began reading, trying to figure out what The Commissioner had been up to.

Har was surprised at the speed of the Mrs. as she flipped through the papers. She wasn't just flipping pages, she was reading, and apparently understanding. Her face began to take on a concerned look, and Har had to keep himself working at his own files just to keep up.

"The scoundrel!" she cried in disbelief, slapping her last file on the desktop. "How could he? I realize I didn't pay any attention to things. That's why I married him, so he could do it all. But this is outrageous. There is file after file of devious dealing with these people. Our people!" She again stamped her dainty foot, then inelegantly plopped into his large leather chair. "Oh, Harold, what am I going to do? These people must hate us." She dropped her head to her more than adequate chest, and although she didn't cry, she did look a bit broken.

Keeping at a safe distance Har asked, "What would you like to do, ma'am?" This was no time to be getting close to The Commissioner's wife.

"This needs to be corrected," she said in full fervor. "I'm not sure how, but I will not let these people be swindled so I can have another shawl. I simply won't." She thought for a moment and brightened. "I will send a letter to my father. He will know how to deal with the man."

Har frowned, and she caught the look, raising her eyebrows at his impropriety.

"If you would, ma'am. I might have a better idea."

Her eyebrows didn't lower, but she turned her full attention to him. "Yes?"

Rhone walked alongside, as Aundrea rode Pasha, hands holding Jewel tucked under her chin. Riding slowly so he could keep up, she spoke quietly to the little rock, as though whispering to a kitten.

"We are going to be the best of friends," she whispered, "and I will keep you with me every day. We will be inseparable. I think I will make a ring where you can be mounted. You are small enough to fit. Would that be all right, my little beauty?"

She wasn't carrying on a real conversation. Stone had told her, through Rhone's translating, that Jewel would need to hear her words for weeks before it learned to understand everything she was saying. So she continued to talk to Jewel, thinking bright pictures of what she was saying. Stone said it was the best method, and that it was working, but other than the first Hello, they hadn't shared thoughts again. There would be plenty of time for that later. Right now, they had to develop their connection.

Aundrea turned to Rhone as he walked beside her. "I ran into a report in the history files that spoke about other stones. Do you think there might be more? You said you were searching for others."

Stone overheard and sent an immediate query to Rhone. *What were the stories? Not every rock is a We you know.* He now seemed a bit cynical about having more We around.

Rhone passed the question to Aundrea, a process he found tiring. It was much easier to talk to Stone for himself. Passing on everything was quickly getting old.

But Aundrea was excited with the idea. "The report mentioned a group, where a ring or rings were set with a glowing stone. It didn't mean much to me then, and I honestly didn't believe a word of it, but now it's a definite possibility."

Rhone looked worried as he asked, "How many?"

Aundrea shrugged. "I don't know. It doesn't say. Only that a group of men attempted to break into The Council's records. Especially those dealing with elections. They all got away and were never found, but soon after that, the term 'The Brotherhood' began to be known, and changes began to occur in the government. I know it's a long shot, but it doesn't matter how long the shot if you get a hit."

"And you think this Brotherhood might have We they're working with?"

Aundrea nodded, knowing it was a dangerous game. "They must have been small stones to be set in rings. Perhaps even smaller than Jewel." She watched to see his reaction.

Finally, Rhone began listening to the incessant noise he had been blocking.

Why were you blocking me? Stone all but sputtered. *I think that was very rude. Did you hear her? She was talking about We. Those of my kind. Now, what are we going to do about it?*

Rhone took a resigned breath, knowing he was going to get a lecture.

"We can't go stealing every piece of jewelry we run into, just hoping it will be a We. It simply won't work." He was frustrated with all the moving, searching, and hiding they had done. Why couldn't they just settle down somewhere and stay awhile?

For the same reason we had to save Jewel, Stone said in annoyance. *My people need to be free.*

It felt as though Stone had stamped his non-existent foot, and Rhone had to smile, but he couldn't argue the fact. They may not be humans, but they were thinking beings.

"Okay, okay, we'll go," he said, relenting. "But can we get Jewel trained first? It might be handy to have someone else around for backup." Not certain he had gotten his point across, he added, "You know. In case something goes wrong, again."

Aundrea smiled at the exchange. It was fun to watch the two interact so well. She could hardly wait.

M ack and Har sat quietly in the dark tavern, feeling old, and a bit worn.

"Do you think we're almost done with this stuff?" Mack asked his old friend.

Har responded thoughtfully, "I've got to admit, this didn't work out the way I thought it would. Any idea where Commissioner Dodge ran off to? Haven't heard a word from him for days, and even his wife doesn't know. But Dad-gummit, I'll tell you what. That woman surprised me. She has a head on her shoulders. If The Commissioner's gone for good, then good riddance. But believe it or not, she just might do a good job of taking his place."

Mack's face showed his surprise. "Didn't think I would ever hear you talk like that." Then with a self-satisfied grimace, he said, "Me, now that's a different story. I'm more of the cultured type."

Har had to shake his head, knowing it was anything but true. Mack's mouth ran away with him far too often. "I sent off a note to Aundrea and hope she gets it soon. If The Commissioner doesn't come back, I'm going to see that his Mrs. slips into his position. I think the town will do pretty well with her there, even if she is a bit showy. Who knows, maybe she can fix things around here."

"Couldn't hurt," Mack agreed. "It can't get much worse than it is, and even if The Council sends someone, it would take them months to set it up and get a new person in place. I'm good for the try, but how are you going to do it?"

"No problem there. I'll put it to the town and let them decide. It's their place. Let them choose their own commissioner...ess." He shrugged. "Whatever works."

"And what about the kid?" Mack asked, mostly to get onto safer ground.

"Honestly, I have no idea. Nobody's seen him since the row with Manny and his boys. I doubt he'll ever show his face around here again. I know I wouldn't."

Once again, Mack couldn't disagree. "It'll be kind of quiet with The Commissioner gone, but it might be nice for a while." There was a long pause as the two sat contentedly sipping their brew. "Har? How long are you gonna stay around?"

Har wrinkled his brows, thinking. "Oh, I'll see Mrs. Dodge into office. Then, I think I'm done. There's a place in the southland I've been thinking about. Might make a good place to settle and let the bones rest. What about you?"

Mack set his glass on the table and turned to face his friend. "Think they could use a new tavern down there?"

Smiling, Har popped his old friend on the back, raising a cloud of dust that drifted lazily through the dusky room. With a cough, he said, "Gosh, Mack. Don't you ever wash that stuff?"

They laughed as Mack poured another cold one, then raised their swirling brews in a toast.

The End

<h1 style="text-align:center">About Strider</h1>

An award-winning author, Strider began his writing career after his twenty-five years as a firefighter / EMT. The emotions and experiences of those calls carry themselves through every story, bringing true 'been-there' reality to the scenes.

With additional years as a general contractor, designer, business owner, wildland firefighter, big game guide, ski instructor, mountain climber, backpacker, sword fighter, and hunter, his wide range of knowledge is intricately woven through the stories.

To date, Strider has written YA (young adult), Old West / science-fi, light steampunk, dystopian (post-apocalyptic), gaslight (early mechanized era), and just good fun reading. Most of his writing is structured to teach, as well as entertain.

Strider and his wife Pam live on an island in the Puget Sound. One of the great benefits of their beautiful woodland home is being only steps from the rocky beach, a perfect place to write and romance.

Contact at: DuramenPublishing.com

or:

DuramenPublishing@gmail.com

Luna – The Adventures of Rhone & Stone

Be sure to read, Luna, book 2 of,
The Adventures of Rhone & Stone.

In **_Luna_**, our young friend moves from his back-country environment of Skragmoore to a life-changing view of the big city. The new eye-widening styles and updated technology of the Steam Era sets him back a step, but his new position as an agent with the OPR gives him plenty to do to catch up.

It's his first assignment, and maybe his last, as he gets sideways with both the Mayor and pirates. Only by using his head, and Stone's vast knowledge, can he find a very uplifting way to win. His astoundingly brilliant method will bring a smile to your face.

A fun read for all young at heart.

⚜

<u>Luna</u>

- **First-place winner of the Chanticleer International Book Awards: Dante Rossetti, Young adult fiction**

- **First-place winner of the BookFest Awards: Fiction > Fantasy - Gaslamp**

- **PenCraft Awards: Best Book of Spring 2024**

And More

Stay tuned for more of The Adventures of Rhone & Stone, as Recalled, book 3, continues the story.

Being recalled, Rhone heads back to The Capital Stronghold, but being waylaid en route wasn't in the plans. Beaten but ever optimistic, Rhone turns his plight into a gain by delivering not only himself but a new compatriot to Aundrea's call.

Join us as Rhone & Stone's mind-boggling interplay leads them from one problem to the next, but who would have considered bugs as anything but obnoxious?

But when they get in deeper than they had anticipated, it's Aundrea who seeks help, calling on Captain Belle and The Lady Luna. With Rhone's new toys, they build a plan to rescue Rhone and deal with the nefarious organization once and for all.

Coming, fall of 2024: Recalled, book 3 of the Adventures of Rhone & Stone.